BY FRANCESCA SERRITELLA

Full Bloom

Ghosts of Harvard

Nonfiction
(coauthored with Lisa Scottoline)

I See Life Through Rosé-Colored Glasses

I Need a Lifeguard Everywhere but the Pool

I've Got Sand in All the Wrong Places

Does This Beach Make Me Look Fat?

Have a Nice Guilt Trip

Meet Me at Emotional Baggage Claim

Best Friends, Occasional Enemies

My Nest Isn't Empty, It Just Has More Closet Space

Why My Third Husband Will Be a Dog

Full Bloom

Full Bloom

A NOVEL

Francesca
Serritella

Ballantine Books
New York

Ballantine Books
An imprint of Random House
A division of Penguin Random House LLC
1745 Broadway
New York, NY 10019
randomhousebooks.com
penguinrandomhouse.com

Hardback ISBN 978-0-525-51039-0
Ebook ISBN 978-0-525-51040-6

Printed in the United States of America on acid-free paper

1st Printing

BOOK TEAM: Production editor: Ted Allen • Managing editor: Pam Alders • Production manager: Meghan O'Leary • Copy editor: Emily DeHuff • Proofreaders: Addy Starrs, Ellen Weider, Al Madocs

The authorized representative in the EU for product safety and compliance is Penguin Random House Ireland, Morrison Chambers, 32 Nassau Street, Dublin D02 YH68, Ireland. https://eu-contact.penguin.ie

FIRST EDITION

Perfume bottle illustration: unorobus/Adobe Stock

In loving memory of Pip
who saw me through

Scent speaks in every language. It is made of flesh and personal impressions. It is tied up with the need to feel alive, a need everyone senses from an early age. The need to live is also a need for perfumes and scents. Inescapably. They are the depositories of our deepest secrets, whether we like it or not.

> —Master Perfumer Dominique Ropion, creator of such iconic fragrances as Givenchy *Amarige,* Mugler *Alien,* Calvin Klein *Euphoria,* Lancôme *La Vie Est Belle,* and Frédéric Malle *Portrait of a Lady* and *Carnal Flower*

I know that words, and even more so smells, do not have the same significance for each of us; all the same, smells are elements that perfumers can transform, bring to life and change. It is because they change meaning that they are alive, and that perfumes are alive.

> —Master Perfumer Jean-Claude Ellena, best known for Van Cleef & Arpels *First,* Cartier *Declaration,* and as the exclusive in-house perfumer for Hermès from 2004 to 2016, where he created such favorites as *Terre d'Hermès, Rose Ikebana,* and *Un Jardin sur le Nil*

Full
Bloom

PROLOGUE

We experience scent for the first time in utero at only twelve weeks, and by birth we are primed to associate our mother's scent with comfort, nourishment, and safety. Scent is always there, its volatile molecules swirling, speaking to us before language, before cognition, before culture. It is our most primal sensory system, bypassing our intellect and directly stimulating our emotional nervous system. Transporting us through memories of pleasure or terror.

Tempting us, warning us.

Yet after just fifteen minutes, humans go nose-blind to any scent. No matter how alarming the odor, if we can't escape it, we get used to it. And once we get used to it, it becomes imperceptible. As if it disappears.

But the danger remains.

So one has a short window to act.

Luckily, young Isaiah Patterson wasn't one to keep quiet.

"What's that smell?" Isaiah wrinkled his nose.

"I don't know." Jayden remained focused on pressing a Spiderman action figure into a toy truck. The boys were playing in the shabby hallway of their apartment building at Hendricks Houses.

"Ah man, it stinks. You farted."

Jayden frowned, hard. "I did not!"

"Did too. *Jeez*, I got to clear the air." Isaiah went to find his big sister, Kiara, who was babysitting them while their mom was at work.

Kiara was in their bedroom. She was dancing in front of her phone, which she had propped up on the dresser.

"We got Febreze?" Isaiah's voice sounded funny because he was pinching his nose.

Kiara dropped her arms with a groan and stomped over to tap the phone. "No. Go away, I'm making a TikTok."

"You got a perfume or somethin'?"

"Leave me alone."

"We gon' play outside then."

Kiara ripped out her headphones. "No, I told you, you gotta stay in the hallway."

"It smells like rotten eggs out there!"

"Then play inside the apartment, you ain't goin' outside!"

Isaiah stomped out of the room, stomps he had learned from his sister.

No sooner had he reached Jayden than Kiara popped out of the apartment. Her face looked different, worried.

"Where's it smell like rotten eggs?" she asked.

The boys pointed to the far wall.

She walked over, sniffing the air like a dog.

"It wasn't me," Jayden said again.

Kiara turned back to them, this time she looked scared. "Boys, you have to go outside, right now, go all the way to the sidewalk and don't talk to strangers. I'll meet you there in five minutes."

"Why? What's happening?" Isaiah asked.

Kiara put her hands on both boys' shoulders. "We have to get out of the building, it's not safe. Go downstairs and outside all the way to the mailbox at the corner, okay? Wait for me at the mailbox."

"What about our toys?"

"Leave them! Go, now! Hurry!" She shooed them into the stairwell and darted back down the hallway.

Isaiah hung his head out looking after her. The way Kiara was banging on the neighbors' doors frightened him.

Kiara and Isaiah lived on the fourth floor; Jayden lived down the hall from them. But Jayden wasn't Isaiah's only friend in the building. When Kiara was too little to babysit him, Ernie used to watch both of them. Ernie always said if something bad happened, Isaiah should come get him.

"Are you coming?" Jayden asked.

"I gotta get Ernie." Isaiah peeled off on the third floor, leaving Jayden on the landing.

"But your sister said—"

"Go on, I'll meet you at the mailbox." He hustled down to Ernie's apartment and knocked on the door with their special knock, then waited for Ernie to walk to the door. Finally the door opened.

"Look at you-uu, taller by the day!" Ernie's signature singsong greeting. Isaiah hugged him while Ernie patted his back with a shaky hand. "Come in, son, come in. I was just about to put the kettle on, do you want a cup of tea? I'll make it sweet."

Isaiah considered while Ernie shuffled to the kitchen stove. "Can I have chocolate milk instead?"

Ernie's hand paused midair above the stove knob. "Why yes. And you're right, it's too hot for tea. I'll get the Hershey's syrup." He opened the fridge instead.

Ernie poured him a glass of a milk and let Isaiah add the chocolate as he stirred. The boy drank half the glass in one gulp. Then he remembered his purpose.

"We have to get out of the building. Kiara says it's not safe."

"Now why would she say that?"

"I'm not sure. She's banging on everyone's doors and telling them. But I wanted to be the one to tell you."

"Oh my, that does sound serious. Your sister is a very bright girl, I'd better go speak to her. Let me get my oxygen." Ernie shuffled to the side of his recliner and wheeled out the oxygen tank. Isaiah thought it looked like a rocket pack, but he didn't like when Ernie put the plastic tubes in his nose.

"Do you have to have that?"

"It helps me breathe. Don't ever smoke cigarettes, son, it ruins your lungs. And food never tastes or smells as good."

They headed down the hall. Isaiah had to slow his footsteps to stay beside the old man and his squeaky, rolling oxygen tank.

"This elevator ain't ever gettin' fixed." Ernie shook his head. "Everything in this building as broken down as me."

"You're not broken, Ernie, you're just old."

Ernie chuckled and they entered the stairwell. "Now you hold onto the banister, son, I don't want you taking a tumble."

Isaiah held the railing with one hand and squeezed his nose with the other. The rotten egg smell was stronger here.

Voices shouted from the hallway above them, then people hurried down the stairs, passing them. But Isaiah stayed with his friend. Ernie's oxygen tank banged against each metal-tipped step behind him. *Clang . . . clang . . . clang.*

At last they reached the lobby. Kiara was at the front doors ushering their neighbors outside when she spotted her little brother. "What are you still doing here? I—"

Kiara's gaze fell on Ernie's oxygen tank and her eyes got wide. Without another word, she lunged for the tank and swept it away like a linebacker, ripping the plastic tubes from Ernie's face and dislodging his glasses. "This can't be near us!"

Kiara repeatedly jammed the button to the elevator, taped off and stuck at ground level, until the doors opened to the garbage-strewn carriage. She shoved the rolling tank into the elevator car and turned back to them as the doors closed behind her.

"Young lady—" Ernie scolded, struggling to right his specs.

"We have to *go!*" Kiara dragged Isaiah and Ernie from the lobby despite the old man's protests. The trio hustled and knocked into each other as she rushed them across the grass, Kiara all but lifting Isaiah off the ground.

Other residents stood on the lawn, frowning at the building or at their phones, unsure of what to do next. Isaiah saw Jayden wave to them from the mailbox on the sidewalk, but that was still a ways away. They weren't at the street yet.

Kiara flailed her arms and hollered at her neighbors, "There's a gas leak! Get back, get away from the building! That smell is *gas.*"

"It's what?"

"A g—"

KA-BOOM!

The force of the explosion hit them like a truck, hurling them to the ground. A white-hot fireball tore through the building, blowing the doors and windows out at once, roaring in fury. The intense heat made the world around them wobble and glimmer, and searing crumbs of glass rained from the sky, burning their skin as they shielded themselves.

Isaiah squeezed his eyes shut as his sister's body covered his and pressed him into the grass and grit. He smelled the noxious smoke mixed with the smell of burned flesh and hair, so strong he could taste it. It made him want to gag.

The only sensation missing was sound. The blast had knocked a fuzzy blankness into Isaiah's ears like cotton. Slowly at first, then all at once, the noise came back. Car alarms wailed. People screamed and yelled. And the raging fire roared, cracked, hissed, and whooshed through the building as it devoured their homes.

At last his sister's voice cut through the ringing in his ears. "You okay, Isaiah, are you okay?"

Isaiah turned his head to the side to free his mouth to reply, but his throat was too scratchy. He saw Ernie lying on his side, his glasses off, grimacing and breathing hard, but alive. All around them, the ground was covered in debris: glass, gray dust, splintered wood, a hunk of couch smoking like an asteroid.

Their homes were blown to smithereens.

But with instinct, luck, and each other, they survived.

And they would never forget the smell.

Head Notes

Head notes, also known as top notes, are the first and most enticing notes in a perfume. They can be sweet, fresh, or even bitter; common examples are citrus, aromatic herbs, and aldehydes. Bright, sparkling, and dominant, these coquettish notes catch attention, flirt, tease, and flit away. That is because these small molecules are the most volatile and thus project a burst of fragrance before quickly breaking down, taking their scent with them.

One

I ris Sunnegren hadn't planned to host her best friend's baby shower one hour after learning that her own fertility was alarmingly low, it just happened that way. She jogged up the red-carpeted steps of the Plaza with the cold *squick* of ultrasound jelly in her underwear and three bags of decorations under her arms. With some effort, she checked the time on her phone. She was running behind schedule.

The Plaza was Iris's favorite building in New York City, a pedestrian pick for someone who works in architecture and design, but Iris had never lost the fondness formed from reading *Eloise* as a child, a book that made being a little girl with missing parents seem enviable, glamorous, and free, instead of lonely or sad. The baby shower plan was to celebrate with a classic tea service in the hotel's famed Palm Court. The dining room was part jewel box, part botanical garden, with a dated glamor that made Iris nostalgic for her and Hannah's millennial childhood. Huge potted palms bordered the room, and neoclassical pillars held up the greenhouse-like stained-glass ceiling. A large circular bar plaited with white trellis detail burst with a profusion of orange tiger lilies, filling the room with their elegant fragrance.

Iris hustled to the maître d' and introduced herself. "I have a reservation for fifteen, the baby shower."

"Welcome, and congratulations!"

"I'm the host, I'm not preg—"

"You're early. Your reservation is for two o'clock, and it's one forty-five. But you're welcome to wait by the bar."

"I'm sorry, but when I spoke with your events team, they said I could have the table at one-thirty to have time to set up my decorations. I'm actually late."

The maître d' said he'd see what he could do.

I'm actually late.

She hadn't meant to repeat the phrase from her fertility appointment, but the conversation with the doctor lingered in her ears. After her blood tests came back from her regular gynecologist in the "yellow to red" zone of fertility freakout, Iris had been desperate to get in to see booked-for-months Dr. Alsarraj of Family Tree Fertility, so when a cancellation opened up this morning, she'd grabbed it.

"So I'm actually late to do this?" she had asked, after he'd laid out a rather bleak assessment of her stats and ultrasound.

"You're not early. Your follicles are underproducing for your age by at least two standard deviations. And you haven't checked your AMH levels or anything fertility-related before this, correct?"

"Well, I was in a long-term relationship, but it ended unexpectedly—"

"I don't mean to pry, I only ask to see if these levels are stable for you or if we're on a downward trajectory. But in reality, all fertility is a downward trajectory." A smile equal parts polite and patronizing crossed his face. "Women today are living modern lives with old-fashioned biology. Why should you be ruled by a primitive timetable? Why should you have to be on a different schedule than your male peers? You shouldn't. And we have a modern solution with egg freezing—"

The maître d' returned, interrupting her rumination. "Follow me."

Iris hiked the bags up on her shoulder and opened her iPhone party checklist. She loved plans, checklists, blueprints—in her work or personal life, they were how she made sense out of the unpredictable, or tried to. Today she had ten minutes and a plan. Iris confirmed the tea platter choices with the server—*check.* She tied pink and blue ribbons on every chairback—*check.* Hannah had requested no gifts but children's books, which had given Iris the idea for the library theme. She laid out the name cards she'd made to look like library ID cards on each plate, along with a mini pencil, a stick-on manila sleeve, and a borrowing card for the guests to write Baby Lefebvre a sweet message in their gift book—*check, check, check.* And she unpacked the retro Polaroid camera she'd bought so they could take pictures to tuck into the books as well. Iris knew how precious old photos could become.

Iris was loading the film cartridge into the camera to test it, the final task on her list, when she heard Hannah's voice and looked up to see her waving eagerly alongside her mom, Cathy. Iris waved back and held up the camera to snap a picture of their smiley approach; the camera gave a nostalgic *click* and *whirr* as it spat out an undeveloped picture—*check.* She lowered it and smiled, though it still took her aback to see Hannah so pregnant. Iris knew the outline of her friend's five-foot-three body at so many life stages; she'd looked for it in classrooms and horse shows and concert crowds since they became friends in sixth grade, after Iris came to live with her grandparents, and it had always changed in step with her own. But now Hannah looked so different and her life was about to change forever.

"Iris, honey, it's so good to see you!" Cathy said, giving her a squeeze. She had been like a surrogate mother to Iris growing up.

Hannah hugged her next and squealed over her shoulder. "Omigod, look at this table!" She and her mother cooed over the decorations, gushing over every thoughtful detail.

When Cathy went to the ladies' room, Hannah pulled Iris aside. "How did this morning go? You okay?"

"Oh, fine. But I've never been so dressed up for a gyno appointment, I had my feet in the stirrups *in heels.* I was afraid they'd think I have some kind of fetish."

Hannah snorted, but she was Iris's best friend because she laughed at her jokes as easily as she saw through them. "But for real, are you up for all this baby stuff today? Because I get it if not. My mom and I can take it from here if you want to go home."

"No! I want to be here to celebrate you and the baby! I told you the one thing I don't want—"

"Is for me to feel weird, I know. But just do a gut check for me. You're allowed to change your mind."

"Gut's good. Promise."

Hannah hugged her. "So did you like the doctor? What did she say?"

"It was a he, and he was nice, but he told it to me straight. If I want to have a biological child, I should probably freeze my eggs, soon. Ideally, like yesterday."

Dr. Alsarraj's blunt words still rang in her ears: "Egg quality begins to decline at age thirty-five, it's not the so-called fertility cliff as was once believed, but the likelihood of getting and staying pregnant does drop." He glanced down at her paperwork while her stomach dropped, too. "And you're thirty . . ."

"Four," Iris answered too quickly. "I turn thirty-five in a few days."

Dr. Alsarraj looked up. "Happy birthday."

Hannah brought her back to the present. "Shit. Okay. Well, at least you have clarity."

Iris sighed. "I guess. I still have to figure out how I'm going to pay for it." The consultation alone was $650, which Iris found to be both outrageous and typical. Her regular gynecologist had prepared her that the full process of freezing her eggs would cost over ten thousand dollars, and the health insurance from her lighting design firm wouldn't cover it. According to Blue Cross, a man's wilting erection was a medical problem, but Iris's waning fertility was because she didn't smile more.

"Did Frank give you a timeline on your promotion?" Hannah asked.

"I didn't ask yet. But I will soon, I swear."

"Do it! He's gonna say yes. You've earned that raise."

"I know. Who else would wait in the office on a Saturday to receive his Peloton?"

Hannah tilted her head. *"And* because you're excellent at your job! Doesn't he call you the 'client whisperer'?"

"Yes, for my preternatural ability to take shit from angry architects and developers without showing any emotion beyond reassuring detachment. Thank you, childhood trauma."

Hannah laughed. "Just don't sell yourself short when you talk to Frank, okay?"

"I won't. With this egg freezing, I'm officially too broke for self-deprecation."

The shower guests arrived in a steady stream of hugs, introductions, and squealing over the setup, until the table was filled with girlfriends from every stage of Hannah's life. Iris knew most but not all; she was the only friend from middle school.

Once everyone was seated and drinks had been served, the waiter came over to explain the tea service. "As you see, we have the étagère of finger sandwiches, cucumber mint and crème fraîche, smoked salmon and lemon butter with dill, Canadian ham and Manchego with Dijon, as well as deviled eggs with salmon roe."

Iris stared at the plate of eggs, boiled and bisected, their yolks creamed and regurgitated into a rosette and topped with sticky orange orbs with red eyes staring at her. She again heard Dr. Alsarraj's voice: "Rule of thumb is harvesting ten eggs will yield one successful live birth, but I like to aim for a dozen. Do you have a problem with needles?"

Iris's seat neighbor reached across her plate to stab a mini ham and cheese with her fork. "Do you mind if I take this one? I hate fish."

"Go for it, I don't eat pork."

"Perfect! I'm Jorie." The two of them caught up on how they knew Hannah (Jorie from PS 89, where they both taught third grade) and where they lived—Jorie lived in Jersey City and was impressed that Iris lived in the West Village, to which Iris demurred, "My parents helped," before Jorie segued into the line of questioning Iris disliked most. "Are you married? Kids?"

"Neither. You?"

"I'm engaged!" Jorie stuck out her left hand and wiggled her fingers, showing off a lovely solitaire with a halo setting.

Iris oohed appropriately. She both loved and hated that she could clock the carat size at a glance—two point-five—but she'd done so much research when she and Ben were designing her ring, before she'd decided to use her mother's stone. Before Ben had decided he couldn't go through with it.

"So, Hannah told me you're an architect, that's cool," Jorie said.

"I'm in architectural lighting design." Iris watched the familiar disappointment and uncertainty register on Jorie's face, but discussing her professional life was still preferable to the personal. "I figure out how light is going to color a space, create mood, direct movement and attention, affect energy costs, etcetera. For example, see this stained-glass ceiling light above us?"

Jorie looked up and smiled flatly. "Pretty."

"Yeah, but how does it make you feel?"

"Um, I mean . . ." Jorie shrugged.

"Right. You feel nothing. It's kind of a bummer."

Jorie chuckled. "Yeah, it is. Why is it such a bummer?"

"The glass is matte, so it's flat and heavy-looking when it should feel lofty. And the color temperature is wrong, a little too warm— which they could tweak, because it's a laylight, meaning an artificial skylight. The original glass dome was built in 1907, *that* was a marvel, made by Tiffany, all leaded glass, which is extra brilliant and gently textured, like what you see in cathedrals. It would've looked like an airy lace veil under the sky. But that was a hundred years ago, it fell into disrepair, was destroyed, built over, and ultimately replaced with this replica like fifteen years ago. It's still impressive, but it's a glass lampshade over a giant ceiling light, and they didn't get it quite right." Iris caught herself rambling. "Sorry, I think about this stuff a lot."

"Please, I'm a teacher, I like to learn!" Jorie sipped her mimosa. "You can't fake nature, I guess."

Iris thought with a pang about making babies with IVF someday. "Well, to be fair, working in lighting is always about electrical engineering, art, and natural light. You need both science and nature."

"True. You'd never know my diamond was lab-grown. It's a real diamond, physically, chemically, it's exactly the same. *Only bigger!*" Her eyes flashed. "I say, life is short, get what you want."

Three clinks of silverware on crystal cut through the din, and they looked up to see Hannah's mom standing with her mimosa, preparing to make a speech.

"First, I want to thank you all for coming and especially to thank Iris for putting together this beautiful shower today. Baby Lefebvre is already so loved. And to my firstborn, and forever my baby, Hannah." Her voice broke and she croaked a chuckle, her eyes glossed with tears. "I'm sorry, this makes me so emotional. I remember the day you were born, and I was just . . . in awe of you. I'd prayed for a girl, with blond hair like mine, and blue eyes like her daddy's, and there you were, my dream come true."

Iris thought of her own mother. During the appointment, Dr. Alsarraj had asked about her mother's history of fertility. "Did your mother have a hard time getting pregnant?"

"I don't know. I'm an only child. I'm not sure if that was on purpose."

"It's worth asking her. Many women of her generation kept these types of troubles private, but genetics can be as big a factor as any in fertility."

"She's passed. Both my parents have."

"I'm sorry to hear that. Any relevant medical history there? Cancer?"

"House fire."

"Oh, I'm very sorry." It always threw people, but Dr. Alsarraj recovered quicker than most. Iris supposed a doctor of infertility was used to the ordinariness of unthinkable tragedy. He spoke frankly. "Considering your current values and unknown variables, and the fact that our window to intervene is closing, I'd advise you to act now."

Cathy continued, "They put you in my arms and I thought, I cannot be happier than I am in this moment, because I had everything I ever wanted. But now I look at the beautiful, amazing, surprising woman you've grown into, who exceeded all of my dreams, and I think I will be even happier when my first grandchild is born. Hannah, I love you so much."

Hannah stood up, teary too, and they embraced. The guests clapped, several dabbing their eyes. Iris never cried with people around, but she did feel a lump in her throat. First, because she loved Hannah and her family like they were her own, and they deserved every ounce of this happiness. But also because getting *everything she ever wanted* felt so far away—it always had, but today farther still. Since her parents died, Iris had learned to moderate her wants and wishes, cutting them down to fit what was reasonable, realistic, and attainable. If she didn't ask for too much, she couldn't be disappointed. And as long as she planned for the worst, she couldn't be surprised. Not again.

Yet somehow, as of this morning, she'd discovered she might have to renegotiate her expectations once again.

About what she wanted most of all.

Two

Rain in the city felt like the first squeeze of the painter's sponge, more purge than cleanse. Summer rain in particular released as many smells as it rinsed; like the difference between a dry dog and a wet one, New York City was a filthy animal. Iris had recently learned there was a word for the scent of rain: *petrichor,* a pleasant, refreshing note with a cool mineral glint—but this rainwater wasn't running through green grass or skipping over smooth river rocks. A city shower ran through the sieve of overstuffed municipal trash bins, drenching their contents to fetid sludge; it flushed over soot-scuffed curbs and sluiced into the gutter carrying cigarette butts, the bones of cabbies' chicken wing dinners, and a discarded condom like shed snakeskin; it flooded the rat warrens under sidewalk flower beds and sent dog-piss-soaked mulch chips floating away like tiny stinking barges.

Plus, it made Iris's hair frizz. Worse with her new haircut. She had fallen victim to the evergreen scam that a bob will change your life, but so far her life still needed a straightening iron.

Iris had been tempted to postpone this first date, but that fertility consult scared her into open-mindedness. Chris Hinge (app men had to earn their surnames in her contacts list) seemed fairly promising: thirty-eight years old, lives in South Slope Brooklyn, looked roughly the same in his profile pictures as he did in Google Image Search, with an interesting-sounding job at a film studio. He was not a convicted criminal and he was on LinkedIn—that was all the verification a girl could get these days. But his best feature, as far as Iris was concerned, was his adorable brindle-coated rescue pitty named Lola, cuddled close to him in multiple pictures. As a single dog-mom to a beloved rescue beagle, Iris took this as a great sign of character.

Iris arrived at the designated cocktail bar on MacDougal Street and shook off her navy umbrella printed with dogs she liked to think were beagles but were more likely foxhounds, and deposited it in the bin. She had already received Chris's "Here" text, so she scanned the room for him. A row of men and women sat hunched over glowing phones, surely waiting to meet a prearranged stranger just as she was. Bars like this no longer felt like places to meet, mingle, and see where the night took you; dating apps had transformed them into dimly lit WeWorks for socio-sexual job interviews.

Identifying someone from photos in real life was always a little uncertain, but Iris thought she recognized the curly brown hair, five-ten-listed-as-six-foot man from her phone. "Chris? Hi, I'm Iris."

Likewise, he took an extra beat to register her. "Oh! Hey!" He stood and they hugged lightly, hips apart. "Your hair was longer in your pictures."

"Oh yeah, new haircut. Sorry, should I leave?" she joked, making him laugh. He had a pretty good laugh—she cared about that more than height.

"No, no, it looks nice. You look great."

A fragile bubble of optimism formed in her chest as she took her seat. They placed a drinks order and got through an initial round of small talk before Iris landed on her favorite topic.

"Your dog is super cute. I *might* have swiped right mainly on Lola."

"I get it. She's way cuter than me. I named Lola after the Jacques Demy New Wave film," Chris explained, like it wasn't a top five popular dog name. He cut the pretension by showing her some puppy pics on his phone.

"Beyond. So how old is she now?"

"Almost five. She was my pandemic puppy, I wouldn't have made it out of lockdown without her. That's my baby girl right there."

Iris felt herself warming to him. "Aww, that's so sweet. I rescued my dog Hugo when he was around two, and I wish I had baby pictures of him! He's thirteen. I hate that he's aging, but he's only getting cuter to me."

"Old dogs are saints."

"I agree." Iris smiled; it was something she would say. "We should get them together sometime."

"For sure. Thing is, Lola mostly stays at my parents' house in Bedford now, she's like *obsessed* with my mom. But my mom visits with her fairly often."

"So you have shared custody?"

"Lola's still *my* dog, but she just lives with them. You know, it was great having a dog during lockdown, but now it's not so easy, I mean, I still work from home, but my schedule is all over the place. And I *love* to travel; getting inspiration from the world around me is essential to my creative psyche. But it's not fair to Lola."

Iris nodded politely while her image of a devoted dog-dad crumbled.

Just then the waiter arrived with their food, a slate of assorted charcuterie and cheeses, a ramekin of olives, and a basket of airy French bread.

Chris took the board but waved off the basket. "Thanks, we don't need the bread."

Like she hadn't already eliminated him for dog-child abandonment.

"I'm sorry, did you want the bread?"

"Nah, I could skip it."

"I've completely cut out sugar and refined carbohydrates, best thing I ever did for myself." He proceeded to tell her about a billionaire who wants to live forever so he built a ranch in Wyoming where he raises all his own meat without antibiotics and believes bread is "literal poison."

"Wow," Iris replied, unwowed.

Chris pulled apart a piece of prosciutto with his fingers, used it to pick up a piece of comté cheese, and popped both into his mouth at once, not waiting to swallow before adding, "Nutrition is super important to me. I've tried all the diets: intermittent fasting, the bulletproof coffee thing, total-thirty, paleo, I mostly eat keto anyway—not for weight loss but for mental clarity. The mind and body are not separate. You have to optimize your body's health and performance to optimize your brain, you know?"

"Totally." Iris took a swig of her cocktail.

"But you know what was the real game changer for me?"

Iris shook her head and wondered if she could yawn without opening her mouth.

"Enemas."

She nearly choked on her gin fizz.

"I know, it sounds crazy. But what you take out is as important as what you put in. Have you tried it?"

"Not on the first date."

Chris laughed his mediocre laugh. "Our natural cleansing system developed when we were basically animals, eating only whole foods in the wild. Our gut biome hasn't evolved as quickly as modern food processing. You need to help yourself detoxify."

"Sometimes I drink cold brew, does that count?"

"Sadly, no. I grew up with this stuff. My mom is all about wellness and homeopathic medicine, she's the one who got me into nutrition in the first place. She does it for me."

"Does what?"

"The enemas."

"Wow." She meant it this time. *Good God in Freudian hell.*

"I'm sure she would comp you a session if you want to try it."

"Thanks, but I'll pa—" *pass away from this conversation,* she might've finished, but from the corner of her eye, she saw him: her ex, Ben. He had just walked in, as if summoned by her humiliation, and he wasn't alone. He was beaming down at a tiny blonde hanging on his arm. The girl was laughing with his denim jacket draped over her shoulders—a denim jacket Iris had bought him years ago—adorably soaked from the rain so that wet tendrils of her hair stuck to her décolleté and rendered her white tee translucent and even more clingy. She looked fresh out of college. Meanwhile Ben looked, infuriatingly, great. Worse, he looked happy. Worst, he looked up.

"Shit." Iris snapped her head back to the table.

"But you really don't see any—" Chris continued obliviously.

"No, I have a thing! I just forgot, then I just remembered, and I have to go. I'm so sorry." She hadn't seen Ben since they broke up six months ago. She was *not* going to see him and his new girlfriend for the first time while on a date with Enema Oedipus.

"You have to go *now?*"

A nearby server briefly shielded her from view of the entrance. "Very now. Right now." She began snatching up her things. "I'm so sorry!"

"I'll get the check and walk you out."

The server moved; she saw Ben speaking to the hostess, who waved a hand in their direction. *"No!* It's on me, please." She tossed twenty-one dollars on the table, which hadn't covered two cocktails in Manhattan in years, but it was all the cash she had. She was already slithering out of her seat and trying to sidle past him without fully standing up. "Sorry meeting you—sorry, I mean, *nice* meeting you, sorry. 'Bye!" She left Chris sitting in shock, his eyes blinking like a cleansed anus.

Iris kept her head low and drafted behind a busboy striding swiftly to the kitchen. Stealing glances at Ben, whom the hostess was leading to a table dangerously close to her old one, validating that she really had no choice but to act like a psycho. As Ben and Co. headed to their table, Iris made her escape.

She hit the sidewalk so giddy with relief that she didn't immediately register the raindrops pelting her head. It was pouring. And her umbrella was—

"Iris!"

Currently over Ben's head. He was standing with it outside the bar, looking at her with earnest concern, like he hadn't just busted her cowardly retreat. He popped the umbrella above him like Mary Poppins. "Isn't this your Hugo umbrella?"

She sighed in defeat and jogged toward him with her cardigan flopped over her head. "Yes, I just forgot it." Sharing the shelter of the umbrella, they stood closer than they would otherwise, at least since their breakup. She felt his nearness like an electric charge. "I was in a rush."

"No kidding. I recognized the umbrella in the bin as soon as I came in, and I wondered if I'd run into you. But then it was you who was running out. Is everything okay?"

"Totally." An absurd answer, as she was so obviously out of her mind. She looked down at her leather sandals darkening with rainwater, because looking up at Ben's face felt like she might kiss him, if only out of muscle memory.

"I won't keep you, I gotta get back too. But you've been good?"

Iris longed to be the type of ex-girlfriend who appeared indifferent and cool, an ice queen *but thriving*. But in the presence of this man who knew her intimately, and after the day she'd had, she found it impossible to posture. "I've been better."

Ben smiled kindly. "How's Hugo, does he ask after me?"

Iris shook her head. "Actually, no. He was only in it for the socks."

He laughed that great Ben laugh, and it set her aglow that she could still make him break.

"I suspected as much, but dammit, it still hurts." He clutched at his chest as if wounded.

Her smile fell. His play-acting at heartbreak curdled her mood. Reminded her that he was the one who had rejected her, blindsided her, wasted so much of her time, and wounded her so deeply. She couldn't chuckle at him pantomiming the visceral ache she still felt for him. They weren't friends yet. And it wasn't his joke to make. "Can I have my umbrella?"

"Oh yeah, sorry." Ben handed it to her, seeming to register the change in temperature with a new formality in his tone. "We should catch up properly sometime, when you're not busy."

"Sure." She had to hold it high, since he was taller than she, and the wind made it unwieldy. The rain blew on her cheeks, like the tears she was holding back.

Ben took the openness of her posture as an invitation to hug her goodbye. She stiffened at first. But pressed to his Oxford shirt dotted with rain, she inhaled his familiar skin scent, a mix of Ivory soap and fresh bread, warm skin under cool cotton, and she exhaled all the tension in her body. She wanted so badly to give in to that safe scent of home in the crook of his arm.

Instead, Iris said goodbye and spun on her heel to walk briskly in the wrong direction from home, leaving Ben to jog back to the shelter of the bar. And she held back her tears successfully until Houston and Sixth.

CHAPTER
Three

A ll the emotion she had suppressed since Hannah's shower came bubbling to the surface. The anger and hurt to see how Ben had taken their breakup in stride, with a new girl on his arm, as easy-breezy and jokey with Iris as ever—no shame, no awkwardness, no remorse. Their breakup had cost him nothing. Meanwhile Iris had spent the morning in a doctor's office with her feet in cold stirrups, stuck with an ultrasound wand, about to spend thousands of dollars to pay for the years he wasted, if she could come up with the money, and even then it might not work. Ben was an eligible bachelor, and she was damaged goods—the injustice.

And the betrayal. By Ben, obviously, whom she had trusted that they were building toward a family together, but now betrayed by her own body. Iris had always felt at war with her physicality, which was always recalcitrantly too big, too wrongly shaped, or too hungry—and now to desert her in its most basic feminine function. Iris had gone her whole childhood bereaved of a family, dreaming of the day she could start her own, only for her body to secretly and unilaterally decide she didn't need those eggs after all. Just like it did the night of the house fire, when Iris was terrified but her body froze instead of fled. Why couldn't she control her own body? Why couldn't she count on her body to perform its most basic biological imperatives—to procreate and to survive?

And the absolute worst part was, Iris hadn't seen any of this coming.

Blindsided. That was the word for it. And Iris hated surprises.

Ben's proposal to Iris was never going to be a surprise, it was a sure thing. They had been dating for five years total, living together in her apartment for three, and when a couple shares six hundred square feet for that long, surprises are the first to go. Ben was the archetype of marriage material, the type of man who owned and used an iron before Iris even met him. He was the youngest of four with three older sisters, his mother joked that his feet didn't touch the ground until he was five, and he had the confidence and benign narcissism of a favored and only son. But being raised by so many women, even indulgent ones, had also conferred on him emotional intelligence and a people-pleasing nature. Ben basked in praise. He wanted to do the right thing, and he wanted people to see him doing it. That sense of responsibility was something he and Iris had in common, although attention made her uncomfortable.

His family loved her, and the feeling was mutual. At least part of the reason Iris fit so beautifully into Ben's family was because she had none of her own to complicate her assimilation. Although the Bergen clan could be overwhelming, Iris had fallen in love with their traditional, boisterous holidays: the Rockwell Thanksgivings, the matching PJs at Christmas, the giggly girl-energy that ran the household and encircled Ben and his dad, who pretended to be put-upon and outnumbered but were doted upon. It was so unlike Iris's family of origin—she was an only child, then an orphan, raised by grandparents on a Pennsylvania farm; her childhood had been happy, then tragic, then quiet.

Iris and Ben had discussed marriage, romantically, with tangled limbs and bedsheets, and also sensibly, fully dressed, over meals, even once with a lawyer, since Iris's late parents' and grandparents' estates were a complicated merger, not that Ben needed any more family money. They had designed the ring together, using the center stone from her mother's engagement ring—Iris's idea—plus two additional baguettes and a white gold band, so it would have their own unique touch and more wattage—Ben's idea. He didn't let her see the finished product, but she saw the velvet box every time she put his shorts away in their top drawer, and she impressed herself by never peeking.

So she waited. And waited. As each holiday, birthday, getaway passed without a proposal, Iris began to dread the expectant questions from his family and her friends that would follow. But she wasn't worried.

They had a plan.

Last winter's holidays came and went, though she knew Ben wouldn't propose over Christmas, he knew that that holiday had too much baggage for her to be rehabbed into a happy memory—but Ben's Christmas gift to her was booking them a trip to Cabo San Lucas for a week in February including Valentine's Day. Iris was so excited, she preplanned whale watching, snorkeling, a cooking lesson, tequila tasting, *except* on Valentine's Day itself—Ben had asked her to leave that day to him for a "surprise."

Iris booked a manicure through the hotel for February 13, and Hannah had been sending her links to white bikinis and lingerie all month.

But one snowy night in late January, while Iris was in bed reading with Hugo snoozing over her blanketed feet, she noticed Ben open his top drawer and take the small box out of it.

Iris sat up a little taller in bed and her heart began to pound. Her long brown hair was in an alligator clip, no makeup, she was wearing her glasses. Her nails looked like shit.

Ben sat on the bed beside her, the box in his lap. He looked so nervous, she actually felt sorry for him.

"I know we were both thinking I was going to propose on this trip," he began. "I had a huge thing planned for the beach, private dinner, drone photographer, but . . ."

Iris nodded. In an instant, she revised her vision of the proposal; it was better this way. The beach on Valentine's Day was too contrived. A private proposal at home was truer to their life together. Ben was the romantic, Iris the realist. She never needed anything fancy or Instagrammable. She only needed him.

Ben slid the ring box toward her and let it sit on the coverlet, closed. "I want you to have this, but I can't give it to you."

"What?" Iris genuinely didn't understand.

Ben started to cry, and suddenly Iris knew: it was bad, and it was real.

"I've been feeling this . . . detachment, like I'm watching myself go through the motions of doing everything right, but it's not me, or not real. I kept trying to psych myself up with things that would get me excited and make it feel like I always thought it would. The ring design, Cabo . . ."

Her heart raced as she listened to him name every action she had taken as proof of his love and certainty, only to learn they were . . . the opposite—manifestations of his lack thereof.

"I thought if I set up the perfect proposal, the feeling would come. But maybe that was always ass-backwards, I don't know. I know I love you, and I want to make you happy, the last thing I want to do is hurt you, but . . ." He looked at her with red eyes full of tears. "Iris, you deserve someone excited to marry you."

Her face was so flushed with disappointment and shame, she could feel her pulse in her ears. She managed to choke out, "And you're not?"

"Fuck, I'm so sorry." His voice croaked in a snotty sob.

Iris rose to get him a tissue. She put a hand on his arm and rubbed his back, steadying herself by comforting him. She could still fix things. "So you're not ready to get married. That's okay. You know I never gave you an ultimatum. I can be patient. Or maybe we never need to get married, there are no rules. All that matters is that we're together. It's okay. We're *fine*."

Ben looked miserably at her. "If I'm not ready now, when will I be? I swear, I'm thinking of us both, I think. I care about you too much to sleepwalk into this huge decision or make you wait any longer just to be let down."

"How long have you been feeling this way?"

He shrugged. "I don't know, I don't remember."

Her stomach flipped. *Long enough you don't remember.*

"It's not you. You're everything I could ask for, you're a perfect girlfriend, my family loves you, you did nothing wrong, you do everything right. I feel like we're already married."

"Is that so bad?"

"Nothing about us is bad, that's how we've coasted for so long—"

Coasted?

"But is not-bad good enough for forever? Don't we both deserve to feel something big, something powerful to *move* us to the next level? You know, that feeling when you want someone so much, you can't get enough—"

"That's not realistic. We've been together a long time, it doesn't stay like that. Our love is stable and mature, and maybe that's not the most exciting, but that's the kind of love you can build a life on. Do you know how rare that is?"

Ben looked her straight in the eye for the first time since he sat down. "Can you really tell me that I make you feel *enough* to get married?"

Iris blinked, her eyes tearing. "Yes, of course I can. I love you. You make me feel comfortable and safe, and when I'm with you, I feel like I'm home. That's all I've ever wanted."

Ben was quiet for a moment, his face crumpled like the tissue in his hand. He wiped his eyes roughly, leaving his cheeks streaked with pink, and looked back at her with eyes full of apology. "I want more."

I ris walked into the office of Candela, the boutique architectural lighting firm that had employed her for nearly a decade. Iris loved her job and her boss and mentor, Frank Morro, and she put up with the pirate band of male colleagues that comprised their ten-person company. Iris was one of only two women, the other being their unseen, off-site accountant. Architecture had a sophisticated reputation, but it was a boys' club like most building-related fields, and Candela was too small to afford the HR department it so desperately needed. Still, Iris had enjoyed remarkable job security at Candela, unlike so many of her friends who had been forced to change jobs and even careers, and Iris valued stability.

She was extra loaded down today, carrying her laptop bag over her shoulder, a cardboard tray with two large coffees, and a box of a dozen Magnolia cupcakes.

Ana, a member of the building's janitorial staff, spotted Iris as soon as she got off the elevators and rushed over to help her.

"Just take both coffees for a minute while I set these cupcakes down." Iris had gotten in the habit of picking up a coffee for Ana at Dunkin along with her own, as Ana was typically the only employee who got in as early as Iris. Iris liked to get to the office early on the days she didn't work from home. It gave her a chance to focus and start her day while the office was still quiet, before her coworkers arrived.

"*Gracias, amor.* Who has birthday this time?"

"Me."

"Ay! Happy birthday! I should bring you something instead of you me. Why you no remind me?"

"Please, I'm thirty-five, I hardly want to remember it myself. How's your coffee?"

"Perfect. Light and sweet like me." Ana chuckled.

"I don't know how you drink hot coffee in this weather. You have to let me get it iced for you at least once." Iris had a cold brew addiction, black.

"Coffee is supposed to be hot." Ana took a grateful sip even as sweat beaded on her brow.

"Let me drop these in the breakroom." Iris took the cupcakes into the breakroom and refilled the Keurig with water while she was there, although she rarely used it. It was a habit from her early days, and she had come to notice that if she didn't fill it, it never got filled.

Iris was settled in her usual seat in their open plan workspace, reviewing her models for an upcoming design pitch, when the rest of her co-workers trickled in. She thought of the core group as "the frat": Jesse, Theo, Max, and Lawrence. They were tolerable individually, but together they became a pack of dogs. They spoke crassly about the women they dated, took clients to strip joints "ironically," and prided themselves on an ethic of "work hard, play hard" long past the age when such a catchphrase was sufferable. Most days, Iris felt like their beleaguered homeroom teacher.

"Yo, Iris. Are you on your period?" Max asked, loud enough for the room to hear.

"Excuse me?"

"Bruh." Lawrence gave him an admonishing look. Lawrence was Black and at least occasionally on Iris's side.

"No, it's not what you think." Max rubbed both hands over his face. "I'm only asking because I need Advil. I'm hung over, my head is splitting. Girls always have Advil in their purses when they're on their period."

"I don't have any Advil," Iris replied.

"Dude, that's Midol," Jesse said.

"Midol, Advil, it's the same thing."

"You've taken Midol?" Theo snickered.

"It's the *same!* I have sisters."

Iris sighed. "Check the first aid cabinet in the breakroom."

"Will you look for me? The lights in there are too bright," he mewled.

"No, I'm working." *You should try it sometime,* she thought.

"Who designed these lights to be so fucking bright?" Max groaned.

"You needed better light last night so you could see who you were taking home!" Lawrence teased.

"She was all right."

"You sure she was a she?" Jesse quipped.

"I mean, she gave birth to you, so . . ."

The boys erupted in laughter.

"*Guys.* C'mon," Iris chided.

"Yeah, guys. You're disturbing Iris," Theo said in her mock defense.

"Uh-oh, Mom's mad," Jesse sniggered.

Iris tried to breathe slowly through her nose. She didn't want to give them the satisfaction of her frustration.

Another colleague, Nate Childers, emerged from the break room with a cupcake and landed by Iris's desk. He set down the red velvet and clapped his hands once like a coach to catch Jesse's attention. "Yo, my email. I need that price sheet before I can get back to the client, and they're up my ass. Don't let me get fucked on this one."

"I got you." Jesse wheeled his chair back to his desk.

Iris looked up at Nate. "Why do they listen to you?"

"Because I speak idiot." Nate smiled.

If Iris was the office Mom, Nate was Dad. He wasn't much older than the others, around forty, but he was more mature, married with a daughter, and he took his job seriously. He and Iris had hit it off right away when he first started working there, and she considered him her friend and ally.

"I should be used to the frat by now." Iris rolled her eyes. "I just need one of those paddles to whack 'em."

"They should be embarrassed, but that would require self-awareness. But I lived in a frat house in college, and trust me, this place smells a lot better." Nate gestured to her laptop. "How's it going? Are those your designs for the Wolff pitch?"

The Wolff Dev building was going up at 270 Eleventh Ave in Hudson Yards. It was expected to be the latest jewel in the crown of Wolff Development, continuing Jonathan Wolff's reign as the It Boy of New York real estate. Wolff was hoping to repeat the success of his Tribeca glamazon tower known as the Pebble Stack for its tiered stories and rounded edges. But the Hudson Yards project hadn't been as smooth; it was a gamble to bet so much capital on the rising but not yet coveted neighborhood, then Covid hit, halting construction and spooking initial investors. The project had recently found new funding, but only after an ambitious redesign and major internal shake-up. Wolff Dev was now seeking a new lighting designer, and Candela was among the many lighting firms eager to make a bid for it.

"Yes, I feel like I've been designing it in my head before I even knew we'd have a crack at it. I was just talking with Frank about it, landing this would be huge for Candela."

"And for the lead designer, a career-making gig. That's why everyone and their mother wants it."

Iris sighed. It was a long shot, especially for a boutique firm like theirs. Still, Jonathan Wolff had a reputation for being guided by instinct, valuing passion over blue chip legacy firms; it was part of what made him the most exciting developer in New York.

Nate gestured to her laptop. "May I?"

"Sure." She swiveled it toward him and Nate peered down at the screen, clicking through the three-dimensional REVIT model.

"Nice, really soft and organic. I like how the underlighting directs your awareness upward."

"Thanks, the airiness of the lobby height and the lines were my favorite part. And since the building is all about the river view, I wanted to bring that reflective quality of the sun on the Hudson inside."

"You achieved it. It looks . . . tranquil." Nate nodded. "I'd live there."

"Thank you."

"But I thought Frank said they only needed the lighting redone for the hallways and residences, the amenities spaces were going to stay as is."

"I know, but I have this idea for a whole reconceptualization of the building via the lighting. Their post-Covid remodel has an emphasis on privacy and private outdoor space, with all these sections and dividers. But it totally changed the vibe, it's almost brutalist now. And the interiors are stuck in that 2019 sleek luxury hotel look—the whole thing is too cold. I think they have to bring *life* back into it, and the common spaces are a huge part of that. What I've come up with would let them rebrand as a 'wellness residence,' not just compliant with health standards but redefining them."

"A 'wellness residence'? Sounds very Goopy."

"Gwyneth Paltrow gets hate, but Goop is far from a flop. I mean, wellness has become a multi-billion-dollar space."

"I guess, my wife loves it. But you know Wolff's going to be selling these apartments to tech bros, right? Facebook is moving in next door."

"I try not to take design advice from anyone in a gray vest and a lanyard."

Nate laughed. "Touché."

Iris continued to justify herself. "I don't know, I'm into this human-centric lighting, where we can create light that mimics natural circadian rhythms. And I've been researching 'indigo clean' 405 nanometer light that actually disinfects the air. The sanitizing effect is undetectable, but we can direct it above the sight lines anyway, and it disinfects the air as it circulates."

"Feels a little gimmicky."

"You think? I mean, maybe a little. But I think I can pitch it as high tech, you know? It fits in with the Silicon Valley transplants and appeals to the luxury market. Their old plans emphasize the 'hospital grade HVAC,' which is a negligible filtration improvement for a high cost, and who wants to live in a hospital? Wolff can redirect the money into what I'm proposing and still save."

Iris thought she had him convinced when Nate titled his head.

"But you're stepping out of the lighting lane. And that chilly hotel look is Wolff's whole thing."

"He set the bar, but now there are copycats all over, so it doesn't feel new anymore."

"You want to tell Jonathan Wolff his brand is stale?"

"Well, no. I would say it differently." Iris felt the heat rise in her cheeks. "It's a bigger piece of the budget for lighting but a lower cost overall. It would save them money."

"But would it save them face?"

Iris deflated. "You're probably right."

Nate shrugged in a way that communicated the opposite of doubt. "Don't listen to me, go for it. Fortune favors the bold." He took a bite of cupcake. "Found these in the breakroom if you want one."

She waved him off, though she suddenly felt low-sugar.

Nate pointed back to her laptop with some icing on his lip. "Lead with the lobby images. They have a wow factor, a real signature. You're talented, Iris. If Wolff's open to the idea, that's the moment he buys in. Men are visual."

Iris nodded.

Her cellphone vibrated on her desk. "Excuse me, I have to take this."

Nate indicated that she should, and she mouthed "Thank you." Iris waited until he was back at his desk, out of earshot, to answer it. "He-eyyy," she said, grinning at what she knew was coming.

"Hap-py birthday to-oo ya'aah! Hap-py bi-irthday . . ." It was Roman, singing his annual rendition of the Stevie Wonder birthday song. Roman was her other best friend; they'd met a decade ago when they were both baby designers, Iris in lighting and him in interiors, though he'd since become a real estate agent.

Iris laughed. "Thank you, baby."

"I hope my singing softens the blow, because I have bad news. I can't make your birthday dinner tonight! I'm sorry!"

"Oh no!"

"I know. You know I wouldn't miss it if it weren't major, but did you hear about that gas explosion in the Hendricks Houses projects a few days ago?"

"Yes, just reading about it gave me a nightmare. Two people died, right? Awful."

"Well, James"—James was Roman's live-in boyfriend—"James's sister and her kids *live* there, or they did. His niece and nephew were home alone when it happened."

"Omigod! Are they okay?"

"Yes, thankfully. His niece Kiara actually smelled it and got other people to evacuate in time."

Iris gasped.

"But that's not even all. So the New York housing authority is providing the displaced residents with emergency housing, *except* Veronica and her kids don't qualify, because she's been in some eviction dispute and now they're using this to push her out. It's a mess. So they're currently crashing with us."

"Aw, that's terrible. But it's nice of you and James to help."

"It's a whole thing, I'll tell you about it when I see you. But today, I gotta help them get settled. Would you hate me if I missed dinner tonight with you and Hannah?"

"Oh no, I completely understand. Can I do anything to help?"

"No, James and I got it. We might need an extra pair of hands when they allow them to go back to the building to get their stuff, but it's all shut down for the explosion investigation right now."

"Okay yeah, let me know."

"Anyway, I'm sorry to miss your birthday celebration. I was dying for a martini and that ricotta cheesecake. But we're still on for the Kusama exhibit, right? We'll celebrate then."

Iris replied, "Yes, don't worry about tonight. Go, be a good boyfriend!"

"*I'm trying!* Happy birthday!"

Iris hung up and looked at the clock. It was just about time for her much-anticipated meeting with Frank to ask for a promotion. Iris had requested the meeting, drafting and redrafting the email, letting it marinate in her Drafts folder before she hit Send last week. She reminded herself she deserved this promotion. She had been courted by other firms, but she had stayed loyal, and paid her dues twice over. It was only fair.

Frank had the only private office on the team, and the door was shut. Iris knocked, no answer, but she could hear a rhythmic thumping and whirring sound. She knocked again, louder.

"Come in!"

She entered and found Frank in a tight tank and bike shorts, legs spinning atop the Peloton beside his desk, pumping along to Bruce Springsteen music and a chirpy woman's voice. The room smelled ripe. "I'm sorry, should I come back in a bit?"

"Nah, it's fine. I was in the cool-down anyway. Please, sit." He lifted his rimless glasses and wiped his face with a hand towel. "This was my only hour to get this in today. I'm training for the Labor Day centennial ride. Madison here is very encouraging." He gestured to the tiny blonde onscreen before finally muting her whoops of affirmation.

Iris took a seat in the chair opposite his desk and swiveled it to face him, albeit awkwardly lower than his perch on the bike. "A hundred miles, that's very impressive."

"At my age, just trying to stave off death." Frank was in his sixties with close-cropped silver hair and a short, wiry physique. He slipped his feet from the cycling shoes, hopped off, and began to stretch his quads in his sweat socks. "Before you say anything, let me go first. I have something for you."

Iris's heart leaped at the potential reprieve from asserting herself.

Frank swung his leg high on the seat to get his hamstrings and pointed behind his desk. "See there, on the floor, the pink bag? That's for you."

She retrieved the gift bag herself and opened it. "A candle."

"Happy birthday! It's scented. Aromatherapy. Susan picked it, so you know it's good."

Her shoulders sank. Frank had been like a father figure to her ever since he took her under his wing just a few years after grad school, but she wished that today he was thinking of her professionally, not personally. Still, it was kind that he remembered her birthday, she scolded herself. Iris gave the candle a sniff. "Mmm, lavender. Thank you so much, and thank Susan, too."

"You should thank yourself. You put everyone's birthdays into the GoogleCal."

"Oh, right. Ha." She had done that a couple of years ago so that someone other than her would think to bring in treats on birthdays, and so that Frank might notice that Jesse was always suspiciously "sick" the day after his. Neither wish was achieved.

At last Frank sat at his desk. "So what's up?"

"Well, I was just wondering if we could revisit a discussion we had a while back, about my role here, and the possibility of having the opportunity to advance into more of a leadership role here." *Damn,* and she'd had it so succinct in her bathroom mirror.

"Ah yes, the promotion." Frank tented his fingers. "Here's the deal. You're terrific. You're a workhorse, and you care about this firm as much as anyone here except me."

"Thank you."

"You're dependable and consistent. You have good taste, your ideas fit the budgets, I can trust you not to screw up, which is more than I can say for some of these yahoos." He gestured to outside his office. "You're a good influence on the guys. It's impolitic to say, but the truth is, sometimes men need a woman in the room to behave themselves."

"They're old enough not to need a babysitter."

"Of course you're right, I should give them more credit."

That wasn't what Iris meant.

Frank leaned forward in his chair. "There's a thing in cycling called drafting. In cycling racing teams, they ride in a line to minimize drag. You have a great rider in the front of the pack, and other riders can draft behind him, literally using him as a shield against the air resistance, and they all take turns being the lead. Drafting lets the whole group go faster while conserving energy overall. You've been at the head of the pack, grinding it out to the benefit of the whole. Rest assured, I see you, I appreciate you. But I need you there."

"In the lead?" Iris said, hopefully.

"At the head. See, if I pull you out of the pack, move you up and on your own, that group benefit is lost. They'll have no one to set pace."

"Won't it make space for a new person to go to the front of the pack? Nate's good."

"Nate does his own thing, he may not stick around. And the rest of the group is still maturing. I feel like we're on the cusp as a company, I don't want to throw off the team dynamic right now."

"Well, we forwent the bonuses the last few years, which I understood, but I really think based on my time and effort, I feel like I've earned, well, I'd like to be considered for a raise."

"Everyone at the same level gets equal pay, only fair."

"But I've been at this level the longest, and like you said, they're drafting behind me, so—"

"Seniority isn't the only factor. You can't expect to advance by simply waiting it out, this isn't a royal engagement."

Iris winced.

"Listen, I feel your frustration, but it's nuanced. The person at the front is putting in slightly more effort than those drafting behind, but he—*or she*—isn't actually faster. He isn't a better rider, necessarily. You're in the lead but not yet a leader, that's the difference."

Her face flushed, but Frank barreled on.

"We've got some people here who aren't as disciplined as you, but they have other strengths, like creativity, initiative, balls—figuratively speaking. I think those are areas you have room to grow. But the road doesn't rise to meet us, Iris. I need to see more from you first, then we can revisit promotion. Fair enough, kiddo?"

Iris nodded, her mouth dry with disappointment.

"That said, if you're looking for an opportunity, Wolff Dev looking for a new lighting team is huge. If we win this bid, and it's a big if, it would be a game changer for Candela. I'd need to rely heavily on our lead designer for the project, a big effort for a bigger reward. Today we have our in-house meeting to brainstorm pitches and decide who I'll take with me to Wolff. Put your best ideas forward. If you were the one to win this contract for us, that would certainly warrant a promotion. So, impress me this afternoon."

Fresh hope hit her like caffeine; she'd been pouring in time on her idea for the Wolff redesign for weeks. "I will. You'll see."

She exited Frank's office to see Max shoot a wadded-up piece of paper toward the waste bin across the room and miss, it landed on the floor. Jesse booed him. Ana, passing nearby, bent to pick it up.

"Oh, there's Ana—Ana!" Max beckoned her over. "*Mamacita,* will you do me a favor, *por favor?*"

"Yes, Mr. Gelman."

"Can you see if we have any Advil or headache medicine in the breakroom or somewhere?"

"I have some in my bag."

"Ohhh!" the frat burst into laughter and jeers.

Ana smiled despite not being in on the joke. "I get it for you, one minute."

Iris hated them.

Later that afternoon, they all gathered in the conference room. Iris put the box of cupcakes in the center of the table and set up her laptop next to Frank.

Frank clapped his hands to open the meeting. "As you know, construction on Wolff Dev's latest luxury building, Oasys at 270 Eleventh Ave, has been on pause as they reconceptualize the design. The previous lighting design plans are incompatible with new layouts and with the new air filtration system, and apparently Wolff has soured on Lumi, so they won't be working with them for the renovation. That means we are getting a second chance at this project. This is a big fish for us, but I believe our team can do it and pave the way for future growth. I want to put in a bid as soon as possible. But I can't take you all with me to pitch Jonathan Wolff, so first you need to pitch your idea to me, and we'll see who will take the lead alongside me."

Max started talking first. "I think they could allow more natural light by incorporating Japanese-style screen doors made with frosted glass—"

"Frosted glass?" Frank made a face. "Dated. People don't want to live in a giant bathroom. Think bigger."

Iris raised her hand.

But Lawrence jumped in, "We keep thinking of the way the light tracking has to avoid the air filtration system, framing them as oppositional systems trying to occupy the same space in the structure.

But what if we could combine them and kill two birds with one stone?"

Frank looked interested. "You came up with a plan to combine them?"

"No. Not yet, but—"

"It's a good idea, but the whole challenge is the execution. See what you can work up for me by Friday. Does anyone else have an idea like that, big picture, ready to go *now*?"

Iris raised her hand again but Frank was looking the other way.

"Indigo clean," Nate said.

Iris's head snapped in his direction.

"It's light that actually disinfects the air. The optical and sanitizing effect are unobtrusive, we can direct it above the sight lines. It's high tech, it's tied to wellness, it's a new angle. Wolff needs a fresh take if he's going to stand out in this buyer's market. Getting an official designation as a 'wellness residence' could do just that."

"It's gimmick," muttered Theo.

"It's a *hook*. A wellness residence. Exceeding clean living standards. And indigo clean lighting actually works, and it's cheaper than HVAC."

"That's a very interesting idea," Frank said.

"Iris gave it to me. I made a joke about Gwyneth Paltrow's company Goop, and she rightly chided me for it, saying that wellness is a multi-billion-dollar industry. Sure, it's typically marketed at women, but everyone should sit up and listen, unless they want to leave money on the table. There's no reason that value shouldn't extend into real estate, and women have a lot of influence over real estate decisions. If mama ain't happy, ain't nobody happy, amirite?"

The men at the table laughed.

Jesse tapped her shoulder. "Hey, pass me a cupcake?"

Iris caught up to Nate as soon as the meeting let out. "Nate, what was that?"

"What do you mean?"

"Indigo clean? You pitched my wellness concept."

He frowned like he was totally puzzled. "Wait, you're not *mad,* are you? I mean, c'mon, I credited you! I literally said you gave me the idea."

"You credited me with defending Goop, but you passed the design concept off as your own."

"Whoa." Nate put his hands up as if she had a gun. "I really think you're overreacting. It came up! Frank was pushing us for more ideas in the meeting, and I thought of our conversation. I mean, I'm sorry if you felt like I stole your thunder or something, but I didn't want to let the moment pass. Why didn't you say something in the meeting?"

"I was so surprised to hear you saying it, I couldn't react fast enough."

"I wish you had, I was all alone in there. But look, no worries." He put his hands on her shoulders. "I got you. We're a team. We're trying to come up with the best pitch for the firm to win the bid. I really thought you'd be happy. Frank loved our idea, I think he's gonna go with it."

Iris exhaled in a mirthless chuckle. *Our idea.* But Nate was right about one thing.

Her moment had passed.

Five

I ris burst out the doors of her office building fueled by anger. But the lion's share of her fury wasn't at Nate, or at Frank, or any of the guys, it was at herself. Raising her hand like a schoolgirl while the boys steamrolled her, again. And *right after* Frank had said he wanted to see more from her, *right after* she'd told him he would. Why hadn't she shut Nate down right then? Why did she always freeze when she needed to act?

Iris stepped into the flow of end-of-workday commuters that streamed down Sixth Avenue toward the subway stations on the corner. Six in the evening and the weather remained chokingly hot and humid, and the prospect of squeezing into a sweaty subway car felt as appealing as crawling into an armpit. Speaking of which, she wanted to avoid pit stains at her birthday dinner, so she treated herself to an Uber to the restaurant.

Iris had hit the final location confirmation for her Uber when she received a text from Hannah:

> I'm sooo sorry to do this, I was TRYING
> to rally, but I have been vomiting
> non-stop, I don't think I can hold it
> together for dinner tonight. I'm sorry!!!
> Preggo problems. But I'll make it up to
> you! Birthday brunch Sunday?

Iris's shoulders sank. This was shaping up to be the worst birthday in memory. But she knew Hannah felt bad already, so she texted back:

> No worries! Sorry you're sick 😔
> Sunday's good!

> Yay! Sry again about tonite. I know
> Roman will take good care of you!
> Have fun! xo

She double-tapped Hannah's text to add a thumbs-up to it; white lies were easy via emoji.

Shoot, Iris remembered the Uber—currently one minute away, but redirecting it to drive her home would take forever in rush hour traffic and be way too expensive. She canceled the ride, but a pop-up informed her she'd be charged for the late cancel. The fee was still cheaper than the ride, so Iris grudgingly hit Accept and descended into the grimy sauna of the subway.

Waiting on the crowded platform with only her elbows' width of personal space, Iris cancelled her Resy app reservation for dinner that night, incurring a late cancel fee—Accept. Then she opened WoofIt, her dog walker app, and canceled the seven P.M. walk she'd scheduled for her dog, with another late cancel fee—Accept.

Then one more text chimed in from Hannah:

> Forgot to ask! How did promotion
> talk go???

The A train screeched into the platform like Iris's frustration made manifest, screaming for her.

Iris put her key in her front door and eased it open an inch at a time. A neighbor she didn't know passed by in the hall and shot Iris a quizzical look; Iris smiled, aware that she appeared to be sneaking into her own home. In a few more inches, she was confident enough the other side was clear and entered.

The stocky beagle was snoring against the wall of her front hall, his tail flopped over the doorstop. Hugo always slept by the front door, waiting for her to return. But he was thirteen years old now and sometimes he no longer heard her come in, so she had to be careful not to bump him.

Getting home to her dog earlier than expected was the sole upshot of the day. Iris stepped out of her shoes, set down her purse, and crouched beside him. His cinnamon muzzle, now sugared with age, quivered with a dream. One of his ears was turned inside out, showing the faded blue number tattooed inside. Before Iris adopted him from the beagle rescue, Hugo had spent his early life as a test subject in a laboratory. Iris named him in homage to Victor Hugo's *Les Misérables,* because like the hero of that story, he didn't let an unjust imprisonment corrupt his pure soul. He was the sweetest baby.

Iris lightly stroked his smooth head, warm as an egg beneath a hen. On the second caress, he awoke with a start, the floor side of his face still smushed. She hated when she startled him awake, hated to think she'd triggered his puppyhood trauma. But Hugo never stayed scared. As soon as his twitching nose inhaled her scent, his tail thumped against the floor, and he hustled to press into her waiting arms.

On her way out with Hugo, Iris saw her cute neighbor David and his dog, a fawn French bulldog named Gronk, because, as David joked, "He makes every catch." David hailed from Boston, and dogs couldn't help it when their namesake players got traded. David and Iris often seemed to be walking their dogs around the same time, their schedules loosely synced. She liked it. It had engendered a camaraderie between them; they bonded over politics, whispered gripes about their surly super, Ervin, and of course the dogs. David wasn't Tom Brady, but he was tall and around her age, with a laid-back affability, and since Ben moved out, Iris's neighborly affection had budded into a crush. On the days she just missed them coming home as she was going out, she was always sorry. She wondered if he was sorry too.

Hugo was a great wingman. He tugged toward David in the lobby, tail wagging, and as soon as Gronk spotted them from one googly eye, he planted himself for playtime in a wide-legged stance. David and Iris had no choice but to say hello. "Hey, David."

"Yo, Iris and Huuug!" He bent to greet Hugo, who was preoccupied with trying to sniff Gronk's butt while the bulldog spun with snorty excitement, nails clacking on the polished floor. David laughed. "Let's get them out."

They dragged the dogs outside and started walking in the same direction.

"Ervin finally came to fix my air conditioner yesterday, only eight days after it conked out," David said.

"Ugh, this week was one of the hottest. How did you survive?"

"Multiple cold showers a day and basically stripping naked as soon as I walked in the door," he said, making Iris blush. "But it's Gronk I was worried about; Frenchies can't handle the heat. I put him in doggy daycare so he'd stay cool during the day, and he wouldn't leave the bathroom tile all night."

"Aw, poor little guy." Her esteem for David went up a notch. "I'm glad Ervin fixed it."

"Oh, he didn't fix it," David corrected. "But he satisfied himself that it was actually broken and not just my helplessness and called the commercial repairmen. They came today."

"I'm sorry to laugh."

"Once, I called him when my toilet kept running, and it was a really easy fix, and he's never let me forget it. He thinks I'm soft."

"He never gives me a hard time about needing help. Sexism for the win!"

"He's old school all right."

"But I'm actually pretty handy with home stuff, so the next time you have a problem, feel free to knock on my door, I'm 1-F."

"You wanna fix my toilet?" David smiled at her like she was nuts.

"Well, no, I mean—" she stammered.

Frenchie grunts drew their attention down to the dogs playing again. Gronk opened his clamshell mouth, baring the wonkiest tiny teeth, and Hugo held his ears back and tried to engage in some friendly humping.

"All right, you horndogs, break it up."

They passed the nylon leashes to and fro, their hands coming close to touching, but not.

"Gronkster, we gotta get down to business. See you around, Iris."

" 'Bye," Iris said, disappointed to have let the conversation die.

But her awkwardness was a mercy. Even single, she would never act on her crush. Not with someone in her building. There was one social rule even dogs understand: Don't shit where you eat.

Iris walked Hugo alone to the next block, to the more historic part of the West Village, where the boxy apartment buildings of the 1980s gave way to the elegant brownstones of the 1880s. Though she could never afford to live in one, these were the homes that had made her fall in love with the neighborhood. On these night walks, her favorite thing was to pass a lit window and glimpse the glowing diorama inside, like a life-size dollhouse. She told herself her interest was professional and not merely voyeuristic, as from her lower vantage point, she could mainly see the top half of the rooms, ornate crown molding and crystal chandeliers, midcentury modern Nelson bubble lights, fine art worthy of its own tiny lamp. But it was the lives beneath the lighting that Iris longed to know and liked to imagine. Still, she figured, you were entitled to be nosy about people wealthier than you. She wondered if the residents left their curtains open on purpose, forgetfulness as a form of noblesse oblige.

She should feel more guilty for peeping, but to be a voyeur in New York City required one only to open one's eyes. Manhattan was home to 1.6 million people stacked on top of each other like an ant farm. Precious "units" of real estate, obscenely priced by the square foot, were pressed flush against, above, below, and beside other people. You could smell the neighbor's cooking, hear the couple on the other side of the wall making love or screaming at each other, see someone undressing in the apartment across the street—but you abide by the city's cardinal rule: Mind your business. For the residents beneath the penthouses and beside the brownstones, privacy is a social contract rather than a physical barrier.

This definition of *private* as merely *unacknowledged* was tested every day when you passed someone unsheltered, doing what others did behind closed doors, you afforded them privacy with your inattention. Even if they called out to you directly, with Bible verses or psychosis, even if you gave them what they asked, you did so with eyes averted. You told yourself that that was a kindness.

To stare was rude.

To care was untenable.

That was how the city's population could be at once so cramped and yet so atomized. The sensory overlap was unavoidable, but you ignored it completely or, as a second choice, complained about it, fruitlessly, to friends. What other choice was there? There were simply too many people to comprehend, too many wishes and desires, fears, problems, and needs jammed up in one place for everyone to stay connected and still get by. It was a numbers problem.

For all the crowds and false privacy in this town, there was real loneliness. But acknowledging *that* was more embarrassing and transgressive than walking naked before an open window.

To live in Manhattan required willful dissociation.

Normally Iris was better at it.

Iris ate her dinner straight from the takeout containers beside the pamphlets from Family Tree Fertility spread out before her. Candela provided her basic health insurance but none that covered fertility treatment. On the back of an envelope, she had added up the expected costs of the egg freezing process and circled the total: $16,000.

Without the promotion, it felt out of reach, or at least unwise. She had always been careful with money. On her eighteenth birthday, Iris gained control of her late parents' estate, although she let her grandparents manage it while she went to Penn State. On her twenty-first birthday, instead of planning her drink order, Iris sat across from her grandfather for a serious talk about money. She remembered him saying, "Buy your home. No matter what people say, buy it outright. Debt is dangerous. Your friends can go home and live with their parents if things go sideways, but not you. Find a place you love, no more than you need, and live off the money you make. Property is always a good investment. And I won't rest easy unless I know you've got a roof over your head."

It was good advice. Iris graduated with her master's in architecture from Stuckeman and landed in New York City. She felt as if her grandfather was watching over her when she found a great deal on a first-floor apartment in the West Village. So, at twenty-four, Iris bought her first home, all cash. The sellers must have thought she was an heiress; technically, she was, but it took nearly all the money she had.

She didn't regret it, even if she was house-poor. When she and Ben wanted to move in together, there was no question, he was moving into her place, and when they broke up, he was the one who had to move out. And her apartment had certainly gone up in value—but only if she sold. Her net worth on paper didn't make paying for this egg freezing any easier.

For most of her life, Iris had felt rushed ahead of her peers, forced to grow up fast and privileged to land her dream job and home in her early twenties. Somewhere along the way, her milestones stalled. Today's thirty-fifth birthday did not look the way she had imagined.

But she was here. Her parents got to only thirty-eight and forty. Iris always thought of them on her birthdays, and she owed it to them to celebrate. She started a new order at Seamless.com, found Raffaela's restaurant, and tipped five bucks on an order that included only one item: a single slice of ricotta cheesecake.

In the Special Directions section, she typed: If possible, please include one candle, thanks!

Iris brought up a streaming episode of *Sex and the City*, her comfort show. The salsa theme music began to play, and before she could hit Skip Intro, her phone pinged with a new message. She opened it, expecting a confirmation of her order.

It was from Ben: "Happy birthday!"

CHAPTER

Six

"I'm sorry, Iris. We are supposed to be celebrating your birthday, and you are in my shitter."

"That's the vibe of this birthday so far, to be honest." Iris was standing on a ladder and troubleshooting her neighbor's antique toilet. She held a small flashlight between her teeth in order to reach both hands into the tank. "*But dish, I can fixsh.*"

The neighbor was Mireille Rapacine, an elder, but not elderly, Frenchwoman whom Iris had come to know on her dog walks. Madame Rapacine, as Iris called her, was a neighborhood character. She lived nearby in the first-floor apartment of a stately brownstone on Bank Street and often sat in a lawn chair on her building's stoop, as if it were a porch in South Philly instead of a twelve-million-dollar townhouse in the coveted West Village. But she did so with Parisian style: black sunglasses, Hermès scarves, and in the summer, a hand fan—though never, ever a cigarette. Iris might have found her intimidating, but Hugo adored her; he whined unless Iris let him up the brownstone's front steps to press his snout into her waiting hands.

During the pandemic, Iris's first thought was for Mme Rapacine. She looked in on her every few days during lockdown, brought her groceries, prescriptions, anything that couldn't be delivered. But they really became friends when Iris herself caught Covid, or, technically, just after. Long after her worst symptoms had passed, Iris's anosmia—loss of smell—persisted. She could never have anticipated how disorienting and depressing anosmia would be; it didn't help that this was soon after she and Ben had broken up. She couldn't even eat her feelings, as the anosmia had ruined her enjoyment of food—popcorn tasted like Styrofoam, and her beloved Frosted Mini Wheats were wet, wadded tissue paper. Worse, it made her feel alienated from the world; she felt numb, disconnected, and alone.

Only then did Mme Rapacine reveal that she was a fourth-generation *nose,* a master perfumer, now retired, and she insisted that Iris come over every afternoon for smell training. They would sit together before her "organ," a classical perfumer's desk whose tiered shelves, reminiscent of the musical instrument, held rows of brown apothecary bottles of various fragrant essences used to "compose" a perfume. Rapacine would dip thin strips of white paper into different scents for Iris to practice identifying them, instructing her to smell them *comme un lapin,* like a bunny, with short, rapid sniffs to coax her olfactory receptors into functioning again. In a month, Iris's sense of smell and its accompanying pleasures had returned, along with something else: hope.

Madame Rapacine had brought her back to life.

The least Iris could do was repair her toilet.

Rapacine's powder room was as charming and eccentric as the rest of her apartment. The close walls were papered in pale blue and forest green *toile de Jouy.* The toilet at issue was a bona fide Victorian antique—the type with a wooden seat and wooden tank mounted high on the wall with a brass chain pull. And before Iris came over, it had been running for a full day and night.

"Normally I give it a tickle and it stops, but this time it is relentless. The super never answers my calls. My new landlord would prefer I drown," Rapacine snipped.

"*Jhuh cha*—" Iris removed the flashlight from between her teeth to speak properly, "Sorry—the chain inside gets twisted and the flapper doesn't close fully. But don't worry, it won't overflow as long as the drain is clear." She stepped carefully down the ladder and turned the water valve to open it again. "And you can always turn this valve to stop the water flowing through the pipes, or in this case, to restart it. Okay, let's try and flush it now."

Rapacine pulled the chain, they held their breath as the flush slowly whirlpooled down, and at last the toilet began to refill normally. Rapacine clapped in delight. "Brava, Iris! *Merci,* you're brilliant."

"Nah, just good at fiddly home mechanics. And they don't make them like this anymore. This is the *real* old New York. Before they did a slapdash reno for every new buyer." Iris washed her hands. Upon closer inspection, she noticed that the wallpaper scenes were not pastoral but marine, featuring mermaids waving to ships, pulling sailors and pirates underwater, and communing with sea creatures like giant octopuses and whales. "I'm in love with this wallpaper."

"*Toile des sirènes.* Designed by a friend."

Iris loved that everything in Rapacine's apartment had some story or personal connection to her. Iris admired that she lived a full and extraordinary life, with a creative, cultured, and interesting circle of friends. Though Iris hadn't met any of them.

"You have earned a glass of wine. I have a perfect Sancerre in the *frigo.* Come."

While Mme Rapacine retrieved the wine, Iris lingered in the living room. There was a Louis XVI chaise longue upholstered in ochre damask that contrasted beautifully with the peacock blue walls and an Eames armchair in cognac leather, worn as a catcher's mitt, begging for a rainy afternoon and a book—of which she had plenty. Her wall space was covered by packed bookshelves and framed art. The one item of the modern era was the small flatscreen TV tucked on a bar service behind a row of Baccarat barware.

The strange thing was how dark Rapacine kept the apartment. The windows were covered by double-lined shantung drapes, which she kept drawn, blocking what could be abundant natural light from the bay window. It pained Iris, both as a lighting designer and an envious apartment dweller. But Mme Rapacine insisted darkness was absolutely necessary, as sunlight degraded fragrance, and the eye-level tier of every bookshelf displayed volumes of her vast collection of perfume bottles filled with creations from her long career, scents composed by famous noses she counted as friends, vintage perfumes, and other rare fragrances. Iris had once asked Rapacine why she displayed no personal photographs, and she'd gestured to her perfume library and replied, "These are my photographs."

It was a small miracle that one of her cats hadn't knocked any of the bottles off by now, but perhaps even the animals recognized their special value. Iris *pssp-pssp*ed and Chéri's marmalade head popped up in slow-blinking wakefulness from a large wicker basket on the living room floor. She found them both curled up inside, Chéri, the orange tabby boy, and Jasmine, a deaf white female, still asleep, the two of them forming a Creamsicle yin and yang. Jasmine felt her brother's movement, and soon both were yawning and stretching, emerging from the basket like pulled taffy. Iris crouched to kiss Jasmine's snowy head and caught a whiff of faintly floral perfume.

"How do even your cats smell good?"

"It is not the cats, but the basket," Rapacine called back from the kitchen.

Iris bent to sniff the empty basket, and sure enough, the woven wood itself was fragrant: floral, sweet, and a little vegetal.

Rapacine reentered the living room, drying her hands with a towel. "When I was a girl in Grasse, we lived beside the flower fields, jasmine, mimosa, Rose de Mai. That was one of the pickers' baskets, it has cradled decades of flower harvests, tens of thousands of freshly plucked jasmine heads. I used to keep my lingerie in it."

Iris smiled inside.

"But then the white kitten liked it so much, I surrendered it and named her Jasmine."

"I can't believe it holds the scent after all this time."

"My father used to say the only thing that smelled better than the pickers' baskets were the pickers' arms—an accord of dewy jasmine mixed with sweat and the musk of warm skin. He would know, he slept with most of them."

Iris followed Mme Rapacine around a paneled Chinoiserie screen and passed into the kitchen at the back of the apartment, where the sunlight was allowed to bounce off the yellow-painted walls. Rapacine stood at the butcher block island and opened the bottle of wine.

In the light, Iris was struck, as always, that Mireille Rapacine was beautiful. One might reflexively add "for her age," which had to be somewhere in her seventies if not eighties, but that would be wrong. She was beautiful, period. She was petite and slim, but not frail; she had the posture of a dancer. Iris had never known someone with such deep-set eyes, and although her lashes had grown sparse, the better to admire her piercing blue eyes. She didn't make any of the conventional choices for women her age: she left her hair long and gray, shaded like an oyster shell, and she wore it either up in a twist, or, as she did now, loose and wavy, kissing her shoulders. Rapacine dressed like a cross between Manon des Sources and Steven Tyler, favoring soft peasant blouses and slip dresses and an excess of jewelry, scarves, and the occasional feather. She rarely hid her freckled décolleté but decorated it with necklaces. She adorned her slender wrists in gold bangles and stacked rings on every knobby finger. She didn't appear to care if her signs of aging were on display. Instead, she wore her skin so proudly that her age all but disappeared.

"It was your father who taught you to be a nose?" Iris asked.

"Yes, against his own wishes. My father was a typical Grassois— passionate, provincial, romantic but chauvinistic. He intended to instruct my elder brother, but alas, *mon frère* was such a good student of masculinity that he broke his nose in a fight and then suffered from nose blindness that was incurable. *Alors,* my father had no choice but to teach me." She retrieved two wine glasses from her cabinet. "To his further chagrin, I was better than all of them. Should we have our wine inside or in the garden?"

Chéri meowed at the back door, eager to be let out.

"*Bonne idée, mon Chéri,* the garden it is."

Iris opened the door and it was like opening a portal to Eden. A trellised entrance presented a veil of wisteria, but the purple-flowered tendrils parted to reveal a walled garden, lushly planted. The cats shot out ahead of their human, and Rapacine took a seat at a small wrought-iron table beneath the shade of a Chinese maple tree. Back here, the city noise was muted, soundproofed by climbing roses. The only sounds were birds chirping and bees buzzing—when was the last time Iris had heard a bee in Manhattan?

Rapacine raised her own glass to toast. "*Bonne anniversaire!* Belatedly."

Iris limply clinked glasses and thanked her. "Thirty-five."

Rapacine rolled her eyes. "You know it is a myth that women lose their power as they age. A lie invented by men afraid of being challenged. Youth has currency, but not power. Every perfumer knows you do not pick green buds. A flower's scent, its power of attraction, is most potent on the cusp of decay."

"Yeah, well, 'decay' needs a rebrand." She stroked Jasmine's tail as the white cat wove under her chair legs. "I'm not where I thought I would be at this age. I thought I'd have progressed in my career. I thought I'd be married with a kid by now."

"To Monsieur Khaki? Would that be preferable?"

Iris chuckled. "*One time* he wore pleated khakis in front of you."

"You two had no heat. Who could with that man? Gutless, bloodless."

Ben's words haunted her, *I don't feel excited.* "What if I'm the bloodless one?"

Rapacine blew air through her lips in a very French dismissal.

Iris watched Chéri stalk a butterfly. "My animal instincts have always been blunted."

"Impossible. You simply stopped trusting them."

"I told you about the house fire when I was a kid—I remember seeing and smelling the smoke from my bed, I was awake, but I froze. A family member had to come save me, otherwise I would've just laid there and died."

"Freezing is also an instinct. We cannot blame ourselves for what we failed to do as terrified children."

She was glad Mme Rapacine had turned to yank a weed after she said it, because her words released a swell of emotion that pricked her eyes with tears. Iris didn't easily feel compassion for her young self, so the older woman's validation caught her off guard. Most often, the memory of Iris's savior brought her shame, but she didn't want to get into that now. She blinked away the vulnerability before Rapacine turned back.

"And you know, you can have a child without a partner."

"I'm looking into freezing my eggs, but I was counting on this promotion at work to afford it, and I'm not sure that's gonna happen now either." She shook her head. "I've always dreamed of having a family of my own, but this isn't how I imagined it. I wanted it to happen *naturally*, with someone I love, not in a petri dish or a doctor's office. It's depressing."

"Do you know how we fertilize the Rose de Mai?" Mme Rapacine reached to an abundant rosebush behind her, tilting her chair up on its two back legs, making Iris nervous. She grabbed hold of the thorny stem of a glorious bloom, light pink but vibrant, like the inside of your lip, and pulled its profusely petaled head forward. Its honeyed, piquant fragrance caught the air, even from across the table. "Also known as the Rosa Centifolia, the hundred-petaled rose, the Rose de Mai is the pride of Grasse, a legendary material in perfumery the world over for its powerful yet delicate fragrance. But it is a sensitive flower, very difficult to grow. So perfumers developed a surgical method: We make an incision into the stalk of a common shrub rose and graft the bud of a Rose de Mai and bandage them together. The wound produces extra sap to feed the bud, while the hardy shrub shelters it as it grows to glory. *Et voilà*." Rapacine snipped the flower, and the branch sprang back, swaying all the heavy blooms together. She handed the lush rose to Iris. "Sometimes nature needs a little doctoring."

Iris brought it to her nose and smiled. It did make her feel better.

Rapacine clapped her hands. "I have a birthday gift for you. *Un moment.*" She went into the apartment and reemerged with a small brown paper box tied with kitchen twine, a bloom of purple iris tucked into the string.

"Aww, you didn't have to do this."

"I wanted to. I don't do anything I don't want to do." She smiled serenely. "Open it."

Resting inside the box lay a bottle of perfume. The bottle was a wonder: jade-green crystal in the shape of a winged insect, at once naturalistic and poetic. The central vessel was frosted to a soft semi-opacity, but it was enclosed by translucent wings of polished crystal, carved like lace, draping elegantly down the body of the bottle. Iris turned it in her hands, enjoying its pleasing heft as the sunlight caught its facets. When she set it down, the wings cleverly provided a wider base of support, so that the interior flacon appeared to hover, balanced only on a pinpoint.

"A *cigale,* I forget in English, the singing bugs in summer."

"A cicada."

Rapacine snapped her fingers. "*C'est ça! La cigale* is the symbol of Provence, where I come from. To the Greek poets, they are a symbol of death and rebirth because of their life cycle—they bury themselves underground to emerge years later to sing, to fly, to make love, and *then* to die, as one does." She chuckled. "They have been depicted on perfume bottles since René Lalique made his first crystal flacon for Roger et Gallet's fragrance Cigalia, and they have always been a resonant metaphor to me, and I think for you as well. This flacon is French, late nineteenth century. I collect them, and it's a good one."

"It's stunning, thank you."

"The bottle is not the gift. *C'est le parfum.*"

Iris delicately pinched the top of the stopper, shaped like a flower at which the cicada was about to sip, and hesitated. "I'm afraid to break it."

Rapacine took it and demonstrated the twisting motion to unstop the bottle and remove the blotter. She took each of Iris's hands, turning them to expose the thin, pale skin of her wrists and tracing the cool blotter along her blue veins, leaving behind a tingly sensation and an oily sheen. Mme Rapacine dipped the crystal blotter again into the bottle, then gestured to Iris to expose her neck by tilting her own jawline up. Iris mimicked her, leaning in and lifting her chin, so for a moment they sat like two swans, arching their necks toward each other. Rapacine lightly touched the crystal to the pulse points of Iris's neck, where the drops clung and alerted her entire body to the caress of the breeze.

Then the first, effervescent head notes of the scent began to tickle her nose like champagne bubbles. She was awakened by a tart and refreshing zest coupled with sweet floral nectar like honeysuckle, bright, transparent, and airy. She closed her eyes and imagined a blast of sun and sky carrying the finest spray felt from the edge of a sailboat, but one cresting waves of rosewater instead of brine. Iris had to laugh, embarrassed by the pleasure of it.

"Oh, it's *beautiful.*" It was a helpless understatement. "What's in it?"

"You tell me. Remember your smell training."

"Something bright and juicy at the top, but I don't think it's berga-mot, it's not citrusy." Iris closed her eyes. "I see pink, like a sweet, tart berry . . ." She opened them. "Currant?"

"Lychee, because like you, it has a prickly shell belying its sweet, tender interior. What else?"

"No, please, you do the rest. I love when you tell it." She sounded like a child asking for a story.

"Like any good fragrance, it's greater than the sum of its notes, and I must guard some secrets. But I will share the primary notes of its olfactory pyramid. In addition to the aquatic freshness of lychee fruit, the head has neroli, the flower of bitter orange. It is delicate, a little green, and more aromatic than citrus, and known for its purify-ing qualities."

Iris thought the neroli must be the juicy nectar and the lychee the rosy pop.

"Then a voluptuous floral heart. Tuberose, *la fleur charnelle,* the carnal flower, whose narcotic femininity was once believed to be so powerful that it could send young women into spontaneous orgasm if they smelled it after dark. Next, the flower that raised me, jasmine, a tiny white flower with an enveloping sweetness, warm and reso-nant as a cello line. And Osmanthus, what the Chinese call the flower of wisdom, whose scent evokes an apricot's velvet flesh, at once blushing and innocent yet strapped with a leather nuance."

Iris sniffed her wrist again. The floral facets were already unfurl-ing as it settled, and she felt drawn into its warm depth. "And some spice?"

"*Brava,* your nose has gotten better. There is a touch of cumin to bring harmony to the floral chord, a carnal romance at the heart of the fragrance." Rapacine reached for Iris's arm and smelled the fragrance on her; a satisfied smile spreading on her face. "And at last, a sensual and animalic base: ambergris, salty and erotic; sandalwood, milky and sacred, and . . . I couldn't resist an iris note, but iris is a mute flower, the bloom will not give its scent—"

"That tracks, I'm a mute flower at work, too."

"No, you misunderstand. Live iris has a scent, but its scent is impossible to extract like other flowers. Iris guards its fragrance fiercely. What I used in the base is orris, a material that is made from the iris root, which takes years to mature, that is tender, powdery, and intimate. You are named for a rare and precious fragrance, one whose character is both ethereal and yet rooted in soft earth."

Iris was in awe.

"*C'est un parfum vivant,* a living fragrance. It will bloom on your skin differently depending on your body heat, your hormones, even your mood. Changes within you will change the dance between you and the *parfum. You* are the final ingredient."

"What's it called?"

"It is untitled. It is your story to write."

"You composed this just for me?"

"And only for you. Iris, this is no ordinary perfume."

Iris had buried her nose in her arm. "It's amazing."

"No, it is *extraordinary.* This perfume will change your life."

Iris glanced up, incredulous. Madame Rapacine was not one for self-deprecation, but this was a bit much even for her.

"I've gotten to know you well these years we've been friends. You are smart and kind. You are a thinker, you live in your mind, your worries, your plans. You are very good, but you are not very happy. When was the last time you relied on instinct? When was the last time you acted on your desires? When was the last time you knew them?"

Iris snorted.

"When you connect to your sense of smell, you awaken your body's intelligence, its desires, its repulsions, its instincts, its memory. I made this perfume because I want you to feel your power and to show the world what you're capable of. But above all, I want you to get what you *want*."

"I'd settle for just getting what I deserve."

"Who's to say they are not one and the same? You deserve everything you want."

The thought pushed Iris back in her seat.

"An old friend, the great nose Dominique Ropion, said 'Perfume is a language that all can understand but few can speak.' I created this fragrance to speak to you and for you. To be bold when you are cautious, to be seductive when you are shy, to make manifest everything that is inside you!"

Iris lifted her brow. "That's a tall order for a perfume."

"Not for one of mine." Rapacine's eyes flashed like opal. "To those near to you, you will be captivating. You will arouse all kinds of desires, not always sexual, but whatever someone feels or wants from you, they will want intensely. Your scent will speak to the part of them before language, beyond logic, and beneath their awareness. For a woman to be desired is both empowering and imperiling. Deploy the fragrance as you wish. Know it will neither make princes out of frogs nor wolves out of lambs. It will simply be a spur in the flank of their animal within—and yours."

"But you taught me that fragrance is subjective. How can this work the same way on everyone?"

"It won't, that's what makes it so exciting! No two people will respond in exactly the same way. But no one will be impervious to it, unless you are too far to smell. It's a pure *parfum*, with good *sillage* and longevity, but keep in mind, it will wear down like any fragrance."

"So I'll turn back into a pumpkin at midnight?"

"What good is a perfume that can't perform overnight?" She popped an eyebrow. "But you still think I am joking."

Iris stifled her smirk. "I'm sorry, I'm listening."

Rapacine leaned forward and cupped Iris's head by the base of her skull. "That oldest part of your brain, the limbic system, which processes scent, memory, and emotion; the part that we drown out with rules, distraction, and shoulds—this perfume will be its microphone." She released her. "It will increase your natural animal magnetism. It will amplify your desires and lower your inhibitions. Who would you choose if you could have any man? What would you say if you had everyone's attention?"

"For that it would have to be magic."

Another puff of dismissal. "I don't believe in magic. But I believe in you."

CHAPTER

Seven

I ris floated down the steps of Rapacine's brownstone, enjoying
the scent bubble of her new perfume. She didn't know what to
make of Rapacine's exaggerated promises, but the fragrance was
spectacular. Iris felt lovelier and lighter than she had in months,
maybe years. The scent was such a mood booster; it made Iris more
keenly aware of the pleasure of her surroundings: the sun filtering
through the leaves, dappling the street and warming her bare shoulders, the soft breeze against the nape of her neck, the charm of the
manicured hedges and flower boxes of the neighboring brownstones.
She was newly grateful for this beautiful Saturday in her beautiful
life.

Iris caught sight of her reflection in a shop window. She didn't
look any different, she didn't even look particularly good. She was
wearing the easy house clothes of a weekend morning: cuffed over-
alls, Birkenstocks, and a cotton tank, with her hair on its third day
yanked up in a clip with a handkerchief as a headband. But in her
new mood, the look felt effortless, insouciant, even sexy. She wasn't
a person who tried too hard, she was just herself, and it turned out
herself was adorable.

Iris stepped onto Hudson Street and sniffed her wrist again with
a smile. She turned the corner to where the weekend brunchers at
Oscar's Place were dining al fresco within a little border wall of
painted plywood and topped with potted geraniums. Iris caught

whiffs of the salty, fatty bacon and syrupy French toast as she walked by, making her stomach growl. But what she didn't catch was the diners' heads lifting in the wake of her scent, pausing mid-date-recap, a hand halted on its path to steal a French fry, for something in their lizard brain telling them to stop, to notice, and to seek the source of a smell more delectable than anything on the plates before them. They might not have realized that it was the average-looking woman passing by who had attracted their attention, only that they'd lost their train of thought. Once Iris was a few paces beyond their checkerboard tables, her scent trail dissipated, and with it their curiosity, and focus returned to their companion's fries.

She popped in to the nearby health food store where the air-conditioning was uncomfortably cold, so she beelined around to gather her items from the maze of narrow aisles. She and a male employee shelving stock had to do a wordless do-si-do for Iris to reach a bewildering array of nut butters. He asked her if she needed any help.

"I'm just looking for normal chunky peanut butter."

He shook his curly hair off his face. "I got you, it's right . . . here." He handed her the jar, then pointed to the container of raspberries in her arms. "You know, we just got a fresh produce shipment, haven't put it out on the shelves yet. Can I get you fresher raspberries?"

"Oh, these seem okay, I'm about to check out."

"Perfect! I'll bring it straight to the register, gimme one second, I'll meet you up there." He snatched her old berries and ran off to the back of the store.

He reminded her of a high school boy eager to carry her books, and he didn't look much older than one—not that Iris had ever gotten that sort of attention in school. She'd been coming to this grocer off and on for the last five years, and never once had any of the employees spoken to her unless she explicitly asked for help.

There were two long lines at checkout, but before she could take her place at the back of one, the stocker came jogging up and opened a new register to ring her up so she wouldn't have to wait.

"Do you live in the neighborhood? We offer free local delivery."

"I do, but it's just one bag, and I don't meet the minimum for delivery anyway."

"That doesn't matter. We're not busy today."

"Well . . . do you mind if I add a pack of those?" She pointed to the boxes of La Croix seltzer stacked at the endcap. "Then I'll meet the minimum at least. Or am I just making it heavier for you?"

"That's not heavy for me at all." He puffed out his chest.

She chuckled.

Back on Hudson Street, she passed by PS 3, the local grammar school, where a gaggle of elementary-aged campers in sunny yellow shirts had gathered on the sidewalk, like dandelions dotting the pavement. When Iris got closer, she paused to admire the chalk artwork of two little girls crouching to color in a pastel butterfly. One of the girls squinted up at her and asked, "Are you a fairy princess?"

Iris laughed, then bent to whisper, "*Shh, in disguise!*" She pantomimed tapping both girls with a magic wand. "And now you're both secret princesses too!"

The girls squealed. Iris walked away feeling more magical than before.

Strains of Latin music thrummed from somewhere up Christopher Street, and she detoured on her way home to check it out. She found a street fair on Bleecker abuzz with streams of people and stalls lining both sides of the street. She passed a fruit smoothie stand as one of its workers chopped up a whole pineapple using a hand ax with mesmerizing speed and skill, releasing atomized juice with each whack; it was glorious to catch wind of the tropical sweetness. She sniffed her wrist again, noticing new fruity facets of the perfume. Though that was just one of the riot of aromas that surrounded her: fragrant steam billowing from the sizzling cooktop of a Cuban sandwich vendor, carrying the mouthwatering scent of pulled pork; the peaty, mossy smell from a vendor selling potted plants and bonsai trees; the earthy patchouli of the CBD head shop; the buttery, slightly sour notes from racks of leather jackets and purses; all laced with the piquant odor of sticky summer bodies moving slowly past one another. She figured her perfume wouldn't stand a chance here.

The music was coming from a dance floor set up in the intersection with West Tenth Street where the salsa group Baila Nueva York had two couples of trained Latin dancers performing alongside passersby who had joined in. Iris recognized the group's name; they hosted sunset dances by the Hudson River some nights. She had always wanted to try it out with Ben, but he wasn't into it.

She marveled at the professionals whirling around one another, moving their bodies perfectly in sync to the beat and with each other. Of the amateurs, there was an elderly couple dancing as though they hadn't missed a beat in forty years, and two college-aged kids who leaned heavy on the spins. Only the couple dancing with their arms around their chubby-limbed infant in a papoose gave Iris a pang of envy.

At a break between the songs, one female pro dancer had stepped offstage, leaving her partner alone when the music started back up. He spotted Iris and reached his hand to her in invitation. On impulse, she accepted, and he pulled her up onto the stage easily.

He lifted her right hand in his left and placed his right on her upper back. Her other hand rested naturally on his shoulder, and she felt the heat of his body through his shirt. He was wearing a long-sleeved button-down, the top three buttons undone to reveal a tan chest, a corner of a tattoo on his pectoral, and a crucifix on a gold chain. He was barely taller than she, but trim, muscular, and glowing with sweat.

"I don't know what I'm doing," she shouted over the music blasting.

He grinned and lifted her arm over her head to spin her and pull her back toward him. "Your body knows! Just feel the music and follow me."

And so they danced. He started leading her in a gentle retreat and advance to the music, and she surprised herself that she was able to follow instinctually. Soon she was mimicking the swivel of his hips, and adding her own flourishes, laughing when he raised his eyebrows in approval. She stopped thinking and let the rhythm of the drums and the euphoria of the horns take over her being. As her partner was winding and unwinding her in his arms, guiding her close and away as they spun around each other, she would catch only glimpses of the world around her, his pursed lips, his brow glistening in the sun, the crowd of people and color.

Iris got down, flushed and exhilarated, as the small audience applauded. She wasn't used to calling attention to herself, but her shyness was eclipsed by pure joy.

She made a mental note to look into salsa lessons.

She wandered farther along the street fair, pausing often to poke around a stall. She stopped at a table of Tibetan jewelry, drawn to the silver, lapis, and coral like a magpie. She asked to try on a collar-style necklace but struggled with the clasp. The elderly proprietor slowly rose to help her. Iris lifted the hair off the back of her neck while he gently clicked it into place. He held up a small mirror for her to see it. It was bolder than the delicate jewelry she normally wore, but she liked that. She felt strong. She could see herself wearing it with a crisp white shirt, asking Frank for a raise and getting it.

She thanked the man for his help and got the necklace off by herself. The handwritten sticker price was blurred. "Does that say seventy dollars?"

"For you? Forty."

"Aw, no, it definitely doesn't say that."

He nodded. There was a softness in his face and a glistening in his eyes. "You smell like my wife on our wedding day. More than fifty years ago. She sent you from heaven to say hello and to make me feel nineteen again." He closed his eyes for a moment and inhaled deeply. "If I could give it to you for free, I would."

It was enough to make Iris choke up.

And so commenced an argument where Iris was haggling to pay more for the necklace. In the end she managed to press two twenties into his hands and toss a third onto the table, then run away before he could get his cane to chase her.

Iris paused to retie the bandanna in her hair. As she raked her fingers through her short waves, she caught a whiff again of the perfume, only now the sunny top notes had mellowed, no longer effervescent but a tangy glaze over the rich florals. There was a salty note, too, that made the scent soft, warm, and close. She loved it even more. It perfectly suited this gorgeous day waning into twilight. The sun had begun to sink in the sky, beaming its warm golden light across the street at every intersection while the short blocks rested in cool blue shade. A cellist sat in the amber glow on the corner of Perry and Bleecker, and the instrument's yearning tones floated above the din of the crowd. Iris dropped the few dollars she had left into his case with a smile, and he gave a nod of gratitude. She was imbued with a deep appreciation for this city's people, colors, tastes, smells, and music.

As Iris sidled through the streams of slow walkers, distracted trying to remember the dry cleaner's weekend hours, someone grabbed her backside, hard. Her brain raced through rationalizations: someone had bumped her, it was an accident—but in her gut the violation was obvious: Someone had groped her. She spun to see who but was faced with an anonymous crowd, people moving around her in every direction, every one of them invading her space by necessity but none of them reacting to what had just happened to her. It wasn't a big deal, she told herself, she shouldn't overreact, this wasn't the type of scenario in which one would scream. Was it? No, the threat was gone. But it hadn't been playful, it had hurt. She should have said something, cussed—at least a stern "Hey!"—but she hadn't reacted fast enough. She didn't even see him. Maybe it was that man in the Oakleys, but he was with a woman, but maybe that didn't matter? Or that guy on the skateboard rolling away, some punk faking nonchalance? Or that guy with the backpack, was he walking away strangely fast? There were many men in the crowd, which suddenly made her feel claustrophobic. It could have been any of them.

Iris hurried home.

Eight

The next day Iris walked up Ninth Avenue to meet Roman and help James's sister move out of her damaged apartment at Hendricks Houses. She had Hugo in tow, which she had resisted but Roman had insisted he'd be "like a therapy dog" for James's niece and nephew while the adults packed up what was salvageable from the apartment. It would be the kids' first time back since the explosion. Iris had offered to help because she knew something about what Veronica and her kids were going through, but now that the day was here, she found herself anxious. She'd put on Rapacine's perfume that morning for a boost.

Before the destroyed building was fully in sight, her nose caught the acrid, nauseating smell of smoke and charred building materials. It had been nearly twenty-five years since she'd smelled it, but the odor piqued her memory like it was yesterday. It got stronger and stronger as she approached, and by the time she and Hugo were standing before the Hendricks Houses explosion scene, every muscle in her body had tensed, because she *remembered.* The visceral, emotional experience of returning to the most familiar of settings—your home—and finding a new, strange nightmare in its place. The four walls that had once meant safety turned into a kill shed. The internal parts of a building strewn across the ground like entrails, body horror of the home. She might have been eleven years old again.

But Iris knew today wasn't about her, and this wasn't her heartbreak. In the clarity of the present, the scene she took in was completely different from that of her childhood house fire. For one thing, the scale was enormous. An apartment building five stories tall with a giant bite taken out of it at the bottom, a third of it collapsed into a pile of bricks. Also, the level of police presence as well as FDNY personnel. The entire area was crisscrossed with caution tape fluttering in the wind and officials tasked with keeping residents, neighbors, and looky-loos at a safe distance. She texted Roman that she was here.

Iris spoke briefly to an officer at the perimeter and he let her through. A minute later, she felt Hugo tug at the leash, his tail wagging. She looked ahead to see Roman waving at them from across one of the courtyards. He was easy to spot, even though he was wearing an N95 mask, as he was a six-foot-three white guy with California surfer blond hair (never mind that he grew up in New Jersey). He stuck out everywhere, especially here.

Roman pulled his mask down when he reached her. "Ah sorry, I was coming to let you in. Did the security give you a hard time? They've been dicks all day."

"Not at all, the cop let me right in."

"He did? Huh." Roman frowned.

"Must've been Hugo. The cute dog card never declines."

"Anyway, thank you for coming, you're the best." He gave her a hug and sighed into her hair. "Finally, someone that doesn't smell chargrilled." He drew back, still holding Iris by the shoulders. "Wait, you smell better than nontoxic. You smell *amazing*. What is that?"

"Oh, thanks, it's this new perfume my neighbor gave me. She says it's gonna change my life." Iris smiled and rolled her eyes.

He made a stank face normally reserved for new Beyoncé. "It might change mine. I'm still gay, but barely. That's why the cop let you in."

"You think?"

Roman motioned her to follow him. "We're around the other side. Although, I feel bad, I probably should've called you off today, there's less work than expected."

They rounded the corner of the block to the least impacted side of the building where security was directing parking for a temporary loading area and residents were lined up along the fence sorting through their boxes of belongings or pitching what they weren't keeping into a big construction dumpster. Many people wore masks and blue surgical gloves. The staff that was escorting people in and out of the building were in full white paper hazmat suits and gas masks.

"Asbestos," Roman explained. "They're giving them out, we'll get some for you if you want. But we already got in and out of the apartment."

"You did? Am I late? I thought you said—"

"No, there's just . . . not much left."

They had arrived at where James and his family were stationed, and a round of introductions were made between Iris and his sister, Veronica, and her two kids, Kiara, a teenager, and Isaiah, who looked about eight, and Iris expressed her sympathy for all that had happened. She could see the family resemblance immediately, something that always delighted Iris. Veronica was rounder and fuller-figured than her younger brother James, but as James was a sinewy and lithe professional dancer, that didn't take much. They all had slender long legs without being tall, and their faces had apple cheekbones and wide-set, smiling eyes. Isaiah looked like his uncle's mini, sharing James's camel-like eyelashes that seemed to curl up to his brows, and Kiara looked just like her mom, with matching dimples in their perfect heart-shaped faces, although neither was smiling much.

Hugo tugged toward Isaiah and the boy jumped back with a tiny yelp. Iris quickly reeled her dog in.

Veronica put a hand on her son's shoulder. "Sorry, he's a little scared of dogs. He's just not used to 'em."

"Oh no, I'm sorry. I should've been holding him. But he's very friendly." Iris shot Roman a look of reproach. *Therapy dog.*

"I'm not afraid," Kiara said, stepping forward. "What's his name?"

Iris told her as Kiara scratched his ears, making Hugo's back leg beat on the sidewalk in happiness. Not to be outdone by his sister, Isaiah tentatively approached.

"Put out your hand, baby, let him smell you first," Veronica said.

Isaiah stuck out his stiff little palm, from about four feet away. Iris carefully let Hugo get closer, but still left enough space that Isaiah could be the one to close the gap.

But Hugo beat him to it, giving the boy's outstretched hand a quick lick. Isaiah jumped back once again, but this time with a giggle. After that, both kids were Hugo's new best friends.

"So how can I help?" Iris asked.

"Well, it's mostly this." Veronica gestured to a picnic blanket they'd laid out on the grass with their things on it.

Iris couldn't believe how little they had left. Two trash bags full of clothes, three cardboard boxes of loose items, and a few piles of random things they were sorting through on the blanket. And more than half of it looked utterly soaked, wrinkled, or hopelessly soiled.

Veronica explained, "I was thinking fire. I didn't think of the water damage from the sprinklers and hoses. The water really got everything. We just have to see what's worth keeping."

Isaiah had a little pile of toys that looked like they'd been through a war. Kiara was filling a trash bag and tried to take a truck whose dump attachment had snapped off, but Isaiah snatched it back like a much younger child. "Mine!"

"Excuse you?" his sister said.

He covered his pile with his body. "I'm keeping all my stuff."

"Let him keep it. We'll see what we can wash at Uncle Jimmy's," Veronica said.

Kiara shook her head. "You baby him."

"I'd baby you, too, if you let me." Veronica tried to touch her hair, but Kiara ducked away. She dropped the trash bag on the grass and said she was getting a water and walked away.

James smiled after his niece. "She's just like you when we were kids."

Veronica tsked. "I didn't want that. I wanted my kids to grow up slow."

With the kids out of earshot sorting through their own belongings, Veronica filled them in on the latest from the building management, which was holding firm to their decision to exclude them from emergency housing.

Iris was wrapping dishware in newspaper, outraged for them. "If they couldn't legally kick you out before, they certainly shouldn't have the right to do it now. Do you have a lawyer?"

Veronica scoffed, "If I had the money for a lawyer, I'd be renting somewhere else."

Iris felt sheepish to have suggested it. But she made a mental note to ask Hannah's husband, Mike, a real estate lawyer, about taking the case pro bono. She would shoot him a text about it on the way home.

While Iris was hauling some trash to the dumpster, she noticed a commotion on the other side of the police tape by the wreckage. A crowd had formed, including a meager press spray of photographers and reporters; the focus of their attention seemed to be a political type taking questions. Iris walked over just as all the cameras began to go off at once. She weaved through the people to get a better view.

A robotic creature marched haltingly toward the destroyed building. It was the size of a Great Dane, with four black metal legs curved and jointed like an animal's and gripper prongs in lieu of paws, a wasplike tapered yellow body, and, disturbingly, no head. As a police officer with a remote control walked slowly behind it, the mechanical creature moved with eerily precise strides, anatomically canine but lacking the natural fluidity of a real live dog.

"What is that?" Iris asked a man in glasses next to her.

"'Digi-dogs,' search-and-rescue robots. The NYPD got two of them for seven hundred fifty thou. See the one over there painted like a Dalmatian? That's the FDNY's. Our tax dollars at work."

"Jeez. A trained golden retriever would be so much cheaper, and cuter."

The man chuckled and looked at her for an extra beat. Iris noticed. He continued, "It's news that they're here. Digi-dogs were banned in public housing under de Blasio, because the tenants' organization thought the cops would only use them to spy on residents. Or worse. But the current admin is more police-friendly."

No wonder Isaiah is afraid of dogs.

Iris watched as the Digi-dog took three steps up onto a mound of rubble before toppling over, moving its stiff animatronic legs in the air like a beetle before a fresh chatter of photographs. A few onlookers laughed as it took two officers to right the heavy machine.

"Looks like we're safe from our robot overlords," Iris said.

"For now." He pushed his glasses up his nose. "I'm Josh, by the way."

Iris saw a press pass around his neck—JOSHUA KEATON, NEW YORK TIMES—and she got an idea. If the perfume was working in her favor, she wondered if she could use it to the Pattersons' advantage. She flipped her hair for extra wafting and feigned surprise. "You're Joshua Keaton? I know your name from your byline. I read you all the time. I'm Iris."

"Really? Thank you." He flushed. "I'm not used to getting recognized."

Iris almost felt bad for lying, but it was for a good cause. "Are you writing a story about this?"

"Everything that's fit to print. NYCHA and housing are my beat."

"Do they know what caused the explosion?"

"Gas leak caused by neglect. No shocker, unfortunately, this will probably get bumped to D-fifteen, if I'm lucky. If you know the kind of shape these buildings are in, it was only a matter of time before something like this happened. The outdoor CO_2 meter has long been broken, and down in the basement, police said the Dante valve was missing."

"The what?"

"Oh, the regulator on a gas pipe—it's called a Dante valve, because if you open it, you open the gates of hell, like in *The Inferno*. Who knew pipelayers were so literary, right?"

Iris thought it a grim name, but she smiled and set about her agenda. "Actually, I have a good news tip for you. My friend's teenage daughter, Kiara Patterson, was the one who first identified the smell and called 911, and then she got her neighbors to evacuate. She saved a lot of people. But NYCHA is excluding her family from the emergency housing because of some rent dispute. So literally her reward for saving lives is being made homeless."

"Hmm. That's good. Patterson is the last name?" He started taking notes; Iris spelled it for him. Then he looked up and smiled at her. "So I'm pretty much done here and free the rest of the afternoon—"

"That's a good story, no? Do you think you could write about them? It's so unfair what's happening to this family, you could help bring light to the injustice."

"Sure, right. Maybe." He scrunched up his nose, either in consternation or to fix his glasses. "Problem is, the girl wasn't actually the first person to report the gas. A resident called in the smell to building admin earlier that morning, and someone was supposed to check it, but no one ever did. Like many public housing complexes, Hendricks uses an outside contractor for maintenance, and as usual, the guy didn't show. I'm more interested in potential corruption and outsourcing to crony contractors, although like I said, this was an accident waiting to happen, so it might not be the best example."

"Oh." Iris didn't hide her disappointment.

"But 'hero to homeless' is still a great angle," he added, eager to regain her attention. "I can pitch it to my editor, for sure. Maybe we could talk more about it over drinks? Let me give you my card . . ." He was handing it to her when his cameraman called to him from a few yards away. "I gotta go. Text me!"

Iris was left holding his card, not particularly hopeful he was going to be of any use to the Pattersons.

Roman and the kids were playing with Hugo on the lawn while Veronica was taking waterlogged items from the "Keep" box and doing her best to dry them. Iris knelt beside her to help. After laying out some books in the sun, Iris pulled out an upholstered bulletin board crisscrossed with purple ribbons and photos tucked inside. The water had made the ribbons bleed blooms of violet across the photographs, whose edges had gone soft and pulpy, but the images were still clear: Kiara with her girlfriends dressed up; she and her mom showing off manicures; Isaiah taking a selfie too close to the camera, squeezed next to an old man, maybe a grandfather.

Iris carefully slipped each photo from the damp, inky board and brought them over to Veronica fanned out like playing cards. "I found these, but I'm afraid if I stack them, they'll stick together."

"Ooh! Thank you." Veronica took them carefully.

"Did you find your photo albums?" Iris knew those were the only items that mattered.

"Yes! That was my prayer for the day, and I got them. They're even in pretty good shape." Veronica regarded her. "James said you lived through a fire as a child, but you lost your parents. I'm so sorry. That's why I keep saying we can't feel sorry for ourselves, we are so lucky no one got hurt. What about the rest of your family, siblings?"

"I'm an only child. But my older cousin was living with us when it happened, Jacob. He saved my life that night."

"Wow. Like Kiara, springing into action. I'm so proud of her, but I'm so afraid this will change them."

Iris thought uncomfortably of Jacob. That holiday break his freshman year of college, he'd been sleeping on the pullout couch in the living room not far from where the Christmas lights started the fire, he could've run out the front door to safety immediately, but he got eleven-year-old Iris first. While carrying her downstairs, he fell and broke his back but still managed to get them out alive. They were both hospitalized for smoke inhalation, burns, and, in Jacob's case, a fractured lumbar spine. He recovered with the help of a prescription for oxycontin.

And he never got free of it.

He didn't graduate from St. Joe's.

He graduated to heroin.

Veronica cut into her reverie. "Did you ever get to feel like a kid again, after it happened?"

Not even close. But Iris smiled. "I had a lot of happy times living with my grandparents."

Veronica nodded, not likely fooled.

I ris walked to her bathroom to take a shower, and Hugo toddled after her. She pulled her shirt over her head and caught a whiff of the perfume on her collar—buttery white florals, warmed by sandalwood and vanilla—it was so comforting. She needed that feeling after the morning.

Her phone rang, and Iris hurried to answer it, expecting Mike's reply about the Pattersons' case. But the screen showed an incoming call from Beth Miller, her aunt. Iris couldn't remember the last time she and Beth had spoken on the phone, and she had the irrational sense of having summoned the call by mentioning Jacob to Veronica earlier—a jinx. On the last ring, she picked up.

"Hello?"

"Hi, have you spoken to Jacob recently?" Beth asked abruptly.

The words hit Iris's ears like an accusation. Iris had always planned on reconnecting with Jacob when he got clean, but that day never came, or at least it never lasted. She hadn't seen him in years. She and his mother, Beth, were barely in each other's lives, save for liking posts on social media. But Beth, her husband, Clay, and Jacob were the closest living family she had left.

"No, I'm sorry."

"Clay thought he might have reached out to you."

Why would he? Iris felt on edge. "He hasn't. Is everything okay?"

Her voice broke. "He's missing."

"Oh, no." Iris softened immediately. "I'm so sorry. For how long?"

"He was in rehab in Fort Lauderdale, but he left the program early last week. No one knows who picked him up or where he went. None of us have heard from him. This isn't the first time he's gone to ground, but, call it mother's intuition, I have a bad feeling this time."

"I'm sorry, Beth, I hope you find him safe soon."

"Will you try calling him? I know you haven't been as close as you once were, which makes me very sad, but you two always had a special connection, you always will. You have a bond that can't be broken." Beth always talked about them this way.

"Gosh . . . we haven't talked in such a long time. I don't think I have his current number."

"I'll give it to you. Call him, or shoot him a text, whatever you kids do these days. You remind him of his best self. The *real* him."

Iris hesitated for only a moment before Beth added, "Don't make me beg."

"Of course. I'll try. Text me his number."

A minute after they said goodbye, Iris heard the text chime in, but she couldn't bring herself to open it right away; the thought of contacting Jacob filled her with anxiety. What could she say? Her mind drew a blank. She'd think better in the shower.

Under the soothing streams of hot water, Iris's thoughts swirled around Beth's request. She'd long sensed that Beth found her insufficiently grateful to Jacob for saving her life and, relatedly, insufficiently engaged with his recovery. Beth was under the impression that Iris held the key to summoning Jacob's better angels, that she was living proof of his true character and a touchstone that could inspire him to get clean. Although Iris didn't agree, she could track Beth's belief to the intervention she participated in over a decade ago. An experience they interpreted very differently.

She was twenty-three years old. Iris couldn't remember having been so nervous as she was sitting on that couch with her handwritten letter to Jacob on her lap. She had followed the addiction specialist and facilitator Randy's instructions, mirroring the formula on the worksheet, although writing her own version had still been difficult.

She had struggled to find the right words, so fearful of saying the wrong ones, and in the end the letter had come out short, sweet, and rather generic. Not life-changing, but safe:

Dear Jacob,

Ever since I was a little girl, I looked up to you, and you looked out for me. You were more than my cousin. When you lived with us, you were like a brother to me. And during the worst night of my life, you were my hero. You saved my life. But ever since you became addicted to drugs, we have not had the close family relationship that we used to, and that I wish we could have again. Will you accept the gift of treatment today?

Iris's stomach dropped when Jacob walked in with his mom. He looked like Death itself. His black sweatshirt shrouded his gaunt frame with the hood pulled up, under which he wore a knit hat despite the mild weather. His skin was dull, his cheeks were hollow, and his eyelids were at half-mast, so all the parts of him that might connect—his eyes, a smile—were buried under layers or withdrawing from the world.

He saw the rest of them seated in the living room and gave an empty laugh, instantly registering what was going on. He didn't even look surprised. Until he spotted Iris.

"What are you doing here?" Jacob lifted his eyebrows like they were heavy. He seemed as taken aback by her appearance as she was by his. "You grew up."

"Hi, yeah, it's been a minute." She stood and hugged him, and found herself fighting the urge to recoil at his smell, something she couldn't put her finger on. "It's good to see you, Jacob."

"I fuckin' doubt it." Jacob slumped on the couch between his mother and father. His father swiped the beanie from his head in a gesture of both admonishment and affection—capturing the tone of the day. Jacob was seemingly too exhausted or too high to put up a fight.

Randy, the facilitator, kicked them off, explaining the purpose of their gathering. Jacob made the expected protestations—"I take pills for pain. I have a back injury. I got prescriptions. You'd die if you had pain like mine"—but, as instructed, they didn't engage with him. Randy spoke frankly of how the sympathetic origin of Jacob's drug problem might have become an obstacle to his sobriety, as he used it to hook his mother into enabling him. Iris stole glances at her aunt Beth. Randy called out how his father, Clay, took a harder line with his son, but Clay's own drinking was something Jacob had learned to throw in his face as deflection. Clay sat stone-faced. Randy said addiction was "a family sickness," and they were here to listen and heal as a family. Iris didn't know where she belonged in the equation, but it felt like someone was cranking a Jack-in-the-box that she was sitting on top of.

When it was time to read the letters they'd written him, Beth read her heartfelt one through tears, ending with "I will no longer participate in the destruction of your life. I will not love you to death." Iris was moved. His father read a short one that could've been paraphrased to "Man up!" Little seemed to be getting through to Jacob, who appeared to nod off at times, but at least he was being quiet and calm. Then it was Iris's turn.

Iris looked down at the notebook paper that trembled slightly in her hand; her mouth was already dry. She began, "Dear Jacob—"

Jacob cut her off, "You don't gotta talk."

Iris looked up and Jacob was staring at her, more alert than he'd been yet. He held her gaze with his Husky-blue eyes and gently shook his head. She felt frozen like a rabbit, unsure of what to do next.

Randy stepped in. "Your cousin wants to share her experience with you, Jacob. All we ask is that you listen."

Jacob sighed audibly and leaned over his knees. "Whatever."

The facilitator nodded to Iris.

"Dear Jacob, ever since I was a little girl I looked up to you, and—" Iris ran her tongue over her teeth and swallowed. "And you looked out for me. You were more than my couthin—cousin." Her lip caught on her tacky teeth, distorting her enunciation. "When you lived with us, you were like a brovher to me." Her lips, teeth, and tongue felt tangled and stuck, the natural choreography of speech suddenly clumsy and disobedient. As her cheeks burned with embarrassment, Iris wiped the corners of her mouth, if only to replace her lips over bared teeth. "Is there water?" she asked from behind her hand.

But Jacob turned to his mother, suddenly outraged. "Why'd you bring her into this? She's got nothin' to do with this. What is she here for?"

Beth put a hand on his arm. "We're all here because we love you and we want you to get help. Iris knows the man you really are, and she came a long way to say this to you. Please listen. Iris, go ahead, honey, say your piece."

Jacob crossed his arms over his chest, his knee bouncing.

Iris took a breath through her nose, trying to summon all the calm and saliva she could. "And on the worsht nigh' of my life, you ... you were ..." She could not get the next words out. Iris felt like she was choking. "Shorry," she croaked. "Water?"

Randy heard her request this time and cracked a plastic water bottle for her. But just as he reached it across the coffee table, Jacob sprang to his feet, overturning the table, and bashed the bottle out of Randy's hand. Iris flinched as water sprayed her, Beth screamed her son's name, and the two older men stood, Randy with a stern authority and Clay in wordless fury, while Jacob loomed over them all and roared.

"What the fuck is this? What are you trying to do? Dig through my whole goddamn life to show me I'm a piece of shit? I don't need to hear any more, I know already, I fucking *know*!"

"Whoa, whoa! Let's relax," Randy said, hands up.

"Why drag my cousin out here, like she has any idea about anything, kicking up old shit. For *what?*" The veins in Jacob's neck and temple bulged.

"Sit down," Clay said through clenched teeth, going chest to chest with his son.

Jacob looked at him, eyes bloodshot and wild. "Or *what*? You want everything out there? Tell me, why'm I like this? *Huh?*"

Clay grabbed him by the collar, twisting the cotton hoodie in his hands.

"No, let him go! Nothing good comes from getting physical." Randy tried to jam himself between the men. But Clay held fast to his son, unblinking, fists clenched so tight his knuckles were white.

Jacob was panting with agitation, but his expression started to crumple. "Who made me this way, huh?"

"Enough!" Beth cried, now standing.

Clay released him and Jacob stumbled backward.

Jacob's fury spent, he adjusted his warped sweatshirt as if he was straightening a suit jacket. He nodded with a snort that curled his nose. "It *is* enough. This is over. I'll go to rehab, okay? That's what you want, right? Fine. I'll go."

Instantly the mood shifted. Aunt Beth erupted in a grateful sob and threw her arms around her son, Randy clapped a hand on his back, even Clay muttered a few words of praise and pulled his son in for a hug by the back of his neck.

Only Iris had remained frozen in her seat, gripping the chair arms like a roller coaster ride.

Iris rinsed the last of the conditioner out of her hair and turned the water off. She blotted her face with a towel, letting its softness press the upsetting memory from her mind's eye. She had always felt that she had triggered Jacob that day, that she was responsible for his outburst, though it didn't stand to reason. She knew addiction could cause erratic and agitated behavior; she just wasn't used to being around it. But Aunt Beth remembered the intervention differently. She saw Jacob's breakdown as a breakthrough, and although the sobriety that followed that rehab stint hadn't stuck, she viewed Iris as the lucky charm for Jacob's compliance.

But then Iris thought of how scared Beth sounded on the phone. And who was she to second-guess a mother's intuition?

After toweling off, Iris picked up her phone. She opened her text messages, copied the number from Beth's text, and pasted it into the field of a new one. Jacob's name popped up; turned out she did have the number. She told herself not to overthink it and typed a message that was, again, not life-changing, but safe:

Hey, it's Iris. Been a long time, but I hope you're well. Your mom is worried about you, everyone just wants to know you're okay. Please get in touch. ♡

CHAPTER

Ten

Iris joined Roman at the art gallery on the far west side of Chelsea for the Yayoi Kusama exhibition "Every Day I Pray for Love." As they explored the installations, they caught up on how Roman's living situation with James and his family was *really* going.

"It's cramped. I mean, I'm happy we can help, but it's five people in a one-bedroom. But it's temporary, that's what I keep telling myself."

"Right. Although Mike, Hannah's husband, got back to me, and unfortunately he can't take the case because his firm does work for the city, so they're conflicted with NYCHA."

She and Roman entered a pitch-dark room with a glowing green neon ladder jutting from a barrel in the center of the room and reaching all the way to the ceiling—actually, it appeared to ascend *into* the ceiling.

"Thanks for trying. Honestly, as chaotic as it is having them stay with us, I don't mind the distraction right now. At least it changed the subject."

"From what?"

"James wants to get married."

Iris grabbed his arm. "Omigod! He proposed?"

"No. It was more like 'Hey, asshole, when are we getting married, or do you not love me?'"

"Oh. Have you guys discussed that before?"

"No! Well, a few times, postcoitally, which doesn't count! But he was dead serious. It caught me off guard."

"Did he give you an ultimatum?"

"No, I think he knows I wouldn't react well to that kind of pressure."

"Whoa, look down," Iris interrupted. They peered down into the barrel, which wasn't truly a barrel but a mirror, and the neon ladder seemed to plunge into an elevator shaft infinite stories deep. The illusion made Iris queasy with vertigo.

"See, this is how talking about marriage makes me feel," Roman said.

Iris looked back at her friend. "But you and James are so good together."

"Exactly, why mess with it? He's not really ready for marriage anyway. He just wants reassurance." The color of the neon ladder shifted from green to red, rendering Roman's face a human stoplight.

"He isn't ready, or you aren't?"

"*We* aren't ready for it. We moved in together less than a year ago! He's always been anxious, I'm avoidant—it's our secret sauce and our kryptonite. I think he sees marriage as a status marker of stability that he didn't have growing up. But my parents have been married for forty years, and all it got me was a front-row seat to their kitchen cage match. No, thank you."

"So what did you say to him?"

"I put his dick in my mouth and he forgot about it."

Iris chuckled and they walked on.

The next room they entered featured sculptures spread out across the floor like quicksilver that had spilled in giant drops and pools. As the gallery guests walked among the pieces, the globular mirrors distorted their figures.

"You know I'm on your side, but after what I went through with Ben, I can't help but sympathize with James here. If you're never going to get there with him, you should cut him loose."

"Who said *never*? I only know how I feel now. I love him, I'm embracing his family, I'm showing him with my actions how serious I am about us. Why isn't that enough?" He stopped beside one of the mirror blobs, and his reflection shrank to an angry dwarf.

Iris's frown stretched down to her torso. "Just make sure you're honest with him."

Finally, they reached the immersive installation that had gotten the most buzz, the "infinity room"—and the line to view it. The infinity room was a large mirrored cube at the center of an all-white room, and two gallery employees stood beside it like bouncers meting out entry to small groups, five minutes at a time. Iris and Roman were admitted with an attractive straight couple ahead of them. The man had his muscular arm draped over his petite girlfriend, who clung to his waist, their bodies flush together, as if they were running a three-legged race.

Once the door had closed behind them, the immersion was complete—and breathtaking. All the interior walls, floor, and ceiling were mirrored, which created the illusion of boundless space in every direction. It was lit by countless pendant lights, small orbs that dimmed and brightened irregularly, shifting colors and temperatures from warm white to cool blue, then fiery red. Iris turned off her lighting professional brain to experience it as Kusama intended, mysterious and sublime.

"This is crazy." Iris used her dressing room whisper, aware they were in close quarters even if it felt like being lost in space.

"Okay, c'mon, we're doin' it for the 'gram." He snapped a couple of pictures of them together in the surreal surroundings, then stepped aside. "You should take some solo pics for Hinge."

Iris regarded her reflection in the twinkling universe, but she had more than one double lurking elsewhere. It took a moment for her to recognize her own back facing away from her over there, and farther still she spotted her profile turned another direction. It gave Iris the uncanny feeling of glimpsing herself in different timelines, her life going other ways: one engaged to be married to Ben, one where she had never met him and wasted her time, one where she was already a mother, one where she was still someone's daughter. But she returned to her double whose level gaze met her own, a reflection of how she often felt: alone, untethered, floating above herself, in a beautiful and perplexing world.

But she was not alone. Iris felt the faint tickle of being watched, like someone blowing on her ear. Elsewhere in the mirror, she spotted a reflection of the man staring at a reflection of her, like a little movie. While his girlfriend was distracted, Iris watched his eyes scan her backside approvingly. It was like her skin awoke under his gaze, and she felt goosebumps as she took in his own pleasing form. Then, in the mirror, their eyes met. That embarrassed them both enough to break the spell. Iris turned away.

And bumped straight into his chest, the *real* him. She chuckled, cheeks aflame. "Whoops, sorry."

He steadied her with a hand on her arm. "'S all good."

His girlfriend appeared at his side, and he dropped his hand from Iris's elbow, breaking the electrical current. But places where his fingers brushed stayed warm after he let go.

"Babe, I'm ready to go," she said.

On cue, a corner of the room suddenly swung open and flooded the space with blinding light. Like waking from a dream, the illusion shattered and the room was revealed to be nothing more than a hundred-square-foot box.

An employee poked her head in. "Thank you for coming," gallery-speak for "please leave," and the four of them filed out.

"That was amazing, wasn't it? I loved it." Iris squinted at Roman, her eyes still adjusting.

"Yes, and I loved the little drama that played out, too. That hot guy was checking you out so hard. I thought his girlfriend was gonna take her earrings out."

Iris blushed. "I did notice that. And I feel dumb saying this, but do you think it's the perfume?"

He tilted his head. "You know, I could really smell it in those close quarters."

"Is it too strong?" She smelled her wrist to see if it had changed on her, but maybe she had grown nose-blind to it. "You'd tell me if I smelled like a cheap whore, right?"

"No, it's not like that at all, it's gorgeous, it's . . . sexy."

"It actually makes me feel sexy, which is rare." She laughed.

Roman frowned. "What are we doing in a museum? We should go out."

"It's a gallery, and there are two more rooms."

"Pumpkins and polka dots, we get it. If we're really gonna test this perfume, we need to take it for a proper spin."

Eleven

Twenty minutes later, they were standing in a different line, this time outside the popular nightclub the Jane Ballroom.

"Aren't we too old for this?" Iris scanned people ahead of them, who looked like rich kids from NYU.

"No. Now we can afford the drinks."

Two beautiful girls walked past them, each wearing a dress that barely covered her ass, high heels clicking in stride. They strutted straight to the front of the line, spoke to the bouncer, and went in.

"That's the move." Roman took Iris by the hand and pulled her from the line, ignoring her protests, until the naked vulnerability in her voice made him pause:

"Roman, I don't *look* like them."

His expression softened. "Okay, first, they were basic. Second, we're great! You're beautiful, and I'm a gay seven and a straight ten. And third, we wanted to test this perfume, didn't we?"

Iris sighed. "You're at least a gay eight."

"Thank you. Now go make that man smell you."

They walked up to the bouncer, a sour-faced bulldog with an earpiece and an iPad. Before they could say a word, he barked, "At capacity."

Roman shoved Iris forward. "It's her birthday!"

"Not on the list, back'a the line."

Iris got an idea. "Can I at least get a birthday hug before we go?"

His scowl cracked slightly, and he opened one meaty arm to her.

They embraced for a moment. She could smell the bouncer's cologne; she hoped he could smell hers.

When they broke, Iris was beet red. "Well, thanks, have a great night." She and Roman exchanged a glance of defeat and began to walk away.

"Wait." The bouncer gestured with his iPad. "I found you on the list." He smirked. "Happy birthday."

Iris and Roman bounded up the steps of the hotel, positively giddy.

"The hug was inspired!" Roman pulled her close, bumping her side.

"There was wind, I had to get close!"

They entered the ballroom, a mashup of Victorian colonial style and hipster cool: a sweeping walnut bar tended by mixologists dressed like Wes Andersen bellhops, and a giant disco ball sparkling over a dance floor packed with the young, rich, and beautiful.

Iris grabbed the small menu from the bar. "Ha. Well, we got what we deserved for weaseling our way in here. Twenty bucks for a cocktail."

"Oh honey, we are not buying." He leaned back against the bar and surveyed the crowd. "*This* is a controlled environment. No wind, plenty of guys. This is where we conduct our experiment." He patted her shoulder. "You know my order."

"Wait, how am I supposed to get a straight guy to buy *you* a drink?"

He tut-tutted. "Where is the ingenuity I saw outside? You get two *different* straight guys to buy you a drink, one for you and one for me. Now go."

"You're not coming with me?"

"I'll only cockblock you. But I'll keep an eye from afar, like Secret Service."

Embarrassed in advance, Iris slow-walked the length of the bar, scanning for a man not obviously with a date, half-hoping she wouldn't find one. She arrived at a trio of preppy-looking guys and slotted into the bar top beside them. She had to look thirsty, so she raised her hand to wave when she knew the bartender wasn't looking. It worked; the man nearest to her turned. "You need a drink?"

She smiled nervously. "That's the idea. It's hard to get their attention."

"I can't imagine it's hard for you to get anyone's attention. I'm Asher. What can I get you?"

Within five minutes of small talk with him and his friends, Asher had bought her two drinks, one for her and another for her unseen friend. Iris was stunned. It was *that* easy.

And so began a whirlwind of Iris going back and forth, getting rounds of drinks for both herself and Roman. Sometimes she didn't make it back to the bar before a man would strike up a conversation with her. Normally she disliked attention from strangers, she rarely wore anything flashy or revealing, it made her too self-conscious, but this was different. Because Iris wasn't attracting eyes, only noses. She didn't feel objectified, she felt . . . fascinating. These men couldn't put their finger on what drew them to her, but they were intrigued. Iris had never felt so popular, charming, funny, and beautiful. It was a rush.

Iris returned to Roman's couch setup with the latest round, two flutes of champagne. "That last guy thought my name was ISIS, and he still bought me both of these."

Roman laughed and they toasted. "Bravo!" He took a sip and brightened. "Ooh—guess who's here tonight? *Rhys Elliot.*"

Iris blinked at him.

"He was in that movie. And now he's in some show about a small town and a sex trafficking ring preying on wayward teens. It's called *Truck Stop* or something?"

"That describes like seven shows."

"With the hot rookie detective who partners with the cranky old one."

"That describes ten. I only like the ones where the cranky detective is a woman—and she prefers to work alone." Iris ripped a champagne burp.

"Anyway, Rhys plays the hot detective, and he is sitting right up there." He gestured to the mezzanine balcony.

Iris looked up. In a cordoned-off section, a group of people were clustered around a particular couch, and she saw a man who had to be Rhys Elliot. He was drop-dead gorgeous.

"I met this guy, Sam, who's the costumer, they're friends! They're having their wrap party, and Sam said he can introduce us."

"No," Iris said, using the same tone she used on Hugo when he got into the trash. "I can't. He's too famous!"

"You didn't even know who he is. *And* you've got the perfume!"

"Roman, it's a perfume, not nitrous oxide. He's too hot for me. He probably dates models!"

"Who cares? You don't know what he likes—what about *you*? Think with your dick for a change! I swear, women are so disadvantaged that you can't feel yourself get hard."

Iris rolled her eyes. "We do have a counterpart to that."

"Then listen to it! Now tell me, do you want to meet the hottest guy you've ever seen?"

Soon they were upstairs, where Sam escorted them to the VIP area. Rhys was even more breathtaking up close. He was over six feet and built like a collegiate rower, biceps straining at his casual chambray shirt. But his face is what set him apart from the ordinary humans. Perfectly proportioned and symmetrical, a jaw chiseled like a super-hero's, pouty lips a man didn't deserve, and the hypnotizing hazel eyes of a mountain lion. When he smiled at Iris for the first time, she thought she was going to throw up.

Roman stepped in. "This is Iris, and I'm Roman, we're big fans of *Interstate*." They'd googled the show on the way upstairs.

Rhys chuckled. "It hasn't aired yet, but thanks."

"Oh, right, but I mean, the buzz is incredible—can we get a selfie?" He snatched Iris's phone from her hand.

Rhys politely obliged. Iris figured out Roman's ploy when he added, "Squeeze in tight now, all three of us"—he was making sure Rhys was in her scent bubble. After he snapped the picture, Roman returned Iris's phone and excused himself, leaving them alone.

Rhys turned to Iris with interest. "How'd it turn out? I'm happy to take another if you don't like it."

But fragrance didn't come across in a photo. "I'm sure it's fine. I don't like having my picture taken anyway."

"I don't either."

Iris tilted her head. "Are you being sarcastic?"

"People want selfies, but they take them at terrible angles, and if I look bad, I feel like I let them down, and they're still gonna post it."

"So you want to make sure *you* look okay?" Iris teased, disarmed by his insecurity. That he was human made him even hotter.

He laughed at himself. "But the real worst part about selfie culture is, as soon as someone sees me, they turn their back to take a picture. They'd rather interact with the image than the person. You think fame will make you popular, but I miss talking to people."

Taken over by her new delusional confidence, Iris leaned toward him and put her hand on his knee. "So let's talk."

And they did, as though no one else was there. Iris thought Rhys did seem a bit out of practice, going on about the new show, on-set jealousies, panic about an upcoming *SNL* hosting gig. He didn't ask many questions, but he was so pretty to look at, Iris didn't mind.

"Sorry, I'm rambling. There's just something about you, Iris. You're a real one. I didn't ask, how do you know Sam? Are you an actor?"

"God no. I'm a lighting designer. Not for film or anything like that—for buildings."

"That makes sense."

"Why?" *Because I don't look like I belong in front of a camera.*

"Because you changed the mood in here as soon as you came in."

Iris smiled into her drink as her whole body blushed. It was such a line, but from his perfect mouth, the words didn't matter. She didn't say anything but let her gaze soften on his face, the way his eyelashes cast a shadow over freckled cheeks, the glint of gingery stubble, his lips curving into a smile.

It was Rhys who broke the tension, "Was that so corny? I—" but Iris stopped his mouth with a kiss. Her desire and instinct had taken over, she wanted to devour him, and he responded in kind. She felt his fingers run through her hair and settle on the back of her neck, pulling her close as his other arm slipped around her waist, gathering her into his lap as all her nervous tension melted into her center.

They made out like teenagers on the couch, oblivious to the swirl of people and drinks and loud music. When at last they came up for air, Iris's eyes immediately found Roman, who was looking at her like a proud papa. And when Rhys invited her to "see the view" from his suite at the Standard, she thought the way Roman had encouraged her to.

While Rhys closed out the tab, Iris went to Roman sitting with Sam and others. "So I think we're gonna go," Iris said, trying to contain her glee.

Roman burst into the biggest shit-eating grin and sprang up from the couch to hug her. "You're doing amazing, Moana," he said into her ear, before dissolving into giggles.

"You're such an idiot," she said the way only best friends can insult each other with deep love.

"Go! Have fun! Call me in the morning first thing!" They hugged once more and she was about to go when he hissed in a stage whisper, "Take a picture with him when he's asleep!"

The next morning, Iris woke up early, thanks to the floor-to-ceiling windows in Rhys's hotel room. She squinted in the sunlight and peeked at her bedmate, who was sound asleep. He lay in repose like an artist's model, free of self-consciousness and bedsheets, a well-muscled arm thrown across his eyes, perfect pecs, washboard abs, and everything else on display. Iris eased herself out of bed, careful not to wake Sleeping Beauty, and tiptoed across the room, gathering her strewn clothing. The room was like a solarium, she had no cover, even the bathroom was open concept. It was a flex for any Manhattan hotel: views so unobstructed by neighboring buildings that its guests could indulge their exhibitionism kink. Iris wouldn't have thought herself the type, but the body-shaped smudges on the windows told otherwise.

In the mirror, her dark hair was a tangled bramble at the back of her head, her eye makeup was smudged, her cheeks imprinted with sheet lines. Only her lips looked better than the night before, swollen and pink, and she had a bona fide hickey on her neck; Rhys Elliot was a biter. Iris looked far from her best, but she couldn't help but smile at her reflection.

Iris washed up and was patting her face dry with a towel, trying to at least smear last night's eyeliner upward, when she noticed something—or rather, the absence of something. She sniffed her wrist and didn't smell anything. It was time to go.

She called Roman on the walk home.

"You *left* without saying *goodbye*?" his voice boomed from the phone.

"I had to! The perfume was gone, I'm slutty Cinderella, my coach is a pumpkin, I'm back in my rags."

"But you should've left a note with your number or something."

"He lives in LA and they film in Atlanta. It was the perfect one-off. I fooled him once, I'm not gonna push it."

"What? Iris, you didn't *fool* him. Maybe the perfume got things rolling, but I bet you're a million times more interesting and real than the Hollywood plastics he usually meets." He sighed into the receiver like a disappointed parent, or pimp. "You could've been his go-to NYC hookup."

Iris shrugged. "Hmm."

"Did I just hear a 'meh'? Omigod, was he *meh*?"

"It was fun. He was exuberant, I'll give him that. Creative positions, good energy."

"You're saying he wasn't that great in bed."

"A guy who looks like that never has to learn what works, you know?"

Roman cackled into the phone.

Twelve

The first week wearing the perfume was like the doors to a different world were gallantly held open for her. The city felt more charmed, spontaneous, and romantic than the one she knew before, and every close encounter was a meet-cute waiting to happen. She had been asked out by the man on the next bike over at spin class, as well as the man whose schnauzer had gotten tangled with Hugo's leash, and her dry cleaner said her clothes smelled so good he didn't want to launder them. She'd had only one scary experience, when a chatty Uber driver suggested they go somewhere other than her destination, and when she got out of the car at the next light, he shouted after her that she was a "stuck-up bitch" who was "not even hot." The creep didn't hurt her feelings—if anything, she wanted to yell back, "I know!"

She had chosen not to wear the perfume to work.

Until today.

Today, she and Nate were pitching *her* design to Wolff Development. Although Nate had presented the idea to Frank as his own, Iris was the one who had actually done the research and prep work, so he had to bring her along. Iris hoped to assert herself in the meeting and show Frank she was the brains of the operation. Whether she got her due credit or not, if Candela landed this project, there would be more money for Frank to reconsider that promotion. And she needed the confidence boost. This morning, she had blotted it conservatively, once on each wrist and her sternum.

. . .

The offices of Wolff Development were in One World Trade Center. Iris arrived and found Nate already at the marble reception desk in the lobby.

"You made it," Nate said flatly.

"Sorry, subway trouble." Two men on the 1 train had nearly gotten in a fistfight over the right to offer her their seat, and she'd missed her stop trying to evade them. "Is Frank here yet?"

"No." Nate noisily blew his nose, giving the results a peek before wadding up the tissue. "It's not Covid, it's hay fever. And it's worse than ever this year. My eyes are killing me."

"You know why pollen is so bad in cities? Male trees. Female trees drop fruit, which requires municipal resources to clean up. So urban landscapers plant only male trees instead. But males spread their seed, in this case, pollen, and with no female trees to receive it, the excess causes allergies."

Nate's lip curled. "I have botanical jizz in my eye?"

Iris saw Frank striding toward them, bike helmet on his hip. "Woof, it's a hot one outside, this A/C feels good. Let's get checked in and head on up."

The three of them waited for the elevator for floors 28–42 alongside another businessman. As soon as they got on, the businessman turned to Iris. "What floor can I get for you?"

Before she could answer, Nate shoved his finger onto the button for 39. The man gave him a dirty look before exiting at his floor.

Frank glanced in her direction. "You look especially lovely today, Iris."

"Thanks." Iris discreetly plucked her shirt to get some air and caught a blast of the fragrance. The hot subway ride had made her modest dab of the perfume explode on her skin.

Nate gave another juicy blow into his tissue.

Once they'd exited the elevator, Frank huddled them up. "Now listen, Jonathan may or may not be there. Don't be discouraged if we end up pitching to Marilyn Hruska, his executive assistant. She's been with him for years, and he holds her in very high regard. Do we remember our game plan?"

Nate answered, "Yes. Frank, you'll introduce the team, then I'm going to outline our wellness concept and budgets and the rest. And Iris, if I forget something, don't be shy this time, jump in."

Iris smiled. "I will."

Marilyn greeted them at reception. Iris was relieved to see she was a polished middle-aged professional and not some twentysomething poached from a nightclub hostess stand. Iris had worked in architecture long enough to know that many of the top developers were absolute pigs, treating their female subordinates like just another prestige property—anything to make themselves look like the alpha male in the concrete jungle.

Marilyn led them down a glass-walled hallway and opened the door to the corner conference room.

Frank entered first. "Jonathan! Good to see you again."

Iris was taken aback—the man rising from his seat was nothing like she was expecting. Jonathan Wolff was younger than most at his level, early forties, or just in great shape, and undeniably handsome. He had thick wavy hair and a suntan that made his eyes pop a Caribbean blue. Her heart began to race with nerves, or something else.

He greeted Frank warmly. "Frank, how are you, old man?"

"Join me again on the next centennial ride, you'll see who's the old man." Frank chuckled and gestured to his team. "Let me introduce you to two of my best designers, Nate Childers and Iris Sunnegren."

Jonathan greeted them both with a handshake and eye contact so direct it made Iris look down. She noticed he wasn't wearing a wedding ring.

He invited them to sit wherever they wanted to at the long table surrounded by sweeping views of the Hudson River. A young woman appeared to take their coffee orders, while Marilyn vamped with some friendly small talk. Iris poured herself a glass of water to drown the butterflies in her stomach.

Jonathan Wolff was far from the typical corporate silverback, some thick-bodied executive who'd rather be golfing. The man at the head of the conference table looked more like an Italian film director. He wore a linen jacket the color of sandstone over a tan-striped shirt left open at the collar. In lieu of a necktie, he had draped a light camel-colored scarf with eyelash edges in tissue cashmere so fine Iris feared she might snag it just by looking. And for his last trick, he was somehow pulling off white slacks, albeit an elegant ecru, cuffed at the bare ankle. He looked as if he had come to this meeting straight from his yacht.

From what Iris knew of his success, perhaps he had.

Frank opened the pitch with an expression of gratitude, praise for recent Wolff Dev projects, and a graceful highlight reel of Candela's own recent awards and accomplishments. He also included flattering bios of both Nate and Iris, which were nice to hear. Iris noticed that Marilyn was listening intently, Wolff less so, occasionally distracted by his phone and the woman who returned with the coffees and a tray of pastries.

Iris had planned to jump into the pitch as soon as Frank finished, but he explicitly indicated Nate to speak: "Nate, why don't you get us started?"

Nate had done his homework. He opened with a detailed financial analysis of the market, then turned to the project budget, the layout for their plan, and its comparison with nearby buildings. He talked about the tax benefits accorded to designated wellness residences. It was an impressive amount of memorized content and seemed serious and competent, but a lot of dry facts and figures.

Eventually, Wolff interrupted. "You have to know this isn't the most cost-saving package I've seen from other lighting firms. So if your best argument is money, you've been beat."

"I'm not sure what other packages you've been pitched—"

"I am, and I just told you what you need to know." For all the softness of his clothes, Wolff's tone was razor sharp. "How do you justify the cost of this sanitizing element? People think the pandemic is over, or at least they don't want to hear about it. Paying a premium to remind them of a health hazard doesn't appeal to me."

Nate looked down at his papers. "I think this is something that could create excitement and novelty in a competitive market. It's buzzy, it will get write-ups, attention."

"So this is a PR strategy?"

Nate was floundering. "Well, this is also an updated aesthetic, as your signature sleek luxury has become commonplace—"

"My taste needs upgrading?" He smiled over his shoulder. "Marilyn, am I 'basic,' as my daughter would say?"

"No, not at all. Um"—Nate nervously rubbed his already red nose—"Marilyn, do you like Goop?"

Iris stepped in. "Wolff Development has set the bar for design in your category. Your choices have been copied, but you have yet to repeat yourself, and we're here to partner on your latest reinvention. You're right, this is not the bargain basement plan other firms may be presenting. But what are they offering you beyond cost cuts? Where is the value added? What I'm suggesting—"

"What *we're* suggesting, at Candela, is a holistic approach," Nate cut back in. "We view ourselves as your creative partners in creating a product that will be both novel and durable in today's challenging market . . ."

Iris glared at him for interrupting her with his industry-jargon slam poetry, but Wolff had seen right through it.

He waved Nate quiet. "When is the market *not* challenging? Tell me, why should I listen to a lighting designer's take on my sales approach when I have an entire team of overpaid real estate marketing analysts working for me on that very thing? Ms. Sunnegren, what's the connection here?"

Iris's heart leaped into her throat, but she was confident in her pitch, and in herself. "I'll put it this way: Lighting is a language everyone can understand, but few can speak. It dictates our sense of well-being on a subliminal level. Other high-end finishes matter, but everyone's taste is different. The connection between light and emotion is primal and universal."

Wolff's arms remained crossed over his chest, but it was the first time during the pitch that he didn't cut in with a quick retort, which Iris took as a good sign. With his turquoise eyes trained on her, she continued: "You don't sell just any product at Wolff Development, you build *homes*. What we're pitching is as much a statement of purpose as a design plan. The biometric lighting coupled with the health benefits of indigo clean underlines the essential truth that light is the life force of any space. It's the mood, it's the color, it's the character. Light has always been the protector of a home's health and wellness.

What's the first thing you do when you come home? When you need to feel comforted? What do you adjust when you're hosting a guest or setting a mood? Lights on means home safe."

All three men stared at her, quiet for the moment.

Only Marilyn smiled.

"That wasn't our game plan." Nate said, dabbing his nose with a sorry-looking tissue. He and Iris were outside on the sidewalk, after Frank had praised them both and hopped on a Citi Bike to zip down-town. "Frank thought I'd be the best to lead the pitch to Wolff."

Iris hiked her bag on her shoulder. "And you did. But Jonathan wanted to hear what I had to say."

"Already on a first name basis?" He snorted and shook his head. "I didn't stand a chance."

"What does that mean?"

"Jonathan *liked* you."

"Come on." But a hot flush of embarrassment splotched her chest. "If I did well in there, it's because I knew my stuff. I've put a month of research and work into this concept that was a 'jumping off point' to you just last week. I did the legwork, and it showed."

He smirked. "Legwork. Is that why you brought high heels in your bag?"

Her flush turned to anger. "I didn't invent professional attire for women. But yeah, I bring a change of shoes. You try running up sub-way stairs in heels and get back to me."

Nate sneezed again. "*Ugh,* this hay fever is killing me. Look, I'm busting your balls, it went well. I'm just saying, we should try to co-ordinate better, present a more united front next time—if there is a next time."

He wasn't kidding, he hadn't been kidding, Iris knew that Nate had meant what he said. What she didn't know was whether she agreed with him. She was more prepared, she had rehearsed that pitch and nailed it. And she had deserved to take the lead in the first place.

But she *was* wearing the perfume.

Was that an unfair advantage? Even if she was more qualified, did that legitimize the edge the perfume gave her? She didn't think Wolff seemed attracted to her, he was merely engaged with her plans—they were good plans! Nate was talking out his ass, his pitch was full of filler and empty jargon, and anyone as successful as Jonathan Wolff could smell the difference.

But had he smelled *her*?

Thirteen

"Oh, you smell good," Hannah said as she hugged Iris hello. "Thanks, I have so much to tell you."

They were meeting at their favorite coffee shop, Merriweather, halfway between Iris's West Village apartment and Hannah and Mike's new place in Tribeca with good caffeine-free options for pregnant Hannah. They sat at one of the outdoor tables on the sidewalk of Hudson, in the dappled shade of the generous ginkgo trees whose roots splintered the concrete bed like balsa wood.

"I'm sorry I look like I just rolled out of bed. I've been up late working on this new project at work."

"The big new development—you got it?"

Iris nodded, Hannah squealed, and they high-fived across the table. Hugo barked in excitement.

Iris recounted the Monday afternoon when Frank called her in to his office, reliving every detail:

Frank had said, "You knocked his socks off last week. Jonathan loved your pitch for 270 Eleventh Ave."

Your pitch—Iris broke into a smile. "That's awesome!"

"It really is. And he was particularly impressed by you and your vision for the project. Now, I know this was sort of a joint thing between you and Nate—"

"Well—"

"But Jonathan is a particular kind of developer, he picks his people and he works them, hard. He dresses like he's perpetually on vacation, but the man doesn't sleep. Not when there's money to be made. And for all the growth Wolff Dev has had in recent years, he keeps his team lean. He hates waste, he can be very exacting. And he wants you."

Iris swallowed.

"Unfortunately, Nate kinda rubbed him the wrong way."

Now she knew she liked him.

"But a redesign of this size, it's a lot for one person. Do you feel comfortable taking on this project on your own?"

"Absolutely. I'm prepared, I'm ready to work."

He clapped his hands. "Wonderful. Thank you for stepping up, Iris. This is big. But I think you can rise to this occasion."

"Thank you, I will."

"This is profile-raising for Candela. I shouldn't speak too soon, but if things go well with Wolff Dev—I'm ready to promote you to partner."

She nodded, radiating with ambition's toothy joy. "I won't let you down."

"Only problem is, we gotta figure out what to do about Nate. I'm going to let him take over your account with Harry Winston, so the added commission will soften the blow."

And cut into Iris's total compensation. "You know they're so picky. I don't know if Nate has the patience for them."

"But now that we know what they like, the account is on autopilot. And believe me, you're gonna have your hands full with Jonathan."

At this point Hannah groaned. "Wait, why does Nate get a consolation prize for making a bad impression? Typical man, failing upward."

"I know. But I wanted to pick my battles, and Wolff is the prize. Plus, Frank is right, it's a lot of work. I've wanted this opportunity, but now that I have it, I'd be lying if I said I wasn't a little intimidated."

"Aw, well, that's normal. But this brilliant Wolff guy wouldn't have chosen you for no reason."

But was it the right reason? Iris thought of the perfume.

"Don't make that face. Iris, this is a *good* thing! Don't be afraid to bet on yourself!"

"You're right, and I am. With Frank's promise on the promotion, I decided to take the plunge and officially move forward with my egg freezing. I start at the end of my cycle."

"Omigod, yay!" Hannah clapped. "I'm so proud and happy for you! I think this is a really great call."

Iris nodded. "Thanks. It was the push I needed. That, and seeing how Ben has moved on. I have to too."

"Exactly right. To moving on!" She lifted her lemonade for a toast. "Speaking of, is this an okay time to tell you that Mike wants to invite Ben to his birthday party?"

"I guessed that was a given." Mike and Ben's friendship predated either relationship with the two women. Iris and Ben had introduced Hannah and Mike, and Iris had envisioned a lifetime of couples trips, another dream shattered in the breakup.

"But if seeing him makes you uncomfortable, I will use my I'm-ruining-my-body-for-your-seed veto power to ax him from the guest list."

Iris waved her off. "It'll be fine."

"You're taking this better than I thought. You sounded so sad after you ran into him, but now you seem so much . . . lighter. I'm loving it, but what brought on this new unbothered vibe?"

A smile curled on Iris's face like a feather on a cat's lip. "Well, that's what I really wanted to tell you about, but you're not going to believe me."

Iris filled her in on Madame Rapacine's gift and its miraculous effects, including her night with Rhys Elliot.

Hannah screamed in delight, startling the people at the table next to them. "You slept with a bona fide celebrity? Tell me everything! I'm hard up. These pregnancy hormones have me so horny, but Mike has turned into a nun."

"He doesn't want to have sex?"

"No, and I never thought he'd be like this! He's always had a healthy sex drive, and he's always been so cool about having sex on my period—sorry, overshare—I thought he would be into it. But now he's like a nineteen-fifties husband, all weird about the baby 'feeling it' or something. I'm like, the baby is *not* in my vagina, you have a law degree, how can you be this ignorant?"

"Men can't resist the fantasy that their dick is so big it could dislodge a baby."

Hannah chuckled before her expression darkened and she made a little pout. "I can't help but think it's about my body not being attractive to him like this."

"No! It's not that. You look beautiful."

"Let's be real, I look different. I look big. I feel enormous. Weird thing is, this is the first time in my life that my sex drive has outpaced my body insecurity. Normally I only want to have sex when I feel attractive. Now, with all the hormones, I want to have sex even though I feel like a whale. I'm a horny whale."

"Aw hon, you're being too hard on yourself! Have you tried talking to him about this more explicitly?"

"Like sexting?"

Iris chuckled. "No, I mean like an open discussion about feelings."

"Of course not. I rub my butt against him in bed, and when he doesn't instantly get hard, I feel rejected and say nothing and resent him the next day. And if Mike truly loves me, he will learn to read my mind!" Hannah banged her hand on the table, making Iris laugh again and startling Hugo.

"Talk to him. Maybe he doesn't know you're in the mood, or he worries your body is uncomfortable right now. I feel like ever since I got this perfume, I've learned that attraction is not as visual as we think. This scent is speaking to some subliminal, primal stuff, and it's more powerful than if I were the hottest girl in the room."

"Iris, it's a beautiful fragrance, but that's not what got your groove back. You're healing, you're feeling yourself, and it shows."

Iris shook her head. "You're wrong. I can look like absolute shit, like right now—"

"You do *not* look like shit."

"Bana, you know I do." Iris only used Hannah's childhood nickname when she was really being ridiculous. And right now it was appropriate, because Iris was wearing her giant, tattered Penn State tee, basketball shorts that used to belong to Ben and came down to her knees, and the beat-up Dansko clogs she normally relegated to dog walks. Her dirty hair was half yanked up in a Pebbles Flintstone ponytail, she wore no makeup except last night's eyeliner, and her glasses were smudged. "But it doesn't matter. I'm wearing the perfume, so I can get any guy."

Hannah narrowed her eyes, then her gaze traveled somewhere above Iris's head. A sly little smirk appeared on her face. "All right, Bike Hottie in the blue shirt."

Iris looked over her shoulder and saw the man she was talking about. A super fit guy wearing a tight blue Under Armour T-shirt that showed every muscle. He was sitting on a bench, tapping away on his phone, his ears plugged with earbuds. His bicycle was propped against the bench beside him.

"I dare you to go over there and get his number."

Iris snorted. "Hold Hugo."

Iris sauntered over to the man and sat down on the bench next to him. He didn't seem to notice her, and Iris didn't elicit his attention in any way. Instead, she sat back on the bench and stared right back at Hannah, a bored expression on her face.

Thirty seconds later, Bike Hottie looked up. He glanced over at Iris, almost puzzled. He took out his earbuds, ran his fingers through his hair, and stole another glimpse of Iris. After another moment of fidgeting, he smiled and said something.

Hannah couldn't hear what they were saying, but the body language was clear: this gorgeous man was, a little nervously, chatting up her friend. And in just a few minutes, they were exchanging phone numbers.

Then Iris pointed at the bike.

The guy laughed again, and Iris touched his arm and said something else close to his ear. Bike Hottie nodded. They stood, hugged, and then Iris took his bike by the handlebars, swung her leg over, and rode it back toward her astounded best friend.

Hannah's jaw hung open. "Are you effing kidding me?" She pushed herself up from the table and laughed in shock. Hugo whined at her feet and tugged the leash toward his mom. *"He gave you his bike?!"*

Iris smiled, growing wobbly again as she slowed down and hopped off the seat. "He lent it to me. His name is Joe. He's a personal trainer. He said he'd come get it tomorrow if I let him buy me a beer."

"I can't believe it. Neither can the baby, they're kicking like crazy"

"I told you, it's the perfume! But hang on, I gotta give this back to him now. I didn't give him my real phone number."

Iris returned to their table, where Hannah was waiting with her most mischievous grin.

"Okay, we *have* to use the perfume at Mike's birthday party. I mean, this is revenge body in a bottle!"

"I thought we just toasted to moving on."

"We want Ben to eat his heart out. We don't want him *back!*" Hannah often used the best-friend version of the royal "we" when discussing their problems; their perspectives were always in sync.

"Totally." Although this time she wasn't sure she was on the same page.

CHAPTER

Fourteen

On her way home, Iris picked up a few items at the farmers market for herself and Madame Rapacine, including a bouquet of flowers to thank her for the perfume. Outside her brownstone, Hugo did his thirteen-year-old version of bounding up the steps, akin to a bunny hop on his stiff hind legs. He seemed extra keen to visit today, sniffing wildly at the front door.

Iris punched in the code for the vestibule, and as soon as she opened the door, the sickly-sweet stench of garbage smacked her in the face. A row of bulging trash bags slumped along the wall; one by the staircase had oozed a mystery liquid onto the checkerboard tile. She swatted a fly buzzing around her and tucked her nose into her collar to muffle the stink.

Iris tied Hugo's leash to the brownstone's railing so he wouldn't try to "help" with the trash and got to work hauling it to the curb. After several trips, she'd taken it all out, retrieved Hugo, and knocked on Mme Rapacine's apartment door. She waited to hear the rattling of the chain and various clicks from the other side.

"*Salut,* Iris!" Rapacine answered the door with an Hermès silk scarf tied around the lower half of her face like the world's most elegant bandit.

"*Salut,* Madame, do you want me to put on a mask?" Iris still kept one in her purse.

"No, it's—ah, it's gone!" She yanked down the scarf.

"I took the trash out."

"*Merci!* But you shouldn't have. Come in, come in." After exchanging the customary double air-kiss, Rapacine scowled over Iris's shoulder like she was angry at the hallway and welcomed her inside.

Hugo was good with cats, collectibles less so, so they went straight to the back garden, where Iris saw Rapacine had company. A muscular, shirtless man was pouring a large bag of soil out by the border of the rosebushes.

"William, come meet my friend Iris."

William dusted his hands off and walked over. With his long blond hair, shirt tied at his tapered waist, and skin glistening with sweat, he looked like he'd sauntered off the cover of a romance novel. Rapacine introduced them.

"I'll head out, let you two catch up. And I'll get that trash on my way out."

"*Ma'm'selle* beat you to it."

He looked disappointed but gave Iris a nod. "A'right, babe. Text me." William bent and kissed Rapacine on the lips.

It was all Iris could do to contain her laughter until he disappeared inside the apartment. *"Babe?"*

Rapacine leaned her cheek in her hand. "I told him not to get attached."

"Well, he's good at his job. You and the garden are glowing. More flowers are probably the last thing you need." She presented her with the bouquet and a pint of fresh strawberries.

"They are beautiful. And I often cannot cut my own darlings. I'll get a vase."

Iris let Hugo off the leash with a telepathic plea, *No digging,* and watched him toddle off to snuffle Jasmine, who lay stretched out on the patio, unbothered by the old dog.

Rapacine returned to arrange the flowers in the vase and rinsed the strawberries with the garden hose before laying them on a cloth-napkin-covered plate. She poured Iris a glass of iced tea from a pitcher. "You know they put the trash there to torment me."

"Your neighbors?"

"The neighbors are gone, ousted. I am the only one left in the building. My tormentors are the new landlords and their bastard henchman manager. He is the one who takes the next-door neighbors' trash from the curb and piles it outside my door."

"Why would he do that?"

"They want to drive me out. I've lived here since 1979, the original owner was a friend from Paris, and it was *rent-controlled.* The building has changed hands several times since then, but I am the grandfather inside."

"You're grandfathered in?"

She snapped her fingers in approval. "Previous owners have tried to buy me out, but I say no, this is my home, it's priceless to me. These new ones hate me. They want to sell the whole building to some hedgehog."

"Hedge funder?"

"You've been here five minutes, already you must correct my English?"

"You've been here since seventy-nine, I thought your English would be better."

She laughed and clasped her hands, jingling her stacked bracelets.

Iris took a sip, pleasantly surprised by the bite. "Ooh, is that lemonade in it?"

"Yes, but you probably taste the whiskey."

Iris chuckled. "Hot gardener, spiked iced tea, you live right."

"Alors, I forgot the mint." She darted over to the herb section of her garden and returned rolling a sprig between her fingers. She tore it right above Iris's glass, releasing the most refreshing aroma, a relief tantamount to smelling salts in this heat, before dropping the torn leaves into her glass. "I asked William to cut the grass and prune before the rain, so that the plants could drink more deeply. A beautiful scent, no?"

Iris breathed in through her nose, savoring a tender sweetness, a hint of peppery spice, and the lemony taste of a chewed clover that reminded her of peaceful childhood summers of green knees, grazing ponies, and lazily tearing grass blades between her fingers.

"The smell is the grass *screaming.*" Rapacine popped a strawberry into her mouth as though she hadn't said something completely bat-shit.

"Huh?"

"The aroma chemicals emitted when a blade of grass is cut are a warning call to the others that there is danger afoot and to adapt. All living things speak with fragrance, plants included."

"Now I feel bad for grass? I need more whiskey in my tea."

Rapacine chuckled. "I mean to say that scent is a channel of communication. It has guided our lives for millennia, helping us to survive and evolve to today's point of overthinking. That is why I'm always telling you to trust your nose."

"Speaking of scent, that perfume you gave me . . ." Iris widened her eyes.

"I noticed you are wearing it today. It is as special on you as I'd imagined."

"I honestly didn't believe you when you gave it to me. But you're right, people are relating to me completely differently, especially men."

"Men are very suggestible."

"I have to thank you. I've had the most amazing couple weeks wearing it. It's so good, I feel a bit guilty."

"I don't believe in guilty pleasure."

"But is it . . . wrong somehow? Maybe manipulative? It's like a superpower, I'm not sure I know how to wield it responsibly."

"It is a perfume, not the atom bomb."

"I wore it to work," Iris said sheepishly.

"Why is your face?" Rapacine mimicked her wince.

"I wore the perfume the day my company was making a pitch to this big developer. And the developer loved my ideas, I won the bid. My boss was super happy. But my co-worker dinged me over it, he thought the developer just loved *me*."

"Your co-worker is also a man?"

"Yes, Nate. We used to get along, but—"

"This Nate did not succumb and step aside for you simply because of the perfume?"

"No."

"So whatever appeal you had that day did not make him abandon his self-interest. Do you think so little of men as to imagine they are so easily overcome by feminine wiles? If that were so, women would be in a much more powerful position than we are in this world."

"That's true."

"And what is professional attire for you at the office? What kind of shoes?"

"Sometimes flats. But on pitch days, we dress up more, so I wore heels."

"So a shoe that lifts your ass. And hair that looks shiny and touchable. And a face that is pleasing. 'Professional' for women is a combination of a mother, temptress, and nun, on top of your actual role. And if the balance of any one of those roles is off, according to someone else, you are blamed for it. You see, the game is already rigged against women, because men made all these rules. Just because you found a way to win doesn't mean you are the one cheating. Was your idea the best?"

"Yes."

"So don't question it. You waste time wondering whether they recognized the idea's merit or your physical appeal. So what? They could just as easily overlook your idea's merit *because* of your physical appeal. You cannot make your body and mind exist *à la carte*. You are a package deal."

Iris pondered the truth of what she was saying. "They *have* done studies that show taller men get promoted faster."

"Of course! The things men admire in other men are always valued. The things men desire in women are used to undermine women so they retain the upper hand. Don't fight back with one of yours tied behind your back."

Hugo barked, making Iris jump up. But Hugo was only play-bowing before Chéri, who, despite his eyes wide as an owl's and ears pinned, had his orange paw splat atop the dog's head. Hugo's tongue lolled with joy, relishing his submission.

"You see? Power is a game. Play well," Rapacine said.

Iris sat back down. "But wait, you didn't finish the story about the apartment. The new owners can't just abdicate management because they want you gone. Dumping outside trash at your door is tenant harassment. Who is this new landlord?"

"No one, it is not a person, it's a *société écran*."

Iris searched her memory of high school French, but came up empty.

"*Comment dit-on? Euhh...*" Rapacine swirled her hands trying to conjure the word in English. "A company created to hide one's identity."

"A shell corporation."

"*Oui.* This shell of a person bought the building and also secured the air rights. So if they could get me out, they could tear the whole thing down and build something bigger that would make them gobs of money."

Iris had heard of this kind of thing, landlords antagonizing residents in order to get them to break leases and move out. "I'll ask my friend who's a lawyer if he knows anything about this type of thing. Maybe you could sue them."

Rapacine puffed her cheeks in *horreur*. "I don't have the money to wage a legal battle against the likes of them. *Non*, if I am to get the better of them, it won't be in a courtroom."

"He takes some cases pro bono. What they're doing might be criminal, you have rights."

"Iris, you must listen to me carefully. You and I both are without family to protect us or to fall back on. And that's all right, sometimes family is who one needs protecting from. But it takes a certain tenacity. It takes strategy. You can trust only yourself. And you must get what you need, by hook or by book!"

"By hook or by *crook*."

"That's what I said!"

Iris pondered a moment. "Why don't you make yourself a special perfume like mine to get the landlord to change his mind about letting you stay in the apartment?"

"I cannot make one like yours for myself."

"Why not?"

"Because regardless of my skills as a nose, I cannot escape one fundamental human fact: We are nose-blind to our own natural scent. A *parfum* like yours, its transcendence lies in its perfect harmony with your personal scent. I calibrated it specifically to you. That alchemy of flesh and fragrance is what takes it to the next level. *You* are the final ingredient. I could make myself a stunningly beautiful perfume, but not one as transformative as yours."

"I'm sorry. I wish I could give you the gift you've given me."

"I've lived longer than you, and I have learned the lessons of my senses. You still have a way to go."

CHAPTER
Fifteen

I ris sat on the toilet scrolling—nay, stalking—on Instagram, but she was very careful with her fingers, as an accidental Like in this deep would be deadly. She was on the profile of the woman she believed was Ben's new girlfriend, Madison McKee. According to her bio, she was a "Certified Peloton Instructor. Certified Personal Trainer. Yogi. FSU grad. Scorpio. Christian," each noun followed by a corresponding emoji. So far, Iris had learned that Madison celebrated her twenty-sixth birthday last fall, broke up with someone hotter than Ben about a year ago, and started filling her lips in 2022. And although Iris achieved brief gratification from deducing the month and year that she got breast implants (August 2020), the knowledge did nothing to diminish the undeniable: Madison was stunning. She was like the AI result for "hot girl." Sure, she'd had some enhancements, but she hadn't needed them. Her face was beauty queen beautiful, and her body was tanned, taut, and tiny. Nearly all of her pics showed off her physique, a spinning carousel of beach, gym, and suggestive yoga poses. But despite the repetition and inane product tie-ins, her thirty-five thousand followers apparently couldn't get enough. Her every comment section looked like an emoji wildfire, and as the Insta algorithm bolded for Iris under the recent photos, "Liked by ben_bergen89."

Iris regarded herself in her bedroom's full-length mirror. She was nine years older than Madison and felt like a different species. Her eyes clocked all her well-worn insecurities: the slight dimpling on her stomach she wished was flatter and firmer, the indent on the side of her hips she wished was smoother and rounder. Her breasts looked nice when she pushed them up and together, but they didn't hold themselves up like Madison's.

Iris eyed the perfume bottle on her dresser. She dabbed the blotter on each part of her body she hated. Her thighs. Her belly. The empty space between her breasts. Then she closed her eyes, and it was as though she was remembering a version of herself she hadn't been yet. She was clothed in something more luxurious, a silk kimono slipping off her bare shoulders. With her eyes still closed, she caressed her body, imagined someone else doing the same, finding her skin smooth, supple, and delectably creamy. In her mind's eye, she saw rumpled white linens, glowing skin, and a vase of flowers on the bedside table, filling the room with their delicate fragrance. With a deep inhale, the body she touched was no longer flabby, it was soft, yielding, and beautiful.

Then she opened her eyes. It was dark outside, and her messy room was lit only by her reading lamp. She saw Hugo lying on a small pile of dirty clothes on the floor; his tail thumped the ground when he caught her looking at him. The laundry reminded her, she had a set of sheets likely ready in the communal dryer.

Iris shuffled down the hall in her fuzzy slippers dragging her empty canvas hamper to the second-floor laundry room. Her sheets had a few minutes left on their cycle, so she decided to wait. The room was small, not much bigger than an apartment galley kitchen, with the machines on one side and a peeling poster of directions on the opposite wall. The air was close, heated by the thrumming dryers and scented with the clean, synthetic musk of dryer sheets.

Her neighbor David appeared at the door holding a giant cushion on his hip. "Oh, sorry, I can come back later if you're using the washers."

"Nope, just emptying the dryer."

He hesitated in the doorway.

"I won't bite." It sounded like someone else's line, Iris was instantly embarrassed to have said it.

But David smiled. "I didn't think I'd run into anyone. I'm not dressed for company." He was wearing Adidas slides, basketball shorts, and a white T-shirt. He reminded her of the guys she used to crush on in college.

Iris wore a tattered T-shirt from the now defunct Spotted Pig restaurant and an even older pair of gray Soffe shorts reading CAPE MAY across the butt. "It's a laundry room. If we had better clothing options, we wouldn't be here."

"Gronk barfed on his dog bed." He shuffled over to the washer beside hers. "Sorry, I don't know why I just blurted that out."

"I'm glad you did. I want to know the designated barf-washing machine so I can avoid it forever."

He chuckled. "You can use it for when Hugo ralphs on your stuff."

"He has such a long windup, it gives me plenty of time to move him to some wipeable surface."

David looked at her, puzzled. "Windup?"

"You know, the—" She commenced a truly exemplary imitation of a dog gagging.

He cracked up. "How are you still cute doing that?"

Her blushing cheeks stifled her laughter.

The dryer beeped, and she opened it and pulled out her hot bedsheet. She struggled to fold it without letting it touch the dirty floor.

David stepped in to help. "Okay, we're folding it hot-dog-style first."

Iris frowned in confusion. "You mean lengthwise?"

"Yes, excuse me, I didn't realize you went to *private* school."

They stepped back from each other to pull it taut and make each long side meet at the corners.

"Okay, now *horizontal,* or hamburger-style, if ya nasty."

Iris giggled as they stepped toward each other to make their corners meet, holding the top of the sheet high above their heads so the bottom wouldn't touch the ground. Although they were hidden from each other by the bedlinen curtain, Iris felt David's hands close around hers as he gathered her corners with his. But as soon as their fingers touched, he stepped back, and they were pulling it taut again. With each fold, they drew closer and closer, and the curtain separating them dropped lower and lower.

"Perfect," he said, looking directly at her.

"Thanks." She held his gaze for a moment before placing the sheet in the hamper. She could feel him take a step closer behind her. She smoothed the folded cotton while contemplating her next move.

David beat her to it. "So, did you break up with that Connecticut guy?"

"A while ago. But he wasn't from Connecticut."

"Could've fooled me." He poured detergent into the machine.

"Do you have a girlfriend?"

"Single as a Pringle."

"Pringles are literally the only chip that comes spooning other chips."

He scrunched his face into a pout. "That's why being alone hurts so bad."

She laughed and gave him a playful shove; his tee was so thin, she could feel his body heat. "So then why don't you ever flirt with me?" she asked, uncharacteristically bold.

"I have no idea." He turned to face her, leaning on the washer with one arm. "Why haven't you flirted with me?"

"I'm shy."

He laughed like she was being sarcastic, although it was the truth. Until recently.

"And we live in the same building," she added.

He took a step closer. "New Yorkers don't talk to their neighbors anyway."

The kiss was both unexpected and inevitable. And neither of them wanted to stop there.

"What about the dogs?" she joked, as he was devouring her neck. "I don't want it to be awkward for them."

"How 'bout, outside of the laundry room, we're just friendly neighbors with clean clothes?"

"What happens in Laundry Room A stays in Laundry Room A?"

"Exactly."

Her face eased into a smile, and they resumed their make-out. David lifted her butt up onto the whirring washing machine, sending pleasurable vibrations through Iris's thighs. Her arms draped over his shoulders from her newly elevated height, as David nestled himself between her knees.

"One more thing." He pushed off her and reached a long arm to the laundry room door, turning the lock. Then he flipped the lights off. In the dark, the digital displays on the machines glowed an unearthly blue like spaceships.

Iris giggled again as he slipped her shorts and underwear down her legs. She stopped giggling when she felt his stubble between her thighs.

Iris hurried back to her apartment on jelly knees, overcome with extreme giddiness and embarrassment. She could not believe what she had done, or rather let be done to her in that laundry room. Even with Ben, she would let him do that for a maximum two minutes before relieving him from what she imagined was a sexual chore, despite Ben's protestations to the contrary (though he never protested much), and reciprocating. She was a giver, after all. She had convinced herself that she didn't really like it, anyway. Other women might, but not her.

Today, she liked it.

Mentally, she couldn't believe it, couldn't bear thinking back on it. But her body had loved it, was still loving it, and she couldn't *stop* thinking back on it. It occurred to Iris that she had never before gotten out of her head while getting head.

And she didn't know if David got off, maybe he did, maybe he didn't, she didn't ask! He seemed to enjoy himself—it was his idea, anyway. When he stood back up, he whispered in her ear, "We're gonna get caught if we stay here any longer." If that had been an invitation to go back to his apartment, it had gone over her head. Being reminded of getting caught doing something so out of character, so naughty, so obscene, had triggered her flight instinct. So she got dressed, grabbed her hamper, and bolted.

Was she a horrible, selfish, greedy slut? No, she wasn't that bad.

But she was close.

And she liked that, too.

Sixteen

I ris was meeting at 270 Eleventh Ave, the building site of Wolff's Oasys project, for her first official walk-through since she got the job. Although Rapacine had made a good case for wearing the perfume, she hadn't been able to shake Nate's accusation that Wolff only wanted to work with her because he was attracted to her. So she'd decided *not* to put on the perfume that morning. Today, she was just Iris, au naturel.

Opposite the perimeter, Iris was greeted by a twelve-foot-tall blow-up rat with red eyes, painted teeth bared and Frankenstein arms extended as the machine inflating it whirred with an angry growl. Iris was somewhat surprised that Jonathan would use non-union workers, though she understood the tyranny of the bottom line. Still, she took care not to enter the site within view of the union protesters.

Once within the privacy of the painted green plywood barrier, she spotted Marilyn at the perimeter, deep in discussion with one of the contractors. Her dyed-red hair captured the sunlight like the red-purple shade of Rapacine's Chinese maple tree.

They greeted each other, and Marilyn introduced Iris to Eduardo, the head contractor.

"Is Mr. Wolff on-site today?"

"Unfortunately Jonathan won't be joining us, he has his daughter today. Allegra trumps everything."

Iris softened hearing that a busy man like him would take the day off to prioritize his kid. She was only disappointed that she wouldn't get to test her perfume-free abilities on him.

"But I'll give you the tour."

Knowing it was a construction site, Iris had chosen to wear sneakers. Marilyn wore black pumps but gave the impression she could scale Machu Picchu in heels.

"Before we start, we'll need to get you a hat, and I need you to sign a couple of forms, a liability waiver to be on-site and an NDA, standard operating procedure." She handed Iris a pen and a leather folder with the papers already tabbed, then motioned to Eduardo.

Iris nodded and signed both.

Marilyn took the folder back and plopped a hard hat on Iris's head. "Follow me."

Iris gasped when they entered what would become the main entrance and lobby. Even with only framing and drywall, she could *feel* the space, and it made her heart skip a beat. She had previously engaged with the building only in the REVIT virtual system, and though that program modeled the project with down-to-the-millimeter accuracy, the rendering failed to capture the striking impression of being in the space. Iris had never worked on a lobby so grand; her imagination had undersold the soaring lofted ceiling, the drama of the curved staircase, and the *light*. Sunlight poured in from the wall of glass, and her eyes were drawn upward to the skylight, now an open square of blue, cloudless sky. Her challenge as a lighting designer was atypical. Instead of bringing light to a dark space, she would have to bring a feeling of comfort and home to an atrium. This was the type of design project she had dreamed of in grad school. It would get press, it would put Candela, and herself, on a new tier. Iris wasn't just stepping into the lobby, she was stepping into her future.

Marilyn noticed that Iris had stopped in her tracks. "Everything all right?"

"I'm just taking it in. I can't tell you how grateful and honored I am to work on this project. I think this building is going to be spectacular."

"Everything Jonathan does is spectacular. He doesn't have another setting."

"How long have you worked with him?"

"I don't want to date myself, but suffice it to say, since I was his only employee. Let's go 'upstairs.'" Marilyn put air quotes around the *upstairs.*

In the next moment, Iris understood why. Their mode of ascent was an external construction elevator, basically an open-air cage that shook when they stepped into it and rattled as its gears carried it upward.

Marilyn spoke over the clatter, unfazed. "When I met Jonathan, I was a single mother without a college degree and with a bad Jersey accent—well, worse. I was in debt, working as a broker for rentals in Brooklyn with my baby strapped to my chest. Most developers took one look at me and said 'Walking disaster.' Jonathan saw a multitasker. This spring, my son Patrick graduated from Rutgers with honors and zero debt. And in the fall, he'll join the team at Wolff Dev." Love softened Marilyn's expression when she talked about her son; her eyes glistened and she beamed with pride. "Meeting Jonathan changed my life. And if you impress him, he can change yours."

Iris smiled. Marilyn was a smart, unpretentious, no-nonsense kind of woman, and she admired that Jonathan valued that. "It seems he really respects women, which is so refreshing, honestly. Architecture and design can feel like a boys' club."

"If architecture is a boys' club, real estate is the Playboy Mansion. I've met more pigs in this business than when I used to bartend at Scores—I never danced, for the record."

They exited at the top floor, also bare-bones but impressive. "And this will be the penthouse floor."

"The view alone is worth twenty million."

Marilyn scrunched her face. "We're asking thirty-five."

Iris laughed. "You'll get it. And I'm so excited to be a part of this, thank you for trusting me to be a part of the vision."

"Cover of *Arch Digest,* that's your mantra. Jonathan has spared no expense."

"I thought developers were always trying to cut corners."

"Not on this building. This is his baby. We'll be lucky to break even."

Iris smiled, unsure if she was joking. "That can't be true. Can it?"

"You know this project has been through the wringer. First costly delays from Covid, supply chain problems, but he was unwilling to compromise."

"Did the shareholders push back?"

She shrugged. "They'll get more than their due. We have a robust portfolio of projects and properties with fatter profit margins. This will be the showpiece. This is what drives the Wolff brand. Jonathan liked your pitch because it showed you understood that brand's value."

Iris warmed with pride, already envisioning her work on the cover of a glossy magazine. Maybe she'd even be nominated for a LIT Award. Frank should make her a partner.

Marilyn's voice cut into her reverie. "But are you up to the task?"

Iris opened her mouth but it took a beat. "Yes, absolutely."

"I hope so. Because Jonathan saw something in you. I trust him, but I'm not sure I see it yet. Today you look like the dog that caught the car."

"Oh!" Iris gave a nervous laugh—and she'd thought they were getting along so well. "Sorry."

"Don't apologize. Maybe I'm just a bitch."

"What? No, I, I don't think—"

"What I mean is, don't let my feedback make it worse. You don't even know me. Give yourself the benefit of the doubt. Take your own side. That's what men do that women don't." Marilyn's navy-lined eyes scanned Iris up and down, her lips pursed in a polite smile. "How you carry yourself matters. Attitude is everything. Act like you belong here, look 'em in the eye. It's primal. Just be sure to bring back that spark you had in the pitch meeting. You owned the room that day."

Iris nodded.

Marilyn leveled her gaze at her. "You're a wolf now. Act like one."

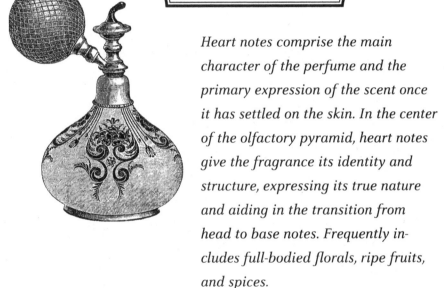

Heart Notes

Heart notes comprise the main character of the perfume and the primary expression of the scent once it has settled on the skin. In the center of the olfactory pyramid, heart notes give the fragrance its identity and structure, expressing its true nature and aiding in the transition from head to base notes. Frequently includes full-bodied florals, ripe fruits, and spices.

Seventeen

I ris was having dinner with Roman and his boyfriend, James, at
Gusto, a bar-bistro in the East Village where tables were tight,
and Iris's chairback was pressed against the man's behind her.
Something in the couple's overly solicitous negotiation of shared appetizers gave Iris the feeling that she'd been invited that night as a
buffer. When Iris asked about James's family, Roman said that the
search to find them an affordable apartment within any reasonable
radius of the city had so far come up empty, and James fell uncharacteristically quiet. She knew their home life was stressful right now.
As coveted as a reservation at Gusto was, she wondered whether
trading tight living quarters at home for tighter ones at dinner had
been the best idea.

Obliged to be the evening's distraction, Iris made her stories from
the last couple of weeks as juicy as possible. For once it didn't take
embellishment.

James snapped his fingers in approval. "Wash-and-fold me over,
baby, why doesn't that ever happen in my laundry room?"

"Because we send out," Roman said.

"Iris, you got a new air about you, a new *aura*. I'm an empath, and
as soon as I hugged you today, I said, something different about this
girl." James rotated his hand in front of his face and inhaled theatri-
cally. "You know what I smelled?"

Had Roman told him about the perfume?

"Freedom!" James cried. "You finally got Ben out of your system.

That L.L.Bean motherfucker was dragging you down, sapping your power. Now look at her! She's open, she's radiant, she's magnetic, she's *read-dy*!" He swayed his body with the rhythm of his words, and Iris joined to match him. They both ended in laughter, until James snapped his attention back to Roman. "I just want to make sure *you* aren't *my Ben.*"

Iris had to take up for her friend. "Not possible."

"No, I know, that's right." James put a hand on Roman's shoulder before adding, "He'd never shop at L.L.Bean!"

She and James laughed. Roman looked irritated. Iris changed the subject. "How's the new musical coming along?"

James had recently left his years-long gig leaping through *Hamilton* to be the head choreographer on a new musical based on the work of Langston Hughes. He lit up talking about it, and even his gesticulations possessed the grace and artistry of years of classical ballet.

As Roman listened, his face softened with admiration. "I'm proud of you. I know you've been under so much pressure lately, starting this new project and then Veronica and her stuff at the same time, but we'll figure it out. And I know all your hard work is gonna pay off, this is your time. Cheers to the first steps on a whole 'nother level." He raised a glass.

"Thank you. And to Iris's new gig, too—to being booked and busy!"

The three clinked glasses.

"This musical has to work out, because I can't go back to the touring contracts, the travel, always chasing the next gig, just a body for hire."

"I'd hire your body." Roman bumped his shoulder.

"You do, baby, you pay my rent. But it's a new phase of my career, I want to be more settled, mature. It's my personal life that's falling behind."

Roman shook his head. "Are we really starting this again *now*?"

It appeared they had run out of *Let's have a nice night* energy.

"Is it so terrible, my being ready to make a home with you?"

"We have a home together!"

"It's your name on the lease, not mine. I'm a guest."

"And so are your three relatives! The latest of the many ways I support you that apparently don't count."

James glared at him and the table fell silent.

"Which I am *happy* to do because I *love* you. Okay?" Roman gave a dry little laugh.

Suddenly all the lights went out in the restaurant. The diners murmured in surprise, the servers froze, and the bartenders groaned as the POS screens went dark. Only the small votives on the tables illuminated the restaurant.

The din of conversation and utensils resumed, as the patrons were happy enough with candlelight, but the staff looked increasingly agonized. Staying quiet felt like the lighting engineer equivalent of ignoring *"Is there a doctor in the house?"* Iris excused herself.

Iris passed a server carrying a trayful of lighted votives like a birthday cake and approached a man huddled with two kitchen staff members. She arrived as one said, "I have two hours on the fridge before I have to throw everything out."

"Hi, I work in lighting, can I help you troubleshoot this?"

"Oh, thank God."

The manager, Robert, explained the power outage's extent, while Iris scanned the ceiling. She zeroed in on the single cord snaking along the exposed beam ceiling, meant to power all the pendant lights in the dining room, including a striking glass chandelier. It was a play on a traditional rustic antler chandelier, only each "antler" was a hollow curving horn of amber-colored glass with lightbulbs nestled among the pointed branches. Even dark, it was an impressive piece, muscular yet irreverent. She loved it.

It was also likely the problem. "Is this chandelier new?"

"Yes, how did you know?"

"You have all these pendant lights daisy-chained to one another, plus the chandelier with incandescents, that's likely overloading the circuit."

"Don't tell me I have to take it down, it was a bitch to get up there."

Iris shook her head. "Long-term, you'll need more amperage, but I have a short-term fix. Do you have a ladder?"

"Yes! I'll get it. And let me send your table drinks or dessert on the house."

She thanked him and pointed to where her friends were sitting. Roman and James looked absorbed in conversation. Iris hoped they weren't fighting.

The manager set to reseating those under the chandelier as wait-staff swept the tables and chairs out of the way, and a busboy brought a twin ladder and set it beneath the chandelier.

Iris began to climb, eyes fixed upward. Halfway up, she glanced through the ladder's steps and was surprised to find a man's face across from hers.

Sometimes Iris experienced her emotions like shifts in lighting, and the man across from her glowed, golden and warm, like someone holding a giant buttercup under his chin. His dark eyes creased at the corners as he met her gaze smiling, with a bottom lip so ripe it made Iris bite hers just for looking. Longish black hair that fell soft around a jaw sharp enough to cut glass, the sparkle of stubble making it look like it already had.

He gave her a small wave with a big hand, "Hey, I got this," and climbed higher.

"Oh, no." Iris too ascended. "It's okay, I work in the field."

The man tilted his head to peer at her through the slats, a boyish dimple appearing under regal cheekbones. "You're the electrician?"

"No. Are you?"

"Definitely not." He climbed another couple steps. "But it's my fault, so I have to fix it."

"How's it your fault?"

"I never know." He smirked. "So what *is* your field?"

"Ladders," Iris deadpanned.

"How's this one, in your professional opinion?" He took her pause to offer suggestions: "Tall, well-built, sure of itself but not cocky—"

"Crowded."

His deep laugh made Iris feel like she'd won something. They were closer now, having climbed in tandem, and faced each other overtop the apex.

The manager addressed Iris from the floor, "Miss? You can come down, I'll have one of my guys help Gabe get the chandelier down."

"I'm Gabe." He grinned and stuck his hand out across the top rung.

"Iris." She shook it, and when their hands touched, a frisson of electricity coursed through her. "And we don't have to take it down—" the *we* slipping out unintentionally. "You just have to unplug it from the daisy chain. I can tell you what to do."

"Put me in, Coach."

Gabe climbed as high as he could, until the ladder's apex was at his hips, which put his crotch at the level of her face. Iris tried not to look.

She directed Gabe on where to disconnect and reconnect the extension cords. He reached his muscular arms over his head, exposing a lean slab of lower abdomen upon which dark hair trailed down into his black jeans, belted low. When he had completed Iris's instructions, she told the manager to try the fuse box switch again. For the next minute, they waited in suspended animation, Gabe on the ladder, Iris on the ground. And then, *voilà*! Every pendant but the chandelier illuminated at once.

The entire restaurant broke into cheers and applause. Gabe descended, Iris beamed, and as soon as his foot hit the floor, without thinking, they hugged. He smelled smoky, though not like cigarettes or weed, but some happy summer memory, a campfire or beach bonfire—an accord of woodsmoke, fresh air, and salt. She could still smell it when they parted.

Rob clapped a hand on Gabe's back. Iris craned her neck to check on Roman and James, but they weren't at their table. She overheard Rob tell Gabe, "Don't apologize, we could never have afforded that piece if you'd charged us what it was worth."

Then Rob turned to them both. "What can I get you two, on the house?"

Gabe and Iris spoke over each other:

"Well, do you—?"

"I should find my—"

"Your friends?" interrupted the server who had waited on Iris. "They left while you were fixing the lights. But we comped your table anyway, so there was no bill."

"Oh, okay, thanks." *They were definitely in a fight,* she thought in dismay. She looked to Gabe, who had his hands in his pockets, bushy eyebrows lifted in expectation. "Didn't you come with people?"

He shrugged. "They'll find their way home."

Gabe was, by every measure, too hot for her. His face was a marvel of natural symmetry, she could have studied his bone structure in architecture school. His body was long, lean, and broad-shouldered, with a surfer's laid-back athleticism and easy masculinity that could carry chin-length hair and a saffron-yellow shirt. That he had marked his tan, sinewy arms with haphazard tattoos like stickers on a locker door seemed to underscore his genuine modesty. He had beauty to burn.

And yet Gabe was looking at her with intensity and delight, listening to her, laughing easily, raking his hand through his hair more than necessary. Iris rubbed her nose to discreetly sniff her wrist; the perfume was still strong. It emboldened her to flirt as if she talked to male models all the time.

She noticed his hands were a mess, calloused palms and skin crisscrossed with pale scars. Iris took his hand in hers—any excuse to touch him—and teased, "What do you do for a living, shuck oysters? Repair garbage disposals? Are you the piranha keeper at the zoo?"

He laughed. "Worse, I blow glass." He saw her puzzled look and elaborated. "I made the chandelier. Cuts and burns are an occupational hazard."

"You *made it?*" Iris was shocked. "I thought you just sold it to him and installed it, badly."

"That too." He chuckled. "I'm full service."

Their conversation flowed as easily as breathing. He seemed genuinely curious about her, asking lots of questions, and when he heard she had a dog, had to see pictures. And she learned Gabe grew up in Brooklyn, got a scholarship to RISD to study graphic design but fell in love with glassblowing and stayed on for his MFA. He'd been honing his craft ever since. He was a little younger than she at thirty-one, which Iris secretly hated.

"Why glass? Of all the mediums, it seems the most punishing."

"It keeps you honest. There's no bluffing or pretense in front of a two-thousand-degree furnace. Your mind can't wander for a second. You're totally present."

"Sounds intense."

"It is, but for me, it's a relief, like meditating. I get in a zone when I do it, everything else ceases to exist."

"Do you ever get close to the end of a big, elaborate piece and then it breaks?"

"All the time."

"And that doesn't make you want to tear your hair out?"

"Oh, it's the worst! I swear like a sailor, I feel sorry for myself. And then I let it go, start over. That's life, right?" He sipped his drink. "What about you? Why lighting?"

"When I started grad school, I was all about structural engineering and building safety, but the farther I got into my program, the more drawn I was to lighting design for the creativity and, I don't know, the . . ."

"Emotion?"

A smile spread on her face. "Yes, light is emotional." She surprised herself by opening up more than usual: "I survived a house fire as a kid, and after it happened, I got really afraid of the dark. My grandparents got me a little night-light that I used every night until I went to college, it was embarrassing. But it made me feel safe, when I really needed to feel that. I realized I wanted to make spaces that feel inviting, or dramatic, or emotional, and above all, safe for people."

He nodded. "You make me want to do more lighting pieces."

"You should. That chandelier is incredible."

"Thanks. I told Rob my inspiration was his fragile masculinity."

Iris gave a laugh that extinguished the votive candle between them. "Shoot, I blew out our candle." The wick had burned way down to the bottom.

"Watch." Gabe produced a lighter from his pocket and sheltered the smoke with his hand so that its tendrils corded together, snaking up from the votive like a cobra from a basket. Well above the candle's lip, he cracked the lighter beside the writhing smoke, and in an instant, the wick deep within lit itself.

Iris's jaw dropped. "How did you do that?"

"I like to play with fire." He popped his brows.

"Oh please." She gave him a playful shove. His shoulder felt rock solid, and she wanted to touch him again as soon as she'd let go.

"It's just chemistry. I'll show you. First, blow the candle out."

She reached to pull the votive toward her, but the hot glass seared her fingers. "Ouch!" She shook out the sting.

"Here, I'll hold it for you, the nerves in my fingertips are dead or used to it." He lifted the votive and held it in front of her chin like a birthday cupcake. The candlelight's reflection made his brown eyes sparkle as the flame flickered with their breath. He looked from her lips to her eyes. "Make a wish."

She smiled and leaned in. It was the closest their faces had been all night. She puckered her lips and extinguished the flame with a gentle puff.

He set the votive on the bar and handed her the lighter. "Now, light the smoke."

Iris chased the twirling smoke trail high above the candle, took a few tries to start the lighter, and—*gasp!*—it worked! The flame leaped into the bottom of the candle.

"I did it! Did you see?" She turned to him, elated.

Gabe was already gazing at her like she was the magic. "I missed it. Show me again."

And they went back and forth, creating fire, feeling like tiny gods.

It wasn't until the servers turned up the house lights and began to stack chairs on tables that Iris and Gabe realized they'd been talking for hours. She would barely remember the conversation the next day, she would remember only the feeling. And the feeling was that she had been meaning to catch up with this stranger for her entire life.

After tipping the bartender generously, Gabe walked Iris out into the warm summer night to get her a taxi home. As they approached the corner, she got increasingly in her head. Iris always botched goodbyes with men. She got nervous and rushed them. And Gabe made her very nervous.

Luckily, he seemed like the type who had never been nervous in his life.

He hooked her hand with one finger. "So, can I get your number? You know, in case another lighting emergency occurs?"

"Did you make enough faulty chandeliers for that?"

"I can break the ones that work." He pulled his phone from his pocket.

She tapped in her number. When she handed it back to him, instead of taking the phone, he slid his fingers down her own, over her wrist and arm, until his thumb grazed her elbow crease. They locked eyes for one suspended moment, asking, knowing, before their mouths met in a kiss as instant as the flame jumping into the candle. It felt easy, natural, unthinking, but the thrill—*there* was the proof it was a first kiss, *the* first kiss, as if she had never kissed or been kissed properly by anyone before. Every sense was heightened in a swirl of pleasure; the woodsy smell of his skin, the bittersweet Campari on his tongue, the warm envelopment of his presence even as he touched only her lips and her elbow, the sight of fireworks behind closed eyes, and the sound of the world falling silent. A cyclone of sensation overloading her system, and the two of them, alone together in the eye of a beautiful storm. It was a good thing he'd left his hand on her arm, because by the end of the kiss, he was keeping her on earth.

When they broke, it was like two magnets pulling apart, first hard to separate and then all at once. They rocked back on their heels and locked eyes in shared wonder.

"Take me home," Iris whispered.

Gabe glanced over her head and whistled loudly to a passing cab. The cab braked and pulled over ten yards ahead of them. He grabbed her hand and they ran, giddy as kids, toward the taxi's blazing taillights.

Eighteen

"So did you have an orgasm?" Hannah asked.

Iris fitted the screw into the hole and power-drilled it into the particleboard, buzzing to a satisfying thud. "That you have to ask tells me you haven't been listening."

Iris was sitting on the floor of Hannah's nursery in progress, surrounded by slabs of white IKEA particleboard and the crumpled assembly instructions for a changing table. Hannah was overseeing from her new nursing chair, writing out shower thank-you notes and folding tiny clothes into tinier squares. Hugo was stretched out on the flattened cardboard boxes, happy to be included. The room was painted a soothing soft green, like the underside of a leaf, and Hannah had stenciled a border of flowers and butterflies along the top. Despite the whimsical innocence of the setting, their conversation was anything but.

"He was really that good?"

Iris's memory flashed to being with Gabe: her hands on his smooth, chiseled chest, the strength of his tattooed arms winding around her like a python, lifting her onto his lap, holding her as she draped over him. "I can't even describe it, honestly. Words fail."

"You can't hold out on me. I am a horny preggo! At least tell me, was he a good kisser? I can see your chin is all pink from stubble burn."

Iris held the drill to her chest. "Oh my God, the kissing. *The kiss-*

ing! That could've been the best part. I mean, it wasn't, because the rest of it was insane, but with another guy, it would have been."

Hannah squealed in delight. "People don't make out enough anymore! Even if Mike is too weirded out to have sex with our fetus present, I'm gonna propose more make-out sessions. Tell me more!"

"It's weird. It's like I can't remember the details, I was so in the moment. Normally the first time with a new guy, I'm totally in my head, observing myself, my body, grading his moves, imagining him judging my body, all that noise. Last night with Gabe, I was just . . . blackout."

"Drunk?"

Iris laughed. "No, like, sensory overload. I wasn't thinking about it, I was just feeling it. And it felt fucking amazing."

"Wow." Hannah patted the stack of onesies on her lap. "In other words, his dick is big."

They both dissolved into giggles.

Iris dropped her shoulders. "I blew it at the end, though."

"Really? I usually blow it in the beginning."

Iris threw a Styrofoam peanut at her. "I don't even want to tell you. The secondhand cringe could send you to early labor."

"You'd be doing me a favor. What happened?"

"So this perfume can't last forever—"

"It was *not* the perfume!"

"Hannah, I could not pull this guy on my own. Anyway, after a marathon night with him, multiple rounds, multiple orgasms, I'm sure I sweated it off. And I hadn't intended to fall asleep at all . . ."

Iris recounted how the morning had played out, reliving her humiliation. As soon as the sun's first rays hit her face, Iris's eyes shot open, pupils tightening in the light and panic that morning had come and she was naked—without the perfume. Gabe lay similarly bare, but at peace; he was facedown, his breathing slow and steady, the sheets tangled beneath him, exposing his perfect buttocks like two scoops of caramel ice cream. And as much as Iris wanted to take a bite, she knew she had to hightail it out of there.

She summoned all her mediocre Pilates skills to rise from the bed without bouncing the mattress and set to gathering her belongings strewn across Gabe's studio apartment. She hastily dressed—bra, sundress, the bangle bracelets she slipped silently into her purse, but she couldn't find her underwear. Leaving them behind was not an option; these were *not* date night panties. She couldn't leave proof that she laundered the underwear the dog chewed instead of throwing them away. It was no wonder she couldn't find them now, Iris had been so eager to get them out of sight she might have chucked them into space.

That jogged her memory—she *had* flung them with some height. She redirected her search upward and spotted her granny panties hanging from the fin of a surfboard mounted on the wall—*Called it on the surfing*—but they were too high to reach. She glanced at the kitchen counter for some sort of utensil. She pulled a long chef's knife from the block and used it to catch the elastic band of her undergarment and lift it off the fin.

"You were going to stab me without saying goodbye?" Gabe asked from just behind her.

"No!" Hannah cackled. "He catches you creeping around his apartment with a *knife*? You absolute psycho."

"It gets worse. So I tell him . . ."

"I'm sorry, I never do this, I'm bad at it."

"Homicide?"

"Sex with someone I just met. Well, that's not completely true, I *used* to never do this. Lately I've been on kind of a tear."

"Thanks, I feel special."

"You were the best, like, ever!"

Then he *really* laughed.

So did Hannah, doubled over now. "Stop, I can't take any more. You did not say that!"

"I was trying to say something nice, and I accidentally told the truth."

"You never need to feel bad about being mean to a hot man. They cut their feelings with their carbs, he probably ghosts hookups all the time."

"I don't know what came over me. It was like I couldn't lie to someone so beautiful. Remember that poem in AP English? 'Beauty is truth, truth beauty'?"

"Keats, 'Ode to a Grecian Fuckboy.'"

Iris laughed. "Actually, he's Asian. And I don't know if he's a fuckboy. We made plans to see each other again. He was a very generous lover. And he's creative! You should've seen this glass chandelier he made."

"Ooh, defending him already? So you *like* this one."

"Ugh, I think I really do."

"Why do you say that like it's bad?"

"It's a bad time to start anything. I begin my egg freezing cycle next week."

"So what, you can't have sex? Why is everything related to baby making so ironically prudish?"

"I don't know, I have to ask the doc what the rules are. But I meant more, how can I keep the egg freezing a secret from him?"

Hannah shrugged. "So tell him about it."

"Oh right, guys love that after a first date. 'Hey, nice to meet you, just FYI, my eggs are about to dry up and I'm desperate to have a kid someday, so I'm undergoing fertility treatment. Can we circle back?'"

Hannah laughed. "We'll workshop that text message. But seriously, you're both adults."

"It's embarrassing, and it's private!"

"Girl, he knows how you *taste*. Now you're gonna get shy?"

Iris shielded herself with a children's book. "Please, not in front of *The Velveteen Rabbit*. Anyway, it's my business. He's not entitled to my fertility stats."

"That's fair. Just as long as you know you have nothing to be ashamed of. I think you're making a smart and empowered choice."

Iris tilted her head. "But is it a *hot* choice?"

Hannah chuckled.

"The irony is, I'm doing this so I don't have to rush having a baby, and yet talking about fertility makes you sound baby-crazed."

"Maybe you're right. You don't have to tell him. Just do you."

Iris stood up and tested the completed changing table, giving it a push with her hand. It held firm. "Yay! I think this is solid. I just have to slide in the lower shelves."

Hannah cooed in gratitude. "Aw, that makes it really feel so real. Speaking of, I officially told the school I wasn't coming back in the fall."

"How do you feel?"

"Mixed emotions. You know I loved my job, even if it wasn't the easiest these past couple years. But I'm excited for this new chapter, and obviously, I'm grateful, I know it's a huge privilege to be able to stop working . . ."

"Bana, it's just me."

She smiled. "I'm freaked out. Even if I'm just swapping teaching other people's kids for raising my own, it feels like a change in my identity. You know I always supported myself, no matter how shitty the apartment, you remember."

"Oh, yes. The Bushwick studio? Those roaches owed you rent."

"It started to change when I moved in with Mike, but I was still making money then. Now it's like, fully different. Better, obviously, and compared to what Mike makes, my contribution was a drop in the bucket. It was more for my pride than anything."

"Your pride is allowed to count."

"I guess now I'll take pride in being a mom. I just hope I'm a good one."

"Hey." Iris reached over to touch her knee. "You're gonna be the best mom. This baby is the luckiest."

"I found out the sex."

"You *did*? I thought you guys wanted to be surprised."

"Mike wants to be surprised. I was dying to know. He couldn't make our last appointment, and I caved."

"So?"

"I can't tell you. I feel bad enough I went behind his back, I'm so afraid I'll let it slip around him, I have to keep my mouth shut from here on out. I didn't even tell my mom."

"I understand. But we never have secrets!"

"I know, I hate it, this will be the first and the last secret, pinky swear." Hannah stuck out her smallest finger, and Iris reached up from the floor to link pinkies.

In another room, the front door opened and closed. Hugo lifted his head and sniffed the air.

"Mike's home." Hannah called to him that they were in the nursery.

A moment later her husband appeared in the doorway, looking ruddy-cheeked in sweaty athletic clothes. He was tall, fit, and freckled, with bright blue eyes and strawberry blond hair the color of a BBQ potato chip. "Wow, you two made progress!" he said as Hugo ambled to greet him, nails clicking on the hardwood.

"Iris did. She built the bookshelf and is almost done with the changing table—"

"But not the crib," he interrupted.

"Not the crib, because you told me to leave that to you." Hannah gave him a look.

"Yes, I'm going to build the crib. If not tomorrow, then next weekend."

"You should want to—"

"I do want to!" He softened his tone and smiled. "That's why I asked you to save it for me to do. I promise. I want to be a part of the nest making."

"I told him that." Not that Hannah needed to clarify; the tension in the air made clear this was not a new discussion. "Male birds help build and feather the nest for the baby just as much as the females."

"What if I pay someone else to build it, does that count?"

"I'm thinking of you! Mothers get all this bonding time during pregnancy while the baby is inside us, and then it comes out, and there's nursing and all these chemicals and hormones to bond. I don't want you to feel left out."

"I won't. The first time I hold our baby, I'll be all in, hundred percent. It's instinctual."

Hannah pointed a finger. "Iris was telling me about her hot new guy."

"Nice. Bring him to my birthday party on Friday," Mike offered.

"Thanks, but it's very new. Like, less than twenty-four hours."

Mike shrugged. "Good enough for me. I don't know if this is a factor, but Ben will be bringing Madison."

Madison. Hearing him say her name was like ice water on her scalp. Ben's new girlfriend was *established* in their friend group. She wondered if Hannah and Mike had met her.

"Ew, no! Michael." Hannah shot him a look like a power drill.

Mike put up his hands. "He just texted me asking. I didn't know what to say! That's why I'm giving her the heads-up. Should I tell him he can't?"

"No," Iris interjected. "It's fine, don't say anything to Ben."

Hannah groaned. "Iris, I'm so sorry."

"It's okay, really. We broke up six months ago. I knew he moved on."

"And so have you," Hannah pointed out.

"Bring your guy! Have a battle of the new SOs, or don't. I think showing up unbothered is the flex." He sniffed inside the collar of his T-shirt and scrunched his nose. "Woof. I'm gonna hop in the shower and then get dinner going."

"He means order takeout," Hannah said.

Mike had just left when Iris remembered Rapacine. She excused herself and caught up with him in the hallway outside their bedroom.

"I hate to ask you for another legal favor, but I have another friend in need . . ." she filled him in on Madame Rapacine's landlord problem. "I don't even think she wants to litigate, but she could use some legal advice. That said, I know you're busy with the baby and all, so please, please feel free to say no."

"I don't want to say no!" He pulled his shirt off over his head, and Iris caught a rank whiff. "I felt bad we couldn't help with the NYCHA thing because of the conflict of interest. But a landlord from hell? That's no problem. Give her my number, and my summer associate Tony will look into her case."

She thanked him and left him to get his shower.

A s Dr. Alsarraj invited Iris into his elegant office overlooking a leafy cross street between Fifth and Madison, it was clear she had entered the privileged world of elective healthcare. Family Tree Fertility was located in a posh Upper East Side building, and his spacious private office had built-in bookshelves with leather-bound volumes bookended by crystal professional awards. Iris took a seat in one of two matching wing chairs that faced the doctor's imposing mahogany desk. Dr. Alsarraj was in his fifties, fit, with thick, dark, wavy hair—"like Omar Sharif," Iris could hear her late grandmother say. He wore a silk tie with a gold tie clip, and as he navigated with his computer mouse, Iris noticed enameled cufflinks peeking from under his white coat sleeve. Behind him hung his framed degrees from Yale College and Columbia Medical School, and a Certificate of Excellence for the practice. Everything about this process made her anxious, but Iris reassured herself that this was out-of-network money well spent.

Dr. Alsarraj was saying, "So we're on track to begin your egg retrieval cycle next week. From there, the entire process will take about two weeks: twelve days of injections for ovarian stimulation, then a special one called a trigger shot, and forty-eight hours later, a short outpatient procedure to retrieve the mature eggs. During those weeks, you'll visit us for frequent monitoring appointments, which will include ultrasounds, blood tests, or both. This way I'll keep a close eye that everything is moving along as it should and tailor your medication levels exactly to your needs."

"I'm a little nervous about doing the injections myself."

"It's very straightforward. Nurse Dani will walk you through exactly how to do it. Side effects of the hormones and ovarian stimulation are minor but worsen toward the end of the cycle. Bruising at injection site, cramping, bloating, mood swings, think PMS on steroids. Normally, an ovary is the size of a walnut, but as we're turbocharging ovulation to make them overproduce, each ovary will eventually swell to the size of an orange. Hence the bloating and tenderness."

Iris reflexively crossed her arms over her body, imagining her internal organs more than quadrupling in size.

Dr. Alsarraj continued, "So my general advice is to be gentle with yourself. Avoid high impact sports or activities, because if you incur trauma to the abdomen, there's an increased risk of a ruptured follicle or ovarian torsion, which is extremely painful. These complications are rare, but we want everything to go smoothly so you have a great result. Any questions?"

Iris had almost lost her nerve to ask. "If I'm seeing someone, what's your advice on . . . intimacy?"

"Meaning, penetrative intercourse with a male partner?" Dr. Alsarraj bluntly clarified. "When I was a resident, my attending used to tell his patients, 'Don't do anything that bounces your ponytail!'" He chuckled.

Iris recoiled.

"That hasn't aged well, has it? But you get the idea, nothing too strenuous. Sex is safe early in the cycle, provided you use a condom— the hormone therapy will control the release of your eggs, but juicing ovulation, there's a danger of ectopic pregnancy. I do recommend abstaining in the last few days before retrieval to guard against torsion, but I doubt you'll be in the mood at that point."

Iris nodded. So maybe she could get away with keeping this to herself.

"And you will need pelvic rest for five days after your retrieval. So tell your guy to get it out of his system now and in the first half of your cycle. After that, easy, tiger."

Iris smiled politely and opted not to clarify that *she* was the tiger.

She thanked him and he said she could schedule her next appointment on the way out. Iris had just reached the door when Dr. Alsarraj stopped her:

"One more thing, I was reviewing your intake questionnaire, and I see you've checked one prior pregnancy three years ago, but you didn't indicate its result—live birth, still birth, miscarriage, or abortion."

"It was very brief. Maybe it doesn't even count."

"Would you be comfortable sharing the details with me? It could be relevant history."

Iris forced a shrug. "I was a few weeks late, had one positive home test, and then a few days later, bleeding. Nothing, really."

"I see. And you're right, nothing to worry about. Even in perfectly healthy women, early miscarriage is very common."

Her heart winced. "I thought it might've been a false positive."

"In any case, it won't affect our course of treatment."

Iris hadn't worn the perfume to the appointment, so she descended into the subway station at Sixty-eighth and Lex and boarded the downtown 6 train, average and invisible.

The shushing and rocking of the subway car lulled her as the memory returned. Ben had just moved into her apartment, half his things still in boxes as they tried to jigsaw two lives into one. And she found herself on the toilet, holding a positive pregnancy test, and her first thought was, *Fuck.*

Then, *I shouldn't have taken this test,* as if unknowing it could undo it. But it didn't make any sense, she was on the pill, and she was only a week late on her period. It was overkill to buy the pregnancy test at all, she bought it on impulse, on a whim.

Or intuition?

And now it read positive.

How would she tell Ben? She didn't want him to feel tricked or trapped. It was an accident. It was a fluke.

Or a miracle?

She remembered standing at the edge of the living room looking at Ben on the couch, separated by boxes of his unpacked belongings like cardboard ice floes. He had his hat on backward, tufts of his brown bangs sprouting out the front as he bent over his phone. He looked more like a teenage boy than a dad.

"Ben?" Her heart pounded with nerves.

"Yeah." His head stayed down, and his thumbs tapped furiously like the phone was a Gameboy. "Sorry, this partner doesn't understand the concept of a weekend." The *whoosh* sound of a sent email coincided with his sigh, and finally, Ben looked up. "What's up?"

Iris couldn't find the words, so she just said, "Look."

His jaw dropped when he read it. "*Fuck.* Sorry, that's not what I meant. Let me start over, catch me up. Can this be real? I thought you were on the pill or something."

She stammered, "I was, I mean I am. But I ran out of refills last month, and it was the weekend, so my doctor's office was closed and so I couldn't renew the prescription right away, I only missed a couple days, that's happened before and it was always fine . . ."

He put a hand on her shoulder as much to calm her as to lean on her for balance. His exhale puffed out his cheeks. "This is a lot."

"For me, too."

"You! Yes, God, even more for you, you're—" another puff of breath, "Whoo, damn!" He took off his hat and raked his hands through his hair. "Shit, I never swear this much. Why can't I stop swearing? Fuck me." He laughed. "I mean, what the hell? This is great, right?"

"Is it?" She often looked to Ben first, his emotions were so much easier to read than her own.

"Of course it is! Holy shit, we're having a baby! I love you— c'mere!" He pulled her into him and hugged her tight. "That's why they call it a love child. It's our *looove* child." He said it in a silly voice. "We're having a *loo-oove* child."

Pressed against his chest, Iris thought maybe it *was* a good thing.

Ben surprised her by instantly embracing this turn of events. Right then, he finished his unpacking, newly energized to nest. And he was more doting, more affectionate, more lustful. It was as if he became infatuated with Iris all over again, and she felt herself blossom under the attention. His positivity was infectious, and Iris quickly adopted the new narrative, that this accidental pregnancy was just proof of the kismet quality of their union, messy and down-to-earth, yet written in the stars. This was the story they'd tell their child one day: that even if his or her arrival wasn't planned, it was ordained.

That night they made love and stayed up talking, wrapped up in each other on top of the bedsheets. Ben was marveling at her body, which was completely unchanged from the outside. "I can't believe my mom doesn't know."

"I know." Iris couldn't believe her mother didn't know either.

The next night, the same amorous routine, and Iris felt like everything in her life had fallen into place at once. Until Ben's pillow talk upped the ante.

"We should elope!"

"Elope? Your mom would kill us."

"She'd kill *me*. She might actually stop liking *you* so damn much, which would be nice. I miss being Mom's favorite. But she'd forgive us when she saw the baby." He met her incredulous mouth with a kiss.

"She'd forgive *you*. No, when we get married, we'll do it right, with family and all our friends there."

"Why bother? We can't do it in a church now anyway."

Iris playfully shoved him, and he caught her and pulled her onto his chest.

"What if we got married at the courthouse this weekend? Surprise everyone!"

"You don't mean that."

"I do! See? I just said *I do,* by accident! Let's go tomorrow!"

She grinned but eyed him warily. "I don't think you can just walk up and do it, it's not Vegas. We have to get a license, and I think a blood test or something."

"All right, let's get a blood test and *then* get married! Why are you finding reasons to say no, when we have such a good reason to say yes?"

"I just don't want an unplanned pregnancy to be the reason we get married. I want you to have thought it through."

"I'm a guy, this is not the first time this scenario has crossed my mind, and since I was young, I always knew I would do the right thing."

"'Do the right thing?' Ben, I don't want you to do it out of your Eagle Scout sense of duty. I want us to *choose* each other."

"We haven't chosen each other?"

"Of course we have. Look, the pregnancy is a big enough thing to process. I just don't want you to do something impulsive that you'll regret."

"I'll regret, or you will?"

The next morning, things were tense between them. Iris hadn't slept, she had stayed awake thinking of how she might have phrased her words differently. Ben went to the gym in the morning, and she gave him space to reset his mood. The more Iris thought about it, the more she softened her position. She decided that if he brought it up again, she might say yes.

But he didn't.

And on Monday, she started to bleed.

Iris remembered how she phrased it to Ben when he came home from work: "It turns out I'm not pregnant, I guess." She couldn't bring herself to add another loss to her tally, even if it felt like one.

"Are you okay?" Ben searched her face.

She nodded, but the tears came. He dropped his bag and hugged her, holding her for a long while, letting her cry.

"Good thing we didn't tell anyone yet."

Iris nodded dolefully. "I'm sorry."

"You have nothing to apologize for!" He squeezed her. "It wasn't supposed to happen in the first place. You were right. We were getting ahead of ourselves."

"I don't know why I'm so sad."

"Don't be. We'll do it right someday, all planned out like you like."

Iris, the planner, had planned herself right into being alone. She had thought back often to that day since they broke up. At the time, she reassured herself that it wasn't the right order of things, and she wanted everything to be perfect to set them up for success and happiness. But in retrospect, she saw how she might have burst his bubble. Her reticence read to him as rejection. She didn't tell him she was scared, she told him he was silly. And in that misunderstanding, she had squandered their chance at forever.

Iris wished she had explained to Ben that she needed more reassurance that he wanted to marry her without the pregnancy, not only because of it. That he would love her in a way that was solid, with a foundation that would last, that the family they were building together would be strong enough to withstand the anxiety, fear, and loneliness that had hounded her since childhood.

If she had been as impulsive as he, as free with her words and her love and her trust, would they be happily married today? Maybe the leap of faith would've saved the pregnancy, signaled to the universe that they were all in—as if Nature cared. Maybe they'd have tried again and had one or two children thereafter. Would she have gotten the home and family she wanted?

Or would she have called his bluff? Said yes that night only for him to get cold feet on the colder steps of the courthouse, just like he did last winter? Or would they be *unhappily* married, as she'd feared? And she'd be wedded but unloved, stuck with his resentment and second-guessing. Who's to say he wouldn't have stopped "feeling it" after she was saddled with his kid?

No, Iris couldn't have counted on Ben to build a family with. He was still the man who changed his mind about her.

She never made up hers.

The subway car screeched to a halt, and Iris peered out the dirty window to find she had missed her stop.

CHAPTER
Twenty

I ris had come to learn that Frank wasn't exaggerating when he described how micromanaging working with Wolff could be, although it wasn't Jonathan who called Iris every morning, it was Marilyn.

On Monday: "Good morning, Iris. Jonathan was sorry to miss you at the walk-through. He can do lunch Wednesday. Do you have any dietary restrictions or preferences?"

"Oh great, Wednesday works for me." Not that Marilyn had asked. "And no restrictions. I'm not a big meat eater, but I can find something on any menu."

"Prefers pescatarian. I'll email you the details by end of day."

"Great, thanks." Marilyn's ultra-efficient energy made her nervous. She reached for a Post-it and jotted "find new word for GREAT" and stuck it to her computer screen.

On Wednesday: "Good morning, Iris. Unfortunately, Jonathan has a conference call with the London team, so lunch today doesn't work. He'd like to do dinner instead."

"Tonight?"

"Yes. He apologizes for the change. I'll arrange a car to come pick you up and drop you home."

"No problem, dinner would be—" she glanced at the Post-it—"lovely."

"Excellent. We have your home address. The car will arrive at seven. Jonathan is looking forward to seeing you."

"Great." *Gah!*

. . .

The change of plans gave Iris enough time to overthink things at home. Iris had never been so high up on a project to be on the receiving end of a free meal. She wondered if she should change clothing—*no*, she was already wearing her carefully chosen Mr. Wolff lunch outfit, it was good enough for a Mr. Wolff dinner.

The real question was, should she wear the perfume?

Since Marilyn had told her to "bring back that spark," Iris had begun wearing the perfume every day. But smelling good at lunch is incidental; smelling good at dinner is a signal, one she wasn't sure she wanted to send.

But the perfume gave her something more than sex appeal, it gave her confidence. It gave her a sense of control over herself and her surroundings. She needed the invisible suit of armor. Jonathan Wolff had money, power, and summer-weight cashmere.

She was deliberating when her apartment buzzer rang.

Her doorman's voice crackled through the intercom: "Car here for you."

"Thanks, Sammy. Be right out." She crossed to her window and peeked out the blinds. A gleaming Mercedes sedan idled beside the parked cars on her street.

She blotted her neck, each wrist, and only one elbow crease—the bandage from that morning's blood test tugged at the other.

They were meeting at a restaurant not far from the building site, Estiatorio Milos, inside the Hudson Yards luxury shopping complex. The Mercedes pulled up around the back, giving Iris a close-up view of the Vessel, a sixteen-story open-air honeycomb structure that was supposed to be an architectural "attraction" until it fatally underestimated humanity's capacity for despair. Since its opening in 2019, it had been forced to close repeatedly after its open levels, intended as lookout points and photo ops, had been used by four people to leap to their death. Iris thought grimly of one of Frank's favorite sayings, "Think like a person! Not like a designer. Great design serves human nature, bad design succumbs to it."

"The restaurant is on the top floor," the driver said without turning. Iris noticed the cartilage of his ear was puffy like a boxer's, she forgot what they called it. "I'll wait here to take you home."

"Oh, no. You should get yourself dinner. Do you have a card so I can call you when I'm done?"

"It's no problem. I'm Mr. Wolff's private driver."

"Oh, okay." She was surprised and a little sheepish for thinking it was a generic hired car and for bogarting the boss's ride. "I didn't catch your name."

"Esdras."

"Thank you, Esdras."

"Enjoy your evening, Ms. Sunnegren."

Iris pushed through the rotating glass doors, which seemed to exhale as they deposited her onto the glossy tile of the shopping center. The luxury stores had closed for the evening, but the emptied window displays remained spotlit. Iris passed by the bare busts of Van Cleef & Arpels and naked mannequins of Dior and Fendi, like headless women for sale.

On the elevator to the top floor, Iris saw she'd received an Instagram DM from someone she didn't follow, @AliAlways, it read: "Hey Iris, can you give me a call at 610-555-7648? It's about Jacob." She guessed it was Alison Cooper, a second cousin on Clay's side whom she'd met only a few times. She'd deal after dinner.

What Iris saw when she emerged from the elevators on the top floor was no ordinary mall restaurant. In fact, the dining space was secluded from view, only the wine bar was accessible from the main floor. Iris waited her turn to speak to the modelesque hostesses stationed in front of a grand white marble staircase that wound upward in a nautilus spiral, with warm, glowing step lights.

"Hi, I'm meeting Jonathan Wolff."

"Ms. Sunnegren, welcome. They're waiting for you. I'll show you to your table." She stepped aside as another beautiful employee took her place and gestured for Iris to follow.

They? Maybe Marilyn was joining them. Iris followed her upstairs.

Milos was a sweeping space with white marble floors and white tablecloths, evoking the sun-bleached limestone of Mykonos. The focal point was the wraparound view of the Vessel and the sunset over the Hudson River, made more glittering by the reflection of the tables' candlelight in the glass walls. The exposed kitchen at her left was bordered by a coastline of chipped ice displaying fresh fish that glinted silver and orange, crab claws the size of dinner rolls, and one wilted octopus, its lifeless arms tumbling down like tendrils of wet hair. And yet the space was devoid of any fish smell—a reminder that you could excise the unpleasantness from any experience, for market price.

In a shark-gray dress, the hostess glided through the tables as the servers darted out of her way, fleet as minnows, clearing their crowded path. Iris followed in her slipstream through the first level, down onto the premium tier of tables along the windows. The hostess extended her arm to indicate the table front and center, where Jonathan Wolff was deep in conversation with two other men. It took a moment for Iris to realize that one of his guests was the mayor of New York City.

Iris stood back from the table, not wanting to interrupt. It took a moment, but Wolff registered her presence and stood to greet her. He remained disconcertingly good-looking in a fine-knit crewneck in lapis blue. He introduced her to the mayor, who clasped her hand in both of his and flashed a megawatt smile before apologizing that he couldn't stay. Iris mumbled she was honored and hopefully something more normal.

When he left, Iris said, "Wow, that was cool. He's a friend?"

Jonathan leaned in. "Everyone's a friend with an election coming up." He graciously pulled out Iris's chair and introduced her to the guest that remained. "Bill, this is Iris Sunnegren, my lead lighting designer for Oasys, my new residence going up on Eleventh. Iris, Bill Hargrove, executive vice president for real estate development at NYCHA—did I get that title right, Bill? Bill and I are at the start of a very important new project."

Jonathan went on to explain that Wolff Development had just won a bid to take over the renovation and management of one of the many public housing locations that had fallen into dangerous disrepair. Attempts at a private-public cooperative solution had been percolating since Bloomberg's administration but had been stymied over politics. Now, at last, the logjam had broken, and a pilot program was approved with Wolff at the helm.

"The deal is, we rebuild brand-new apartments for NYCHA residents on the existing site, and in exchange, we're permitted to build an additional apartment building that could be offered to mixed-income renters. I think it will be a game changer for the benefit of all the residents, and I hope it's the first of many Wolff-NYCHA collaborations." He raised a glass to Bill.

Iris was surprised to hear Jonathan had been gunning to work with NYCHA, when his previous work had been exclusively high-end. "What drew you to public housing?"

"I'm passionate about housing equity and building safe, quality homes for all. It's part of why your lighting pitch spoke to me so much."

Iris's cheeks bloomed.

"What's happened to NYCHA housing in this city should bring shame to us all—no offense, Bill. You've been fighting the good fight much longer than I."

Bill nodded. "Sadly, we've reached a breaking point. New York State has underfunded NYCHA for decades, the last federal infrastructure bill slashed public housing before passage, and it's only gotten worse. Since the pandemic rent moratoriums, we've been in a rent shortfall of half a billion dollars. We need outside investment to do the needed repairs. I'm glad they finally saw that partnering with private developers was the only way forward."

Jonathan tsked-tsked. "The irony has always been that NYCHA owns some of the most valuable open land in the city, and yet the program's broke—because they can't sell it."

Bill took a swig of his drink. "Worse than broke, our capital backlog for needed repairs exceeds forty billion dollars." He saw Iris's eyes go wide. "I'm not kidding, that's the real number. We project that by 2027, ninety percent of NYCHA apartments will be effectively totaled, meaning it would cost as much to demolish and rebuild as it would to repair them."

She looked back to Jonathan, aghast. "How did it get so bad?"

Jonathan shook his head. "Politics. The poor are not a powerful constituency, so public housing gets shortchanged at every turn. Albany is too broken to fix this problem. That's why they need us. NYCHA can't afford repairs and the tenants can't afford to leave. Worsening income inequality combined with how rents have skyrocketed in the city, the tenants are trapped." Jonathan's face darkened. "Just like they were trapped that day of the Hendricks explosion."

The table fell silent for a moment.

"It infuriates me that it took a preventable tragedy for politicians to listen to what I and many others have been saying for a long time. Last year, I told the city council they were allowing 'demolition by neglect' in public housing. Toxic mold, lead paint, asbestos, broken elevators, no heat in winter and no air in summer, and now a fatal gas leak. They should've let me start a year ago when I wanted to."

"Thank you again for your generous donation to the Hendricks emergency shelter fund. It's much appreciated," Bill said.

Jonathan waved him off like it was nothing. "I can't wait to start their rebuild."

"Wait, *Hendricks* is the site you'll be working on?" Iris asked.

"Yes. It's been my dream to revitalize the downtown-west area in a way that serves communities at every income level, from Oasys to Hendricks Houses."

"My friend's family lived there."

"Your friend?" Bill asked, lifting an eyebrow.

"Thankfully they weren't hurt, but they lived close to the blast. Actually it was my friend's fifteen-year-old niece who smelled the gas and warned her neighbors. She helped a lot of people get out in time."

Jonathan sat back. "A teenager did that? That's heroic! She should be on the news."

"That's what I said!" Iris shook her head. "But they were excluded from the emergency housing because his sister was in some prior eviction dispute. So now they're homeless and crammed in my friend's apartment. It's terrible."

Jonathan touched her arm, his eyes full of concern. "Please email me and cc Marilyn with their names. I'll look into it personally."

His generosity, or his touch, flustered her. "Oh, I didn't mean for, you don't have to—"

"I do mean it. Please do as I ask. I want to help."

Iris was moved. "Thank you, I will."

Food began to arrive, and from the first bite Iris knew this was the best restaurant she had ever been to. The appetizers: a tower of paper-thin fried zucchini and eggplant; a large plate of Greek salad with chunks of vibrant tomato, cucumber, and ribbons of purple onion and parsley; giant scallop sashimi served on a Little Mermaid–sized shell. Then the show-stopping entrée of a large whole fish baked in mounds of salt like a snowdrift, accompanied by an array of grilled vegetable sides. As they passed the family-style dishes around the table and the drinks flowed, the conversation got looser and lighter.

"I'm sorry I missed your walk-through. I know it's a bigger project than you've headed up before. Marilyn told me you seemed a bit overwhelmed."

"Oh, no . . ." *It's giving frenemy, Marilyn.* But Iris remembered what the older woman had said about acting the part. "Not at all. I was moved by the canvas you've given me. I have a decade of experience. I'm young, but I'm not green."

Jonathan smiled. "'Green.' Are you an equestrian?"

"I grew up riding."

"My daughter, Allegra, is eleven and officially horse crazy, so I'm in the market for a pony. Her riding instructor recently taught me the meaning of 'green'—it means 'gives Daddy a heart attack.' Maybe you can advise me while I try to find the equine equivalent of a babysitter."

Iris laughed. "Anytime. It's a wonderful sport for a young woman, it builds confidence. Time spent in the saddle gave me my happiest memories."

Bill swirled his drink and smirked. "You know what they say about why girls love horses?"

Iris knew exactly where he was headed; she had always hated this joke.

Jonathan looked wearily at him. "Careful, Bill, this is my daughter we're talking about."

She hated this rejoinder too. It was a scummy way to talk about any young girl, the ones with fathers and without.

"All right, Allegra excluded. But Iris knows what I'm talking about. The friction . . . ?"

The heat radiating off Iris's blotchy chest sent a waft of the perfume up to her flaring nostrils. "People who think riding horses gives women orgasms don't know how to do either thing right."

Both men burst out laughing, Jonathan harder than Bill. Iris, too, but only in disbelief—had she really just said that, *aloud,* at a work dinner?

And had she gotten away with it?

"I think I heard a mic drop," Jonathan said.

"I see why you like her," Bill replied.

Like her—as a designer or as a woman? She wondered how exactly Jonathan Wolff had described her to Bill before she arrived.

"Excuse me, I gotta go to the little boys' room." Bill rose from the table and left.

"I'm sorry about that, Bill's something else. But I needed him for this deal."

"It's fine."

"You handled him perfectly. Men like him are all ego. Humiliation is the only boundary they respect."

They had finished dinner and were walking toward the glowing staircase when Iris saw an incoming phone call from her aunt Beth. Bill and Jonathan were talking, so she excused herself to quickly answer it. Only it wasn't Beth on the line, it was Alison, and she cut straight to the point.

"Jacob is dead."

Iris held one hand to her ear to close out the mall noise. "What?"

"He OD'd. They found him in a motel in Tampa. It was too late to do anything."

Her heart was racing but her body felt frozen, her thoughts voided.

"I'm trying to help Beth and Clay get the word out to family, since they're overwhelmed, obviously. Beth needed a break from her phone. It looks like the funeral will be on the thirteenth near their place. I'll forward the details as soon as I know them . . . Are you there? Can you hear me?"

"Y-yeah," her voice cracked. "I'm here."

"I know this is a shock. I mean, we knew it could end this way, he was killing himself for a long time, but . . . I can't believe it's really over." The detachment in Alison's voice told Iris that after twenty years of addiction, Jacob had burned every bridge in the family.

"Was anyone with him?"

"Someone he was with called an ambulance but bounced before they arrived, a real hero."

Iris felt flushed and hot.

"I'm sorry, I know you guys used to be close." Then Alison added, softer, "I don't think he died alone, if that's what you meant."

Iris didn't know why she'd asked it or what she meant. She rubbed her brow. Her hand was shaking.

"Iris?"

"Thanks for calling. Give my sympathy to Beth and Clay," she said before hanging up. She couldn't continue the conversation.

She'd texted Jacob last week but never heard back. A gnawing feeling told her to double-check. She opened her text messages, searched his name, and tapped the conversation. Her message to him remained typed in the entry field beside the blue arrow, still waiting to be sent.

Iris shut her eyes against the cluster headache that gathered like a storm. When she opened them again, she steadied her focus on the brightly lit fish, caught in the unseeing gaze of a pink snapper that curved out of a pile of chipped ice, its glassy amber eyes staring, mouth agape in a silent scream.

"Everything okay?" Jonathan appeared beside her.

Iris meant to nod in the affirmative.

Instead, she fainted.

Twenty-one

I t was her first real date with Gabe, and Iris had changed her outfit four times before leaving her apartment. She had briefly considered testing their connection without the perfume. Then
she'd dabbed it on her pulse points, cleavage, thighs, and anywhere
else she wanted him to kiss. Infatuation was a fragile bubble, she
didn't want to pop it.

They were meeting at Cervo's, an Iberian restaurant in Chinatown
where the summer evening painted Canal Street in an ochre glow.
Although the restaurant itself was tiny, its outdoor seating had
sprawled out across the street like a block party, with tables dotting
the asphalt underneath string lights like miniature setting suns.

Iris spotted Gabe leaning against the restaurant's brick exterior
with his hands in his pockets, taking in the scene. It was unusual;
no one just looked for the person they were waiting for anymore. If
you had the misfortune of arriving first, all the more reason to affect caring less. You texted "Here" and kept your head buried in
your phone until your date found you; even a lifted chin was too
vulnerable. Better to be tapped and feign surprise, "Oh, it's you, I
almost forgot."

But Gabe spotted her from far off and straightened with a smile.
His steady gaze made her shy, and she glanced down at her feet. But
then she let herself look back at him. The golden hour lit his skin and
made his eyes sparkle, and she felt aglow with his attention. They

were happy to see each other, and suddenly Iris couldn't recall why this had ever been something to hide.

When she closed the distance between them, the last few feet were charged by their delicious anticipation. She bit her lip. "Hi."

Gabe bent and kissed her cheek. She'd noticed he rarely spoke when an action would do. Iris breathed in his scent, less woodsmoke than the night she met him, now he smelled fresh and clean, like crisp bitter orange softened by the musk of his skin.

The wait to sit outdoors was too long, so they sat inside at the counter, which faced the open galley kitchen only two cooks wide. The drinks menu offered a vermouth service, and Gabe said the negronis were great, but Iris disliked Campari.

"Try the Cocchi Americano, long," Gabe suggested. He ordered a white negroni with the same.

The vermouth arrived on the rocks with soda and a twist of lemon. She took a sip. It was sweet, aromatic, and refreshing.

Gabe read her face. "Nice, right? Fruity and something herbal that cools it all down, I don't know what, it's like . . ."

"Cardamom." Iris remembered it from Madame Rapacine's smell lessons.

He stole a kiss. "Mmm, I think you're right."

They ordered a parade of tapas and shared everything: petal-pink yellowfin tuna with bright orange habanada peppers drizzled in olive oil and sprinkled with sea salt crystals the size of snowflakes; melt-in-your-mouth clams drenched in butter, white wine, and a confetti of parsley, and when the clams had been eaten, Gabe read her mind and ordered extra bread to sop up the sauce; a small bouquet of crispy shrimp heads—at first glance Iris recoiled at their black eyes unseeing beneath a heavy dusting of red spice, but Gabe dug right in, crunching as carelessly as a lion. Iris stalled and hesitated over trying one, laughing as Gabe cheered her on, yelping when the whiskery antennae tickled her nose, until she finally gave one a hasty chomp. Gabe was right, it was delicious—a riot of different textures and tastes such that she savored her next bites—even if she did leave the eyes uneaten. And finally the piri piri half chicken, the aroma alone evoked a future longing before the first bite was taken.

They talked so easily about anything and nothing that they didn't get to the typical questions until the end of the meal, when Gabe asked, "What are you up to this weekend?"

Iris's shoulders tensed. "I have to go to Pennsylvania tomorrow. Family funeral."

"Oh, I'm sorry. Who died?"

"My cousin Jacob. He was only forty-two."

Gabe swore. "Brutal. That's too young. I'm sorry. Do your parents live in Pennsylvania?"

They had arrived at Iris's least favorite moment of dating someone new, when she had to tell them about her family. Although she had perfected the art of tragic story aftercare: telling a joke to clear the air, releasing people from their misguided fear that they alone had reminded her that her parents were dead. This evening had been so breezy and fun, she considered lying, saying "Yes, they live in Pennsylvania." But she didn't want to hide things from Gabe—well, other than the perfume and the egg freezing—she didn't want to hide anything *else*.

"Actually, both my parents have passed, I lost them when I was eleven. I was raised by my grandparents. Who are gone now too."

He swore again. "That fire you survived..."

Iris sat back. "You remembered."

"Not the kind of thing you forget." Gabe shook his head. "But damn. That's like superhero origin story territory."

She laughed, surprised and delighted to have someone else cut the tension.

"But that's horrible, I'm sorry, no kid should have to go through that. I didn't mean to joke."

"I don't mind, really! Most people act like I'm a fragile doll when I tell them."

"People are so stupid. As if the sheltered people are the toughest."

"Right? Usually I tell someone and they get all frozen and freaked out, and I end up comforting *them* about my dead parents."

"They do the same thing when I tell them I'm adopted."

Instantly the smile dropped from her face.

He glanced at her. "Yeah, just like that."

She covered her mouth. "I'm sorry!"

"And I know what you're thinking: 'But Gabe, I thought China only gave away baby girls to white Americans, which (a), what makes you assume I'm Chinese, you racist? and (b) you're right, I am Chinese, the twist is, I was just a lackluster baby.'"

Iris laughed, even as she recognized that this was Gabe's adoptee-tight-five.

"But I got adopted by great parents, Italian American, so my name and face are a bait-and-switch, but at least we share a noodle culture. My mom's still here, she lives in Brooklyn. We lost my dad when I was twenty, pancreatic cancer, but he packed in at least forty years' worth of love and smacking me in the head, so . . ." He shrugged, but the emotion showed on his face.

She expressed her sympathy too.

He thanked her, then asked, "So who are you going with?"

"To the funeral? No one. I mean, I'll have family there, obviously."

"Do you want company?"

She was taken aback. "It's not exactly gonna be a good time."

"Oh, it's not one of those party funerals?" Gabe smiled. "Look, we just started seeing each other, I know I'm not your first-string support player. But if you need a ride, someone to park the car, just someone to sit with . . . I'm up for it."

Iris searched his face for a sign of reticence, smarminess, or any indication it was meant only as a gesture. But his expression remained open, his gaze steady, utterly relaxed. She felt her shoulders ease in response.

"I do hate parallel parking."

"I'm your man."

CHAPTER

Twenty-two

G abe held Iris's hand in the car as they left the funeral service
and headed to Jacob's parents' house for the reception. Only
they weren't in his hot shop van like they'd initially planned,
but in the back seat of Wolff's Mercedes with Esdras driving. When
Iris had notified Marilyn that she would be unavailable Friday due to
a family funeral, the next communication she received was a text
from Esdras informing her that he would be at her service to take her
and any friends or family members wherever they needed to go. The
next morning, a three-foot-tall vase of calla lilies from Jonathan was
delivered to her apartment. But it was Gabe who had made the difference on the day, providing an oasis of calm and steady companion-
ship. He looked as clean-cut as he could, wearing a simple black suit
and his hair in a low, neat ponytail like an artist's brush. It was an
unusual support system Iris had cobbled together—a new barely-
boyfriend and a generous quasi-boss—but she would take what she
could get.

Iris hadn't been to her aunt Beth and uncle Clay's house in twenty
years, which sounded weird when she said it to Gabe. She knew her
maternal grandparents tried spending Thanksgiving together exactly once, when Iris was about thirteen, a bleary memory that Jacob
had turned up late and probably high, and Iris recalled that she had
thrown up after dinner, so they didn't stay overnight as planned. Iris
remembered lying down across the back seat of their station wagon,

sick to her stomach, while her grandmother reached back to hold her hand from the passenger seat. They never went back.

As they pulled up today, the house looked smaller and shabbier than she had remembered. It was a single-level ranch house in need of a fresh coat of paint, with a faded American flag fluttering over the porch. Iris noticed a For Sale sign on top of the mailbox.

"I'm afraid I'm not going to be very good at introducing you to people. I haven't been back in so long." She didn't want to say she didn't remember her own relatives' names, but it was the truth.

Gabe gave her hand a squeeze. "I'm here for *you*."

They entered the small house packed with mourners. Iris felt ashamed to recognize so few of the faces, especially as many were elated to see "Johnny's girl." Iris was a living memento of the family's golden boy, her late father, John Sunnegren, but she hadn't seen most of them since she was ten. Luckily Gabe was marvelous at introducing himself first, eliciting the other person's name, and thus allowing Iris to go in gracefully for a familiar, name-knowing hug: "Deirdre, good to see you."

Deirdre, an older woman with feathered short hair, identified herself as a distant cousin "on the Irish side" and cooed over Iris, "Oh, it's like looking right at Johnny's face again. Those cheekbones! You know I taught him how to drive stick. He was so bright, he didn't need me. I remember sitting in the passenger seat, looking at his profile thinking, this boy is going places." She flipped the page of a photo album set out for the occasion. "And I loved your mother, Amy. From the day I met her, I knew they'd get married. They were a perfect match, like cake toppers." She tapped a pink nail over a wedding photo of her parents that Iris hadn't seen before.

Iris's heart swelled when she looked at them. Her father was tall and broad-shouldered, she had him to thank for her height, though she would rather have had her mother's petite figure. He had classic dark Irish looks, nearly black hair, blue eyes, fair skin with few freckles, and looked dashing in a tux. Her mother was a Jersey girl, golden tan with sun-streaked chestnut hair and brown eyes. On her wedding day she looked fresh-faced with her hair pulled back in a barrette. Iris blinked back a tear; they looked so young, early twenties. She was glad they had found each other early—they didn't have much time.

Deirdre muttered, "Wish Beth had made a better match, but she never did listen to anybody."

"I saw the For Sale sign, are Beth and Clay moving?"

"Such a shame. My son helped them take out a second mortgage just last year. Clay thought that contracting work would pick back up, but . . ." Deirdre *tsk*ed. "Beth is hoping they can move closer to Maria-Elena and the baby. But they'd be lucky to break even on what they owe."

The baby? But Iris didn't want to reveal further how poorly she'd kept up with their family news. "I'm so sorry to hear that. I didn't know they were struggling."

"Forgive me for saying it, but how could they not?" Deirdre peered over her glasses. "Jacob's treatment—all those years of rehabs and sober living? *Whoo*—it all but bankrupted them. I told her, let him go to jail and dry out there. But you know Beth, such a softie, she couldn't let him hit rock bottom. She loved him too much."

"That's heartbreaking," Iris said, meaning it.

They circulated a bit more before Gabe sussed out the potluck dishes: pasta salad, chicken salad, tuna salad, and slices of watermelon being sampled by a housefly or two. Iris wasn't hungry. She was getting herself a cup of coffee from the samovar when a large man tapped her shoulder.

"I hear you're Iris." The man put out a hand. "Phil. I'm sorry for your loss."

"Phil, thanks, you too."

"I was Jacob's sponsor. I wish he had called me that night, I coulda been there for him."

She shook her head, wanting to absolve his guilt. "He struggled for so long."

"He told me about you. It gave him comfort to know you were doing so well."

Was she doing so well? Iris thought, before catching herself. Of course she was, compared to Jacob, who had never pulled himself out of the trauma of the fire, the addiction. Her life might not be where she wanted it, but she scolded herself for taking it for granted, especially here. "Jacob and I lost touch, which I regret. I was so young when the fire happened, and afterward I moved away to live with my grandparents. Not to make excuses." Iris took a tight breath. "I could never repay what he did for me. He gave me the chance to live my life. I hope he knew how grateful I was. I should have told him more often."

"Don't." Phil shook his head. "He was the one who should've reached out. But I never could get him to truly work the program, he had some demons he couldn't stare down. What I hope you know is that what happened wasn't your fault."

"Thank you." Iris noticed Beth looking at her from across the room and thought, *If only everyone agreed with you, Phil.* "I see my aunt Beth, I should give her my condolences. It was nice meeting you, thank you for all you did for Jacob."

He gave a nod and dumped four packets of sugar into his coffee.

Iris was making her way to Beth when she spotted Gabe on the floor by the entrance to the kitchen, kneeling before an elderly woman with a walker. She approached and realized he was replacing one of her walker's tennis ball feet.

"He's nice to have around," the elderly woman said to Iris in a quavery voice.

"Isn't he?" Iris smiled.

"I'm your great-aunt Cecilia. You used to visit my house when your parents lived in Narberth. Do you remember?"

"Oh, sure." Iris didn't, not in the slightest. "It's good to see you."

"You were very young, you probably don't. But you were the sweetest little girl. I would serve you rainbow sherbet, and you loved it so much, I made sure to always have some in the freezer, in case your daddy brought you by."

Iris's polite smile slackened with recognition. Her mind was flooded by the sense memory of swirling raspberry, orange, and green sherbet slipping off an ice-cold silver spoon. She had never had that dessert before or since, but she could almost taste it now. And the nostalgia for the period of her childhood that felt truly carefree put a lump in her throat. "Aunt Sissy?"

Aunt Sissy nodded and beamed up at her, as much as her stooped back would let her, and she opened her frail arms for an embrace. Iris had to stop herself from hugging the tiny woman too tight, but she was overcome with emotion, surprisingly, for the first time that day.

At last Iris spotted Beth again. "This is the hard one," she said to Gabe with a heavy exhale. "Jacob's mother."

"You got this."

They crossed the room to see her, and Iris exchanged hugs and condolences with her aunt and introduced Gabe, who offered his sympathy as well.

"He's up there with Johnny now." Beth pointed up and her blood-shot eyes looked heavenward. "I know your dad is giving him a hero's welcome for saving his little girl."

Iris had no memory of Beth in which she did not bring up her debt to Jacob. Iris knew she blamed her for her son's addiction, and now death. It barely got to Iris anymore, she just felt numb.

Gabe put a hand on Iris's back. "You know, in the Jewish faith they say, to save one life is to save the world entire."

"You're Jewish?" Beth regarded him quizzically.

"No, I just always thought it was a beautiful proverb."

"I haven't seen Uncle Clay yet," Iris said.

"Outside on the porch. It's too much for him." Beth choked up again. But she saw someone over Iris's shoulder who seemed to make her brighten. She beckoned them to come over. "Have you met Jacob's fiancée, Maria?"

Iris didn't know Jacob had been engaged. But a young Latina woman who was quite pregnant approached them. She was beautiful and petite, making her belly look even larger.

"Nice to meet you, Maria, I'm Iris, Jacob's cousin. I'm so sorry for your loss."

"It's Maria-Elena," the woman corrected as she shook Iris's hand. "Thank you, same to you."

"Engaged to be married, starting a family, his dreams were finally coming true . . ." Beth shook her head and began to cry.

Iris noted a remoteness from Maria-Elena and a lack of an engagement ring. The girl didn't move toward Beth during her outburst, it seemed they didn't know each other well.

Beth touched her swollen belly. "Thank God we have this little one on the way, a piece of my Jacob to live on."

Maria-Elena quietly excused herself.

"She's very shy," Beth said in a low voice. "I wasn't sure about her at first, her background, *cultural* differences, but she's sweet. We're gonna take care of her, like Jacob would have wanted. And I can't wait to love on that baby."

Iris caught up with Maria-Elena on the couch, away from Aunt Beth.

"When are you due?" Iris asked.

Maria-Elena smiled. "End of October. I'm hoping she comes Halloween, it's my favorite holiday."

"Aw, a girl, that's wonderful. Baby costumes are the cutest."

"I know, I want her to be a pumpkin." Maria-Elena rubbed her tummy. "You don't look like you live around here."

Iris told her she was in from New York.

Maria-Elena nodded and stared straight ahead, thinking for a moment. "We were never engaged, me and Jake—Jacob. Beth maybe thinks I'm embarrassed, but I feel worse lying."

"Oh, that's okay." Iris didn't know what to say.

"We weren't even together. We agreed I was gonna raise this baby without him. He didn't want to be a dad, didn't want no custody, nothing. I never even met his mom before he died, now she wants to be involved with everything, the doctor's visits, the delivery, she even offered to move in after she's born."

"Do you want that?"

Maria-Elena shrugged. "I mean, it's nice of her. But we don't have room. Help would be good, my mom works and I want to finish school, but . . ."

Finish school . . . Iris wondered how old she was.

"I'm not comfortable here. I don't know these people, this isn't my home," she said, before adding, "No offense."

"None taken." Iris felt the same way.

"Jake wanted me to have an abortion, but I wouldn't. We hadn't spoken in months," Maria-Elena confided.

Iris heard herself mindlessly quoting his sponsor: "He had some demons he couldn't stare down."

Maria-Elena nodded. "He wasn't all bad, though. He saved a girl's life once."

Iris fell silent.

"He wouldn't really talk about it, though. He said the real him could never live up to the story."

Gabe returned from the food table carrying two plates of mayonnaise-slathered beige salad. "I was told one of these is chicken salad and the other is tuna, but honestly, I can't tell which is which. I'll eat whatever you don't want."

"I think I'm ready to go."

Gabe's face softened. "I'll tell Esdras we're ready."

Before they left, there was one more person Iris needed to see, and she wanted to do it alone. She wasn't ready for Gabe to see the most hard-edged member of her remaining family. She stepped outside and found Clay sitting in a rocking chair on the porch, smoking a cigarette.

Clay was in his late sixties, and with his square jaw and light blue eyes, he might have been a handsome man if life had been kinder to him, or vice versa. But his skin was textured from acne scars and sun exposure, and his hair had gone thin and gray.

Iris never felt more softness for her uncle than right now. She greeted him gently and offered her sincere condolences.

Clay's eyes rolled up at her. "You brought your own chauffeur to a funeral?"

"It's a company car service. I don't own a car."

"City gal." The smoke plumed out his nose. "Glad to see you're doing so well for yourself."

"I'm trying."

"You know what I think's rich? When your parents died, your dad didn't leave a cent for his big sister."

"They didn't expect to die so young, I don't think either of them even had a will."

"Don't you think if your dad knew that Jacob saved his little girl's life, he would've wanted to leave him something?"

Iris felt her stomach flip. "I was eleven, I had nothing to do with their estate."

"You didn't have to, it all went to you anyway. Life insurance, home insurance—"

"Uncle Clay—"

"Uncle, now? *Now* we're family."

She tilted her head at him in dismay. "We're always family."

He looked her dead in the eyes. "Then help us."

She frowned at him, not understanding, or thinking she understood but hoping she was wrong.

"You owe us, you owe Jacob. That little baby will have less of a daddy than you got, and a lot less to show for it. You owe Jacob a great debt. You've hid from us for twenty years because of it."

"That isn't true—"

"You know, when your parents died, Beth and I, we wanted to take you in. Even with everything Jacob was going through with his injury, we were fully prepared to raise you and love you as our own."

Iris didn't know that.

"Your grandparents fought us, went to court. I didn't think a young girl should have to grow up in an old folks' home, but the judge sided with them. Money always wins."

Her heart twisted as she thought of her wonderful Nan and Pop. They were the perfect soft place to land after the tragedy. And it had nothing to do with money. "It all worked out for the best."

He snorted. "Did it? I just buried my son."

Iris began to apologize, "I didn't mean—"

Clay's blue eyes were cold. "Then why don't you get back to me, when you know what you mean."

Twenty-three

The Mercedes door shut with a cushioned *thud,* insulating Iris from the drone of summer insects and stifling heat.

"What was that about?" Gabe frowned beside her.

Iris exhaled inside the air-conditioned interior. A moment ago with her uncle, she had bitterly regretted accepting Jonathan's chauffeured car. But as she sank into the car's smooth leather seat, temperature-controlled to sixty-eight degrees and ready for a hasty getaway, she decided alienating her remaining family was worth it. "Can we make the A/C higher, Esdras?"

"Absolutely. You have your own controls in the rear console."

Iris thanked him and busied herself poking at the blue display, cranking the blow speed to the max until the fan sound replaced the silence of her not answering Gabe.

"Iris, are you okay?"

"Yes, sorry, I'm just hot." She buckled her seatbelt.

Esdras offered them bottles of water, still or sparkling, as if they were in a restaurant.

"I didn't want to interrupt you with your uncle, but it sounded like he asked you for money. That had to be awkward, I thought you hadn't seen them in years."

"I haven't." When Iris saw Gabe still puzzling at her, she reached to explain—without telling him the answer. "They saw the car, they think I live this big life in the big city, you know, Manhattan is like a movie set to them."

"You haven't exactly had an easy go either. Of all the people to ask for help. Was he drunk?"

"Do you want to stop for food on the way home?" Iris didn't want to discuss any of this in the car with Esdras, or with Gabe, or ever, really. She held the water bottle against her forehead. She just wanted to feel cold. Colder than cold—*numb*.

Little more than a half hour into the drive, Iris fell asleep, from the letdown of a stressful day or the carb crash of fast food. When she awoke, they were already in Brooklyn.

Iris wiped the corners of her mouth and apologized for falling asleep.

Gabe's brow furrowed with sympathy. "Even in your sleep, you looked worried."

"I guess I was a little stressed by . . . everything."

"We're almost to the city. You'll sleep better in your own bed."

Iris shook her head. "Nah, I got enough rest. I think I'll clean out my fridge, maybe organize my closet. I always clean when I'm anxious."

Gabe looked at her, his dark eyes searching her face with concern, then brightened. "If you're not tired, I know just the place to blow off steam."

Gabe directed Esdras through Brooklyn to a rather desolate intersection with a Sunoco station and a La Quinta Inn, far from any bars, restaurants, or charm. Gabe said to drop them off just beyond the gas station, beside a gated alleyway tucked between two faceless brick buildings.

"Where are we?" Iris peered out the window from her slumped position.

Gabe smiled. "Come on."

They thanked Esdras for the ride, and Iris followed Gabe outside, where it was still hot but the skies had grayed with heavy cloud cover. A red neon sign atop the alley's tall metal gate read GATHER ROUND.

Gabe had a key to the gate, which screeched as he opened it. They entered a junky alleyway lined with jalapeño pepper plants in plastic buckets and a few stray lawn chairs. At the end of the alley was an enormous closed garage. Its crusty metal door had an awning of corrugated polycarbonate from which hung a piece of unexpected whimsy—bright neon glass tubing in the bubbly shape of a rain cloud with a rainbow behind it. And underneath that stood Gabe, grinning, like a man-sized metaphor.

Gabe had to shout over the metallic clatter of the garage door retracting. "Welcome to the hot shop!" He draped his arm around her neck. "Step into my office, baby."

The space looked industrial and forbidding. Brick ovens lined the entire back wall, each with fire glowing inside like orange eyes and mouths. Everything appeared hard, hot, dirty, or raw: the unfinished concrete floor; cinderblock walls painted white, emphasizing the black soot that had settled into every crevice and grout line; rolling dividers of dented steel like shields; racks of blackened metal pipes and what looked like hellish gardening tools. The largest, central furnace was a built-out brick structure with a heavy metal facade and a small door around which infernal light escaped like a solar eclipse. It was not clear to Iris how Gabe found this place soothing.

"What do you think?" he asked.

"Uh, I feel like the Brave Little Toaster in here."

Gabe laughed. "God, that movie traumatized me. Not a good movie for abandonment issues." He gave her a quick tour, explaining the three types of furnaces in the room: the biggest and hottest one that contained the cauldron of molten glass; the glory hole, an oven used to reheat a working piece of glass to keep it pliable; and the annealers, kilns that allow a finished piece to cool slowly to prevent breakage. "I'll show you what I'm working on."

Gabe led her to a large annealer that reminded Iris of her grandfather's hunting freezer. But when Gabe unlatched its heavy door, she could feel the waves of heat emanating from the ceramic interior, even from three feet away.

"This is how I pay my bills. It's called 'production.' Useful glass stuff people actually buy."

Iris peered inside, where rows of identical cups stood like little soldiers. She marveled at the neatness and uniformity of them; they looked made from a mold, not a mouth.

Gabe closed the annealer. "But I'll show you what I'm really excited about. It's in the gallery." He walked her across the hot shop, through a door to a cluttered storage room with many shelves of glass creations. But against one wall stood two chopped telephone poles with black wires pulled taut between them, and, to her amazement, the wires displayed glass sculptures dangling precariously off the ground. The pieces were three pairs of shoes tossed over the power line—sneakers, work boots, and laced platform heels—made entirely of glass. Iris got closer and saw the detail on the sneakers, the Nike swoosh embossed on the side, the worn sole just beginning to separate from the body, the Timberland boots with the creased toe box, the tongue curling away from the upper, all rendered in clear glass, yet instantly recognizable. The only part of the shoes that wasn't glass were the laces they hung from.

"This is incredible!"

"Thanks," Gabe said, suddenly shy.

"It makes me nervous, them hanging like that. Are they secured somehow?"

He shook his head. "The peril is the point. Anyway, they stay pretty balanced. You can move 'em. See?" He tugged one glass Air Jordan and it raised the other like a seesaw, causing the wire to bounce and all the pieces to sway threateningly.

Iris yelped. "Sorry," she said, hands over her mouth.

"Art should make you feel something, right?"

"Are you going to sell it, or display it somewhere?"

"My friend is a dancer, her troupe is performing for a charity fundraiser, she was looking for some local artists to participate."

"That's cool, but maybe after, you can shop it around. Gabe, this belongs in an art gallery. This has value."

He shrugged. "The production is what I do for money. The art is for me."

"Have you ever thought of selling to interior design?"

"That's very hard to break into. A small group of artists with well-established relationships to manufacturers and designers."

"Yeah, if only you knew someone in lighting design."

He chuckled.

"You know, Mr. Wolff, who lent us the car today, I'm designing the lighting for his new luxury tower in Hudson Yards. The lobby is my blank canvas, they tasked me with finding a dramatic central installation. I was going to ask you for recommendations, but maybe I should be asking you for a piece."

He scrunched his nose. "Nah, that's your gig. You don't have to get me a job."

"It wouldn't be that easy—Wolff isn't easy to please, that message has come through loud and clear. It was just a thought." Iris didn't want to push it or make him feel criticized. A man's pride could be fragile as glass.

They reentered the hot shop. Iris pointed to a couch against the wall, facing the furnaces, her puzzled look asking the question for her.

"The spectators' couch. For visitors when we have a demonstration or class," Gabe supplied. "Also for hangovers and postbreakage depression naps." He untucked and unbuttoned his dress shirt, then unbuckled his belt.

"A strip show? I'll take a seat."

He grinned, having stripped down to his undershirt and black slacks. "Metal belt buckles get hot. And you're no spectator today. I'm gonna teach you to blow glass!"

He took her to the central furnace and slid open the oven door with a rustic wooden handle to reveal the eye of Sauron. He had to speak up over the fire's breathy roar. "This furnace holds our molten glass, made of silica, lime, and soda, and it burns hotter than any other, about twenty-three hundred degrees. It takes a week for the temperature to get that high, and then we have to leave it running to keep it there. Take a look, but go slow. When you first get close to it, it can trigger your flight response."

Iris hesitated. Even the sound of the fire echoed in her memory, but she wanted to fight it. She stepped closer.

The wall of hot air hit her like a truck. It made her heart race. The furnace's metal lip was coated in drips of glowing orange glass, like electric drool. She could see no flames inside, only a white-hot, blinding light, so bright it hurt to look at. But when she closed her eyes, she was back in her childhood bedroom, the door a glowing rectangle limned in fiery orange, and Jacob—

Gabe's hands landed on her shoulders. "I'm here. Just breathe."

With Gabe's touch grounding her, she steadied herself and deepened it. He asked again if she was all right, and she said yes. Surprisingly, it was the truth.

"So, this is where we get our 'gather,' the blob of glass to work with. Grab that blowpipe—don't worry, it's cold—and bring it here."

The pipe was surprisingly heavy. Iris gripped it like a protective spear.

"We'll do it together." He clasped his hand on the blowpipe, rendering it light as a broomstick. "It burns too bright to see the walls or depth in there, you can't even see the liquid glass until your pipe disappears into it." Gabe stood in front, closest to the oven mouth, apparently inured to the intense radiant heat, and they dipped the blowpipe in together. He twirled the pipe in her hands, and they pulled it out; a perfect gather of red-hot glass clung to the end like an incandescent light bulb.

They backed up while Gabe kept the pipe spinning in their hands, and he directed her to place it atop a water trough.

Iris was relieved to set it down. "Whoa, that little glob of glass is heavy!"

Gabe quickly poured a pail of water over the pipe, releasing great plumes of steam with a sizzling hiss. "Keep spinning!"

The gather had instantly begun to droop. Gabe came to the rescue from behind, sliding his arms around her and his hands over hers to resume twisting the pipe until the bulbous weight of the glass recentered.

"Don't your hands get tired?" she asked.

"The nerves in my fingertips go dead numb. That's why I have to grab you so tight." He clapped a hand on her butt, making her laugh. "Okay, let's take it to the gaffer's bench."

He led her over to a rudimentary wooden seat where she could rest the blowpipe on the bench's metal arms and simply roll it back and forth with her palm to keep it spinning and level. He sat beside her, and the pipe closed them in like the safety bar on a carnival ride.

The blackened tools laid out beside them looked brutal and medieval: a giant pair of tweezers, long and sharp; different types of shears, one with straight blades, the other's bent and crisscrossed over each other like broken legs; a flat wooden paddle, torched coal black. The only nonthreatening tools were a block of hard beeswax and a folded newspaper both burnt and wet, which imparted a honey-smoked sweetness to the air.

"These are not what I expected for such a fragile material as glass," Iris said.

"Cold glass is fragile. Hot glass is tough. And we use rough tools gently." He picked up the giant tweezers, holding them in his fist pointing down like daggers. "Like, these are called jacks. My old teacher used to say, 'Squeeze your jacks like you're squeezing the foot of a sleeping baby.'"

Iris smiled at the thought.

Gabe instructed her how to use each of the tools, letting her play, poking and prodding the gather to make different shapes while he used the wooden paddle to shield her from the glass's radiant heat. Every time the orange glow dimmed and the glass grew transparent, it was time to reheat it in the glory hole, a smaller furnace. Iris liked that he directed her without taking anything out of her hands, even if on occasion she wanted him to. Letting her struggle with it, directing without taking over, let her overcome her initial aversion and anxiety. In contrast, she remembered when Ben taught her to drive stick. Even just practicing in a parking lot, he grabbed the gear shift every other second, making Iris feel like an incompetent child.

She begged Gabe to give her a proper demo, and at last he obliged. Iris was in awe as he effortlessly and intuitively kept the heavy pipe level and perpetually rotating, navigating the cluttered space around him with ease and grace, and always protected the glass. When he placed his lips on the blowpipe, Iris expected him to give a mighty blow, but instead he gave a gentle one, injecting a bubble of air into the glass that swelled like a balloon. In a move that took her breath away, he stood and spun the pipe around his hand like a bō staff, the centrifugal force drawing out the vessel's shape. In no time, he had grown the piece, attached it upside down to a "punty," a new pipe, narrowed the neck, and smoothed the edges until a voluptuous vase had taken form.

"This is the moment of truth, I need you." He brought it to where she sat on the gaffer's bench and instructed her to roll the punty while he put on two giant dirty oven mitts and crouched beside the spinning vase. The vase was large and radiated more heat than the initial gather had. "Now rap the punty against this metal bar, *hard.*"

"*Eeek!* I can't, I'm scared I'll break it!"

"It always breaks, it's just gotta break right. Trust me. Now!"

She banged the punty and the vase snapped off cleanly at the base, landing safely in Gabe's waiting mitts.

They cheered, exhilarated, and Gabe hustled it into the annealer. When he returned, Iris jumped to hug him and he spun her around. She landed on the ground and raised her arm to high-five him, but Gabe caught her hand.

"Whoa," he said, turning her arm over. The skin on the underside of her forearm was bright pink. "You hung in there like a pro! But I didn't mean for you to take this much heat. I'm sorry. Does it hurt?"

"Not really. It's fine, it was fun!" She hadn't noticed it until he said something. "I have a high pain threshold, I guess."

Gabe held her hand and bowed to softly kiss it. Then he turned it over to kiss the center of her palm, her inner wrist—where she dabbed her perfume, she noted—and he proceeded to kiss a trail up her slightly swollen, flushed skin. By the time his lips reached her inner elbow, all pain had turned to pleasure. As he nuzzled between her bicep and her breast, all heat had turned to shiver.

He surprised her when he flicked his tongue in the crevice of her underarm. Her body caved away from him with a giggle, embarrassed to have liked it.

"Where are you going?" He pulled her back toward him.

"Gross." She smiled.

"Nothing about you is gross." He looked at her, eyelids heavy.

"I meant *you.*"

"Oh, I can be disgusting." In one motion, Gabe picked her up and tossed her over his shoulder as if she weighed nothing. He craned his neck to take a bite of her butt cheek as she laughed, doubled over him.

He set her down before the spectators' couch and lifted her dress off over her head. As he undid her bra, Iris reached her arms around his neck and kissed him, pressing her chest into his, experiencing the softness of her body as it yielded to the firmness of his. He broke from their embrace only to pull his T-shirt over the back of his head with one motion, before he caught her waist again and pulled her close enough to feel his yearning.

But it wasn't his own satisfaction he saw to. Gabe sat and brought her onto his lap, not facing him, but with her back to his chest. He gently pushed her hair off her nape and kissed the back of her neck, her earlobes, her shoulders. From this angle, she could barely kiss him back. She could only tilt her head back and expose her most vulnerable parts to him, and to pleasure.

The furnaces now seemed no more threatening than a cozy, crackling fireplace, and she closed her eyes, enjoying having him explore her body. Gabe slipped his hand down the front of her underwear and cupped her as gently and assuredly as he had the spinning glass bulb, spreading and closing his fingers over her without ever pushing inside. It only made her want him more.

He made her feel beautiful, irresistible, sexy.

He made her feel safe, present, and alive.

He made her feel.

And she wanted to feel everything.

Iris turned on his lap to face him, straddling him as the heat from the furnace warmed her bare back. She ran her hands down his muscled torso to where his skin rippled lightly over his stomach, the soft hair trailing his lower abs to where his dress slacks strained. He kissed her breasts with greater ardor, his bites leaving her flesh pink, but Gabe knew how to use sharp tools gently.

Soon they could wait no longer. Gabe swept her onto her back, slipping her panties down her legs and quickly hopping to remove his own while Iris lay back and watched. He crawled over her, his naked, tattooed body hovering tantalizing over her, so that with one intake of breath, Iris could touch her nipples to his skin and send shivers down his body, and with one thrust of his hips, he could set hers on fire.

But they were done teasing each other. They closed all space between them, melting into one another until every edge was smoothed, their two bodies a mirrored reflection of shared passion and desire. When they came together, the heat they generated was so bright that it obliterated any walls between them, and there was nowhere they didn't meet.

CHAPTER

Twenty-four

The patter of the rain was loud on the hot shop's steel roof over the couch where Iris and Gabe lay naked and entangled. With her cheek resting on his sweat-slicked chest, she inhaled, filling her nostrils with the accord of their warm bodies, the sweet smoke of torched newspaper, and the smell of the rain, cooling and soft as a cucumber cocktail. And indeed, Iris felt drunk, in the best way possible. She felt utterly relaxed, her body's strength satisfyingly spent and all her nervous energy burned off. Only her thighs still vibrated, and her right big toe cramped.

With her eyes on the flames that licked the blow pipes, Iris began to tell the story she couldn't in the car. "They blame me for what happened to Jacob."

"Who does?"

"My aunt and uncle."

"He died of a drug overdose. How could that possibly be your fault?"

"His addiction wouldn't have happened if not for me. If not for what Jacob did for me. That's why Clay asked me for money. Because I owe Jacob a debt. He might even be right."

Gabe continued to rake his fingers through her hair, patient, letting her tell the story at her own pace. A story that had taken more than a year for her to tell Ben.

Iris took a deep breath. "I told you I lived through a childhood house fire that killed my parents, but I didn't tell you *how* I survived. My cousin Jacob saved my life. He was sleeping on the pullout couch by the front door, he could've run right out and saved himself, but he didn't. He ran to my room to get me. And he fell carrying me down the stairs in the pitch-black smoke and fractured two vertebrae. And he still got us out, adrenaline I guess. And when he got treatment for his back, they gave him oxycontin. And from then on . . ." She trailed off. "So I owe Jacob my life. And saving mine cost him his."

Gabe audibly exhaled, and Iris braced for his reaction.

"You don't believe that, do you?"

"What do you mean?"

"Like, it's crazy to think you, an eleven-year-old child, were responsible for the entire trajectory of a man's life."

"But if he—"

"No, I get the concept, you're drawing some butterfly-effect kind of causal chain, but it's just a story. The fire caused his injury. The medication caused his addiction. For various reasons, he wasn't able to successfully recover. And the drugs caused his death. That's what happened."

Iris had never been challenged on it before. She felt defensive, or . . . seen. Maybe both at once.

"You were a child in danger on the worst night of your life. You didn't ask to need saving any more than you asked to have both your parents killed in a horrible fire. It's amazing Jacob was able to save you, yes, it was heroic, but no one should have refused that opportunity."

Hearing him say the words, even if she wasn't sure she entirely believed them, made her eyes film over, not with sorrow but relief.

"What happened to your cousin is sad and unfair. But you shouldn't feel any guilt for accepting that help or causing his problems. It's not your fault. At all."

"Maybe I feel guilty because I cut ties with him. After the fire, I moved in with my mom's parents, and we really didn't see Jacob or his family anymore."

"So you're guilty of not being grateful enough?"

Her breath caught. She had never been able to articulate it so succinctly before in her life. "Well, yes. *Shouldn't* I feel more grateful to him? What's wrong with me? I couldn't even make my fingers text him when his mom asked. That's what they really wanted from me today, they wanted my emotion, my grief, my gratitude. And I had none to give them. Sometimes, frankly, I resent them. And then I catch myself, and I'm shocked at my coldness. Like, I should be in pieces right now, and I feel numb. It makes me ashamed of myself."

Gabe squeezed his arms tighter around her. "How could you be grateful for the most traumatic event of your life?" His embrace eased. "Because I know that feeling. And it can be just as toxic."

They sat up, Iris draped her legs over Gabe's lap as he put his arm around her, and she let him open up.

"I mean, look, I have to say it to myself. I'm adopted. I was asking for someone to save my life before I could talk. And I know I'm lucky. All my life, people have told me how lucky I am. Told my parents how good they are. And I'm not arguing that they aren't! But every other kid got born entitled to their parents' love, but for me, it's like a debt to repay, and a charity I have to make good on. But what made me deserve being abandoned or being wanted any less than any other kid on the planet? My parents, God bless 'em, they never made me feel that way, but the message gets in there." He pointed to his head. "The people I was born to, the ones who were supposed to love and protect me, didn't. Or couldn't. Or nobly sacrificed me to a better future. Or had me ripped from their arms by a corrupt adoption agency. Or tossed me out like trash. I'll never know. And it doesn't really matter, the result is the same. I needed someone to step up. And someone did."

Iris put a hand on his shoulder. "I'm sure you were a wondrous child to love. A gift to your parents. The most wanted."

"What about all the moments I wasn't?" He smiled tightly, his eyes glistening. "Or all the ways I haven't made good on the gift of their love? Does that make me less worthy of it?" He shrugged, but his trembling lower lip seemed to betray his answer.

Iris shook her head *no* and kissed him.

He blinked away the tears, and his words came out steadier. "Every child needs love and protection. Even as adults, it's okay to need someone to come through for you. That's a bond, not a debt."

They both were silent for a few minutes as the truth of it sank in.

"Have you been to therapy?"

Gabe chuckled. "I've just burned and broken a lot of shit."

Twenty-five

I ris checked the time again. She awaited the courier from King's Pharmacy with her first batch of fertility medicine to inject. She wiped down her dining table for the second time so the area was as clean as possible. Based on how often a dog hair found its way into her cooking, she wasn't confident that these were entirely sterile conditions. Hugo sensed her uneasiness and whined for attention.

The buzzer rang, making her jump in her seat. Hugo barked. She fumbled to mute the television and rushed to answer at the intercom.

She was expecting a doggy bag of medication, what she received at the door was an entire box of supplies. She placed the cardboard package on the table and carefully cut it open. The first, jarring item was the special red "biohazard" trash receptacle. She had never seen one outside a hospital, and it was unsettling to see one contaminating her dining table. Her first thought was *Is this medication dangerous to me?* Then she realized the container was to protect other people from *her* refuse. The biohazard was Iris.

Iris laid out the rest of the package's contents. There were alcohol prep pads, gauze pads, multiple syringes, multiple needle heads that required sorting—the "mixing needle" and "injection needle" had different lengths and gauges—and one "Redi-ject" syringe like an EpiPen that needed to be refrigerated. And a small army of glass vials of clear fluid medication.

Iris took a deep breath. She didn't know what she'd expected, but she thought it would be more prefabricated than this. This was a full-on science experiment. And all she could recall from her last meeting with Nurse Dani was her perky encouragement at the end: "It's totally easy!"

It did not look totally easy.

She pulled up Dani's emailed instructions and read every line aloud to herself as she went through it:

"Take four Menopur vials once daily." Was it really four? Four seemed like a lot of medication. Or hormones. Or whatever she was about to inject into her body. It suddenly seemed bad that she didn't know which.

"To dilute the Menopur with the saline solution..." She had to *dilute* them, as in, the vials weren't already at the correct concentrations? Iris groaned. But she remembered back in high school AP bio, she had been good at titration. That was only, what? *Twenty years ago.*

While titrating the medication and saline solution, she chased the last drop of medication around the bottom of the vial, her needle like an anteater's silvery tongue. She questioned if a single missed drop would make a difference. Then she thought about just how expensive each vial of medication was and estimated the price per drop. She kept at it until she got it.

Three more vials to go.

Hugo started chomping on his plush toy, making it squeak repeatedly.

"Hugo, please! I'm trying to focus."

He got in one last squeak for good measure, then settled down to tear the squeaker out.

At last she had the medication mixed and sucked into syringes and the needle heads changed. She pinched a few inches of belly below her navel, the way the nurse had shown her, and wiped the intended spot with an alcohol pad. It smelled like hospital. She then delicately picked up the first syringe and held it over the area. Iris didn't think of herself as squeamish about needles, but she had never injected herself with anything, and her mind revolted at the thought of piercing her own skin.

Just count and do it. One, two, three—

The needle sank into her flesh with eerie ease, as though her skin provided no barrier at all. Had she known that the boundary between her insides and the world was so thin, she would've been more careful.

She depressed the syringe to release the medication, waited a second, and withdrew the needle. A moment later, the burning started. Like a bee sting, a warming, itchy pain spread underneath the skin. She fought the urge to claw at the spot.

And that was only the first injection.

New doubts and questions infiltrated her thoughts. Would this even work? Was it safe and healthy to do? Would she ever find someone who wanted to have a baby with her, much less a baby this way? Would being pregnant make her love her body? Would her body be a safe place for a child to grow? Would a baby make her feel better?

Nearly all her postpubescent life, she had taken medication to keep herself from getting pregnant, or technically, to trick her body into thinking she was already pregnant. Now she was overdosing her body with hormones to release lots of eggs for fertilization in order to freeze them unfertilized. She wore the perfume to trick people into finding her attractive. She injected hormones to trick her body into being more fertile. Could there really be no consequences to tricking nature?

Iris wondered, how much can we fool our bodies before they make fools of us?

Twenty-six

I ris scrutinized her reflection in the elevator doors of Hannah and Mike's apartment building. It was the night of Mike's birthday party, where she was going to see her ex, Ben, and worse, was going to meet his new girlfriend, #PelotonMad. But Iris reminded herself that she had a hot new man in her life, low humidity had blessed her with a good hair day, and her liquid eyeliner had come out symmetrical. And of course, she had splashed the perfume on every pulse point.

She would not be the loser of this breakup.

The elevator dinged as the doors opened to the sixth floor, Iris gripping the gift bottle of whiskey with clammy palms.

"Hiii!" Hannah threw her arms open to Iris at the front door, and they embraced around her baby bump. "Okay, you look *hot*. Spin!"

Bless Hannah for pretending she hadn't been part of the decision committee on Iris's outfit: a short navy fit-and-flare dress that fanned out when Iris twirled, showing off her long legs made longer in brand-new wedge espadrilles. The dress had a high bateau neckline, but Iris dropped her denim jacket to flash the bare back, held together by a ribbon tie.

Hannah squealed. "You are giving French girl fantasy, legs for days, I love it. And I'm not letting you put that jacket back on until you go home. Give it."

"Thanks, you look stunning, like a goddess."

Hannah wore a halter neck maxidress revealing new, ample cleavage and draping gracefully over her bump. "I look pregnant. But the boobs are nice. Ben isn't here yet."

"No?" Iris widened her eyes. "Where does the tracking device say he is now?"

Hannah laughed. "You know I would if you asked."

She led Iris into the kitchen where Mike was chatting with a few guests and muddling mint.

"Happy birthday!" Iris presented him with the bottle with a big bow on it. "And I want to thank you for helping my neighbor Mireille Rapacine, I know how busy you are—"

"Iris, you're family. It's my pleasure." Mike handed her a copper mug. "Mint julep?"

Hannah reappeared. "Babe, we have to show her the nursery!"

They led her deeper into the apartment to the room that just last weekend had been a minor disaster. "Omigosh, it's all done!"

The room had completely come together, it was now neat, organized, and absolutely charming. The sage-green walls were decorated with framed illustrations from *Winnie-the-Pooh,* a photo from their pregnancy announcement, and an empty picture frame just waiting for a first photo. A fluffy cream-colored rug softened the gleaming hardwood floor, and the armchair was newly complemented by a round woven ottoman. The bookshelves Iris had built were filled with the children's books from the shower, a few plush animals, and wicker storage baskets with gingham bows. Her heart swelled with happiness for them.

"And look at the crib!" Iris turned to Mike approvingly. The white wooden slats and snug mattress looked neat as a pin, with a sweet mobile hanging above it of floating sheep, a moon, and stars.

"He did a great job in the end," Hannah said.

"I had my potential divorce as a hard deadline."

Hannah put her arms around Mike, lovingly. "It makes it so real."

Iris nodded. "You're going to be amazing parents." Seeing their future in such vivid color reaffirmed how badly Iris wanted this for herself.

. . .

Iris may have had some pre-party jitters, but soon she found herself having an amazing time. The perfume was the greatest social lubricant, as relaxing as alcohol without the drunkenness. She found herself holding court with a group of men and women, mostly men, telling stories, making everyone laugh. Although she didn't need to drink to feel comfortable, she did, as one of Mike's guy friends was always ready to refresh her glass.

And yet Iris knew the moment Ben entered the apartment. Maybe her nose caught his scent in the limbic part of her brain or her ears recognized the exact frequency of his voice, but her eyes knew to look the moment he stepped through the door.

And he looked good.

He had gotten a haircut since she last saw him, cropped close, so he looked less boyish than his normal floppy brown curls, giving him an uncharacteristic edge. He wore stone-colored khakis and a chambray shirt with the sleeves cuffed over his tanned forearms— one of which was draped over Madison.

Iris had found Madison painfully pretty when she'd been caught in the rain, but here, in her blown-out, lip-glossed glory, she was another level of intimidating. Her long blond hair was curled in *Bachelor*-contestant waves, her makeup looked like a TikTok filter. She wore a cropped tube top exposing a taut tummy and denim cut-offs.

Hannah appeared at Iris's side and said, sotto voce, "Who wears a crop top to a pregnant woman's home? She sucks, I hate her, the end." Then she looked earnestly at Iris. "You ready to say hi?"

Iris took a deep breath and nodded.

Ben peeled off when he saw them approach. "Hey, 'Ris. Bring it in." He greeted her with a light hug.

"Good to see you. I hope you'll introduce me to your date." Iris gestured to across the room where Madison was standing, although she wasn't visible behind the small ring of mostly male fans that had formed around her.

"Of course. I'm sorry, I should've given you a heads-up."

"Not at all. We're all friends here."

Ben beckoned her and Madison strode over, beaming. Ben introduced them.

"I love your dress!" Madison said.

"Thanks. I love your outfit. Very Carrie, season three."

Madison looked puzzled.

"From *Sex and the City*?"

"Oh, I never saw it! My mom wouldn't let me."

'Fuck, I'm old!' Season 4, episode 1. "Well, it's a compliment. Season three Carrie is the best."

Hannah and Mike joined them. Madison began asking Hannah the usual questions about her pregnancy when Iris felt her phone vibrate inside her dress pocket. She slipped it out and took a peek.

It was from Gabe, a picture of himself lying back in his bed, his gorgeous bare torso, a sinewy, tattooed arm holding a pillow over his face, with the message:

My sheets smell like you.

A flush bloomed across her cheeks. Iris typed back:

Careful, you'll smother yourself.

Gabe replied:

Trying to. Least until you come
back and finish the job.

"Somebody just read something good," Mike said, smirking at Iris. "That your new boo?"

"Just because it's your birthday doesn't make it your business." She glanced at Ben and found him already looking at her.

Madison asked, "Ooh, Hannah, how did you and Mike meet? I love hearing how couples met."

Hannah smiled. "Actually, Ben and Iris introduced us. I've been best friends with Iris since middle school, and Ben knew Mike from college."

Madison looked discomfited.

"Ben asked me, nay begged me, to do him a favor and entertain this random chick his girlfriend was bringing on a ski trip," Mike teased. Then his gaze melted. "I had no idea she would be the love of my life."

They looked in each other's eyes for a moment, and Hannah had only to tilt her chin up for him to meet her with a kiss.

Iris smiled, glad something beautiful had been born out of her and Ben's relationship after all.

"How about you two, how did you meet?" Mike asked.

Madison bounced on her toes. "Oh, it's adorable. I was filming content in Central Park, and it was really windy, and the reflector shield thingy blew right out of the photographer assistant's hands like a giant Frisbee."

Ben interjected, "And I wasn't looking—"

"He wasn't looking!" Madison echoed.

"—and it hit me in the head."

"Ben did always suck at Ultimate Frisbee," Mike joked.

Madison jumped back in. "So I ran over like, 'Omigod, I'm so sorry!' But I was in a bikini for the shoot on, like, a freezing day in April, which made *no* sense. And . . ." She looked promptingly to Ben, but he only smiled back. "Babe, say what you said, it's so funny."

He hesitated before adding, "I said I thought I'd died and gone to heaven."

"Isn't that the cutest?" Madison pouted. "And he asked for my number, and here we are!"

Hannah shot Iris a look.

"My boy's got *game*. Speaking of . . ." Mike turned to the rest of the guests and clapped his hands. "All right, everybody, are you rea-*dy*?"

"I was born ready," Iris answered, knowing exactly where he was headed.

"I know, kid, you're my star pitcher." Mike gripped her shoulders and jiggled her.

"Ready for what?" Madison asked, confused.

Ben explained, "Every year for his birthday, Mike insists we play charades."

"Competitive charades," Mike corrected him. "This is not your polite society, participation trophy charades. This is Olympic level, God tier shit."

Hannah rolled her eyes. "It's a really reasonable tradition, he's very normal about it."

"Let the charades begin!" Mike did a rundown of the rules for the classic game, plus Mike's additional "competitive" rules, like that every turn must be timed. "Couples can't be on the same team. So, Hannah, I love ya, but you're on the other side. I call Iris, Iris is on my team, birthday rules."

"She's good," Hannah explained to the room.

"And oh shit, this is the first year I can also have my guy Ben on my team, too. *Awkward!*" Mike sang the last word in falsetto, clearly feeling his juleps. "But bully for me! Ben, get over here."

The teams broke down so that Hannah and Madison were on one team, and Ben, Iris, and Mike were on the other, among a mix of his other friends.

Mike went first and got Iris to *The Sopranos* in under thirty seconds by pretending to get kicked in the balls and then pantomiming singing, assisted by a near-perfect impression of James Gandolfini's heavy sniffs.

"Yes, Iris! This is the hustle I'm looking for!" Mike said through gritted teeth, high off the score.

Hannah had an inspired turn getting her team to quickly guess the song "Shallow" by skipping the word entirely and doing the Lady Gaga nose gesture from the movie. Even on the opposite team, Mike was so proud he squeezed Hannah's face for a smooch.

One of Mike's guy friends put his foot in it trying to convey *Rosemary's Baby* by pointing repeatedly at Hannah's belly and making devil horns, especially uncomfortable because people kept guessing farm animals.

Then it was Madison's turn. She reached into the bowl and pulled out a piece of folded paper. She frowned at it. "I don't know this one."

"Can you just act out the words?" someone asked.

"I don't even know what category it is. I've literally never heard of it. Can I pass?"

"Yeah, she can pass," Ben chimed in.

Madison put it back in the box.

"Well, don't put it back," Mike interjected. "Because now you've seen it, so no one else on your team can use it. So kill it and pull another one. And guys, I thought we knew better than to do esoteric ones."

"What was it?"

Madison read out with deep skepticism, "As I Lay Dying"?

"It's a book," Ben said gently. "I haven't read it."

"Oh." Madison tucked her flaxen hair behind her ear. "Where's my drink?"

Mike's lawyer friend Priyanka raised her hand. "Sorry, my bad. I thought it would be an easy title to act out."

"Don't worry, Mad, just take another," Ben said.

Madison pulled another prompt and brightened immediately. "Ooh, *yes,* okay, I totally got this one."

Mike put up his hands. "Say no more! Don't give it away. Chris, ready with the timer?"

Madison gave the movie gesture, which they all shouted out. Then without warning, she dropped to the floor in a full split. Tanned, toned legs stretched out as flat as a Barbie doll's, her denim cutoffs biting into her ass cheeks, their cotton fringe like strings on a cut of meat. She put her hands on her hips and flashed a megawatt smile.

"Holy shit," whispered the guy next to Iris.

"Oh, oh, that Shyamalan movie . . . *Split!*" Hannah guessed.

Madison shook her head, still grinning, and threw her arms in the air, waving her hands and shimmying her shoulders.

"Damn, I thought I had it." Hannah pouted. "What else with a split personality? . . . *Me, Myself, and Irene?*"

Madison beckoned with an aggressive gesture toward her chest, bouncing her breasts.

"C'mon guys, what else?" Hannah said.

"Sorry, lost my train of thought," a guy joked.

"I'm definitely thinking things, but I can't say them out loud!" said another.

"Can you do *anything* different?" asked another woman.

"What was that one with Demi Moore called?"

"*Hustlers!*"

"How many words?"

Madison held up three fingers.

"*Drop Dead Gorgeous,*" Mike guessed.

"You're not even on her team," chided Hannah.

Madison laughed and shook her head again.

Iris looked at Madison with envy: her perfect ass, without a dimple of cellulite, not even a goose pimple, just smooth, tan skin. Her stomach that didn't pouch or roll. Every sign of youth and sex on display without self-consciousness, Madison owned it. Iris felt so dissociated from her body, like it was a shell she was stuck inside, an intractable adversary that she must battle into submission, to shrink, to tighten, and to resist the powers of hunger, gravity, and time.

That is, until she got the perfume.

But then Iris looked at the other party guests watching Madison. The men leaning forward with too keen an interest, their hungry gazes glued to her from the neck down, teeth bared in grins. From the women's body language, Madison was making few friends among them. Iris scanned the women on the opposite couch, sitting way back, arms crossed over stomachs, raised eyebrows, the exchange of glances. Yes, it was jealousy, but more, it was judgment. Their eyes said that this girl was taking too much pleasure in excelling at the game that held us all back. They saw a try-hard. A pick-me. A slu—

The buzzer went off; time was up.

Madison threw up her hands. "*You guys,* it was *Bring It On.*"

There was a collective groan.

"Why didn't you . . ." one of the wives began. "Never mind. That was impressive."

"Thanks, I cheered at FSU."

"She went to college, that's something," Hannah whispered.

Iris elbowed her. She was actually feeling sorry for Madison. Until she caught Ben wink at her and Madison scrunch her button nose in response.

Mike shook Iris out of thought. "All right, Iris, your turn."

Iris knew it would be a hard one as soon as she read the prompt.

It wasn't currently popular, included an unusual proper name, and it had a tough first word to act out. She got the group to TV show, three words, second word, and effectively pantomimed a telephone so they got "call," but then her team was stuck. Time was ticking. But she had a last resort.

Iris made direct eye contact with Ben, pointed at the lower right-hand side of her abdomen, and buckled in imaginary agony.

"Pain? *ER*? *Grey's Anatomy*?" someone said.

Maintaining eye contact with Ben, she pantomimed clicking a remote control, then smiled in relief.

Ben jumped to his feet. *"Better Call Saul!"*

"Yes!" Iris cried, and they clasped hands in a double high-five.

"What the eff, how did you get that from *that*?" someone asked.

"When I was recovering from appendicitis, we binged that show," Iris explained.

Mike's friend Justin on the other team threw up his hands. "This is why couples can't be on the same team."

"We aren't a couple," Iris and Ben said in unison.

Mike clapped. "I'll allow it! The kick is good. Next up . . ."

Iris sat down with some remorse for throwing her history with Ben in Madison's face. But she couldn't deny the sweet taste of victory.

In her peripheral vision, Iris only noticed the blond blur of Madison's head thrusting forward. She didn't register what was happening until she felt the girl's warm, wet puke splash on her feet.

And smelled the sour odor of salsa, oaky-sweet liquor, and muddled mint.

For the second time that night, Madison elicited a spontaneous "Holy shit" from the crowd.

"I'm gonna be sick." Hannah sprang from the couch, her pregnancy gag reflex on a hair trigger.

"Omigod, I'm so sorry." Madison covered her mouth. "Where's the bathroom?"

"Uh, I think Han just went to the near one, but there's another in our bedroom," Mike began.

"I'll show her." Iris rose from her seat, feeling chunks squeeze between her toes as her weight shifted in her wedges. "We can both clean up."

Hannah and Mike's bathroom had a small lavender-scented votive on the vanity, which Iris lit as soon as they entered, hoping the herbal scent would cancel out the smell of vomit.

"This is so not like me." Madison said miserably from the floor as she flushed the second round down the toilet. "I'm so embarrassed I could die."

"Don't be. It happens. Mike makes those drinks too strong."

"I'll pay for your shoes. Are they the Chloés? I have the same ones. I'll Venmo you four hundred dollars."

"Seriously, don't worry about it." Iris didn't want to tell this girl ten years her junior that they were cheap knock-offs.

Iris helped Madison up and to the sink. "They must have some mouthwash in here." She used her old-friend privilege to rifle through Hannah's medicine chest, and handed a bottle of Listerine to Madison.

"You're so nice." Madison swished and spat into the sink. "I didn't want us to come tonight, I'm no-contact with exes. I was nervous to meet you." Madison wiped her mouth. "But I liked you as soon as we met. I think it's cool that you and Ben are friends. Says a lot about you both."

Iris felt too unworthy of the compliment to respond with anything but a smile.

Madison fixed her hair in the mirror. "It makes me feel even better about him. If I dated one more fuckboy, I was gonna go crazy. I'm in wifey era."

"Pass me the Listerine?" Iris had a bad taste in her mouth.

Iris and Madison returned to the living room, Iris in bare feet, and although Madison had cleaned up better than most, she was ready to go home. The party was winding down, guests were calling Ubers.

Puke has a way of ending a night.

As the group was saying their goodbyes, Ben and Iris stepped aside to have a semiprivate moment.

"It was good seeing you," Ben said. "Thanks for being so cool to Madison even when she barfed on you."

She nodded fake-sagely. "That *was* pretty cool of me."

He snorted.

"What?"

"You know, this whole night I've been trying to figure out what's different about you." He narrowed his eyes at her. "Then you got that text, and I got it." He leaned close to her, the closest he had been all night, and she breathed in his familiar scent, making her heart twist. He whispered, "You're in love."

"That's not it."

He smirked at her. "Oh-*kay*. Well, I'm happy for us both." He hugged her, and as he broke from the embrace, added, "You deserve it."

As Ben and Madison were walking out, hand in hand, Madison pointed at the vintage mirror in Hannah's entryway. "See, babe, that's what I want for our new place."

"New place?" Hannah raised her eyebrows.

"Yes! We're moving to Battery Park City, so we'll be neighbors!"

They were moving in together—already? And just like that, any illusion that Iris had the upper hand evaporated.

After all the guests had left, Iris stayed behind to help clean up. She found Hannah slumped over the arm of the couch, asleep with her mouth open. When she placed a gentle hand on her shoulder, her friend snorted awake.

"I'm up, I'm up!" Her face was creased from a throw pillow, a spot of drool shining on the corner of her mouth.

"Let me take you to bed." Iris helped her up from the couch.

"Mike shouldn't have to clean up his own party."

"I've got it, you need to get some rest."

"I can't believe I fell asleep at a party, and I'm not even drunk!"

"You're partying for two."

Hannah took hold of Iris's arm. "If I'm this tired now, what am I going to do when the baby gets here?"

"You're going to wake Mike up to handle it. And other times, you're going to call me."

Hannah smiled sleepily and mouthed "Love you," which Iris reciprocated, and they hugged.

"I'm putting you to bed, and I'm also gonna borrow a pair of your shoes."

Iris was loading the dishwasher when Mike came into the kitchen holding a big trash bag.

"How was it with Ben tonight?"

Iris shrugged. "Ah, you know."

"New girl's got nothing on you."

"Not if we're talking age or weight class."

"I think you played it really classy. Being hot and unbothered is the flex."

"Thanks." She scraped the remainder of the guacamole into the trash and rinsed the dish.

"And I'm glad you came."

"Of course." Iris was bending over to load the dishwasher when she felt a sudden tug on the back of her dress, and the neckline newly loosened. She clutched the dress tightly against her chest to keep it up. *"Mike!"* She gave a laugh, not because it was funny, but because it was awkward.

Mike cracked up. "I'm sorry, it was there, I had to! C'mere, I'll fix it." He beckoned her toward him.

She turned her back to him so he could make it right—the dress and the air between them.

His fingers brushed the top of her spine as he retied the strings. "It's a sexy dress. Did you wear it for Ben?"

Something in his tone of voice made the hair on the back of her neck stand up. "No," she replied.

His hands slipped from the nape of her neck to her shoulders and he whispered, "Then is it my birthday present?" Gripping her shoulders, he spun her to face him, and in an instant his mouth was on hers. Mike was kissing her, pressing her against the counter, and for a moment she was too stunned to react, and then—

"Ow!" Mike clutched his ear in surprise. "You hit me!"

"You *kissed* me!" Iris was confused to find herself on the defensive. She felt scattered and out of breath. It was out of character for Mike, but even more for her. She had never hit anyone in her life; she had acted on pure instinct. But she had hit him, hard. "Why did you do that? What about *Hannah*?" she hissed.

"She's asleep."

"*So?* That's not the point!"

"No, I know, that's not what I meant." He swore and shook his head. "I dunno, something came over me."

"She's my best friend, we were just in your nursery, are you fucking kidding me?" Iris felt her throat tighten with emotion.

"Stop, c'mon." Mike leaned against the sink counter and looked at Iris like she was exasperating. "You really think I'd cheat on my pregnant wife?"

Iris stared at him in disbelief.

"Look, I won't tell her if you won't," he said.

Fresh anger steadied her. "We're not in *cahoots*. I wanted no part of this."

Mike rubbed his face. "Let's just forget it. It was a drunken moment at the end of a long night. Party foul. Okay? My bad. Sorry."

She threw the dish towel on the counter. "I'm going home. Clean your own damn mess."

Iris waited impatiently for the elevator to arrive, her thoughts a jumbled mess, but all that came through clearly was *This is bad.* Bad for Hannah. Bad for their friendship. Bad for her marriage. Bad for the family Hannah was building. How could Mike throw that into peril? How could he be so reckless and cruel to involve Iris in the betrayal of her best friend? She had known Mike for years, they'd always gotten along well, and Mike had never been inappropriate with her, not even close. Now she felt she didn't know him at all. And she certainly couldn't trust him. What did not trusting him mean for telling Hannah? She could imagine how he might spin it: poor lonely Iris, dumped by Ben, a pincushion for fertility treatments, and all while Hannah and Mike were happily preparing for baby-makes-three. An act of jealousy, sabotage. This nightmare hypothetical had potency, because one part of the lie rang true—Iris wanted what Hannah had.

But not like this. Never in a million years. Iris would never do anything that could hurt Hannah. Hannah was family.

But Hannah had her own family, a growing one, with Mike. She was eight months pregnant and freshly unemployed. If Hannah had to make a choice of whom to believe, whom would she choose?

The elevator paused on the third floor, and a woman in pajama pants entered with a black-and-white Chihuahua on a rhinestone leash. Not even the cute dog could break through Iris's spiraling. Not until the woman asked her a question: "Excuse me. Can I ask what perfume you're wearing? You smell amazing."

"My perfume—"

The woman waited politely, then perplexed, for Iris to finish her thought, and when the elevator landed on the ground floor, she exited quickly. The tapping of the dog's nails receded in the marble lobby.

Iris remained in place, unable to move.

Twenty-seven

I ris had been dodging Hannah since the party, returning text messages only when she knew her friend was likely to be busy or in bed already. She wanted to put off the lose-lose decision between telling Hannah about her husband's behavior or withholding the truth from her best friend for the first time ever. But on Wednesday, Hannah called and said the words no friend can refuse: "I need you."

Hannah was upset after a concerning ultrasound appointment that showed the baby turned the wrong way in utero. The fetus was healthy for now, but a breech birth would be riskier for both of them. At her doctor's recommendation, Hannah was taking a Spinning Babies yoga class that was supposed to flip the baby right side up. Mike was supposed to go with her that afternoon, but he got called to court, and Hannah needed a partner. Iris came straight from the office.

She spotted Hannah sitting on a bench outside the studio door, surrounded by couples, looking like the last kid waiting to be picked up from school. Until she saw Iris.

"Thank you for coming!" Hannah hoisted herself up to hug her. "Mike couldn't make it last time either, and everyone gave me these pitying smiles. Also . . ." she lowered her voice. "The instructor, Talia, is next-level crunchy. She made me her demo partner last time, and it was like I couldn't do anything right. I think she hates me."

"Then I hate her more."

"I love you!" Hannah hugged her again.

Just then the instructor opened the studio door and welcomed them in. Talia was a bit older but very fit in a cropped tank and flowy harem pants, with a shag haircut and microbangs that said *I compost*. She introduced herself and instructed each "couple" to get a mat, a bouncy ball, and a giant stuffed block. Hannah and Iris took a spot near the windowed wall overlooking Holland Tunnel traffic.

Hannah explained their objectives: "I have two weeks to get this baby to turn using these exercises. If by week thirty-eight the baby is still breech, the doctor can try an ECV, where they push on your belly to muscle the baby around, it's supposed to hurt like a mother-effer."

"Oof, like childbirth isn't painful enough."

"Right? And if none of that works, I *have* to have a scheduled C-section, and I *really don't* want that. I want a natural, vaginal birth, that's my birth plan."

"But you want to play it safe."

"Cutting me open and pulling my guts out is 'safe'? American doctors push caesareans because it's easier for the hospital. Ina May Gaskin, who wrote *the* book on birthing, found a tribe in Guatemala that gives birth on all fours when the baby is in breech, and it works just fine!"

"I know you want to give your baby the perfect birth, but any outcome with both of you healthy *is* perfect. I just want you to be okay."

Talia shot a look of reproach in their direction for talking after she'd begun class. They managed to behave themselves for some opening breathing exercises. Then it was time for the warm-up; as per instructions, Hannah lay on her side while Iris jiggled her hip and thigh. Their giggles soon gave way to chatting again.

"So how are things with the sexy glassblower?"

"Gabe's great."

"Oh, he's earned a name! More than just a fling?"

"Definitely. I really like him."

Hannah looked surprised and rolled to her other side.

The next exercise was more daunting, the forward-leaning inversion, where Hannah had to kneel atop the big stuffed block, simulating a couch or bed, and fold her upper body down to a forearm-stand on the ground. Iris stood behind her to hold her hips and support her weight.

"How you doin' down there?" Iris called around Hannah's butt.

"Better with you here, sorry for the view. I could kill Mike for missing this."

"I'm sure Mike would rather be here than in court." *Why was she running interference for him?* Iris helped Hannah to get right side up again.

"I know, he's working his ass off before the baby gets here. I'm probably a hormonal bitch to be mad at him, but—" Hannah sat upright on the block, her face flushed. "I am a little mad at him. The whole point of this class is to learn the exercises so you can do them at home. Maybe after this, you can come over and teach him."

Seeing Mike was the last thing Iris wanted to do. "I'll take some videos today so he can see. And you're never a bitch."

"You'd be surprised. We've been bickering over the dumbest things. The latest fight is how much paternity leave he should take. He thinks four weeks is enough, but they're allowed eight, and I want him to take the full amount."

"That's not dumb."

"And he's got this summer associate, Tony, and he's always talking about how smart he is and how the firm is gonna make him an offer. So I'm like, great, let Tony help cover for you during paternity leave. But then suddenly Tony can't do it without *him,* like a law student needs more babysitting than the baby! I honestly think he's just scared. He hates change. And a baby is the biggest change ever."

"Yeah, it's a lot, for both of you." Iris was grateful when Talia interrupted again, this time to lead the group through some modified cat-cow poses. Iris held the ball steady while Hannah balanced by draping over it like a starfish.

"So how's the new job?"

"Amazing. Jonathan—I mean, Mr. Wolff, the developer—invited some members of his team to his Shelter Island house this weekend. I'm bringing Gabe."

"Wait, Wolff is the mogul who literally caught you when you

fainted at Milos, right? And sent flowers and a car service when Jacob died—"

"Yes, and remember James's sister and kids displaced by that gas explosion? I just mentioned that at a work dinner, and Jonathan got them a lawyer for their eviction case *and* put them up in one of his apartment buildings until it's sorted out. He's an incredibly generous man. I'm so happy to be working with him."

"Is he like, seventy years old?"

"No, he's pretty young, forties."

"Is he a total uggo?"

"He's actually good-looking. He dresses extremely well."

"That's the money, honey! It's like the Bella Hadid meme, you're not ugly, you're poor. To recap, he's relatively young, he's handsome, he's rich . . . he has to be married."

"Divorced. With a daughter he seems devoted to. He wants to buy her her first pony, so he's been sending me horse classifieds to get my take on if I think they sound good. It's adorable."

Hannah rolled off the ball and blinked at her. "So *why* aren't we considering Jonathan as Hugo's potential new daddy?"

Iris chuckled. "Um, because I work with him? Because our professional relationship is the biggest opportunity of my career?"

"You light up talking about him. Do you wear the perfume at work?"

"Sometimes." Lately, always.

"So you *do* want him to like you."

"I want him to like *working* with me."

Hannah's eyes narrowed. "I feel like you're talking yourself out of this attraction because it's risky. But I also feel like you always go for the safe bet when it comes to men."

"Like Ben, who blindsided me after five years?"

"Case in point, Ben *seemed* safe, husband material on paper, but in fact he was a man-child. There really is no sure thing in relationships with human beings. So you might as well go out of your comfort zone."

"Gabe is out of my comfort zone. He's an artist and younger."

"Yeah, but he's safe in that he's a little beneath you, no?"

Iris's heart leaped to his defense. "I don't think so—"

"You described your connection with Gabe as so physical. He's a sexy rebound, and I love that for you! But I want you to go for a man who can make all your dreams come true! And this Jonathan Wolff sounds like a dream guy."

Iris didn't entirely disagree. She wondered how much of her reticence stemmed from the truth that she just couldn't believe a person like her could end up with a person like Jonathan.

"I'm not saying dump Gabe. I'm just saying, maybe don't bring him to Shelter Island. Keep your options open."

The instructor stopped by Iris's shoulder. "Perfect assist . . . ?" she prompted Iris to introduce herself. Talia smiled. "Iris, Georgia O'Keeffe's inspiration, among other things. Glad to have you this week, Anna is doing so much better with you here."

"It's *Hannah*," Hannah said over her shoulder.

But Talia focused on correcting Iris's form. "Now, if you roll her hips forward slightly, you can use her weight to get a good stretch for your back too." She put one hand on Iris's lower back. "Don't tuck, reach with your tailbone toward me. *Yes,* doesn't that feel juicy?"

Iris nodded, and Talia walked away. Hannah rolled back to her feet. "Okay, so she hates me, but she's hitting on you?"

"She's trying to break up our marriage!" Iris joked, and they both giggled.

"The little home-wrecker! You gotta give me some of that perfume. Speaking of which . . ."

Iris froze. How could she be so careless to have made that joke? Iris reassured herself that probably wasn't where Hannah was going with—

"Something happened after the party, and I'm not supposed to know about it." Hannah faced her, her blue eyes like searchlights.

Iris's stomach dropped. *Fuck, fuck, fuck.*

"But I'm torn whether I should tell you or not. Like maybe this is not productive to share. Do you want me to say it?"

Iris's heart raced. What had Mike told her? She knew she should've told Hannah first. He probably snaked her with his version. "I can't answer unless I know what we're talking about."

"Late the night of the party, after everyone went home ... Ben texted Mike about you!" Hannah lifted her eyebrows in scandalized delight. "He asked if Mike had met the guy you're seeing, clearly sniffing out whether or not it's serious."

Iris gasped in relief; it came out like a scoff. "Why would Ben care? He's literally moving in with Madison."

"Good question!" Hannah bugged her eyes out again. "He even told Mike not to tell me, which we both agree is proof it's not a casual question. Ben is *not* over you."

"So much for not telling you."

"Of course Mike told me! First thing in the morning. Rule number one of marriage: No secrets."

Iris's heart yo-yoed in her chest.

At the end of class, Iris was helping Hannah into her sneakers on the bench outside the studio. Hannah's phone rang and Mike's grinning face appeared on the screen. She answered it.

"Hi, baby! Good. No, it was fine. Iris came."

Iris tied her shoes as quickly as possible. She was so close to making a clean escape.

Hannah smiled at her. "Yeah, she's still here. You wanna talk to her?"

Iris shook her head and tried to wave her off, mouthing the words, *I should go.*

But Hannah held out the phone. "Take it, Mike has something to tell you."

Twenty-eight

B ut Mike didn't apologize, or beg her to stay quiet, or interrogate what she'd said to Hannah, or any of the possibilities that raced through her mind in the seconds before she brought the phone to her ear. Instead, Mike's cheerful voice relayed that he'd spoken with her neighbor, Mireille Rapacine, and come up with a plan for her landlord dispute, and he invited Iris to his office to go over it with her. Iris was so desperate for things to go back to normal, she said yes.

Mike worked at one of the old-school, high-powered law firms in the city, Atherton Klein. Iris checked in at a glossy marble reception desk, where a woman already knew her name and directed Iris to his office down a carpeted hall lighted with elegant brass sconces.

The door to Mike's office was ajar. Mike was beside his desk, standing close to a shapely woman in a sleek, sleeveless turtleneck dress. Both their heads snapped toward the door when Iris poked her head in.

"Sorry, are you ready for me?" Iris sensed she had interrupted something, although by now they were both leaning away from each other, the air of relaxed professionalism restored.

"Of course, come in." Mike reached her first and greeted her with a friendly hug. "Iris, this is my summer associate, Antoinette Weaver. She's the ace up my sleeve on your landlord problem."

Antoinette extended her hand. Iris was struck by how beautiful she was. She wore her hair natural and super short, which she pulled off thanks to big brown eyes, high cheekbones, full lips, and deep skin so poreless she could sell cosmetics. "Call me Toni, no one calls me Antoinette outside of a courtroom."

"*Toni*," Iris repeated, shaking the woman's hand. Did Hannah know that "Tony" was an attractive woman? "Nice to meet you."

Mike began, "So I spoke to Mrs. Rapacine—I think I have a crush on her, I mean, that accent! I completely see why you've adopted her. But she's definitely getting screwed here. I think we can get her a buyout."

"She wants to stay."

"I know. That's why you gotta talk some sense into her."

Iris shook her head. "I don't know if she'll listen. She's lived there forever, and she's very headstrong."

"But here's the thing. If the other side thinks there's no way out but litigation, they have no motive to play nice. They'll continue to make her life miserable, and believe me, it can get worse. Real estate in New York is like oil in Texas, they're gonna drink her fuckin' milkshake. If they think she's a die-hard holdout, they'll make her want to die."

"I thought New York City laws were tenant-friendly. And isn't rent control protected?"

"I've been researching," Toni offered gently. "The holdouts that triumph or get a big payday get a lot of press, but they're the exception. Most tenants in this situation leave with a few thousand dollars, if they're lucky."

"But," Mike jumped in, "if the new landlord sees a sliver of hope that they could stop the delay, start the construction, and claim their payday, they'll be inclined to go for it. If they believe negotiating a deal is possible, they'll back off the shenanigans. Then she can at least have some peace to plan her next move, and a reasonable chunk of change to put toward it."

Everything he was saying made sense, but she knew Rapacine wouldn't see it that way.

The multiline phone on his desk beeped and blinked; Mike answered. "Yeah . . . I'll take it in the conference room. Thanks."

"Do you need your office back?" Iris asked.

"No, this will take me five minutes tops, and I'll bring back the docs Ms. Rapacine needs to sign. Stay. In the meantime, ask Toni anything. I'll be right back." He stepped out, leaving Iris and Toni alone together.

The questions Iris wanted to ask couldn't be spoken. "Thank you for your help with this."

Toni gestured openly. "Happy to help a friend of Mike's."

"I'm actually better friends with Mike's wife, Hannah. She's my best friend, really. Have you met her?" She scanned the woman's face for any flicker of a guilty conscience.

Toni only smiled. "No, but I'd like to. Anyone who can put up with Mike twenty-four seven has earned my respect."

Iris gave a laugh, disarmed. But not exactly trusting. "Hannah is about to have their first baby."

"I know. So exciting for them. I'll be assisting with Mike's cases while he's on leave. And I'm looking forward to getting to know the other partners. Mike doesn't like to share."

Iris was pondering what she meant by that when Mike walked back in. He gave Iris the documents for Rapacine and began to small-talk her out the door, when suddenly Iris didn't want to let *him* off the hook so easy. The coward. "Mike, can I talk to you for a second, alone?"

Toni obliged and left them. Iris shut the door after her.

"About what happened at your party, in the kitchen . . ."

He put up his hands. "Don't worry about it."

"No, it needs to be said. It was not cool. And it can't happen again. Ever."

"We were all trashed that night, honestly, my memory is a blur. But sure, whatever you say is right."

"Mike. You remember."

"It's hazy, but look—" he tilted his head with a patronizing smile. "You're going through a breakup, you had to spend the night with your ex and his new girl, you weren't yourself, I totally get it."

"You came on to me."

He scoffed. "That's not how I remember it. But in any case, it's in the past. Bygones! I won't be drinking that much again until the kid is eighteen." Mike crossed to open the door to his office and usher her out. "So, we good? You still want me to help your neighbor?"

Iris was too appalled to speak. She searched his face for any sign he actually believed the bullshit he was saying to her.

But before she could call his bluff, Mike called hers: "And hey, thanks again for pinch-hitting today with Hannah. She really needs her best friend right now."

Twenty-nine

Jonathan's second-string assistant told Iris to be at the East Thirty-fourth Street heliport around four P.M. for takeoff to Shelter Island at four-thirty on Friday afternoon. As she approached the windy tarmac jutting into the East River, Hannah's advice against bringing Gabe lingered in her mind, not because she wanted to seduce Jonathan, but because juggling a new relationship with a new professional team felt imprudent. Looking at Gabe now, right on time, carrying both of their luggage, with his hair pulled back in a cute headband, she had no regrets.

Marilyn was next to arrive with her son, Patrick. Well over six feet, he towered over his petite dynamo of a mother but shared her ice-blue eyes, chestnut hair, and freckled nose. He seemed to apologize for his height with stooped shoulders and an endearing shyness.

"Nice Vans, bro," Gabe said, indicating Patrick's shoes, slip-ons with a dingy black-and-white checkerboard print. "I had a pair just like 'em. Do you skate?"

Patrick's eyebrows buoyed. "Yeah! Now just to get around, but in high school I lived at the skate park."

"Oh, you should've seen his hair back then, down past his shoulders!" Marilyn said. "I used to tell him, that hair makes you look like you need a *job*. I'm glad those skater days are over."

Gabe flicked his own shoulder-grazing hair and put on a sheepish voice. "I dunno, I hear long hair is making a comeback."

They all laughed, and the ice was broken. Iris loved how Gabe could connect with anyone and make them comfortable. Patrick was like a flower that had been watered, he even stood taller as he talked animatedly about his summer travel plans. He was leaving for a month-long European tour starting next week, and Gabe shared recommendations for Venice from his own time studying glassblowing in Murano.

Patrick thanked him. "There's so much I want to see. Jonathan helped me with the itinerary. He's been *everywhere*."

"If you knew the time Jonathan spent on that! I had to force him to focus on his real work." Marilyn chuckled, beaming with pride. "He's so excited for you, honey. Jonathan treats Patrick like a son."

Patrick's ruddy cheeks got ruddier.

"Are you guys staying at Mr. Wolff's house as well?" Gabe asked. Marilyn nodded.

Iris jumped in. "I hope we're not crowding anyone. I told Jonathan we could get a room somewhere—"

"Honey, he can fit all of us and then some."

"There's one other couple on the helicopter, right?"

"Bill Hargrove, NYCHA executive vice president for real estate development, who I think you met at that dinner with Jonathan. A few friends will join us for the dinner party, but they have their own places in the Hamptons."

"Of course." Iris had briefly forgotten this was not a class of people who "crashed" at friends' beach houses.

It wasn't long before a black Lincoln town car pulled up next, and Bill emerged with a woman who appeared in her early twenties. One might have thought that, like Marilyn, he had brought his adult child, but once the woman stepped fully out of the car wearing a whisper-thin minidress and stiletto sandals, Iris realized Bill was a different kind of daddy.

Marilyn handled the introductions. Bill's date, Lindsay, was high-maintenance beautiful, with sleek platinum blond hair she kept having to unstick from her mirror-glazed lips and acrylic nails that clicked together when Iris shook her hand. She smelled like bubble-gummy tuberose and vanilla icing.

They waited for Jonathan and his daughter in the air-conditioned BLADE lounge on the landing deck, whose interior was a mix of Pan Am midcentury and Miami nightclub. Lindsay tugged uselessly at her skirt, which draped over her lap like a napkin rather than an article of clothing, and Iris caught Patrick glancing at her as she recrossed her legs. Bill might've noticed too were he not busy squinting at his phone screen. They were given branded clear plastic sippy cups that contained an internal glass of champagne, so you could pretend you were drinking from stemware without spilling on yourself like a toddler.

"Have you ever been to the Hamptons?" Iris asked Gabe.

He shook his head. "I just go to the Rockaways."

"The drive is the worst part. The traffic on Montauk Highway alone is—" Marilyn pantomimed a gun to her head.

"How much is the helicopter ride?" Bill asked.

"Jonathan wouldn't want you to worry about that." Marilyn smiled, then glanced toward the helipad. "There he is now."

Iris recognized the gray Mercedes as it parked out front. Esdras got out first, opening the back door, and two skinny legs popped out with high-top sneakers. A preteen girl got out of the car, hauling a tall, funny-shaped backpack that Iris recognized instantly. Jonathan emerged from the other side holding two suitcases and a duffel bag, waving off Esdras's offer to carry them. He looked handsome in a crisp, billowing white shirt cuffed at the forearms, but Iris pushed that thought out of her head.

Jonathan never seemed ill at ease, but with his daughter he was lighter and more jovial. He greeted everyone with enthusiasm, clapping a hand on Gabe's shoulder, and proudly introduced his daughter Allegra to the group. She was at that age when a girl is a patchwork of childish and womanly features. She was still narrow-hipped and lanky, a sprite with knobby twigs for arms and legs, but wearing denim shorts short enough that Iris's grandmother wouldn't have let her out of the house. Allegra's dark blond hair was yanked tight in a messy bun, save for the two front tendrils she had pulled out and tucked behind her double-pierced ears. She had a sweet baby face with shiny skin and a matching pair of her dad's big aqua eyes.

Iris gestured to the bag slung over Allegra's shoulder. "Are those your tall boots?"

Allegra's eyes lit up. "Yes, my first pair!"

"Have they broken in yet? Or are they still digging into the back of your knees?"

Allegra kicked one leg out to display the telltale red rub.

Iris sucked air in a show of respect. "That's a good one. But that mark is in the right spot. I promise they'll sink soon."

The girl beamed before self-consciously closing her lips over her braces.

A BLADE employee told them they were welcome to board, and they followed him onto the helipad where a shiny black helicopter awaited.

"Now this is how to head to the Hamptons in style!" Bill said as they approached. "What do you think, baby?"

"It's like *The Bachelor*," Lindsay said, posing herself in her front-facing camera with the helicopter behind her.

The cabin was a tight squeeze, with two bench seats facing each other only a few feet apart. Iris had to thread her knees between Lindsay's to fit. The pilot passed them all bulky headphones to wear, and when Iris turned her head, her earpiece clicked with Jonathan's like football helmets in a huddle.

The propeller's whirring rose to a high-pitched whine as it spun faster in preparation for takeoff. The top half of the cabin windows were open, so the air began to swirl, blowing the women's hair around and making Allegra laugh. Iris hadn't expected the experience to be so visceral. Even with the headphones, the propeller thudding was loud, and Iris could feel the vibrations through her chest. When the helicopter lurched off the ground, she reflexively braced against what was on either side of her, in this case, Gabe and Jonathan. Iris released Jonathan's arm as if it were a hot stove and grabbed Gabe with both hands, prompting him to turn. "You all right?" Gabe shouted over the noise and wind, and she nodded. Jonathan glanced at her with a smile before returning his attention to his daughter.

Takeoff was nothing like the straight, gradual ascent of a commercial jet. The helicopter levitated, then felt like it was falling backward, making Iris's stomach drop, but the pilot was taking a sharp turn toward the water. The chopper pivoted 180 degrees and shot outward over the East River, hovering low over the shimmering water like a dragonfly, before soaring to eye level with the tallest skyscrapers.

The views were breathtaking and felt thrillingly close with the windows down and air rushing in, and after a few squeezes of Gabe's hand, Iris relaxed enough to appreciate them. Manhattan's skyline was on one side, a bulwark of cool, steely blues silhouetted against a late afternoon sun that flashed between the buildings like fence posts, and on the other side, the Brooklyn skyline awash in gold, Williamsburg by way of Tuscany. Iris leaned close to Gabe to peer out his window, then noticed he was looking at her. The sunlight glinted in his eye, and his smile creased his face in the most adorable way. He made her heart flutter, even more at elevation.

But when Gabe took her hand and kissed it, her response was to break from his grasp and replace her hand on her lap. In a different context, this experience would be utterly romantic, but she didn't feel comfortable being physically affectionate around colleagues, much less with her thigh pressed against her boss. No matter how fun or luxurious the itinerary, this was essentially a work trip. She hoped Gabe would understand. She vowed to explain it to him once they were at Wolff's beach house—and make it up to him once they were finally alone.

Thirty

I n a remarkable forty-two minutes, they had landed in Shelter Island. Had they gone by car, on a summer Friday with typical traffic, it could've taken up to six hours. But now they deplaned on a breezy heliport and were seamlessly received by a pair of black Cadillac Escalades with professional drivers and security personnel sitting up front.

Iris had lived in New York City for over a decade, but she still felt intimidated by the Hamptons. The Long Island beaches were so different from the Jersey Shore and Delaware beaches she had grown up going to, and even then, Iris went mainly for day trips or the rare long weekend with a friend's family. Those misty memories were of casual holidays in tightly packed townhomes with alternating Italian and Irish flags, kid-friendly boardwalks selling novelty tees, pet hermit crabs, gooey pizza that scorched the roof of your mouth, and frozen custard that cooled it down. Days that moved as slow as saltwater taffy, and a dress code that allowed for powdered sugar from a funnel cake. She had acclimated to a different sort of beach vacation with Ben, whose family had an old clapboard house on Cape Cod that had a distinctly New England humility and a persistent whiff of mold, even if it was worth north of five million.

If Cape Cod was old money with Puritanical restraint, then the Hamptons were coastal elite wish fulfillment. A place where stressed and demanding New Yorkers could let their hair down without relaxing a single other standard or expectation, and they were willing to pay for it. Where a seven-dollar oat milk latte and twenty-dollar avocado toast arrived with an edible pansy, and fifty-dollar day parking and six-hundred-dollar beach tags were de rigueur. You could buy old-money class and indulge in new-money decadence.

For someone in the field of architecture and design, the Hamptons meant something else: making money. The cash-flush clientele created constant demand for rebuilds, renovation, redesign, and decor. It was a place to sell out, get rich, and settle down. Her peers' occasional snark decrying the cookie-cutter design deployed up and down Route 27 was laced with more sour grapes than the vineyards of Water Mill. Any architect or designer being honest, Iris included, would gladly install trio after trio of geometric lanterns over a thousand kitchen islands if it paid for a vacation home here.

Iris anticipated that Jonathan would own one of the typical Hamptons trophy homes. You saw them all over, frequently with a contractor's sign posted in front of the manicured box hedges and resplendent hydrangea. The preppy palace consisted of a boxy mansion in the traditional style, with bloated proportions fit for today's excess, enrobed in cedar shakes weathered to stately silver—but just as many fresh and blond, telling on their owners—and peaked white pointing, crisp as a collared shirt. Or maybe he'd have one of the beachfront modern megahomes—a vast and character-free glass box overlooking the ocean, a structure whose size and minimalist aesthetic would be as at home in the Hollywood Hills as it would as a luxury car dealership. But in that case it was the outer beauty, not inner, you were paying for: the unobstructed ocean view and private beach access, not the polished concrete flooring and track lighting.

But nothing about Jonathan was so basic, and Iris should have known his beach house would be no exception. The first clue was that they had landed on Shelter Island, a quieter and more grounded, if still ultra-exclusive, outpost. As the Escalade turned down a long gravel driveway, Iris recognized his home's architect instantly: Norman Jaffe. A disciple of Frank Lloyd Wright and a lifelong Hamptons resident, Norman Jaffe shared Wright's modernism, clean lines, multilevel structure, and integration with nature. Jaffe's work utilized local materials and sculptural, horizontal projection so that the home echoed the rocky bluffs. The crown jewels of his Hamptons oeuvre was a triptych of three homes facing Gardiners Bay, and Iris now realized they were pulling up to the finest among them.

They were greeted at the door by two members of the house staff offering them refreshments from silver trays, Arnold Palmer highballs garnished with a sprig of mint and, Iris noticed upon first sip, spiked with whiskey; Allegra's nonalcoholic one was flagged with a floating purple orchid. Once everyone had a cold glass in hand, Jonathan got their attention.

"Welcome, everyone. I want to thank you all for spending your weekend with me at my new home. Tyrell and Bobby will take your luggage to your rooms. And in the meantime, allow me to show off the latest acquisition in my portfolio, this little gem of a midcentury masterpiece."

"Little?" Gabe whispered to Iris.

Jonathan led them down a long glass-paneled hallway that looked onto the lovely pool and patio area, into a sunken yet spacious living and dining space. Although the interior colors were dark and natural, light poured in from glass walls and windows on all sides, and the entire first floor faced a panorama of the sparkling bay and cloudless sky. There was even a skylight. Iris couldn't imagine how she would improve the lighting in daytime, and at night, she might simply do candlelight.

The floors and walls alike were done in rugged flagstone. The living room featured an enormous stone fireplace and a cowhide rug, and every piece of furniture was a lived-in icon of midcentury design—an Eames lounge chair in black leather with a gleaming patina; a Mario Bellini modular sofa in buttoned cream linen, plump and inviting as a cloud; a Noguchi glass coffee table reflecting the blues outside. It was like the Design Within Reach catalog died and went to heaven.

"The home is so well preserved because it was retained by the original owners, who commissioned it in sixty-nine, and they were wonderful stewards of the property. Jaffe even did the expansion in the eighties. Jaffe called this living area his 'wolf den' aesthetic. I mean, how could I resist?"

"It's incredible," said Iris, meaning it.

"It's like a time capsule," Gabe whispered to Iris. Iris shot him a look of admonishment, to which he grinned and did a little shimmy. "What? I mean it's groovy." She was not amused.

Bill asked, "Don't you get the best ROI with new builds?"

"It's not an investment property. This home is personal to me. And besides, there's so much faceless new construction these days, aping the traditional. Tradition is nothing without history. And this house has stories."

Jonathan led them into the dining room, the other half of the massive open concept living space. "Like this dining table. An enormous piece of solid granite, it's so heavy that it had to be lifted inside via crane, and the house was built *around* it."

Iris ran her hand over one of the sculptural chairbacks; it featured a beautiful design of inlaid palisander and ebony wood in concentric circles, such that the burl crisscrossed the back like tribal lines. "Are these Afra and—?"

"Afra and Tobia Scarpa, yes! Their 'Africa' chairs from 1975. I love their work, and their whole story, power couple of midcentury Italian design, co-visionaries defining an era . . ."

"True partners in love and artistic passion. We studied their iconic lighting in grad school. But I've never seen an original piece of their furniture in person, much less eight."

Jonathan raked his fingers through his hair. "Ten. I have two in the basement. But yes, finding a full set in this condition was a challenge."

The rest of the house tour was similarly impressive and impeccably curated, if not without its quirks. The kitchen, for one, was done in head-to-toe black lacquer cabinetry. And with all the flooring in natural stone and the ceilings done in hardwood, it was like a house turned upside down. The layout especially was unusual, roughly a square with an open center for the pool and patio, plus lots of demi-floors separated by only a few steps up or down, and mazelike hallways whose sharp corners were impossible to see around. Just when you were beginning to feel lost, a glass wall would appear to provide reorientation, a view of the bay, pool, or tennis court—or a voyeuristic peek into a room across the way.

When they somehow emerged back into the living room, two other uniformed members of the house staff were waiting to meet them.

Jonathan spoke first. "I'd like to introduce Pilar, my 'chief of staff' as I call her, who is available to help you with anything you may need, whether that be a dinner or tee time reservation, or simply a drink refill by our pool. Likewise, Chef René is available anytime, including for a midnight snack, but he's really going to wow us at tonight's dinner." Jonathan gave a slight bow to the chef before re-addressing his guests. "My only request is that you not take any photos and especially not post any pictures on social media. This house is simply too recognizable, and my family's privacy is paramount to me."

Lindsay raised a hand. "Can we post on Instagram without tagging the location? I'm a content creator."

"Not this weekend." Jonathan smiled.

Marilyn raised her glass. "A toast to our most gracious host."

The entire group raised their glasses to him, but Jonathan made his own toast: "To the Wolff pack!"

Everyone cheered, clinking glasses, and Iris caught the beginnings of a smirk on Gabe's cheek.

They were shown to their guest room, the aesthetic of which was a combination of Scandi-minimalism and yacht interior, and Iris and Gabe were finally alone. Gabe fell back on the bed with a sigh. "This place is something."

"It's iconic." Iris unpacked the formal dress she'd brought and hung it up.

He pushed out his bottom lip. "Not my style."

"Oh no? What's your preferred style of beach mansion?"

"I dunno. Something more . . ." He sat up and pressed on the bed—it didn't give much—"comfortable?"

She didn't entirely disagree. The designer in her loved the interplay of textures, the smooth wood, the rough natural stone, the open invitation to nature via glass and raw materials, but the overall effect was . . . austere. Yet she felt defensive of Wolff. "Guest bedrooms are always a little spare."

He pulled a phone charger from his duffel. "He shut down Lindsay pretty quick."

"Did you see Bill's face when she asked that? I didn't even think of the security threats he must face as a public billionaire. And he's got his kid here. I think it's sweet he's protective."

"I guess."

She and Gabe decided to spend the afternoon at the beach instead of the pool like the others. But first, Iris had one secret thing to take care of.

While Gabe was in their bathroom, Iris unpacked the insulated lunch bag full of fertility medicine she had brought from home. She still hadn't told him about the egg freezing, and it was going to take some scheming to both administer and store her refrigeration-required meds this weekend without Gabe, or anyone else, noticing. She called to him that she was going to get them some drinks to bring down to the beach and left.

Iris walked swiftly down the glass-walled corridor; the flagstone flooring was refreshingly cool on her bare feet. Her first stop was the powder room that she had noted on the house tour. She slipped inside and locked the door.

Iris had the routine down now. She set up her little vials and pre-packaged needles and syringe on the ample counter space and made quick work of titrating her dosage. After giving an RN-professional flick to the syringe, she pinched the flesh on her lower abdomen and did her silent three-count before plunging it into her skin. Afterward, she hiked up her shorts so the waistband wouldn't touch the sensitive spot. She packed everything away again in the lunchbox, including the used needle; she couldn't leave it in the trash, as it looked like drug paraphernalia.

Next, she'd have to borrow some space in the fridge. Luckily, people as rich as Jonathan didn't do their own food shopping or cooking, so she risked only Chef René finding her hormone therapy. When she arrived in the kitchen, however, she saw Marilyn in front of the open refrigerator, loading fresh peaches into one of the unusually clean, clear drawers. Iris thought of turning on her heel and aborting the mission, but she figured that would look more conspicuous than simply putting the small insulated pack in the fridge.

"Hey lion, whaddya need?" Marilyn asked, looking over her shoulder.

"Nothing, I just have some medication I need to keep cold."

"Diabetic?"

"No, um . . ." Iris weighed the costs of telling the truth or a lie. "It's fertility medication. I'm freezing my eggs."

Marilyn's eyebrows lifted, the fast talker briefly rendered speechless, before clasping her in a surprise hug.

"Good girl, that's so smart," Marilyn said into her hair before releasing her. "If I had a daughter, I'd tell her to do the same thing. You know, I had a terrible time getting pregnant. Five miscarriages, and nobody talked about it then. That was the most heartbroken, loneliest time of my life. Finally got one to stick just as my marriage was ending, but nothing could dampen my joy. Patrick was my rainbow baby, my miracle." The softest expression passed over her face as she thought of him. "Is the process hard?"

"I just started. The injections aren't fun, but they aren't as painful as I thought. But sometimes it feels like punishment for still being single."

"No! It's your reward for not being stupid. Believe me, if I could'a had Patrick without my first husband, I would've saved us both a lot of trouble."

Iris chuckled. It was the first moment of genuine bonding she had felt with Marilyn, all the more gratifying for having been hard to earn. She felt safe enough to venture one more confidence. "Is it all right if we keep this between us? I haven't told a lot of people, and it's only a two-week treatment, so soon it will be behind me."

"Of course. Jonathan doesn't need to know. We don't need to give men any more excuse to call us hormonal, right?"

Iris agreed and thanked her, happy to have gotten to the softer side of Marilyn. She always forgot how much she missed that maternal energy until she got a taste of it.

Walking back through the glass corridor, Iris glanced outside across the patio, where she saw Jonathan and Patrick in conversation by the pool. She couldn't hear what they were saying, but Jonathan gently cupped a hand around the back of Patrick's head. It was a familial and comforting gesture, and Patrick seemed to nod gratefully. The scene touched Iris's heart.

Maybe they were all looking for the parents they'd lost or who had let them down.

CHAPTER

Thirty-one

W hen Iris returned to their room, Gabe was shirtless, having just changed into his bathing suit. His physique still struck her breathless. His sinewy arms and chiseled torso, the way his swim trunks hung tantalizingly low on his hips, with that one vein snaking from beneath his waistband over the taut muscles of his lower abdomen. It was hot in their room.

In contrast, Iris had brought a high-waisted bikini to be more modest with work contacts. Speaking of conservative style, as delicious as Gabe looked, she couldn't help but notice he was very tattooed for the Hamptons. She hoped this crowd wouldn't judge him for it.

"Oh! Let's give Jonathan the gift." Iris had obsessed over what to bring Jonathan as a host gift and, with the guidance of her most trusted wine merchant, spent more than she ever had on a single bottle of red. Then she spent the next twenty-four hours obsessing that wine was too banal, until Gabe took pity on her and offered to make a decanter to go with it. She loved the idea and secretly thought, as a bonus, that it would showcase his glasswork and soften Jonathan to consider Gabe for the lobby piece.

So when Gabe reached into his duffel bag and produced a small, newspaper wrapped object no larger than a grapefruit, she was perplexed. He unwrapped it to reveal a solid glass pyramid, or rhombus, or multisided geometric shape.

Her brow furrowed. "A paperweight?"

"Could be. It's a prism. A decorative object. This place could use a few."

"What happened to the decanter?"

"It broke in the annealer, and I didn't have time to make another. I had some prisms already made. They're good gifts. I sell out every Christmas."

"It's nice, but . . . it doesn't make any sense with the wine I brought."

"Wine doesn't need anything to make sense, it only needs people who want to get drunk."

Iris sighed, then summoned a smile. "It's fine. Thank you. He probably has a decanter anyway."

The house had its own private path down to the shore of Gardiners Bay, and as the others had stayed up by the pool, Iris and Gabe had the beach all to themselves. She had begun to rub suntan lotion onto her shoulders when the pleasantly nostalgic smell of Coppertone filled her nostrils. Then she caught herself—would the suntan lotion overpower her perfume?

She closed the bottle cap and handed it to Gabe. "It's late enough, I don't need lotion."

"Yeah, let's go in the water first."

What about the ocean? There's no way the perfume could survive the salt water. But was Iris really not going to enjoy the sun or water this entire weekend? That'd be ridiculous. Her connection with Gabe was deeper than that by now. And she could always reapply back at the house.

They dived in tandem under the bay's gentle swells, and once they'd swum beyond the breaking point, they floated easily and held each other while the sun was hazy and low on the shimmering water.

Iris hugged his shoulders from behind. "What's the deal with Bill and Lindsay?"

"What do you mean?"

"Like how are they a couple?"

"Hot girl dates old rich guy, tale as old as time."

"But is Bill a rich guy?"

Gabe shrugged, bobbing her in the water. "Sure he is. All the guys out here are."

She didn't agree. Bill definitely seemed to *care* about money, but he didn't seem as comfortable in this environment as Jonathan, or even Marilyn for that matter. "I don't know. I think he's trying to fit in here, but doesn't."

"He's Jonathan's friend."

"He's his *connection* for the government housing, big difference. I don't even think Jonathan likes him that much. Jonathan is classy and educated and into art and design. Bill is like a poor man's idea of a rich man. Complete with the sugar baby."

"Oh yeah, I'm sure Jonathan has *never* thrown his money around to get a hot chick into bed."

"Okay, that's the second time you called Lindsay hot."

Gabe chuckled and fell back, dunking them both in the water.

They swam to shore and trudged back to their towels, and flopped beside each other on the sand. Gabe wrapped Iris in a towel and then in his arms as they settled to watch the sunset. Any doubts she had about the weekend melted like the sun into the horizon.

When at last the sun dipped out of sight, she tilted her head back. "We should get showered for dinner."

Gabe kissed her salty hair. "I have an idea."

Iris giggled as Gabe led her to the outdoor shower by the side of the house. "Is this too obvious? What if somebody sees us? Maybe I should go in first, then you."

"No one's around, they're all up at the pool."

"What if someone comes and sees four feet at the bottom?"

He wrapped his arms around her waist and whispered into her neck, "Then I'll lift you up."

The outdoor shower was a weathered wooden stall stocked with Byredo bath products, a new rainwater showerhead over a flagstone floor, and only the clear lilac sky overhead. Iris and Gabe crowded in together, giddy. He kissed her neck and she bit his shoulder. His skin was like a salted caramel, and she didn't want him to rinse off before she got a taste. Even the piquancy of his sweat appealed to her, and as he reached overhead to adjust the sputtering showerhead, Iris kissed a path up the side of his torso to the softness of his underarm.

He pulled the strings on her bikini top and she undid the tie of his board shorts. Seeing him outside, in daylight, naked and aroused, awakened every inch of her body like the cool breeze on her wet skin. Their transgression laced her desire. She couldn't help grinning as he kissed her, and their teeth clicked like pearls. The shower water was warm by now, and they ducked into the stream together.

They kissed and caressed each other as the water made their skin slick with soap and sunscreen. Gabe ran his hands up and down her sides, then gripped the soft curves of her hips to spin her around and pulled her backside close. She leaned into his chest and felt his hardness thump between her thighs, her buttocks, slipping on her soapy body, and she teased him, swishing back and forth like a cat. He reached one hand around her breasts and slid the other down her stomach. When his fingers found between her legs wetter than water, he swore in her ear—an exclamation and declaration of exactly what he wanted to do to her.

Iris glanced up toward the house, where the fear of someone seeing them had morphed to thrill, then fantasy. Unbidden, the image of Jonathan watching them from a window flashed behind her eyes, and then it was Jonathan's tan arm crossed over her collarbones, his hand making her ache. The first wave of pleasure made it hard to hold herself up. She opened her eyes and braced against the wall, her fingernails making fresh yellow scratches in the soft silver teakwood.

She reached for Gabe behind her to return the pleasure—only her hand couldn't find him. She turned to face him and saw he'd lost his erection. Maybe they'd been too focused on her enjoyment, she thought. Iris took a pump of body wash and sensually sudsed down his arms, his torso, before slipping lower to stroke him. Gabe gave a soft moan, but his penis rested just as softly in her hand.

Iris wanted to ask what was wrong, but talking seemed more difficult than doing other things with her mouth. First she kissed him slowly, deeply, like they had all the time in the world, even as her mind was racing. Then she lowered herself as slinkily as possible in the tight space, not wanting to kneel on the sandy stone but feeling awkward crouching. She felt anything but sexy, but she was a woman—she could fake it. She licked him, ignoring the taste of soap, took him into her mouth, coordinated with her hands, and for what felt like the slowest sixty seconds of her life, got absolutely no response while giving a blow job.

"Stop." He gently pulled her back up to standing. "You'll hurt your knees."

Iris couldn't help but feel embarrassed. "Is there something else I can do?"

He shook his head. "Nothing, it's just not . . . I'm in my head, sorry—"

"Don't apologize."

Gabe turned toward the shower stream, squeezing his eyes shut and making a sour face into the water's blast.

"Let me wash your hair." She could still make this shower a pleasurable, sensual experience. She pumped shampoo into her palm.

"I already got soap into it."

"Soap and shampoo aren't the same."

"They are to me." Gabe stepped out of the water and shook his head like a dog. He pressed his lips into a smile and gave her a peck. "I'm not fancy like you."

They do-si-do'ed and Iris took her turn under the water. But no sooner had the cool dollop of shampoo hit her scalp that she saw Gabe tug the towel draped over the stall door and begin to dry off. "You're going?"

"We'll leave separately." He wrapped it around his waist. "Then it won't be so obvious."

She frowned as the shampoo lather slid down her face and began to sting her eye.

"It was your idea, remember?"

Iris tilted her head into the water, gratified only by the knowledge that the towel he'd used was covered in sand. "Bring me a fresh towel from our bathroom, will you?"

He grunted an agreement and slipped out the stall door.

The water had turned cold.

CHAPTER

Thirty-two

B ack at their room, Iris got ready for dinner in the bathroom. She had gotten pretty good at blow-drying her short hair into a swoopy retro-chic thing. Her grandmother used to say she looked like Natalie Wood, but Iris never agreed—even as a teenager she felt too big and tall and her nose wasn't as tiny. Now she realized it was just Nan's way of calling her beautiful. A gentle bay wave of grief rippled over her feet before receding back into the place where she kept all her childhood heartbreaks, wetting her feet with the memory of her grandmother standing behind her at the mirror, her loving face a blueprint of Iris's mother's, smelling of Shalimar.

The perfume. Surely it had washed off from the ocean, and then the shower would've rid her of any trace. Was that the reason Gabe couldn't get it up? A rush of embarrassment stung her cheeks. Was she not desirable without it?

She frantically rifled through her toiletries bag, relieved when her hand closed around the smooth travel vial she'd made. She spritzed herself twice on each wrist, her neck, and her breast. Its familiar floral musk calmed her like a drug. She was impervious again.

Thus restored, her shame curdled to resentment. Was Gabe's connection to her really that shallow? She'd known the perfume had helped her first get his attention, but she had believed their bond had deepened since then, not just emotionally, but physically. Their sexual connection had always been sheet-twisting, belly-quaking, brain-obliteratingly good—until this afternoon—but it also felt special and meaningful. It couldn't *all* be the perfume.

Could it?

She quickly finished her makeup and entered the bedroom. Gabe lay back on their still made bed, scrolling his phone. She stood quietly, regarding him with new doubt. He looked over and smiled at her.

"You look beautiful."

Look or *smell?* "Thanks. I just need my shoes and then I'm ready."

"C'mere a sec." He reached for her with arms outstretched, opening and closing his hands like a child demanding a toy.

"They said dinner at eight, it's ten past."

"Don't rich people do a cocktail hour, or three?" He took her hand and pulled her onto the bed.

It couldn't be more obvious, Iris thought, a fresh dose of the fragrance and now he wanted her. When he tried to kiss her, she turned her cheek. "I just did my hair and makeup. You'll mess me up."

"That's the fun part." He raked his fingers through her hair and tugged lightly, which she normally liked.

But she didn't trust his attraction at this moment and shook him off. "Isn't it my turn not to be up for it?"

She regretted the words as soon as they left her lips, but too late—his chest caved away from her as if from a blow.

She rose from the bed and smoothed her dress. "I'm sorry. I'm nervous. This dinner is the work part of this trip."

"Totally, I get it." Gabe recovered, roused himself from the bed, and gave her butt a little spank. "Later."

They were about to leave the room when she paused. Gabe was dressed in black slacks, a white shirt, and a black vest—she suspected it was his funeral suit minus the jacket and wished he'd worn another, if he had one. Now he wore the white shirt cuffed at the forearms and open at the collar, and his thin Cuban link necklace in lieu of a tie. If he weren't so good-looking, he would look underdressed.

"Do you have a jacket with that?"

"I didn't bring it. It's too hot. We're at the beach."

Not the beach, Iris thought, *the Hamptons.*

Gabe was right, Jonathan Wolff did indeed have a cocktail hour, a grand one. They previewed the party through the glass-walled corridor, and the patio scene looked like a Slim Aarons photograph. Elegantly dressed guests dotted the flagstone around the pool, the archetypal midcentury house to one side and the pink and purple twilight over shimmering Gardiners Bay as backdrop. When they slid open the patio door and stepped onto the cool grass, they were greeted by the spirited melody of live Spanish guitar music and the maracas-like percussion of a cocktail shaker.

When Marilyn had told Iris that Jonathan would be hosting a dinner party, Iris had imagined it would just be the people on the helicopter, minus Allegra, who was at a friend's slumber party, and Patrick, who was visiting college friends in Montauk. But what she and Gabe found was a full-fledged event with more than a dozen guests. Cater-waiters silently circulated around the chatty groupings, bearing trays of sushi—marbled tuna belly, uni fluffy and bright as a marigold, friendly California rolls with real crab—all made fresh by two Japanese sushi chefs set up on the other side of the pool. The pool itself was lit with floating votive candles among purple water lilies and green lily pads. She crouched to touch one waxy petal near the pool's edge to see if it was real when Jonathan came sauntering toward her. She quickly rose.

"I hope you enjoyed your afternoon."

"We did," Iris said too quickly.

"I want to introduce you to some people." Jonathan turned to Gabe. "May I steal her?"

It reminded Iris of *The Bachelor,* and Gabe had no choice but to oblige. "Sure, I'll get a drink."

Jonathan hooked his arm through hers and leaned in to speak to her as they walked away. "I want you to meet Arthur Bellaus, he's one of the biggest real estate investors in New York. He passed on Oasys but I intend to forgive him when he invests heavily in the Hendricks site build. I want him to meet my A-team to seal the deal."

"I don't know if I qualify, but I'd be happy to meet him."

"Your modesty is one of your most enchanting traits."

Iris could feel her cheeks blush.

They found their target beside the deep end of the pool, and introductions were made. "Art" Bellaus was mid-sixtyish and seemed to like to hear himself talk. His wife, Diane, was of similar age but much better-kept, with a forehead smooth as glass and perma-arched brows that replaced interest in her husband's conversation.

Art was telling a longish story about a dispute over his boat slip when Gabe returned from the bar with a negroni for himself and Iris's go-to spicy margarita. Iris took the drink and was waiting for a break in the story to introduce him when Art took Gabe's drink from his hand and said, hardly looking at him, "Ah, thanks, and we need more California rolls over here."

There was a slow second of silence when everyone but Art realized he had mistaken Gabe for a waiter. Iris looked at Gabe's face and saw his nostrils flare and his jaw clench. But when he opened his mouth to speak, his voice was casual. "Sure, man. I'll flag down a server if I see one."

"Thanks, honey, I'm hungry." Iris kissed him on the cheek. "This is my boyfriend, Gabe DiDonato. Gabe, this is Art Bellaus, and his wife, Diane. Art is a real estate investor. Gabe is a glass artist."

"Like Chihuly, do you know him?" Diane asked. It was unclear whether this was her attempt to smooth things over or if her husband's faux pas had sailed over her head entirely.

"He came to speak at my school once."

"RISD," Iris provided, touching his arm.

Gabe stiffened under her hand. "Excuse me." And he strolled off.

Iris endured another few minutes of small talk before she excused herself to go after him.

She caught up to him at the bar. "I'm sorry that guy was an asshole. Are you okay?"

Gabe drank half his cocktail in one sip, so she took that as a no. "You don't have to hand out my CV to impress these people."

"What, the RISD thing? I'm just proud of you is all. It's impressive, I want them to know who they're dealing with."

"I don't give a shit what they think of me. They can keep thinking I'm the help."

She felt terrible for him. "He's just some fossil Wolff is hitting up for money."

"Then why do *you* care?"

"I don't. I care about you."

In the next gulp, he finished his drink.

The dining table was beautifully set with place cards. Jonathan sat in the middle rather than at the head, which Iris thought was gracious of him, with his work wife, Marilyn, across from him. Iris and Gabe were seated across from each other, Iris between Lindsay and the buildings commissioner, a man whose name Iris was now forced to pretend she hadn't forgotten, Gabe between Bill and another big developer named Peter. Gabe looked so vastly different from these white middle-aged bookends. Thankfully there were a few more guests as buffer from where Art and Diane were placed.

Peter leaned back. "So, Gabe, I hear you're an artist. We don't know a lot of those. What's your medium?"

"I blow glass."

Lindsay sniggered.

"Ooh, I love that," Peter's wife, Jen, said, fiddling with a diamond earring the size of a blueberry. "It's so *elemental*. Is it dangerous?"

"Can you make a living doing that?" Bill interjected.

"Not really." Gabe chuckled. "Not like this."

"A true bohemian," Peter said.

Jen looked smitten. "I admire that."

"You wouldn't if you saw my apartment," Gabe said, eliciting a knowing chuckle from her husband.

Iris added, "But you would if you saw his *work*. His art is incredibly powerful. I fell for one of his chandeliers before I even met him."

"Ah yes," Jonathan interjected. "Iris shared photos of some of your pieces. Original, evocative stuff. When we get back to the city, I want to talk to you about a piece for the lobby of Oasys."

Gabe smiled tightly. "That's nice of you to say, thank you. That'd be a step up from the bar Iris saw my stuff in."

Iris wished this granite slab table was smaller so she could kick him.

Marilyn leaned her head around the server pouring her Sancerre. "Do you show at any of the SoHo galleries?"

"My work was last shown in Bed-Stuy, hanging over a dance troupe's performance benefiting PS 26 and Black Lives Matter."

Jen looked even more titillated. "Oh, how wonderful. If you have any pieces left over, I'd love to get my hands on one or two! One for Spence's fall auction, and our guest bedroom desperately needs some edge." She touched her husband's arm. "Pete, make sure you get his card before we go tonight."

"I don't have a—"

"I'll put you in touch," Iris chimed in.

Chef René came out amid a phalanx of servers and introduced the first course as it was set before them with perfect synchronicity: three fresh local oysters, each topped with a generous dollop of glossy black caviar and served with a scallion-and-rice-vinegar mignonette and champagne foam. Iris and Gabe made eye contact and raised their shells to each other in a silent toast before taking the oysters into their mouths. The taste was bright, saline, and refreshingly effervescent. Iris could've eaten a dozen more.

Peter pointed a shell at Gabe. "Bed-Stuy, you said? Your dancers probably performed in one of my buildings. Some of my best investments have been made in that neighborhood."

Marilyn leaned in. "I believe it. I remember from my agenting days that the time to buy is when a neighborhood smells fifty-fifty of fried chicken and roasting coffee," she quipped.

"That's when I got in. Now, with all the NYU grads and their Bernadoos moving in, Von King Park's looking more and more like Washington Square every year."

"Bernedoodles," Jen corrected him. "We've always had schnauzers."

Art slurped his last oyster and turned to Jonathan. "Have you looked at the NYCHA properties over there? Room for redevelopment like what you're doing in Chelsea."

"Bed-Stuy has nine public housing locations," Bill added. "Lot of potential."

Jonathan nodded. "I've definitely looked into it, very similar struggles to Hendricks, and I think we could help. When people live in dilapidated environments, they don't dream better for themselves."

Jen clasped her hands. "That's so true. I just redid my home office, and I feel so much more energized."

"I like the margins, but I'm impatient," Art said plainly.

"Once this Hendricks project gets under way and everyone sees what a boon it is to the community, and we show that private developers aren't the enemy, I think there will be less resistance."

Art gave a thumbs-up. "We'll talk."

Lindsay asked Iris to pass the carafe of water. When Iris reached for it, she sensed in her periphery Lindsay lean toward her, inhale, and softly hum.

"You smell good," Lindsay purred. Iris thanked her.

Chef René was back with dish two: "The second course is a soft-shell crab tempura with miso rémoulade, fresh peaches, and lovage."

"What's lovage?" Jen asked.

"It's what I have for you," Peter replied.

Chef smiled. "It is an herb, like parsley. Only more zesty."

Everyone oohed and mmmed over first bites. The lovage lent a crisp top note of citrus and celery to the deep umami flavor of the miso and crunchy fried crab's creamy inside, while the peaches picked up the sweetness.

Gabe unexpectedly chimed in. "My family lived in Brooklyn for generations, hardworking middle-class people. Now almost all of them are priced out, my mom's about to move and she's heartbroken. And when I grew up there, it was genuinely diverse. Now Williamsburg is just another West Village."

Iris straightened, inwardly surprised to hear him invoke her neighborhood in a negative analogy. And she hadn't known that about his mom.

Gabe continued, "Gentrification is dismantling nearly every long-standing community of color in Brooklyn. Bed-Stuy is the new Harlem. I think it's sad."

"'Cause it was so great before?" Bill crunched through a spidery leg of crab.

Peter tented his fingers in thought. "Gentrification is very misunderstood. The problem isn't one luxury tower going up in your neighborhood, it's that there aren't ten towers going up in mine. There's a dearth of available housing at every level of cost. Blocking new builds only exacerbates the crisis. See, that's something the progressives get wrong. You lump developers together with landlords, when our interests couldn't be more opposed. Developers are trying to meet demand with increasing supply. Landlords want to suppress supply to charge more. Those who can't afford it will be priced out. That's just the way the cookie crumbles."

The third course was halibut, a white brick of fish set on a heart-shaped shiso leaf, with bok choy sautéed in an aromatic broth of zingy ginger and warm garlic. Iris hoped the food could offer an opportunity for a topic change, but Gabe barely registered the dish that had been set in front of him.

"I think we won't fully understand the cultural loss of uprooting these communities until it's too late. It reminds me of what you said about this house, Jonathan, it's the history and human stories that give a place its meaning. The people who made that history should have a say in its future."

"It's history that's so costly to maintain." Peter seemed increasingly energized by the debate, to Iris's dismay. "You'll find most of the allies to your anti-gentrification arguments are rich NIMBYs, 'not-in-my-backyard' liberals who profess progressive goals but refuse to sacrifice to attain them. They're the real roadblock to affordable housing. They scapegoat so-called greedy developers, because we're an easy villain. I invite you to attend one of your local community board meetings, try telling them you support razing an alleyway garden with a bench and some tomato plants in favor of building a tower of affordable units for elderly New Yorkers. Heck, try asking for a homeless shelter. See how they respond. I think you'll find the price of a charming cherry tomato is worth more to them than putting a roof over people's heads."

Iris thought about Rapacine. "Is rent stabilization a solution?"

Jonathan tilted his head. "Rent stabilization is nice for the few who can get it. But their good fortune only drives up the price on everyone else. It doesn't address the cause of the problem, which is housing scarcity."

Iris noticed Gabe had accepted a refill every time the wine server made rounds. She made eye contact with him when he took a first sip of his third glass, not counting the cocktail by the pool, but he didn't seem to read her silent admonishment.

Instead, Gabe continued to battle with Peter. "I'm not talking about the SoHo garden. Historically minority neighborhoods . . ."

Iris could feel herself beginning to stew. Why was Gabe picking fights with these people he'd never have to see again? It was her ass on the line, not his. Even if she agreed with much of what he was saying, he was putting his ego above supporting her in this new job.

Just then, Lindsay bent over to retrieve something she had dropped, and Iris felt her trail her knuckles up Iris's calf. Iris stiffened in surprise. But Lindsay lifted her head with a little hair flip and replaced the napkin over her lap.

Iris needed a break and excused herself, standing for only a moment before a member of the waitstaff anticipated her question and directed her to the washroom.

Iris was shimmying her skirt back down her legs when someone outside turned the doorknob. "Just a minute!" She put her hand out to block the door's swing.

But the glazed-doughnut nails that wrapped around the wooden door were undeterred. "It's Lindsay," she whispered, like that explained something, and pushed the door wide enough to slip inside. They were almost nose to nose; Lindsay met Iris's bewildered gaze with an incredulous one. "What? Girls never go to the bathroom alone."

Iris chuckled, feeling awkward. "I have to wash my hands, then it's all yours."

"Oh, I don't really have to go. I just got so bored."

"With the shop talk?"

"With Bill." Lindsay stood behind her and began to preen in the mirror.

Iris met her eye in the mirror's reflection. "How did you two meet?"

"My job," Lindsay replied without elaboration. She paused to re-apply her lipstick, a mauvy nude that made her full lips look even plumper. "But he treats me like a princess. The hot ones don't pay your rent."

Iris dried her hands. "I guess that's true."

"I think my lipstick would look so pretty on you. Come here." Lindsay placed her fingers lightly, her index finger directing Iris's jaw, her ring finger and pinky resting lightly on her neck. "Open your mouth."

Iris obeyed, and Lindsay dabbed the rosy bullet on the center of her mouth and swept it gently from side to side. Her lashes and spar-kly eyeshadow made a pretty canopy over her eyes as they remained trained on Iris's mouth. "There." Her gaze flashed upward to meet Iris's, though she kept her finger pressed ever so slightly into her neck, making the spot feel hot. "Your pulse is racing."

Iris gave a nervous breath of a laugh. "I don't know why."

In a motion too sensual to be surprising, Lindsay kissed her. Her pillowy lips were soft but insistent, parting Iris's with her tongue in a languid caress before releasing Iris's mouth with a light, glossy smack.

"Sorry, I'm not . . ." Iris suddenly felt so conventional.

"I know. But I wanted to." Lindsay smiled. "And I didn't even mess up the lipstick."

Iris reached for her purse. "Should we head back?"

"I need a bump. You want one?"

And Iris hadn't thought she could feel more square. She said no thanks and averted her eyes while Lindsay retrieved the cocaine from her bag and snorted it. It was the handbag that made her look again—a cherry-blossom-pink Hermès mini-Kelly with icy silver hardware. Iris had only seen its kind on her Instagram Explore page, keeper of all her shallowest desires.

"That bag is major," Iris said, the clumsy slang making her feel old again.

"Isn't it?" Lindsay's big blue eyes flashed. "She's my new baby."

"This might be rude to ask but . . . is it real?"

"The boobs are fake, but the Kelly is *real.* Daddy got it for me."

"Wow. Can I touch it?"

"The boobs or the bag?" Lindsay handed her the bag with a smirk.

Iris laughed nervously and tried the tiny bag on. It was utterly impractical, but Iris did think it made her look fabulous—and rich. "It's to die for."

"Did you smell the leather?" Lindsay slipped her fingers in the tiny bag's opening and buried her nose inside, exhaling with a carnal moan. *"Fuck."*

Iris realized that for Lindsay, the only aphrodisiac greater than her perfume was Hermès. "They're like super expensive, right?"

"It'd be around ten if we got it straight from Hermès, but then you can't pick the color, and I'm a pink girlie. So we went secondary market—I mean, it was brand-new, in box"—Lindsay paused for dramatic effect—"thirty-five thousand dollars."

"Shut up." Iris quickly took the purse off and shoved it back in her direction. "You weren't kidding about Bill! He must be crazy about you."

She giggled. "It's that building deal that went through for him."

"The NYCHA plan? That just got approved a few weeks ago. They won't even start building for a year. No one's seeing profit from that for a while."

"Something else, then. I told you, it's boring, Bill knows not to bother explaining it to me. All he said was 'My ship came in.' Such a cute old man expression. But he definitely got paid. And don't think he didn't treat himself too. He bought a Maserati."

When Iris returned to her seat at the table, where dessert, a deconstructed key lime pie, had been served, she was dismayed to hear Gabe and Peter still debating.

Peter was saying, "Let me tell you a story of how woke do-gooders perpetuate the problem. I've been trying for years to build a major residential development complex on a flailing commercial lot in Harlem. One hundred and fifty affordable units, six hundred more for folks who don't qualify for assistance but still need a place to live. It would've included a community and cultural center *and* a civil rights museum. It was even gonna be green energy compliant, Jonathan will be happy to hear." He took a swig of his wine. "Two months ago, a single city councilwoman, elected by a handful of votes in an election nobody gives a shit about, vetoed the plan."

Marilyn gasped. "No."

"Years of time, money—*pfft*—up in smoke," Jen added.

"Why?" Diane asked.

"There's no pleasing these people. She wanted three-quarters of the apartments to be below market rate, something impossible. Nothing is good enough for activists looking to make a name for themselves out-woke-ing the wokest."

"What are you going to do?" Jonathan asked.

"Let me guess, cue Michael Corleone." Art smoothed his hair back. "'My offer is . . . nothing.'"

Peter raised his glass. "I converted the lot to a big, beautiful truck depot."

"I believe that's called fuck around and find out!" Art bellowed.

"I may recoup some investment by building a luxury condo building, small enough to bypass council approval. But for now, I'm enjoying letting these truckers pump exhaust into the bitch's face. Small price for the money she cost me."

"How much we talking?" Marilyn asked.

Peter pursed his lips. "Seven hundred million."

Jonathan winced.

Gabe interjected, "So the truck thing is like . . . a revenge prank? You know what the asthma rates are in Harlem?"

Peter chuckled. "Kids can stay home. They're safer inside anyway. Wouldn't want any stray gentrification to hit them while they're walking to school."

"My father always said, perfect is the enemy of good." Jen waved a fork in the air. "And comparison is the thief of joy!"

"Or, profit is the enemy of progress," Gabe said sharply.

Jen gasped, looking stricken. Iris briefly thought she was shocked by Gabe's tone until Jen said, "Lindsay, *your nose!*"

Every head turned toward Lindsay. Bright crimson blood trailed out of her left nostril and dotted her décolleté. She seemed as surprised to see it as everyone else.

"Jesus," Bill hissed. "Get a tissue."

Lindsay covered her nose with one hand and fumbled with the other. "I think I have—" She bent forward to fumble for her fallen napkin and her bag slipped off her chair just in time for gravity to pull a mini gush of blood down her front, *dot-dot-dotting* the purse's blush-colored leather in vermilion. "My Kelly!" She picked it up like an injured child.

Bill scowled. "I got you that a month ago and you already ruined it."

Iris handed Lindsay a napkin to wipe it with, but that only smeared the blood. Lindsay sprang up from the table and fled in the direction of the restroom.

"Another bathroom trip is the last thing she needs," Marilyn muttered to Jen, who tittered in reply.

CHAPTER

Thirty-three

A fter dinner had been cleared and Gabe had gone ahead to their room, Iris heard a man's raised voice coming from Lindsay and Bill's room down the hall. Worried, she tiptoed toward their slightly open door. She spied Bill glowering over Lindsay as she sat on the bed. He roughly gripped her face, squeezing her cheeks to make her face him as he berated her. "You *embarrassed* me! You think this pretty face makes you a princess?" Iris stepped out of sight but kept an ear to the door. She flinched when she heard a loud *smack* and one last invective, *"Stupid cunt!"* Then the slam of an interior door. Then silence.

She peeked again. Bill was gone, but Lindsay remained wilted on the edge of the bed, swaying slightly. Iris whispered her name from the doorway until she looked up.

Lindsay's eyes darted to the bathroom, then back at Iris. Then she got up and met her in the hall. "What? What is it?"

Up close Iris could see her nostril was still crusted with blood. "Are you okay? Did he hit you? You can come to my room, we can get someone—"

"Of course not, I'm fine." Lindsay smoothed out her hair. "He gets mad, but I have him wrapped around my little finger."

"That wasn't what it looked like."

"What, are you spying on me?"

"I was checking on you."

"I don't know what I was thinking with you before." Lindsay touched her nose and winced. "I was bored."

The cocaine, the nosebleed. It dawned on Iris. *She'd lost her sense of smell.* "All right, well, I'm going to bed. But for what it's worth, you deserve someone who doesn't treat you like that."

Lindsay seemed to take it in, but when Iris turned to go, she hissed after her. "You think you're better than me? Does your glass blow job make you pay the bill?"

Iris looked over her shoulder at Lindsay, her pity plain. All the power of youth and beauty was good for a handbag, nothing more. And sex appeal had no upper hand against a man willing to raise his. She hoped Lindsay would see that more clearly in the morning, but Iris wasn't getting through to her tonight.

Iris returned to their room, eager to process what she'd just seen, but she found Gabe packing his bag. "What are you doing?"

"I'm sorry. This is not my scene."

"You're leaving? Are you serious? Why?"

"Do you have to ask?"

"So some of the dinner guests were obnoxious. I just think leaving is extreme, we only have one more day, it's late."

"There's still a ferry and trains all night, I checked."

"You looked up the schedule already? So this isn't even a discussion."

He shook his head. "There's not a lot to discuss. It's simple. I'm not comfortable here, I'm not having a good time, so I'm going home. If you want to come with me, you're welcome to. It's totally up to you."

"No, Gabe, it isn't. This isn't a vacation for me, it's work."

"That sucks for you. These people are awful."

"How am I going to explain you leaving in the night? It's rude. It's embarrassing."

"Sorry I'm an embarrassment to you and these rich assholes."

"That's not what I said." She rubbed her face with her hands, her head was pounding. "This is an important weekend for me professionally, and I brought you here because you're important to me too.

And now you're making me choose. You can't act like you're not putting me in a tough spot."

"Tonight wasn't exactly a comfy spot for me either."

"You made it harder than it had to be. You were spoiling for a fight. Why couldn't you just . . . just . . . ?"

"What?"

"Just go along to get along. Do you know how many times in this industry some jerk has said something offensive to me and I had to smile through it? If I popped off or stormed out every time, I wouldn't have a job."

He crossed his arms over his chest. "I'm not like that. I don't suck it up and take it."

That pissed her off, and Iris could feel herself begin to harden. She sat down on the bed without looking at him. She was no longer interested in fighting for him to stay. "How are you going to get home?"

"On the train, like the rest of the commoners."

"Let me drive you to the ferry."

Iris asked Pilar if she could borrow the Land Rover and she and Gabe drove along the pitch-black roads. Their only conversation was Gabe reading the Google Maps directions and telling her to look out for the deer whose eyes flashed in their high beams from the embankments along the way. Her frustration and anger faded during the ride, and a crumbly sadness took its place.

Gabe must have sensed the energy shift as well, because when she put the SUV into Park in the ferry lot, he had softened his tone. "Look, let's not blow this out of proportion. You gotta do your work thing, I get it, I support it, but I wasn't vibing with it. It's not that deep." A few uncomfortable seconds of silence ticked by in the car's cabin. "Believe me, those people do not give a fuck if I'm here."

Iris's heart wrenched. "It's not about them. *I* care if you're here."

Gabe tilted his head at her in a way that felt more placating than sincere. It made her stomach flip. "We're good, okay?"

"If we weren't, would you even tell me? Because in my gut, I feel like we're not."

He looked out the window. "I can't be anything other than what I am. Let's just leave it at that. Not everything is better when you dig at it. Not everything benefits from pressure, sometimes pressure makes something beautiful break."

"Are we breaking up?"

"I didn't say that. I meant like, metaphorically." He said her name in a sigh. "Iris. Let's just take a breath, okay?"

She found it hard to breathe through the lump in her throat. "Okay."

"Text me when you get home Sunday."

She managed a nod. And he leaned over the console to kiss her goodbye. It was closed mouth.

Her gaze followed Gabe to the isolated glow of the ferryman's ticket taker, and he waved to her before boarding. She waved back, a limp-fingered high sign he probably couldn't see, and started the engine. Iris aimed her lonely headlights at the dark road home, wondering if her glass romance had already shattered.

Thirty-four

I ris had a fitful night of sleep after she returned to Jonathan's house. The air-conditioning was too cold, the digital clock display too bright. She ruminated on the argument with Gabe and rehearsed for new ones, running lines with her worst-case scenarios. She should have heeded Hannah's advice; she shouldn't have brought Gabe. It had been a mistake to introduce a new romantic relationship into a new professional one. She could only hope her error hadn't thrown both into jeopardy.

When she finally fell asleep, she had that dream where she's lying in bed but can't move, a version of the recurring nightmare that had followed her since childhood and resurfaced anew since the Hendricks explosion. It always started out as a lucid dream, one in which she can tell herself *You're having a nightmare, this isn't real.* But it doesn't matter, she is still scared. And soon she drops deeper into it, into a realm beneath her conscious control.

She's in her childhood bed, and her body feels incredibly heavy, three times her weight. She wants to get up, she needs to escape, she can feel the panic rising in her belly, clenching her throat, but she can't move a muscle. Her gaze is fixed above the window, where the wall meets the ceiling. There is a stenciled border of a little house, a little barn, and little farm animals lining the room, a design that she and her mother did themselves. Looking at them takes her back there, happily sponge-painting over the plastic shapes with her mom, who stands behind her on the ladder, fencing her in with her arms on either side. You didn't have to be careful with stencils, you could be messy and the picture would still be fine. When Iris's little arms got tired from reaching, they would switch, and Iris would sit on the bed and watch her mother take over.

She is back in her bed now, seeing her mother's back to her on the ladder, and Iris wants her to turn and look at her. Iris longs to see her face, her comforting smile, the reassurance that everything will be okay. But her mother doesn't turn, and she doesn't see. And then the daylight fades and her mother disappears altogether, and it's nighttime in her bedroom again. She can see the neighbor's windows bordered with glowing Christmas lights.

Iris smells smoke. Instinctively she knows it signals danger. She wants to yell, but she can no more cry out than she can move, her body is too heavy, her mouth choked shut, and it is getting harder and harder to breathe. Her eyes water as a trail of black smoke passes over the little red barn and the little blue house, curving around the animals like a beckoning finger. Then all of a sudden, the weight is lifted and she levitates out of bed. She is moving toward her bedroom door, and as scared as she is inside her room, she's more terrified of what's outside it. The door is a black rectangle bordered in glowing orange, her world in solar eclipse. And just as she bursts through, into the searing bright light—

Iris woke up, like always. It's always this moment the nightmare ends. She never gets to the part where Jacob bravely navigates out of the smoke-filled house, or when he falls down the stairs holding her, protecting her instead of breaking his own fall. For some reason, her memory never takes her to his heroism or their successful escape. The dream dwells on her own inaction in bed and goes only as far as meeting the wall of fire. For all her subconscious seems to know, she never got out.

Iris kicked off the blankets, her body now clammy and too hot, and she sat up to try to slow her racing heart. But her mind was filled with the same old recriminations. Why didn't she move the moment she smelled the smoke? Why wasn't *she* the one to heroically warn her parents just down the hall, who never woke up before the smoke got to them? Why did Jacob have to come upstairs and risk his life to get her at all?

She had had some therapy in her teenage years, and had learned to say she was only a child, and that most likely nothing could have been done to save her parents. Their bedroom door was open, and that's why the smoke got to them first, while hers was closed tight until Jacob arrived. Her counselor told her to have compassion for her younger self, and Iris tried. But it was a sympathy laced with disdain, more like pity. Poor kid.

Poor, stupid kid.

Thirty-five

E ven after a shower the next morning, Iris felt ragged. Her un-
dereyes were puffy from tears and lack of sleep. She tried
dabbing concealer but that only made it look worse, so she
decided that fresh-faced (with mascara) was the best she could do.
She applied sunscreen to her nose, already freckling, and plaited her
hair in two short braids to combat the frizz of another hot, humid
day. And lastly, she put on her real armor: the perfume.

When Iris entered the dining room, Allegra sat alone at the grand
granite table with her back to the panoramic view of the bay and
bright morning. The tween was absorbed in her iPhone, which
sounded with rapid-fire pop song snippets and AI narration. Iris noticed she had done her makeup that morning, a wobbly line of blue
eyeliner and some sparkly lip gloss. On her wrists were many bracelets, a Cartier Love bracelet mixed in with colored bead and woven
ones like camp friendship bracelets. Her fingernails were half-covered
in chipping blue polish. She was a particular type of privileged Manhattan preteen, precocious and sophisticated but still a kid.

"Good morning." Iris had directed the greeting at Allegra, who
didn't look up; instead, an attentive member of the kitchen staff
replied in kind and quickly took Iris's coffee order. But Iris didn't
blame the girl for not acknowledging her. It must be strange for her
that her dad's employees and work colleagues were crashing her
weekend with him.

Iris took a seat at the table, which was cold under her arms. The chef had already laid out a beautiful breakfast spread, plates of fresh fruit, a stacked bread basket, fresh-squeezed orange juice and green juice, an electric hot water carafe and a coffret of teas. Through the windows, she could see Jonathan pacing outside on the balcony, talking on the phone. She reached for a croissant.

"Where's your boyfriend?" Allegra asked, suddenly regarding her.

"Oh, um, Gabe had to go back to the city early. He's, he's—" Iris had rehearsed explaining this to Jonathan, not his preteen daughter. "He had to go home early."

"I like the thing he made."

It took a moment for Iris to understand what she was talking about. "Oh, the prism." Jonathan had already regifted it to his daughter.

"This morning it made my bedroom full of rainbows. It's awesome!"

"Oh really? Good, I'm glad." Iris felt a pang of guilt for diminishing it. "I'll tell him you liked it." *If I see him again,* she thought miserably.

The sliding door opened and Jonathan reentered the dining room. He was dressed in a white linen shirt and khaki shorts, and his freshly showered hair had only begun to dry at the edges, curly from the salty air outside. He greeted Iris, and Pilar wordlessly traded him his empty espresso cup for a new one.

He put his hands on his daughter's narrow shoulders. "Al, you want waffles? Chef can do bananas Foster, I told him it's your favorite."

She dropped her head back to look up at him. "That was my favorite when I was like, ten."

"Well now you're *like,* twelve, so forgive me for missing the memo. What's your new fave?"

"I want an egg-white omelet with spinach. No cheese."

"What is this, your mom's order? C'mon, sweetie, you're too young to be on a diet."

"It's not a diet! It's what I like now."

Jonathan sighed and looked stumped. It was funny to see someone give him attitude, and to see him rendered just another helpless dad.

"What about you, Iris? Eggs, waffles, pancakes?"

"Actually, waffles sound amazing, if it's no trouble."

"Not at all. I'll tell him."

Jonathan had just crossed into the kitchen when Allegra looked up. "Dad?"

He poked his head back in. "Yeah?"

"Okay, I'll have one bananas Foster waffle—on the side."

"You got it." He smiled, and his eyes flitted to Iris in a glance of gratitude.

When he returned from the kitchen, Iris beckoned him. "Jonathan, can I talk to you for a minute?"

"Sure. Coffee tastes best on the balcony. Join me."

They closed the sliding door behind them. Iris squinted from the sunlight as much as the discomfort of what she needed to say. She took a deep breath. "I just wanted to apologize for last night if the dinner conversation got at all . . . uncomfortable."

"Don't worry about it. Peter and Art's egos are bulletproof. They like someone to spar with them. Gives their wives a break."

"All right, but sparring certainly wasn't my or Gabe's intention, and I'm sorry if that's how it came off. It was inappropriate."

"Iris, something I teach my daughter is, never apologize for a man. Where's Gabe now?"

"I asked him to leave."

Jonathan looked surprised but impressed. "Ah. Well, Bill and Lindsay aren't up yet, but we arranged for Bill to have a day at the golf club, and Esdras is driving Lindsay into town to do some shopping, whenever she gets up. I'm sure Lindsay wouldn't mind you joining her."

Her answer must have shown on her face, because Jonathan chuckled.

"Point taken. Believe me, nobody's thinking about your guest's behavior after Lindsay's."

Iris lowered her voice. "That's another thing. If I may, I have some concerns about Bill."

"You're telling me. Why do you think I'm paying for him to get out of the house all day?" He sipped his espresso. "I can't stand the guy, personally, but dealing with him is a necessary evil. He's the gatekeeper to public housing."

"I overheard him being pretty rough with Lindsay last night, in a way that makes me question his character. And earlier she said that he's newly flush, spending extravagantly. He told her it had something to do with a recent deal . . ."

He frowned and shook his head. "Not one with me. We're at the earliest possible stage, it will be six months before we break ground."

"No, I know. But what else might he be up to? Maybe he's leveraging his connection with you somehow. I just wanted to flag it for you. I wouldn't want his shady dealings to derail the work you've put into this project."

"I've had some of the same doubts myself, but hearing you validate them . . ." He nodded. "Maybe we do need to distance ourselves, at least put in a firewall between him and us. Thanks for looking out for the team."

"Of course."

Jonathan opened the sliding glass door to let her back inside. As she passed, he added, "And you know, if you're a free agent today, you might join Allegra and me to check out this pony prospect. Allegra's trainer can't make it, but you could lend your expert eye."

"Oh!" Horses always made Iris's heart leap.

"Unless you'd prefer to have the day to yourself, which I totally get."

"No, I'd love to. How fun and exciting!"

"Good attitude. We're a little nervous." Jonathan rolled his gaze to his daughter.

"Aw, I was always nervous riding a new horse. I'd be happy to come along."

Everything about Daley Equestrian Center evoked a happy nostalgia for Iris. The sweet smell of hay and shavings, the swirls of dust kicked up from the indoor arena footing as a rider schooled a chestnut horse over crossrails, the visceral sound of the horse's gut as he cantered by, and the trainer's shouted instructions echoing through the lofty space.

While they waited for the seller to get the pony, Allegra read Iris the listing on Facebook, and although the ad was full of sales jargon,

Iris could tell this was a top-notch show pony with a better résumé than her own:

"Piano Man 'Billy' is an eight-year-old, fourteen-point-three-hand Connemara x Welsh Pony cross. Competed at the Hampton Classic and Devon Horse Show, Pony Club, fox-hunted, and games—always in the ribbons! Fancy mover with scopey jump and auto changes. Personality plus, bomb-proof, hacks alone, no vices. Sadly outgrown. $75,000 OBO. Will go fast!—What's 'OBO'?" Allegra asked.

Iris translated, "Or best offer."

Allegra brightened. "Like if there's a bidding war?"

Jonathan smirked. "Can you tell her parents are in real estate?"

Iris's first pony at her grandparents' farm was "free to good home." The sort of equestrians at Allegra's riding barn would have likely looked down on young Iris's humbler horse girl, one that showed horses in 4-H alongside prizewinning sows. This was the elite hunter-jumper circuit where Allegra would learn alongside the daughters of rock stars and billionaire mayors. But what did it say that a twelve-year-old had the power to intimidate her at thirty-five?

Then the seller's trainer entered the arena leading one of the loveliest ponies Iris had ever seen.

"Pretty animal, isn't he?" Jonathan said.

The pony was out of a fairy tale. A beautiful dapple-gray gelding, snowy white with silvery gray shading on his legs, rump, and the points of his face. Iris could do the horsewoman's evaluation, taking in the animal's superlative conformation, good feet, lovely head with curved ears, delicate nose, and large, well-set eyes of a striking hazel-gold instead of the typical brown. But the assessment by the little girl inside Iris was much simpler: She wanted to throw her arms around his neck.

Which is exactly what Allegra did. "He's sooo cute!"

"Remember we have to make sure he's safe and you like riding him," her father warned.

Allegra mounted up and Iris helped adjust her stirrup length and checked the girth tightness.

Iris put a comforting hand on her shiny new tall boot. "You feel okay?"

Allegra nodded and gave a gentle kick to walk off.

She and Jonathan leaned over the fence of the arena watching Allegra walk the pony around the perimeter, her back ramrod straight and gloved hands hovering stiffly over the pony's withers. Iris could tell the girl was nervous. She willed the pony to behave.

"Does your ex-wife ride?"

"No, we were both city kids until Allegra. She always loved animals, and she was having a tough time with all the virtual school stuff, so Léonie, my ex, enrolled her in riding lessons, and Allegra completely fell in love with it. Riding has given her a lot of confidence, but she's still more anxious than she lets on. She's a perfectionist."

"I wonder where she gets that from."

He smiled.

The trainer's voice carried through the arena. "Change direction across the diagonal, sit a bounce, good . . ."

Jonathan kept his eyes on his daughter. "How happy are you at Candela?"

"I've been there nearly ten years, it's almost a second home."

"I'm sure you've grown a lot in that time."

"Absolutely." *Mostly in the last month.*

"But is Candela 'sadly outgrown,' do you think?"

Iris chuckled. "I'm certainly ready to move up there, that's for sure. Frank has promised to promote me, and I think my work with you will go a long way toward making that a reality."

"I should hope so. Iris, it was your pitch that won that bid, not Candela's, not Frank's. I didn't want to go with a boutique firm, generally I like to have pick of the litter at the bigger ones. I normally think if someone is at a small firm for a long time, they've already found their tribe, and maybe their level. But I don't get that sense with you. There's a restlessness in you. Am I off base?"

Tears filmed her eyes—with Gabe, the hormone injections, and exhaustion, her emotions were in overdrive—she hoped Jonathan didn't notice. "What you're saying resonates, I have felt frustrated with the limited mobility at Candela. But at the same time, it's hard to think about leaving. Frank feels more like a father than a boss."

"Kids grow up." Jonathan looked back to his daughter, piloting the pony over ground poles. "I'd like to offer you a permanent position at Wolff Development. I prefer to work with my own in-house team and have as few changing contractors as possible, and I'm going to need to tighten focus as we take on this NYCHA rebuild, and I hope more like it. I can offer you the type of opportunities Candela only sees once every five years, if that, whether Frank makes you a principal or not."

Iris was taken aback. "Wow, thank you. I'm honored you would consider me—"

"I'm not considering, I'm offering."

"Can I think about it?"

Jonathan shrugged. "Admittedly, patience isn't one of my virtues. But I appreciate your respect for the relationships you've built over many years. I value loyalty above all. But in contrast to Frank, I reward it. So mull it over, let me know as soon as you can. But know that this type of opportunity doesn't come around often, and as the horse classifieds say, 'Will go fast!'"

Iris smiled. Then she noticed Allegra steering the pony toward some crossrails at the far end of the ring. "Is she gonna jump him?"

Jonathan frowned. "She only ever has in lessons with Cheryl, her instructor."

Iris could see she was pitched too far forward on the approach, and her heels weren't down, common beginner mistakes. But the trainer only called out, "Grab mane!"

As Allegra was riding around the corner to the jump, some birds flapped up from behind the rail, and the pony spooked, dropping a shoulder and ducking to the left of the jump. It wasn't a violent reaction, but the abrupt motion was enough to toss Allegra onto his neck, making her lose her stirrups. She managed to hang on as the pony trotted to the center of the ring, where the trainer was already lunging for her dropped reins.

Jonathan ducked under the fence and ran to Allegra. And as soon as he'd established that his daughter was all right, he turned on the trainer. "You said he was safe, he almost threw my kid! You used the word *bombproof*."

"He is, he's been a child's pony—"

"If she'd been hurt, believe me, I'd fucking explode. Allegra, honey, get off, we're leaving."

Allegra's face was bright red and her lip was quivering.

"Let her go around again," Iris interjected.

Jonathan spun toward her. "What?"

Iris spoke carefully, knowing she was on thin ice. "She's shaken up, but she hung on. If she gets off now, her confidence will stay shot. She'll feel even worse on the next horse. I don't think he's a dangerous pony, I wouldn't suggest it if he was. Give her a chance to show herself and the pony she can ride through it."

"I don't know." Jonathan crossed his arms. "I'd feel differently if her instructor were here."

The seller's trainer added, "If she were my student, I'd say the same thing."

Jonathan remained skeptical. "It's up to Allegra." They walked back to where she and the pony were standing. "Al, do you want to keep riding or get off? There's no wrong answer."

Allegra looked embarrassed. "I messed up."

"No," Iris said, putting a hand on the pony's shoulder and looking up at the girl. "You did great. The pony startled and you got taken by surprise. That happens to every rider. You know what, though? A horse can't throw you if you keep him moving forward."

Allegra's blue eyes tilted dubiously down at Iris.

"To buck, to rear, even to spook, he has to stop. So as long as you press your legs on both sides of him and think *forward,* you can kick your way out of trouble."

"He's bigger than the pony I ride at my barn."

"The smallest pony is bigger than any of us. A rider will never win a battle of brute strength. So we don't ride by force, we ride by communicating confidence to the horse. You have to be the leader and convince him that you know best."

"But what if I'm nervous?"

"That's okay, that's normal. Just, fake it till you make it. You can be nervous in your head but still be confident with your riding. Take a deep breath, sit up, shoulders back, *leg on,* and show him how sure you are about going over the jump. You don't have to ask for the canter, keep him at a nice even trot, but whatever you do, keep your leg on and keep him going *forward*."

"Only if you want to, Al," her dad added.

Allegra took a deep breath, and the furrow in her brow eased. She nodded and turned Billy's head back to the rail.

Jonathan walked back to the ring fence. "If she falls, you're fired."

Iris hoped he was joking.

Allegra and Billy picked up the trot at the opposite end of the arena. *Good girl,* Iris thought; she'd have a nice long runway to let the pony settle before they reached his spooky corner. Iris saw the pony's head get higher and his strides shorter as they approached. Allegra too let her shoulders inch up, and Iris began to worry. But when Allegra reached the corner, she kicked her skinny legs like a marionette. The pony's ears swiveled back and forth, listening to his rider, as he quietly picked up the canter and gracefully popped over the low jump with Allegra perfectly balanced atop him.

All three adults breathed a sigh of relief.

Allegra and Billy rode by them, a wide grin on her face. "I got him through it! Did you see?"

"I sure did, you were brilliant, honey!"

"Well done!" Iris said.

"I'm gonna ask him for the canter again!"

"No, ah—*Iris,*" Jonathan said, like she should do something.

But Iris could only smile as Allegra bopped along in a quick one-two posting rhythm to Billy's smart trot and then confidently asked for the faster gait. The pony picked up his proper canter lead perfectly, again passing the trouble spot where the birds had been, as steady as a rocking horse. Allegra was beaming.

"I want to change his name. How'd they get Billy from Piano Man anyway?" Allegra asked as they walked, or in Allegra's case, skipped, back to the car.

Iris was holding her helmet. "It's the name of a song by Billy Joel."

Allegra scrunched her face. "Who's Billy Joel?"

Jonathan put a hand around her shoulder. "Sweetie, there are lots of nice ponies out there. I think we should keep looking for one who isn't so spooky."

"But once I showed him he was just being silly, he listened to me. I really liked him. Everyone gets nervous sometimes."

"Well, you rode him very well." Jonathan shot Iris a look that said *God help me.* "We'll have to come back and see what Cheryl thinks."

"Oh-kay, but I think you should make your best offer."

Thirty-six

T he rest of the day unfolded like a flower. They lunched on watermelon salad and lounged by the pool in the afternoon, and in the early evening the three of them got dinner at a darling historic inn on the island where they watched the sunset from the veranda. It was a pleasure to spend time with Jonathan and his daughter, Iris was surprised at how comfortable she felt. The horse trial had broken something open in Allegra, she was chatty and warm with Iris, revealing how much of her coolness before had been shyness in disguise. And Jonathan seemed off duty in a different way without the others around. He wore a simple gray T-shirt, khaki shorts, and Birkenstocks; he was in dad mode—*hot*-dad mode. They dined on mussels in a heavenly garlic broth, local sea bass Provençal, and the most perfect strawberry shortcake Iris had ever tasted. Iris and Jonathan ate and drank enough that their cheeks matched the blush of the rosé wine.

Back at the house, Allegra retreated to her bedroom, and Jonathan and Iris shared a nightcap. He invited her to take a walk around the back of the house along the beach, saying only "I want to show you something."

They walked along the stony beach, her feet curling over the pebbles. Moonlight shimmered on the rippling surface of the bay, and the breeze off the water carried the scent of brine and the dark seaweed that washed up on the beach like tangled hair.

Jonathan turned his back to the water and faced the house. "Did you know this house is part of a triptych?" He pointed up to his own property and then the two beside it, each one unique but with similar characteristics. "Three friends in the sixties bought adjacent land plots and commissioned Norman Jaffe to design them all together."

"I knew he designed three, but I didn't know they were commissioned by friends. What a dream, to live next door to your best friends in homes as magical as these."

"Can you imagine the parties?"

Iris could imagine it. To be young, in love, rich and fabulous in the swinging sixties, surrounded by incredible architecture and design and this gorgeous setting—the thought alone was intoxicating.

"That's what really drew me to this property. A place designed from the concept of a social community." Jonathan sat down on the sand, facing the house, and Iris sat next to him. "Real estate gets so competitive, and let's call it what it is, dick measuring. Who can build the tallest tower on Billionaires' Row? Whose Hamptons beachfront palace can have the largest footprint? There's such a fierce individualism to real estate development. Maybe it's an American thing."

"Or . . . a masculine one," Iris ventured.

He laughed. "Yes, I'll cop to that! I was that way when I was younger. And still the prevailing definition of luxury is having every possible amenity at your fingertips *within* your home, so you'd want for nothing and never have to leave. Everyone in their own perfect bubble—and we're miserable! Because that's not how humans are supposed to live. We're social animals."

Iris nodded. "I think about that a lot. And how in the city we're all cheek by jowl, living in a side-by-side comparison, literally. The bubble is transparent. You are constantly confronted with what you *don't* have."

"Exactly. But this house, its entire concept was about friendship, about maintaining ties through land and form and home and community. It reminds me that home isn't defined by the property line, it's the security of the relationships that the home fosters, within and without."

Iris was genuinely moved. She gazed at the other two homes, one of which had its lights on. "Do you know your neighbors?"

"No. Not yet." He shot her a guilty smile. "I've been *meaning* to invite them over. I'm a man still under renovation."

"We all are."

Jonathan grew serious. "That's my biggest regret about the divorce, fracturing that home for Allegra. I can build her all the houses and horse barns her heart could desire, but I let cracks in the foundation of my relationship with her mom turn into a disaster. *We* were her home, not some property. And I didn't protect it. She's been more withdrawn ever since."

"She wasn't today."

"No. Today, she was *brave*. And she was proud of herself. Thanks to you."

Iris began to protest.

"I'm serious, that was incredible. It wasn't my instinct. I wanted to tear her off that pony, and then tear the head off that seller. But then you come marching in—"

"I was afraid of overstepping."

"You did! But I liked it. And you were right." Jonathan met her gaze for a moment that made her heart skip, then looked back at the houses glowing warm yellow against the navy sky. "I'm always trying to protect her from the outside in. Today you made her feel safe from the inside out. I think I've felt so guilty about the divorce, I haven't wanted to push her. I wanted to prove to her how good I can make things again. Like, if I make the obstacles she faces small enough, she won't be afraid to step over them. But she's growing up, and cutting her food into tiny pieces only serves to say 'I think you're gonna choke.' Like I have no faith in her, when I really just have no faith in myself."

Iris was touched he would share this with her. "I think you're a wonderful father. You're a natural caretaker. I can see it in how you interact with the people who work for you and even their families." She thought of him with Patrick by the pool. "And a girl will have plenty of people who try and push her out of her comfort zone. From her dad, a daughter just wants to feel protected."

"Thank you." He sounded choked up.

Iris made a joke to cover for him, "We are the only two people on this island who would sit on the beach and face a *house*."

Jonathan laughed. "You get me." He rose from the sand and offered a hand to help Iris up.

She pushed her hair off her face, and her wrist passed over her nose. Iris smelled the perfume's heady florals melded with the remains of a salty summer day on her skin. She felt beautiful and sensual.

As they walked back along the beach, Jonathan asked, "What do you want out of life, Iris?"

"That's a big question."

"I don't really do small talk."

She sighed. "I want to skip to the good part. I feel like I've been working and grinding in my work and otherwise for so long, trying to get to the next level. But every time I think I see it on the horizon, it's like a big wave comes and sends me crashing back to shore."

"Do you want marriage, family, kids? Or is that too conventional for you?"

"Yes, definitely. Did I give you the idea I'm avant-garde? I'm pretty boring."

"You're anything but. Your confidence, the way you command a room—you could have anything you want."

Jonathan wasn't describing her, Iris thought, he was describing the perfume. She recalled her advice to Allegra: *Fake it till you make it.*

He continued, "You just have to live in the moment and trust that the right opportunity, and the right person, will come to you."

Iris's ankle rolled in the pebbly sand, and Jonathan caught her by the shoulders, his palms warm on her cold skin. She turned to face him and he didn't let go. Their eyes locked.

She kissed him.

For a moment Iris was completely lost in the sensation of his mouth, warm and soft, turning her already loose limbs into melted butter.

Then he gripped her shoulders gently and pushed her away, and reality was like the smack of a wave hitting her face.

What had she done?

Thirty-seven

T he first thing Iris wanted to do when she got home was see the only boys who never let her down, Roman and Hugo. Roman and James had dogsat Hugo at their apartment— newly uncramped after Jonathan set Veronica and her kids up with a temporary apartment, rent-free, while a lawyer, also on Wolff's pay-roll, looked into their eviction case. Roman had offered to drop the dog off Monday when he had a showing nearby, but Iris couldn't wait. She took a cab to his place straight from the heliport.

James was at rehearsal, so Iris filled Roman in on the entire week-end over a glass of wine, or two, with Hugo on her lap for comfort.

"So what did Jonathan say when you kissed him?" Roman asked.

"He said, 'Thank you, but—'"

Roman recoiled with secondhand embarrassment. "Oh, not '*Thank you!*'"

"I know. I should've walked into the sea. He said, 'Thank you, but I want to protect our working relationship.'"

"Okay, that's not *that* bad."

"Right, he was nice about it, which makes it so much worse!" Iris cringed so hard that her body felt like it would implode. "He was such a grown-up, and I was so unhinged. I think I was just sad about Gabe, and it was such a lovely day . . . but I don't know what I was thinking. I *wasn't* thinking."

"You got horny for the real estate. I see it every day, I show a client book-matched marble behind a deep soaking tub, and they need a cigarette. It's why we put so much money into staging. That luxe lifestyle is intoxicating."

Iris thought she was attracted to Jonathan's personal qualities, and maybe his azure eyes, but Roman was right: Jonathan's lifestyle was its own perfume. "There's no way he's offering me the Wolff Dev job now. I'll be lucky if he doesn't terminate Candela's contract with Oasys and I lose my job altogether."

"Wolff said he values your working relationship, that sounds like he wants it to continue."

"I'm a walking sexual harassment case. You better find a new place for Veronica and her kids, quick."

"Don't even joke. That's why I gotta give him the benefit of the doubt, he saved our lives with that apartment hookup. James and I are Team Wolff."

"He's a great guy, great dad, treats his employees like family . . . and I *ruined it*!" Iris flopped over on the couch in agony.

"You're being dramatic. He's a straight guy, I'm sure he was flattered. You really think the man had you spend the day with his daughter and then took you on a moonlit walk on the beach because he *didn't* want to get personal? Whether he said no or not, he wanted it."

"Please, the date rape defense is *not* making me feel better." She set Hugo on the floor and began to leash him up. "Anyway, thank you so much for taking care of Huey, you're the only friend I trust with my son."

"Anytime, I'm his guncle." Roman reached over to ruffle Hugo's ears. "But before you go, I actually want to talk to you about something kind of serious."

Iris sat up and listened. She thought Roman looked nervous.

He took a sip and began. "As you know, James and I have been talking about our future for a while. And now that Veronica and them are settled, at least temporarily, we've had a chance to revisit the issue and talk about what we *really* want. And it was a very open and honest conversation, I think you would've been proud of me."

"I'm always proud of you." Iris already guessed that the news was they were splitting up.

"Family is important to us. And although James and I may view marriage differently, one thing we're on the same page about is wanting a child."

Her sip of merlot leaped into her windpipe. "Whoa. Okay, but . . . isn't a kid an even bigger commitment than marriage?"

"Definitely. But commitment isn't our issue. I thought James wanted marriage from a place of insecurity, which felt like moving backwards. But he expressed to me that he just felt like we had stagnated, and honestly, I've felt that too. We love each other, we can get married anytime, or not. The more meaningful next stage of our relationship, the one we want to invest and plan for, is starting a family." Roman frowned at her. "What? What's that face?"

Iris closed her jaw. "No, nothing, I mean, I'm surprised. I didn't know you were considering this. But I'm happy for you."

"You inspired me! I've been so impressed with how you've bounced back after Ben and taken control over your fertility and investing in your future family. It got me thinking, I need to be proactive too. So, James and I went back and forth over whether he should be here for this, but we decided I'd broach it with you first, and you just take your time thinking it over. Obviously, it won't be the last time we discuss it."

Iris was still smiling but her brow began to furrow.

"We wanted to ask you if you would donate an egg to us."

Iris was too stunned to speak.

"And not for free," Roman continued, eyes wide. "I know this retrieval process has been a burdensome expense, so our idea is that we would help you finance it, provided we can use one of your leftover eggs."

Iris struggled to think while her stomach flipped. "It's not like a cookie recipe, you need more than 'one large egg.' The rule of thumb is ten eggs retrieved to produce one healthy, successfully implanted embryo. I have no idea what I'll get with this round. I might need a whole 'nother cycle."

"All right, well, I admit we've only just begun our own research on all this. If you don't get enough, forget it. On the other hand, if a second retrieval would yield more and give us more cushion, James and I would happily help pay for another round."

"I don't think you understand what a physical undertaking this is for me—"

"To be clear, we're not asking you to carry it. We'd get a surrogate. I just figured, it'd be a lot to ask you to go through this process *only* to be our egg donor, but you're doing it anyway, and I can help cover the cost, it could be win-win!"

Iris thought he made it sound like a two-for-one deal. "I'm on high doses of hormones, I have daily injections, pelvic exams, mood swings. It's not a walk in the park."

"Okay. See, I didn't know that—I'm still educating myself! From my perspective, it seems like you're brighter than ever, you have this new energy. I notice it, James has noticed it, maybe hormone therapy suits you."

Then a realization dawned on her with a sickening clarity: *This is because of the perfume.* "Roman . . ."

"But listen, this is a big idea. It means our kids would be half-siblings, and you'd be the biological mother, however we'd handle that—there's a lot to figure out. So just think about it. Don't answer now."

Iris raked her fingers through her hair. "You know, you've never expressed this desire to have kids before."

"I've thought about the possibility. It's not the expectation that it is for straight people . . ."

"But have you asked yourself, why *now*?"

"I told you, because James and I realized we were—"

"Stuck, I know, but a child is not a solution to a stalled relationship. Completely independent from me or my involvement, you have to think this through."

"I am." Roman was beginning to sound annoyed.

"And why *me*?"

"Iris, you're my best friend of more than a decade. And James adores you, he always has. I mean, we've always joked if I liked girls, we'd be married already! It's not a *totally* crazy idea." He chuckled.

Iris remained grave. "Roman, what if it's just the perfume?"

He wrinkled his nose. "What?"

"A week ago, you didn't want to get married, you didn't even seem entirely sold on monogamy. Now all of a sudden you want to make a baby with me? You don't think that's a big swing for two weeks?"

"I'm offended you'd think I'd decide something so important based on how you smell. I'm not an idiot."

"The perfume works without you knowing it! It plays tricks on your mind. How do you not see it? We tested it together!"

"I'm not some stranger trying to get in your pants. I know you're not trying to be hurtful, but this is actually insulting. It's not the fucking perfume."

"You don't know that. It makes sense, the perfume can't change your orientation, but maybe it can still trigger some animal instinct in you to mate with me. So I wear it around you and James, and all of a sudden, *Hey, let's have a kid together.* It's like I inadvertently drugged you."

"You sound crazy right now."

"No, you do! You and James have stopped fighting for what, a *week*? Get real, you guys aren't remotely ready to become parents."

"Where do you get off criticizing my relationship? I can't believe you would judge me like this, you of all people." Roman stood up and began to pace. "When I've always supported you and whatever choices you made in your love life. Did I say shit when you were begging Ben to propose, and at the same time flirting and fantasizing about *Nate*?"

Iris felt like she'd been slapped.

"Yeah, your *married* coworker whose attention you were so thirsty for that you *cried* when his wife got pregnant?"

Shame burned on her cheeks. Iris gathered Hugo's leash and stood to leave. "I told you about those feelings in confidence, and you know I never acted on it."

Roman followed her to the door. "Oh, believe me, I know. Because you never act on anything! You stay right where you are and complain and cry to me! And you hope to God somebody else makes the decision for you."

Iris spun to face him. "You just liked that it was the one time I was almost as messy as you."

Thirty-eight

I t felt like the Mondayiest Monday Iris had had in a long time, although all things considered, she should be grateful she still had a job somewhere. She slumped in her chair at Candela and sucked down her iced coffee, willing it to change her life—or at least give her such a violent brain freeze that she could forget what had happened over the last forty-eight hours.

Gabe, Jonathan, Roman. How had she screwed up with so many men in so little time? Gabe hadn't texted her since giving a tepid thumbs-up to her text saying she was home on Sunday night. The memory of her embarrassment with Jonathan was as painful and vivid as a skinned knee. She thought of Roman and his enormous request and winced at how she had handled it. Although Iris still believed the perfume was the cause of his baby fever, she couldn't account for why she had been so cruel about his relationship. Something about how Roman had discussed the topic had set her off, and it was only when her anger had cooled that she could parse its cause. Roman was the one man she'd trusted to always see her as a person and never reduce her to an object. Fertility treatment was depersonalizing enough; during most appointments, she felt like a faulty car. She couldn't bear feeling like her friend, too, wanted to use her for parts.

Iris heard Nate's voice from across the office floor, and she slumped a little lower so he wouldn't come over. Nate—Roman had to remind her of *that*.

Not so long ago, Nate and Iris had been work–husband and wife, besties within the bubble of Candela's office, gossiping about the others, sharing increasingly intimate details about their lives. He had been her refuge when the office felt like *Animal House,* because he wasn't like the other guys. Nate was slightly older, married, his background in design made him more artistic, which resonated with her. He treated Iris with respect—or used to.

And yes, at some point in their friendship, Iris had developed feelings for him. Or she became emotionally dependent on his attention, she honestly wasn't sure which. She didn't act on her crush, but she didn't fight it either. And she knew it was mutual. Their will-they-or-won't-they tension reached its breaking point when one evening, after a boozy Candela karaoke night, Nate confessed his romantic feelings for Iris but lamented he couldn't step out on his wife with a baby on the way. Iris gaslit him, said she'd never thought of him as more than a friend, that she was in a happy relationship. Nate left confused and embarrassed.

It had ruined their friendship. Iris reacted to shame the way she always did, by shutting down. She pulled up the drawbridge, redrew her boundaries with cold, remote appropriateness.

Nate reacted to humiliation like many men—with anger.

Enough time had passed that the pain and awkwardness between them had dissipated. But still they teased each other like bitter exes.

Like he was now.

"So?" Nate popped over the top of her cubicle and bit into a red apple. Through a frothy chew, he asked, "How was the weekend getaway with Wolff?"

"The *working* weekend was a success. We secured two new investors for Oasys."

"Hope you didn't have to do anything untoward."

Not going there, Iris thought, but she knew how else to make Nate jealous. "Wolff's house is incredible. He owns a perfectly intact Norman Jaffe on the water."

"Of course he does. Meanwhile, my splurge is four days at Disney for Maddie's third birthday."

"Maddie is turning *three*? Oh my gosh, I remember when she was just born."

"I do too." Nate's green eyes fixed on her with intent, but only for a moment. "My brother says it's not worth the money, Maddie's too young to remember it, but it's looking like next year won't feel so strapped."

Iris was distracted by a new email that came in on her phone, but not on her work email. "Is Annie going back to work once Maddie starts preschool?"

"No, Annie's pregnant again, actually."

"Wow! Congrats!"

"Thank you, we're very excited. But I just had a very heartening conversation with Frank." He stuffed the apple in his mouth like a roasting pig.

Iris watched Nate walk away with her blood pressure rising. *That better not mean what I think it means.*

She returned her attention to the message on her personal email account. It was from Marilyn—Iris didn't even know they had this address—and she gasped when she read it:

> As per your discussion with Jonathan over the weekend, your offer for a full-time position and equity stake are attached. Jonathan appreciates you have a long history at Candela, so take your time to think it over. But I think you will find the terms generous and the opportunity unmatched. We hope you'll join the Wolff Pack!

Iris couldn't believe it. Was this a mistake? Had Marilyn failed to speak with Jonathan first? That didn't sound like Marilyn. Iris opened the Docusign attachment and skimmed the contract—she could've punched the air. Relief flooded her veins. So she *hadn't* kissed her career away.

But now she had a decision to make.

Iris waited until Nate had left for lunch to knock on Frank's door.

"C'mon in, kiddo!"

She found Frank strapping in to his Peloton shoes.

"I'm hearing good things from the Wolff team, they're very happy—"

Iris wasted no time. "So, I was talking to Nate . . ."

"Ah, all right. I anticipated this. You two have always been close, I knew you'd talk."

"But it's not a done deal yet, right? You're still considering your options." She managed a smile.

"I haven't made a formal offer, but . . ." Frank trailed off. "I have to do what's best for the company."

Her stomach had dropped to her feet, and she sank into the chair that faced his desk. "No, Frank, why? We discussed this, the years I've invested here—"

"Well, Nate has as much if not more design experience—"

"I did everything you asked. You said you wanted to see initiative from me, and I landed us Wolff, the most high-profile residential building Candela has ever worked on. We beat out all the big firms with *my* pitch."

"But you boxed him out. I know it wasn't your intention, Wolff handpicked you. But the fact remains, Nate was in at the start, and he got benched right before the big game."

"That's not true. It was always my idea."

Frank put up his hands as if she had a gun. "I don't want to get into the he-said, she-said of it all. You know I don't do *drama*."

Iris looked out the window behind him, fighting the tears of frustration that she knew would only undermine her further. "It's not drama, it's my career and it's the truth."

"Look, I hate to see you upset. Don't take this so hard. You and Nate are both highly valued players on this team. But Nate was unhappy with how Wolff went. I had to do something to keep him. He's got a growing family, without seeing movement, he was gonna walk."

"Why don't you think I'll walk?"

Frank raised his eyebrows, rippling the skin all the way to his hairline. "Kiddo, c'mon. We go back. You've been more than an employee, Iris, you're my mentee. I've invested in you *because* I see your potential. And I think I've earned your trust by now that I know what's best. I would never hold you back. But I can't play favorites, and I won't give you more than you can handle just to flatter you."

"You have no idea what I can handle."

He scoffed. "I think we need a time-out. Go to lunch, lower the temperature, and let's talk when you're calmer, okay?"

Iris nodded, her mind made up. "I was offered a full-time position at Wolff. And I'm going to take it."

"Stop that now. I don't like threats."

"It's not a threat. It's my decision and I'm letting you know."

"Jonathan's poaching you?"

"No, Frank. I'm leaving."

CHAPTER

Thirty-nine

I ris stopped at Rapacine's house on her way home, ostensibly to see how her legal consultation with Mike was going, but truly, Iris needed a friend. Mme Rapacine always had a unique perspective, and Iris could use any voice other than the self-recriminating ones inside her head.

Rapacine had opera music playing on a turntable, the apartment smelled wonderful, as usual, and Iris felt the tension in her shoulders ease as soon as she crossed the threshold. She was greeting the boy cat, Chéri, when she glanced to the kitchen and saw Rapacine already had company. A well-dressed brunette sat at her kitchen island.

Iris reflexively apologized and said she could come back later.

Rapacine dismissed her with a wave of her jeweled fingers. "Nonsense. Iris, meet—"

"Sofia Morales!" Iris said in surprise, immediately recognizing the famous face from TV and social media. Sofia was a co-host on a popular round-table daytime talk show, *Between Us,* and the first trans woman host on network television. "Oh my gosh, I love your 'Can I Just Say?' segments, I always agree with you!"

"I'm glad, because I know this mouth is gonna get me fired someday." Sofia laughed warmly, her teeth dazzling white.

Rapacine introduced her. "Iris is a dear friend and neighbor. She is the one who is trying to help me win my case against the evil overlords." She poured Iris a glass of wine, and Iris joined them at the kitchen island.

"Thank God for you, then! Mireille is the Good Witch of the West Village, they can't make her leave!" Sofia joked. "I tried pitching my producer your story as part of a larger housing crisis package, but they didn't bite, I'm sorry. You know they keep me sequestered on the social issues, they give all the hard news to Kaitlin."

"Don't worry about me, but keep trying for your news. You've made your own path so far, why stop now?"

"How do you two know each other?" Iris asked.

Sofia and Rapacine exchanged a look. Then Rapacine answered, "Sofia fostered my kittens before I adopted them."

"That's how we *met,* and Mireille is kind to leave it at that. Kind now and kind then. But I'm not too ashamed to tell you the truth. I was a mess. I had just dropped out of Columbia journalism school, I was early in my transition, freshly cut off from my family, in crisis, and keeping those kittens alive was probably what kept *me* alive. Then I met Mireille, and she rescued all three of us. She let me live here while I got my head and heart straight. She made me believe in myself when I was at my lowest." Tears glossed her hazel eyes.

"I only wanted you to sense in yourself that which I could sense a mile away." Rapacine reached out to cover Sofia's manicured hand with hers.

Then Sofia glanced at her watch. "I should head out. I have an early train to DC tomorrow and I still have to decide on looks with my stylist. I'm going to interview the vice president about trans rights in schools."

Rapacine clasped her hands together. "I'm so proud of you." They hugged.

Sofia pointed at her. "But you can't tell anyone else about it until we promote it next week."

"You know I can keep a secret."

They both laughed.

"Ah, I almost forgot! *Un moment.*" Rapacine went into her bedroom and emerged with a box wrapped in brown paper and a sprig of lavender tucked into the twine, and handed it to Sofia. "Keep it with you." And kissed both her cheeks.

Then Sofia went to say goodbye to Iris, who couldn't help but ask, "Could I get a picture?"

"Not here, sorry. But I'll give you my card, keep in touch."

"Oh sure, no worries. It was nice meeting you." Iris took her pink business card and they hugged goodbye. Sofia smelled so delicious, like caramel cake with lemon icing and something fresh and aromatic—*lavender*—that Iris almost didn't want to let her go.

After Sofia left, Iris said, "I hope I didn't make her rush out."

"She only needed to pick up that package. Her schedule is very demanding."

"I'm sure. She's famous! Crazy that you two are close."

"You want to know more." Nothing got by Rapacine.

"I do." Iris leaned forward. "But I also got the feeling I'm not supposed to know. So, if you don't want to tell me—"

"She smelled good, no?" Rapacine had a satisfied smile on her face. "She is another recipient of my extraordinary perfume."

"She has *my* perfume?"

"Of course not. These rare few are bespoke fragrances for one wearer and one wearer only. But you are not my first."

"That was one of yours . . ." Iris had felt overwhelmed by what she chalked up to Sofia's star power, but maybe it was that spectacular gourmand scent.

"Her secret weapon. She was picking up a fresh bottle. She'll need it if she wants to get Madam Vice President to say anything interesting."

Iris sighed. "Sofia parlayed her perfume into an audience at the White House, and I've somehow made a complete hash of my life. I don't even know if I want to wear mine anymore. But it's my fault, maybe I just can't handle the attention. I failed your perfume."

"*Pardon?* The last time we spoke you had just gotten your dream job and you were dating a passionate artist with a big—"

"It all became a complete mess over the weekend. I can't trust the good things that have come into my life since I got the perfume, I don't even feel like I can trust myself with it. I don't know if Gabe really likes me, I don't know if I'm up to this task at Wolff Dev, it has challenged some of my oldest friendships." Her eyes welled with tears as she took a shaky breath. "I don't know what's real anymore, and I feel like I'm on the verge of losing control of . . . everything."

"And you think you had control before?" Although Rapacine could be quite motherly at other times, when faced with Iris's tears she rarely appeared moved. "Were you in control when your partner of five years decided he did not feel like marrying you? Were you in control when you were toiling at a job for nearly a decade without advancement, compensated by only a pat on the head?"

"Ouch." Iris raked her fingers through her hair.

"I don't say this to hurt you. I say it to wake you up. Most bad things that happen to us are completely out of our control, it is dumb luck. And then some bad things happen to us because we are not claiming the control we *do* have, you give your power away or lay waste to it with worry and self-doubt. You must learn to tell the difference or you won't make it."

"But how can I accept good things if I got them for the wrong reasons?"

"Syndrome of the impostor!" Rapacine shook her head. "You don't feel worthy of these good things, these opportunities, these pleasures, but you *are*. You have always been worthy! Getting what you want can be the scariest thing in the world. Because then you have something to lose."

"But could the perfume be making me *more* likely to lose it? It made me downright reckless with my boss. On the beach with Jonathan, I smelled my wrist and slipped into the fantasy of the scent, and *I* kissed *him*."

"So it made you take a chance."

Iris shook her head. "I was completely unprofessional. I don't know what our work dynamic will be like now."

"You were *human*. You were being yourself, unfiltered."

"No, it wasn't me at all. I'm not impulsive."

"Your entire personality is not superego, don't you want to know the woman *beneath*?"

"Maybe I don't trust her! Kissing Jonathan was a mistake, among others."

"So, make a mistake. Act, choose, err, fuck. To live is a verb, Iris."

Iris didn't know if she could live with the consequences.

"Look at Sofia. When I met her, she had shrunk to the most invisible version of herself, no needs, no bother, a tiny cactus blending with the rocks. I made her a perfume not to change her, but to help her bloom. You cannot hide with a beautiful perfume, it will announce your entrance to a room, fill a space larger than your arms can touch, and linger when you leave—Sofia needed to learn she deserved this presence. To trust that she could live as her authentic self and be seen and desired as such. One could be crass and say that it helped her to 'pass,' but no, it helped her pass *through,* through the fog of self-doubt, and let the world see her as she truly is: a bright, charismatic, and beautiful woman. And now she is fully herself, celebrated for her identity and opinions, an inspiration for others. She has a successful career in television—mind you, no one can smell her through the screen, and yet she is a star! Because she *always* was. She always possessed the qualities that have made her a success, the fragrance simply made them evident."

"To others."

"To herself."

Suddenly, they were startled as heavy metal music began blasting overhead, the bass so loud it shook the light fixtures.

"What is that?" Iris raised her voice over the noise.

"Iron Maiden," Rapacine shouted back.

Iris squinted at her in confusion and discomfort.

The older woman made hand gestures to the words: "Let's go for a walk."

The music could be heard from the sidewalk, but no longer at a volume Iris felt in her back teeth.

Rapacine explained, "It's the latest escalation in my tenant harassment. Although it is laughable that they thought they would scare me with metal music. I lived in London in the seventies, although I preferred the punk scene."

"But the decibel level. Did you tell Mike about this?"

"I spoke to his lovely associate. Toni told me to make a record of every time it happens. Easy, because it plays every day at seven A.M., six P.M., and nine P.M., carefully within the boundaries of noise ordinances. The speakers must be on a timer."

"That's outrageous. You can't live like this."

"I can, and I do. I got excellent earplugs, they can't fully block the sound, but they allow me to appreciate the music. It's not to my taste, but they are excellent guitarists, 'Aces High' is my favorite. Fortunately, Jasmine is deaf, though I do worry about Chéri."

Iris had the idea to walk to an ice cream parlor in the neighborhood, which seemed fun until they got there and Rapacine asked to taste eight different flavors. But she was so charming the server didn't seem to mind. Earl Grey was the winner. Iris got her usual—black cherry.

They sat on a bench outside the parlor and licked their ice cream cones.

"How is it?"

"Delicious. I can taste they make this ice cream the French way, with eggs, so it is more rich. My mother used to make homemade ice cream for us in the summer. She was a brilliant cook, so inventive, she would use flower petals and their essences in her flavoring, roses, or violet, or lavender. The flavor would be so delicate on your cold spoon, but as it warmed on your tongue, the taste would blossom and fill your mouth with such pleasure."

Iris had never heard her speak of her mother. The memory seemed to bring a melancholy tenderness to her expression, Iris couldn't tell whether the sentiment was sweet or painful.

"Perhaps I should have warned you," Rapacine stated.

"About what?"

"The perfume, it can bring difficulties. You are not wrong. Not everyone has Sofia's happy ending."

"How many others are there?"

Rapacine waved off the question. "Now, no woman reaches adulthood without knowing the dark side of some men's desire, you don't need a perfume for that. That's not the problem—not the new one, at least."

Iris listened but didn't yet follow.

"I told you that my father taught me to be a perfumer. I was a prodigy. As a child, merely from watching him compose at his organ, I could make accords for myself and my friends at school. Soon after he began my formal instruction when I was a young teenager, I was creating fragrances that would sell out in his shop. He was as proud of me as he was jealous.

"My father was a gifted nose, but he was not a good husband or father. Often unfaithful and ill-tempered with my mother and we children. He took no responsibility for his actions, if you got hit, it was because you had it coming. When he was unfaithful, it was because my mother did not take enough care in her appearance to excite him. If only we were better children, or she a better wife, he would be wonderful and shine some of his magic and charm on us. He convinced my mother of this.

"She begged me to make her a *parfum* that would reignite his desire and bring him back to us as the loving family man. I was seventeen years old, even at that age I doubted we could change my father, but I loved my mother and I wanted to help her however I could, so I agreed. Because there is no lovelier smell to a child than the arms of her mother, I challenged myself to make a fragrance that would meld with her unique skin chemistry. I worked in secret, experimenting with many formulas, testing them on her arm, until I perfected it. I named it after her, Clémence. On her skin it was transcendent. She wore it every day. People followed her in the street, men, women, everyone wanted to know what it was about her. The priest she confessed to left the parish." Rapacine smirked. "For a season, she was the most desirable woman in Grasse. And the change in my mother was glorious to watch. I saw her bloom from a shrinking and apologetic woman to one who laughed loudly, danced whenever there was music, and finally relaxed. I never saw her happier."

"And your father, did he like it?"

"*Mais oui.* He dropped the other women and spent much more time at home." Rapacine paused, her pale eyes glassy, glinting in the dark. "Three months later, he killed her."

The words hung in the air like the street lamps, harsh and unblinking.

With a pit in her stomach, Iris asked, "Because he got jealous?"

"Because she left him." Rapacine sighed, then glanced over and pointed to Iris's lap.

Iris's ice cream had melted without her noticing; it dripped over her hand and dotted her legs with cold mauve drops. She wrapped the cone with a napkin.

"Not everyone will like your newfound sense of self, Iris. Someone wanting you does not mean they want you empowered. My mother only thought she wanted the fragrance to keep him, but once she had it, she realized he was no prize. My father was always a danger to her, the perfume did not invent his darkness. He had been psychologically killing her my whole life. She had simply numbed herself to every blow, and so doing, she had numbed herself to every joy and passion and beauty in the world. When you don't feel what hurts you, you cannot feel what gives you pleasure. But numbness is not protection, and after the perfume, she could no longer deny the toll he had taken. The perfume awakened her to the pain he had put her through, how much pleasure she could feel free of him, and how much better she had always deserved."

"Do you wish you hadn't given it to her?"

"No. She and I were innocent. I wish only that he had let her go." Rapacine shook her head. "With your perfume, you may learn things about yourself and others, things about the world, that you have not wanted to face. And for all the scrubbing of your skin, you will not be able to forget." She put her hand on Iris's forearm and gripped tightly. "My warning is not to fear that knowledge. My warning is only to widen your feet for when the ground shakes."

CHAPTER
Forty

I ris walked home digesting all Rapacine had told her, especially the disturbing story about her mother, and what it might mean for her. She remained uncertain about the ethics of wearing the perfume. Sofia had good reason to use it; she had other people's prejudice to overcome. What was Iris's justification for using an assist like this? It felt like she was getting away with something—sometimes thrilling, sometimes shameful. But she didn't want to give up the opportunity with Wolff Dev, Jonathan's esteem, or his paycheck.

And Gabe. She didn't want to give him up either. But something told her he had already given up on her.

When Iris got home, she took a shower to wash the fragrance away; she needed a break. She had just changed into her pajamas and was raking some hair oil through her damp hair when her phone rang. The name on the screen made her heart quicken.

"Ben?"

"Hey, are you home? Your light's on." Ben chuckled. "Sorry, I'm outside."

"What are you doing here?"

"I had a drink with a law school buddy in the neighborhood, so I was just wondering . . . have you taken Hugo out for his last walk yet?"

Iris softened. "Sure, give me a minute, I'll bring him out."

She caught sight of herself in her bedroom mirror: no makeup, wet hair, gym shorts and a Penn State tee—a far cry from the carefully curated eat-your-heart-out attire she wore to Mike's party. She glanced at the perfume's flacon poised on her dresser but decided against it. Iris was done wanting what didn't want her.

Hugo caught Ben's scent before they were out of the lobby, quickening his pace, and when the dog found Ben waiting, Hugo wiggled and whined with happiness. It made her heart twist. Hugo was Iris's most loyal companion, but dogs don't understand breakups.

Ben cut straight to Hugo's favorite tushy scratches. "Didja miss your old man? Dja miss me, good boy?" Ben used his Muppety dog voice, and Hugo happily flopped onto his side for a belly rub. "He looks good!"

Iris fought the urge to melt. "Thanks. He's been keeping busy."

"Has he now?" Ben rose from the sidewalk.

"Six C got a puppy, a Cavapoo named Gracie. I think Hugo has a crush—"

"You're so tan," Ben interrupted her shtick. "I love when your summer freckles are out."

The compliment threw her. "Oh. Um, I was in the Hamptons this weekend." She started walking Hugo to break eye contact.

"Oh yeah, who with?"

"My new boss who built this new Hudson Yards building I'm working on. He invited some team members to his house on Shelter Island. The house was spectacular, it was great." Iris didn't know whether she'd left Gabe out for Ben's benefit or her own.

"New boss? You left Candela?" He stopped in his tracks.

"I got a great offer, and Frank was dragging his feet on my promotion, I couldn't put my career on hold anymore."

Ben blinked. "Wow. Congrats. I'm proud of you. You're too good to be on hold for anyone."

"Thanks." Iris looked down at Hugo.

They walked down the block on the route they knew well, and both Iris and Ben wordlessly adjusted their pace to accommodate Hugo's arthritis and compulsively inquisitive nose. As they strolled, she told him about how exciting it was to work with Wolff Development on such a major building, and Ben told her about negotiating the contract for the Knicks, and they were congratulatory and supportive. When they were together, Ben had always accompanied her on the last dog walk of the night. His protective urge made Iris feel cared for and valued in a way that, until this moment, she had forgotten how much she'd missed.

Hugo tugged toward some trash bags on the curb, tail wagging wildly, and Iris let him investigate. The dog nosedived between two bags and flushed out a giant rat. Iris jumped back with a yelp, Ben flailed to grab her, and the two of them collided, the crown of her head connecting hard with his chin.

Ben stumbled backward, holding his mouth, while Iris apologized profusely.

"I'm fine, I just think I bit my lip," Ben mumbled, nearly tripping again over Hugo, who was feral with excitement.

"Is it bleeding? We'll get ice at home."

In her kitchen, Iris wrapped a baggie of ice cubes in a paper towel, and Ben folded down his lower lip to show her the damage.

"Aw, it looks like it hurts." Iris peered at the cut on his inner lip.

"It doesn't," Ben said, belied by the wince he gave when she touched the ice to it.

"Maybe you need the ice more on your chin, I really beaned you." She tenderly touched his jaw, the intimacy of the gesture zapped her fingers like static electricity. She quickly let go and took a step back. "You hold the ice where you feel it most."

Ben held it to his chin and regarded her, his lower lip swollen to a slight pout. "Iris, I miss you."

"Don't—"

He put the ice down. "It's true. I miss you. I made a mistake, and I want to fix it."

"What about Madison?"

"Things with her moved too fast. I thought fast meant it was good, it was exciting! But we both fell for the idea of each other. Sometimes I feel like she doesn't know me at all. And if she did, she wouldn't like me as much."

The last part was how Iris had felt with Gabe over the weekend.

"But now I think I rushed things because I wanted to feel like I hadn't blown up my life for no reason." Ben rubbed his hand over his head. "I was saying to Mike, sometimes you think you're running toward something, but you're really running away from something else."

"What are you saying?"

"I choked. Our future felt like a foregone conclusion. I felt locked in, and I panicked."

"The contract lawyer afraid of commitment."

"You're right! You're absolutely right, because my whole life is litigation over commitments. I was thinking defensively then. But now I'm coming to you with my guard down. Iris, you know me better than anyone. You've seen me at my best and, God knows, you've seen me at my worst. And you loved me. Is there any chance you could love me still?"

Iris stepped back and tried to exhale through the lump in her throat, tears welling, her mind a jumble of conflicting emotions. "Five years, Ben, you had *five years* to figure out how you felt about me. I believed in you, I built my whole world around you, and you kicked it like sand."

"And I'm sorry. I know, I messed it all up. When we were together, all I felt was pressure. Then we broke up, and all I felt was guilt for hurting you. But now I see you're thriving! And that cloud of guilt has lifted, and I'm free to just feel what's in my heart. And what I want is you in my life again."

It had been exactly what Iris had been wanting to hear for the last six months. And yet she didn't trust his change of heart. "What's so newly attractive about me? What if it's superficial, a new haircut, a new *perfume?* What if I'm exactly the same?"

"How could it ever be superficial with us?"

"This notion that you want me back, did it first occur to you at Mike's party?"

"Yes, I haven't stopped thinking of you since."

She scoffed, suspicions confirmed. "Because there was just *something* different about me, right?"

"Because I felt exactly like I did on the day we met."

She looked into his eyes, the same blue eyes that had haunted so many sleepless nights. The ones that crinkled cutely when he laughed. The eyes she had imagined seeing in their children's faces someday. The ones that had looked bloodshot and sorry when he smashed her heart to pieces. And now these eyes were asking to put her back together again.

Ben kissed her, and her body answered. Her chest rose to meet him, inhaling his familiar scent through her nose, at once so painful and comforting that it broke her heart and mended it again. He smelled like *home*. Ben was the home she had chosen, built brick by brick, and planned on living in forever. This kiss tasted sweeter for the broken dreams it restored. It also tasted like blood.

"Your lip—" She didn't want to hurt him.

"I don't care." He wrapped his arms around her so tightly that he all but lifted her off her feet.

They kissed again, more deeply this time. Her tongue ran over the raised ridge inside his lip, and she thought of all the pain he'd put her through with his indecision, his flip-flopping, all the marks she bore he couldn't see. She sucked his bottom lip between her teeth until he flinched.

Iris pushed herself back from his torso, resentment's bitter metal in her mouth. "No. You can't take it back so easy. You can't play with me—"

Ben didn't let go of her waist. "I'm not, I swear, I wouldn't—"

"How can I trust you?"

"Because it's *me*. Because you know me, I know you, it's us. I need you, Iris. Nothing makes sense without you."

She was whipsawed between craving his reassurance and demanding his remorse. The internal battle left her weak in the knees, but Ben caught her in his embrace. As their passion gained steam, he whispered in her ear, *"Not here."* He wouldn't take her in the kitchen like Gabe might have. She wasn't a fling to be rushed. She was someone who mattered. She was *the one*.

She collapsed toward him and he gathered her up into his arms. Iris wrapped her legs around his waist and buried her face in the crook of his neck, kissing the delicate skin there, feeling the butterfly-wing beat of his pulse against her lips, her lashes, as he carried her toward the bedroom.

Their bedroom. Could it all go back like it was?

Ben peeled her top off as soon as her feet touched the hardwood. She was eager and yielding to him but not the aggressor. She needed to see that he wanted her, that it wasn't a passing urge, old habit, or one thing leading to another. Iris didn't help him to undress her. She let him see that her figure wasn't tiny and taut like Madison's. She hadn't gotten a postbreakup revenge body. She wasn't wearing the perfume. She was only herself. Would he still want her back?

And yet Ben cupped her breasts with awe like it was the first time. He took them into his mouth in turn, savoring them, his tongue was delicate on her nipple but his fingers kneaded greedily into the flesh of her backside. She preferred his greed. His validation fed her like water to a wilted flower. She undid his fly and reached into his boxers, and her hand closed around the hard proof of his desire, making him moan. The reassurance of his body responding to her hit her system like a drug, it numbed the agony of their breakup and anesthetized the painful self-doubt and self-reproach that had racked her brain since the weekend. Ben wanted her back, so she had to be all right.

He kissed a trail from her throat to her heart to her belly and below, until he was kneeling before her, a supplicant with a handful of ass. She ran her fingers through his hair as he parted her legs and tilted her head back as he tasted her. The sight of him on his knees reignited her anger without dulling her desire. *You* should *kneel and be sorry, after what you did, fucking beg for me.* His desperation was the turn-on, she craved his penitence as much as his cock. He had wronged her and she demanded satisfaction. She turned her back on him, and without hesitation, he gripped her hips and buried his face in her bottom. His stubble tickled her butt cheeks, his hot tongue tickled her elsewhere. She giggled in embarrassed delight.

Ben stopped when she laughed. "Was that wrong?"

Iris silenced him with one look over her shoulder, and he went back to it. When she crawled farther onto the bed, he followed like a puppy.

Ben pulled over a pillow to slide under her stomach—a signature of their old routine and his favorite doggy position, not hers. But Iris was getting what she wanted this time, and she wanted to see his face when she did. In one swift motion, she swung her legs over him, trading places and straddling him. She rocked back on her heels and in a deliberate, catlike motion trailed the softness of her naked body from his furry thighs up to his flushing neck, teasing him. While he kissed whatever part of her his mouth could reach, she snatched a condom from her nightside and slid it on.

Ben gasped when she brought him inside her, and his brow furrowed in helpless pleasure as she ground deeper onto him. His reaction made her buckle over him, a mewling kitten again.

"Don't you want me? Tell me you want me," she whimpered in his ear.

And he told her over and over again that he did.

She rocked back on top of him, reached behind, and gripped his balls.

Ben's head popped off the pillow. "Whoa there, cowgirl."

She threw hers back to stop herself from rolling her eyes at him. Ben could be so corny, but his dick felt good.

Iris went back and forth like this, yielding all power to him one minute and then clawing it back the next, sometimes with her nails in his back. Ben must have felt he was having sex not with one woman, but two; the first a desperate pleaser willing to do anything to win his approving moan, the second a selfish hedonist who sat on his face longer than a man could do without oxygen. Either way, Ben couldn't get enough. For him it was win-win, but he was the toy, not the player. Iris was battling her own conflicting needs. Did she want his validation, or his atonement?

Iris decided to take both.

CHAPTER

Forty-one

Morning sunlight streamed in through the top of Iris's half shades, casting lemon squares across the ceiling. But Iris had been awake since the morning was still blue. Not Ben, who remained deeply asleep, snoring. Iris stretched like a starfish, reminding herself she could wake leisurely, without a care for whether the perfume had lasted the night. She didn't need it for Ben. He loved the real her.

But other than that, Iris didn't feel as happy as she had expected. The room felt stale, all shut up with the air conditioner never quite cycling on the ideal temperature, condensation clinging to the unit like a cave wall. The rumpled bedding needed changing, doubly so after last night. She rested her face on her hands and observed the man whose absence had felt so acute over the last six months, and whose presence now took up more room in the bed than she'd remembered. She noticed the little things she had missed: his charming bedhead, his long lashes knitted like a toddler's, the freckles across his shoulders that disappeared into his appealing chest hair. But also things she had forgotten: the funky scent of his scalp in the morning, with an inexplicable note of rubber bands; the small, crusty hairs inside his nose visible from this angle; the occasional rumble in his stomach that made her think unpleasantly of his bowels. She scolded herself for being so hard on him. Ben was human! He'd made mistakes and learned from them, as Iris had too. There was a comfort now in knowing, maybe for the first time, that he was as imperfect as she.

But something remained unsettled within her. She wondered if it was discomfort that the clock had been wound back so easily—did she want *more* from Ben? In her gut, her answer was clear.

Ben stirred with a long zip of a sniff in, squeezing his eyes shut before opening them like a hatchling. When his focus found her, his face softened into a sleepy smile. "Hello. It's so nice to wake up to you again."

Her heart felt heavy. "Your lip looks better."

He yawned. "Last night was so wild. *I ate your ass.*"

"You don't have to whisper, and it was for like a second."

"It was several seconds, maybe even half a minute. I was into it! I didn't think I would be, but I was." Ben looked so proud of himself.

Iris covered her face with her hands and laughed.

"See? That's why I know you're the one, because look how long we've known each other, and there's still more to discover." He squeezed her butt. "Unplumbed depths. We can try that next time."

Iris hit him with a pillow. She wasn't sure he had surprised *her*, really, aside from showing up. Though she certainly had surprised herself.

Suddenly Ben pushed back from her, looking down at her belly with concern. "What's this bruise? Did I do this last night?"

Iris realized he was talking about the bruising around her injection sites, a new development. "Oh, no, it's nothing."

"There's another one. Iris, be honest. Did somebody hurt you? I'll kill him."

"No, the truth is . . . I recently started the process of freezing my eggs."

"What, *why*?"

"Asks the guy who dumped me in my mid-thirties."

He cringed. "So you're trying to have a baby?"

"Not this instant. But after we broke up, I didn't know when I'd be in a relationship to start trying, and I don't want to miss my chance. I want to give myself options."

Ben pushed himself up to a seated position and raked his hands over his head. "I feel horrible. This is all my fault."

She had longed for this remorse, but hearing him apologize now, her anger was spent. "Don't. I'm doing this for myself."

"Have you gone through with it yet?"

"I started the hormone injections, hence the bruises, and I have a little over a week more until my retrieval procedure."

"Can you cancel?"

"Ben, no." She gave an irritated laugh. "I've invested a lot in this. The train has left the station."

"But I'm back. You're back on track again. We can do this the *right* way."

"There is no track. There's no right way."

"So, what are you saying? We're back together, but you're freezing your eggs in case we break up again? I know I have to earn your trust, but—"

"No. What I'm saying is . . ." Iris took a deep breath. "Ben, I don't want to get back together. I'm sorry."

Ben stared at her slack-jawed. "Is this about the other guy—?"

"No, that's . . . already over." Her voice caught.

He threw up his hands. "Then I don't get it! What the hell was last night?"

"I didn't know last night. I needed last night to figure it out."

"So last night was some kind of test that I failed?" Ben shook his head bitterly.

"I thought it was a test for you. But it was a test for me." Iris scooted up to face him directly and put a hand on his knee. "Ben, you were right not to propose. We fell in love and we had something real and special for a long time. But somewhere along the way, that love stopped growing. We stopped growing. Back then, all I wanted was your love and your approval, because I couldn't feel any of my own. I made everything about whether or not you would choose me, whether I was worthy of you and your family, like our whole relationship was a yardstick for me to measure myself. So when you didn't pick me, it broke me."

Tears filled his eyes. "I never wanted to hurt you."

"I know. It wasn't fair of me to put it all on you, because something was holding me back too. I couldn't see it then, or maybe I just didn't want to—because any woman would be lucky to have you and sorry to lose you, and I was both. But you were right, something is missing, and we both deserve to want more."

Ben seemed frozen, processing everything, then rebooted with a long, shaky breath. "This is all I wanted you to understand last winter." He looked mournfully up at her. "Your timing sucks."

Iris laughed through her tears. "I'm sorry. Better late than never?"

He snorted and gave a nod. "I'm sad, but part of me feels relieved. I'll still miss you though, and Hugo."

"We can be friends. For real this time."

They shared a sincere, tearful embrace. And for the first time in years, Iris and Ben were in perfect sync.

Ben turned down her offer of coffee; they simply dressed quietly, he in his clothes from the night before, Iris in underwear and an Eagles T-shirt, and hugged one last time. When she finally heard her exterior door latch shut, she fell back on her bed like a squashed bug, and something cold poked her in her back. Iris reached behind her and felt Ben's belt buckle. Not wanting him to have to come back, Iris darted to the window to call to him, but who she saw on the sidewalk below knocked her backward like a punch.

Gabe.

Gabe had locked his bike to the parking sign outside her building and was pacing in front of it, holding a paper-wrapped bouquet of flowers in front of his chest. It looked like he was talking to himself. Iris craned her neck to see the building's awning outside the lobby, and to her horror, Ben had moseyed from beneath it while making unbothered small talk with her doorman, Sammy. With Ben walking backward and Gabe lost in some inner monologue, the two men collided on the sidewalk.

Iris dropped from the window as if ducking gunfire. Then remembered the men were strangers. They knew *of* each other, but neither knew what the other looked like. She peered over the windowsill and saw the two men already walking away from each other. Iris was in the clear. Except:

Why is Gabe here? Duh, to see her. And he had flowers, so he probably was *not* there to say, "I think we should open our relationship and I encourage you to have sex with your ex-boyfriend." She did a quick scan of her bedroom—it looked obviously postcoital. It smelled that way too.

Iris whipped the bedclothes off the bed and crammed them into her hamper. Looking like you hadn't done laundry was better than looking like you hadn't been faithful.

Her buzzer going off made her jump. Then she caught a glimpse of herself in her full-length mirror and the thatch of tangled hair at the back of her head. She lunged for an alligator clip and gathered the hair within it—*not bad,* she thought, why could she never get volume like this on a normal—

Buzzzz!

Fuck. She stumbled over her shoes in the hallway and lunged for the telecom.

"Gabe's here," Sammy's voice crackled, his tone professionally flat, betraying nothing. She made a mental note to up his Christmas tip.

"Oh? Thanks, Sammy, tell him I'll be a minute."

She darted to the bathroom, yanked on a bathrobe, and rushed to open the door.

But it wasn't Gabe standing in her hallway, it was Sammy, holding a newspaper-wrapped pot of purple orchids.

Sammy thrust the flowers in her direction. "Gabe left this for you, there's a card."

She took them, thanked him, and closed the door, leaning against it in relief. Was it relief, or deflation? It felt the same.

Iris pulled the pot out of the box and unwrapped the newsprint to reveal a round ceramic vase painted a rich lapis blue but cut through with veins of gold. She ran her hand over its cool, elegantly curved surface and found that the precious metal had melded perfectly to every seam. The vessel appeared even more lovely and organic than the delicate fuchsia blooms it housed.

She opened the card, a postcard from Brooklyn Gather, and read what Gabe had written in his boyish scrawl:

Dear Iris,

Kintsugi is the Japanese art of repairing broken pottery with real gold, which I learned from a white lady in Rhode Island.

More importantly, I'm sorry I was an ass this weekend. You did everything you could to show me that you were proud to be with me, and somehow I convinced myself of the opposite. I didn't feel worthy to be with you, and the more I felt myself falling short, the more sure I was you thought that too. My cracks were showing, so I did what I always do in the hot shop—smash it and start over.

But I don't want to start anything that doesn't end with you.

I'm not perfect (clearly!) I carry all kinds of baggage and my communication sucks. But next time it gets hard, I promise to stay and fix it with you. If you give me the chance to make it up to you, I'll heal every crack with gold.

Your Kintsugi lover,
Gabe

Base Notes

Base notes give a perfume its depth, longevity, and resonance. These foundational notes take the most time to reveal themselves and linger long after the rest of the fragrance has faded. Sometimes called the "body" of the fragrance, base notes meld with the skin and anchor the perfume's heart and head to prolong the scent accord. This category typically draws from resins, woods, and musks and includes ingredients that may be unpleasant or even offensive in isolation, like civet, indoles, ambergris, or oud; however, incorporated as base notes, their earthy and animalic qualities provide an essential harmony that enhances the complex beauty of the fragrance entire.

Forty-two

I ris was back under the bright lights of Dr. Alsarraj's exam room at Family Tree Fertility for yet another vaginal ultrasound. It was her fourth in the process and they still made her incredibly tense. She distracted herself by mentally redesigning the lighting; if they replaced these compact fluorescent panels in the drop ceiling with adjustable LEDs, maybe she wouldn't feel like a laboratory specimen. Her nostrils itched with that hospital-clean smell, lemony antiseptic and saline. These appointments were the only place she didn't wear the perfume.

"Hm," Dr. Alsarraj vocalized as he peered at the ultrasound screen, delicately steering the wand inside her. The sound was too short to interpret as positive or negative, perhaps he was unaware he had made a noise at all. But in this office, even an unsaid observation could send Iris's anxiety spiraling.

"Hmm?" she intoned upward. "Everything okay?"

"Nothing bad, just . . ." Dr. Alsarraj trailed off, lost in the shifting sonar orbs on the black screen. He moved the wand again, this time at an awkward angle, and Iris let out a little grunt of discomfort—

"Unh."

"Sorry." Dr. Alsarraj grimaced in sympathy but didn't take his eyes off the screen. "Although increasing tenderness is actually a good sign. It means things are growing."

Iris nodded and looked at the ceiling.

"All done." Dr. Alsarraj slipped the wand out and popped off its jellied condom cover with a sticky *squick* and tossed it into the trash.

Iris snapped her knees shut and sat up, the paper crinkled noisily, only amplifying her self-consciousness.

Dr. Alsarraj didn't seem to notice his patient's embarrassment, or he was just used to it. "I'll let you get dressed, and we'll meet in my office to discuss."

Normally the routine of going to Dr. Alsarraj's well-appointed office for the debrief allowed Iris to decompress, but with today's frowning and hmming, the suspense was killing her. Her knee bounced as she sat on the edge of the wing chair.

Dr. Alsarraj took a seat behind the desk and began, "So, we're deeper into our cycle. You have three follicles in each ovary, which is pretty good. But they're lagging in size. I'm going to up the progesterone. You may notice a greater change in your mood and emotionality, you may feel irritable and depressed. Obviously if the depression is severe, thoughts of self-harm, you need to contact my office immediately. But that isn't typical. Have you noticed any of these side effects so far?"

Iris gave a weary exhale. "I've had some more personal drama than I normally would."

"Yes, husbands and boyfriends hate me."

How about ex-boyfriends, bosses, and gay best friends? "I've noticed I've been more impulsive lately. Is that a side effect?"

That *hmm* again. "Most women find their emotions are more at the surface, so you may be more reactive. But not to worry. Very soon, this will all be over, and you'll go back to being your normal, agreeable self."

"I didn't say 'disagreeable.'" Iris didn't mean to say that thought aloud.

Dr. Alsarraj broke into a smile. "Fair! I speak from my daughters' experience. And believe me, a know-it-all dad to his twentysomething daughter on hormone therapy? There is always occasion to disagree."

"She froze her eggs in her twenties?"

"Twenty-five. The sooner, the better." Dr. Alsarraj must have seen her face fall because he added, "But don't worry, you're doing fine. We're going to get you in the best possible shape for your trigger shot and oocyte retrieval at the end of next week. And if we don't get a sufficient yield, we can always consider another cycle."

Iris was on her way out when the receptionist, Kathleen, jogged out from the front desk partition to catch up with her. Kathleen spoke in an extra-hushed tone, even for a fertility clinic's waiting room. "Your credit card was declined for today's medicine order. Do you have another I could try?"

"Oh, sorry, I um, made some large purchases this week, they probably put it on hold for fraud," Iris lied. The way these medical charges racked up, she needed to call Visa and raise the limit. "I don't have another, though, and I'm in a bit of a rush, so can you just add it to my tab? We can get paid up when it's working again."

"Of course! No worries. And you can always pay by check, too."

"Great idea, thanks." Iris thanked her and wondered how soon that signing bonus from Wolff's term sheet would hit her account.

Her phone rang. It was Hannah. She silenced the ringer and quickly exited the office to answer it. She knew something was wrong as soon as she heard Hannah's tearful tone of voice.

"Iris, can you come over? Something terrible happened!"

Iris's stomach dropped. "With the baby?"

"No," Hannah whimpered. "It's Mike."

Forty-three

Iris poured Hannah a fresh glass of iced tea, wishing she could make her friend something stronger. The two friends were huddled close, shrinking Hannah's spacious, grown-up living room to the dimensions of the summer camp bunk they once happily shared. Hannah lay back on the couch with a pillow propped under her knees, one arm draped over her belly and the other draped over her eyes, and Iris sat on the ottoman beside her. Iris tapped Hannah to hand her the glass and helped her to sit upright to take a sip. Hannah sighed gratefully and held it to her forehead, her face blotchy from tears.

"They suspended him, can you believe that? Without even hearing his side of things!" Hannah rolled the sweating glass across her brow.

A sexual harassment complaint had been made against Mike at the firm, a serious one. An unnamed summer associate had accused Mike of making unwanted sexual advances and, when she didn't acquiesce, blocking her from receiving an offer from the firm.

"Where's Mike now?"

"He's meeting with an employment lawyer, someone his dad knows. But I mean, where's the due process? How can they do this? They're *lawyers*!" Hannah's eyes flashed with anger, then her face crumpled. "But the timing couldn't be worse, right before the baby? Like there isn't enough stress."

"That's why you can't take it all on. I'm sure there's a process, and it will get resolved in time."

"It's all a big misunderstanding! You know Mike, he's friendly and he loves to joke around, he's a prankster! He comes from a big family, everyone's handsy and always hanging off each other, it doesn't mean anything. The younger generations are crazy now, so easily offended. I sound like a boomer, but I hear it from the teachers at the high school, they call it 'the victim Olympics.' I didn't used to agree, but . . ." Hannah covered her face with her hands. "I'm really scared."

"I know—" Iris began, but Hannah cut her off:

"I'm scared he's not gonna get a fair shake. This is starting to feel cancel-culturey, you know what I mean?"

"How so?"

Hannah groaned. "I don't even want to say it."

"It's just me."

"We heard the woman who accused him is Black . . ."

Iris immediately thought of Toni, the memories of Mike leaning close when she arrived at their office and how quickly Toni shrank away, or Toni saying she was eager to work with different partners, suddenly cast in a new light.

Hannah continued, "And now, you know, normally her race wouldn't even cross my mind, what difference does it make? I'm a New York City public school teacher, you *know* I'm not like"—she widened her eyes—*"racist."*

"No, I know." Iris's thoughts lingered on how she had misread their dynamic. She had mistaken Toni's facial expression of shame for complicit guilt, while Mike remained so unbothered, Iris had overlooked that he'd had Toni cornered. *How do men always manage to transfer* their *shame to the women they abuse?* But Iris refocused on Hannah. "Sorry, but how do you think race is a factor?"

"I just wonder *if* it is. She's a young Black woman from an elite law school, it can't be easy! But maybe past difficulty has made her a little hypersensitive, so Mike says something stupid, and it triggers her?"

Iris frowned. "I guess that's possible, but . . . sensitive to sexual harassment?"

"Or maybe another way—college and grad schools value diversity, maybe she's used to being a favored applicant, you know? Then she gets to a real-world law firm where the standards are higher, and when she doesn't get an offer, she jumps to a conclusion—racism, sexism, some '-ism' must be the reason why she wasn't picked. And it's sad, because flimsy accusations like this are unfair to the many *real* victims of prejudice."

It pained Iris to hear her best friend go down this track. This wasn't the progressive-minded, big-hearted Hannah she knew and loved. "It's probably more complicated than that. But there are lots of ways a misunderstanding can happen."

"But will it be treated as a misunderstanding? I'm just afraid the partners will want to look like heroes standing up for diversity and equality against the privileged white guy rather than do a real investigation. But he's not a demographic, he's *Mike!*"

"Hannah, I get what you're saying. But I'm sure she's more than her demo too. We don't have enough information."

"We know Mike would never do this. But you're right, we don't know who the accuser is, they're protecting her identity."

Iris faced the cost of her lies of omission, the same she'd foolishly thought would protect Hannah. "Well, I may have met her when I went to Mike's office for Rapacine's case, I think she's his summer associate."

Hannah shook her head. "No, his summer is Tony."

Iris kept her voice gentle. "Toni, with an *i*, short for Antoinette. She's a Black woman."

Hannah's mouth hung open a beat. Then she snapped back, "Okay, so I assumed Toni was a guy, my mistake. But it doesn't matter, because the accusation isn't true! This isn't Mike. I know my husband. He would never do something like this—What, you disagree?"

Iris looked at her questioningly. "I didn't say anything."

"I know, but you had, like, a look, a wavering look. What?"

Iris began to protest but stopped. Hannah might not know her husband, but she knew Iris. "I think he's been under a lot of stress lately, and maybe he hasn't been entirely himself."

"What are you saying? Did something happen?"

Iris's chest was tight. She had envisioned this conversation many times and debated it, mostly on the basis of whether it would hurt Hannah to hear. But now that the moment had arrived, she realized her hesitation was less altruistic. Iris was afraid for herself, afraid of losing their friendship. She feared that Hannah wouldn't believe her, and even if she did, couldn't forgive her.

"Tell me," Hannah commanded.

Iris's hands shook as she told the story. "At the end of Mike's birthday party, everyone had left, you fell asleep on the couch, so I got you to bed. And then it was just Mike and me. I was helping clean up in the kitchen—" She could see each beat so vividly, and she didn't want to leave out any detail that could help Hannah understand. "And remember, I was wearing that halter dress that was tied at my neck? So, I was bent forward loading the dishwasher, and he . . . undid my dress at the back."

"As a joke," Hannah provided, but her eyes were less certain.

"That's what I thought. I didn't like it, but I laughed, because it was a weird joke. And he said he'd fix it, and I let him, because I couldn't hold the front up and untangle and retie it at the same time. And so he did. Tie it."

"Oh-kay."

"But then he took me by the shoulders and turned me around and he kissed me, by force."

"What?" Hannah's eyes flared.

"He pinned me against the counter and kissed me. It happened so fast, it took me completely by surprise."

"Then what happened?"

"I hit him."

Hannah's jaw dropped. "He had a red welt on his cheek the next morning. He said he hit a cabinet door by accident. That was *you*?"

"I didn't mean to, it was just animal instinct. I whacked him, and I told him off, and he said it was a dumb, drunken impulse, and I went home."

Hannah put her head in her hands.

"Please, I need you to know I didn't want it to happen and I didn't reciprocate. I would never, ever do that to you. I don't know why he thought I'd be open to it, if he thought at all—"

"And you didn't tell me?" Tears sprang to Hannah's eyes.

Iris, too, fought back tears. "I didn't know what the right thing to do was, please, I went back and forth, I wanted to tell you, but I didn't want to hurt you."

"This is a huge thing to keep from me."

"I didn't know what good it would do! I thought it was just a fluke. It was a party, his party, he'd definitely drunk too much. It seemed out of character for him. I know he loves you like crazy, so—"

"Wait. You were wearing the perfume that night. Weren't you?"

"Yeah—for Ben, like you and I planned."

"But it's not like it only works on ex-boyfriends. It works on all men."

"Yes, that's another reason I didn't tell you! I thought it could have provoked him, accidentally. Like, it was my fault."

Hannah closed her eyes, and tears slipped down her cheeks.

Iris's entire body shivered with adrenaline. She felt certain Hannah was going to end their friendship over this. It would be a more painful breakup than Ben by miles. Hannah was her chosen family.

Hannah's lips trembled. "You're my best friend, Iris. I consider you a sister."

Iris's heart twisted in agony. "I know, please believe that's why I would never—"

Hannah held up her hand, silencing Iris. She looked livid. "How *could* he? I don't care if you were buck naked and begging to suck his dick, my husband should not even *look* at my best friend like that. That's a bright red line."

Iris was dumbstruck. "You're not mad?"

"Of course I'm mad, I'm fucking furious! But at Mike, not at you. Come over here, I'm too pregnant to get up to hug you."

Iris squeezed beside her on the couch to accept her friend's embrace. She didn't realize how much she'd been holding in until she let go. Her relief was overwhelming. She sobbed in Hannah's arms.

"Aw, honey, I know it wasn't your fault. I don't blame you, truly," Hannah said.

The tidal wave of emotion passed, and Iris dried her face before pulling back to where her best friend could see. She needed to be strong for Hannah now, not the other way around. She managed to croak out a "Thank you" and blew her nose.

Hannah gave her shoulder a last squeeze before she slumped back on the couch. She pressed her hands over her eyes like a child wanting to keep the baddies out. When that didn't work, a groan of frustration erupted. "If Mike doesn't respect that line in our own home, with me asleep in the other room, how can I believe he'd toe the line at work? Help me up, I need to move." Iris got her to her feet and Hannah began to pace. "Does this mean it's fucking *true*?"

Iris didn't know how to answer.

Hannah's hands flew to her mouth. "Omigod, he had me sounding like a racist bitch making excuses for him. I'm so embarrassed."

"I know you didn't mean it. This is a lot to take in. Did you ask Mike about the allegations?"

"Of course I did! I'm not looking the other way, Iris, I asked him directly, and he told me there's nothing to it. *At all.* He was completely blindsided." Hannah rubbed her stomach. "And he was drinking a lot at his birthday, he always overdoes it. I mean, he was trashed when he tried to kiss you, right?"

Iris gave the answer her friend needed. "He wasn't sober."

"And I'm not saying that makes what he did to you okay, it doesn't. But it's an important distinction. And he's obviously sober at work. So."

Iris could only watch as her friend's clarity unraveled. "You don't believe he harassed her."

"I can't." Hannah shook her head. "It can't be true. Not right now."

"Whatever happens, you can handle. I'll help you."

"I can't have a family without him, Iris."

"You can, though."

"I don't want to."

Iris looked down at the floor.

"This can't be true of my daughter's father."

At that, Iris's eyes filmed with a more tender emotion. "It's a girl?"

Hannah met her gaze with a face torn between joy and agony, the last secret between the best friends now revealed.

Forty-four

I ris's nostrils began to flare before she even entered Rapacine's brownstone apartment building. A musty funk filled the vestibule as she punched in the entry code, and Iris surmised the landlord had left garbage in the hall again. But when she crossed the threshold, she found the hallway clean and the stench unbearable. Her hand flew to cover her nose and mouth as her entire body revolted at the putrid odor and the emotion that accompanied it: fear.

It smelled like death.

Iris banged on Rapacine's door and called her name. She had feared this scenario since she first started helping the older woman during the awful early days of the pandemic.

At last the door swung open, and Rapacine stood there in a wide-brimmed straw hat and equally wide-eyed alarm. "What is happening?"

"Oh thank God." Iris steadied herself on the doorframe. "Are you okay? What the hell died in here?"

"You thought it was *me*? I am insulted." Rapacine tutted. "One, I am not *that* old. And two, even my corpse will smell like flowers."

Iris spoke through her shirt she had now pulled up and over her nose. "Please, I gotta get out of this hallway."

"Come, it's better at the back."

. . .

In the garden, Iris let herself inhale. "Have you considered calling the police?"

Rapacine had gotten distracted by some weeds. "For what?"

"For the smell! The garbage was bad, but this is next level. They must have brought a dead animal or something."

"There is no dead body of any species, I can assure you of that. It is merely a malodor. And a stink is not a crime. I googled it."

"How are you so unbothered?"

Rapacine waved her hand in dismissal. "Did you know that no smell is objectively or inherently unpleasant? Scent is the most teachable sense of all. From a young age we learn to associate each scent with a memory and categorize it as good or bad based on that. Scent is our first signal to bond, to our mother, to her breast—or to avoid, a stranger, or a food that made us ill. It is not the smell of decaying flesh which repulses us, it is the *association* of death. It is only our own mortality that repulses us." She put the last of the weeds into a brown paper bag and joined Iris at the garden table. "And anyway, in fifteen minutes, your nose will go blind to it. In about eighteen hours the scent will be gone completely. The building appraiser came today."

"Why would they stink-bomb the place on the day of their appraisal?"

Rapacine poured herself a glass of wine. "Because they didn't make the stink. *I* did."

Iris looked at her, stunned. Then she could only laugh. "I have bad news for your case. My lawyer friend who was helping you, he's been put on leave. And I'm afraid his summer associate will also be unavailable. But don't worry, I'm gonna help you find another tenants' rights lawyer. Mike thought he could get you a buyout."

"If I wanted money, I would've taken their previous offers."

"What previous offer?"

"The last was about one hundred thousand dollars."

Iris mouth hung open. "You turned down six figures?"

"Of course."

"Why?"

"Because I don't want the money! This is my home, it has been for three decades, it is priceless to me. You can't let people push you around. It is not right what they are doing to me, and I will not give in. I will leave on my own terms or on God's terms. Money is not God."

"They're not gonna stop, Madame. And you fighting back is only going to escalate their anger. If you won't consider any buyout, they have no motivation to play ball with you. I don't even know if a lawyer could help you."

"I don't need any more lawyers, and I don't need help. You must recognize when you have power, Iris, and you must not be afraid to use it. Others will try to scare you into believing you are helpless. It's a lie."

"But they *can* overpower you. They're bigger, richer, they can out-litigate you, they can evict you. You have something they want, very, very badly. And they'll be ruthless in their pursuit of getting it. They've already shown a willingness to harass you! I know you love this place, but that's clouding your judgment."

"Love is never a weakness. Conviction has led many outnumbered armies to victory."

Iris threw up her hands. "It's not how the real world works, I'm sorry."

"Ah *vraiment*? I can think of some real-world examples. What does the tree frog do? What does the skunk? If they insist on trying to eat me, I will make myself *noxious*." Rapacine banged her fist on the table.

Iris took a deep breath. Mireille Rapacine was either the dumbest or the most inspiring woman she knew, probably both.

Rapacine was so worked up that she'd sprung from the table. Barefoot in the grass in a linen slip dress, her gray, wavy hair flowing over tan, speckled shoulders, the muscles of her wiry arms flexing as she parried an invisible enemy with a finger like an épée. She looked as delicate as a fairy and as furious as a wildcat. "It is not strong to take without permission. That is brutishness, not strength. Strength is to be the one who is taken from and yet continues on. I am a woman. I have been taken from my whole life. And I am still here. I am a force!"

Forty-five

Iris approached the gate to GATHER BROOKLYN at dusk. The setting sun was bright as hot iron, casting orange light on the alleyway. Gabe was sitting in a lawn chair on the driveway, drinking a beer beside a fellow artist with a shaved head. When Iris crossed the threshold, Gabe perked up like a Labrador.

She held up a hand, a wave of hello and surrender.

Gabe sprang up and bounded to her, his smile softening every edge of his chiseled face.

"I wanted to—" but before Iris could finish, he swept her up in an embrace with such enthusiasm he nearly tossed her over his shoulder. She laughed and gripped his muscled back.

Still holding her bottom in a bear hug, Gabe looked up at her, his eyebrows a gable roof over imploring eyes. "Are you still my girl?"

Her heart felt like it might burst, and she nodded, her tension melting as she relaxed into his grasp.

Gabe sighed and set her down, enveloping her in his arms and his scent, that deep yet tender accord of resinous woodsmoke and skin musk, which stirred her soul.

"Pax, you close up!" Gabe reached into his pocket and tossed his keys to them.

They stumbled into Gabe's apartment in a tangle of arms, kisses, and, for Iris, tippytoe steps. She heard his keys clatter to the hardwood and felt him kick the door shut behind them. Between kisses and nips, they undressed each other with giddy exuberance. The rush of joy and anticipation at being back in each other's arms bubbled between them like teenagers with the house to themselves. They kicked off shoes, tossed shirts, and slingshotted her bra. But when Gabe slid her jean shorts down her hips, he glimpsed the black-and-blue spots and winced in sympathy.

"What's—?"

Iris remembered all she had wanted to say to him before he'd swept her off her feet. "Let's talk a minute."

Gabe handed her his shirt so she wasn't so naked, and they both sat on the edge of his bed in their underwear. No pretenses and, as Iris had decided, no perfume.

Iris began, "Your note and the vase meant a lot to me, because I'm not perfect either, but I hide the cracks really well. And I want to be honest with you, because I want what we have to be real, even if it's not as pretty."

He nodded.

"Those bruises are from injections because I'm preparing to freeze my eggs. So I may have been edgy with you last weekend, I'm on all these hormones. I hid it from you because I didn't want you to think I would rush things or pressure you to get serious. I didn't want you to think I was unsexy, or old, or desperate. I'm none of those things. But I am thirty-five, with lower than average fertility, and I want a family someday in whatever way I can have one. Believe me, I'm not rushing anything, it's too important, but I *am* looking for something serious. Even that, 'something serious,' is so vague—I'm looking for *forever* with somebody reliably great, who will love me the way I deserve. And if any part of that scares you, I get it, no judgment, no hard feelings. You can walk away, the sooner the better, honestly—"

"We're in my apartment."

"I mean it, I—" Iris rose to her bare feet.

"Iris." Gabe caught her arm, but instead of pulling her back down, he stood too. He cupped her face. "I love you. And that makes me not afraid of anything."

They kissed and fell together back to the bed. He undressed her again, and she covered the ugly black-and-blue marks with her hands. But Gabe gently removed each hand one at a time and kissed her palms. Then he lowered himself to kiss each bruise with lips as light as falling leaves. There was no question tonight that he wanted her, his body thrummed with desire from the fluttering pulse in his neck to the bulging veins snaking down his lower abdomen, but from then on, he was careful with her, delicate. He touched her not as if she were fragile, but precious.

The lighter his caress, the more hypersensitive she became; goosebumps shimmered on her arms, her chest swelled, and her nipples tightened and rose, every inch of her skin yearning to reach him. Gabe didn't tease, but he moved slow. Her belly quaked as a shiver of pleasure sped down her spine. When he guided her onto his lap, he gripped her hips securely but never let his thumbs press one of the painful spots. Instead, he slid his hands up her waist to almost lift her, so she felt weightless as she rocked on him. When she arched back, he held her, and when waves of sensation made her cave toward him, he met her chest to chest. When they rolled and he hovered over her with his muscular arms on either side, she didn't feel caged, she felt protected.

Iris knew there was still so much untested between them and uncertainty that Gabe could be the man she wanted and needed him to be. They would have more fights, more misunderstandings, more discussions. And she knew she hadn't said "I love you" back. She felt the emotion coursing through her, but she couldn't trust it yet. Her heart was still tender, even if its bruises didn't show.

But for now, words were superfluous. Whatever needed to be said could be touched, whatever needed to be heard could be felt. Asking with a fingertip, answering with raised hips. Apologizing with softly parted lips, accepting with tightening thighs. The message was equally if not better expressed that way. Not loud and clear, but deep and warm.

Until all was understood, and all was forgiven.

.   .   .

Iris awoke the next morning with a deep sniff in before she opened her eyes. She inhaled the cottony musk of their bedsheets, warmed by their bodies and the sunlight that now slipped through the cracks in her knitted lashes. She roused herself, stretched her arms wide, and patted the soft rumpled bedding beside her to find Gabe missing. Her first thought was like ice water—that he had changed his mind and abandoned her. But then she smelled something else, an aroma that put a smile on her face: coffee.

Gabe rounded the corner of the sleeping alcove, surprising her by being fully dressed in Levi's, a white tee, and her light scarf around his neck. He was holding two cups in one hand and a large brown paper bag in the other.

"Mmm, you got coffee," Iris cooed. "I like the accessorizing."

Gabe set the coffees down on the bedside table. "It smells like you." He drew the scarf across his face with a smile. "And that perfume you always wear."

Without a sip of caffeine, she was wide awake. "I'm not wearing any perfume."

"Maybe it's just you, then. I can't get enough of it."

When he kissed Iris hello, she slipped the scarf from his neck and brought it to her nose. She smelled the faint but familiar contours of the perfume, like an echo of the scent—this time it filled her with despair. She didn't want to believe it had played a role in Gabe's feelings last night. So she lied, "I don't smell anything."

"Maybe you're too used to it."

She frowned at the thought that it might smell stronger to him. Now she wondered anew if she could trust her nose—or her boyfriend.

"Hungry?"

Iris pushed the doubts out of her mind. It was only a scarf, it had spent most of the night somewhere on the floor. "Now that you mention it, starving."

He reached into the bag, pulled out a white cardboard box tied with string, and handed it to Iris. "Get it while it's hot."

She took the box; it was too heavy to be muffins or croissants, and the cardboard bottom was so warm, she felt the heat on her thighs through the sheets. She shot a puzzled glance at Gabe, who remained impishly silent, and pulled the cotton string. She opened it to reveal a fresh-baked whole pie, releasing a mouthwatering aroma of toasty, buttery pastry and a caramelized berry sweetness that was bubbling through the golden-brown crust in dark veins of sticky sugar.

Her stomach growled in response. "Do you have a knife? I'll cut you a slice."

Gabe produced two forks and handed her one. "Who needs slices anyway? This is just for us."

He stripped naked and jumped into bed, bouncing her as she giggled and kept the pie upright. They cozied up next to each other, sitting up against the headboard, and dug in, Gabe first. It felt sacrilegious to defile a pie this way. But it simply smelled too good to resist, and she too poked her fork in the center, shamelessly breaking the sparkly sugared crust and digging into the soft, steaming blueberry filling. Her fork was no match for this glorious pie, and each juicy bite sent a few blueberries tumbling like black pearls, dotting the box and bedsheets in royal purple. The sweet ink of a delicious memory that would excite Iris for years to come.

CHAPTER

Forty-six

I ris was still with Gabe when she got a phone call from Rapacine.
She had never heard her friend sound so distraught, or so French.
"They took Jasmine, *mon chaton,* they took her!"

"Who, the landlord?"

"Or one of their maggots—Iris, they took her *from my home!* Jasmine was outside on the patio, she likes when the sun warms the stone, *et ma bichette,* she sleeps there after she takes breakfast. But that toilet *de merde,* I heard it running and I went to fix, and when I returned, she had vanished!"

"Okay, don't worry. I'll come and help you look for her—"

"No, she is not missing, she was taken! I saw! I saw him take her on the ring!"

Iris didn't follow. "What ring?"

"Roh!" Rapacine growled in French frustration. "The video camera! My neighbor next-door, she has the camera ring, all rich people have cameras! And so I ask her, please show me this morning on the video, *et voilà!* He is there, *fils de pute,* sneaking up on my Jasmine, *la pauvre,* she is deaf, *tu la connais,* and he snatch her and he shove her in a trash bag, a black trash bag, and he took her!"

Iris's stomach dropped. Gabe had been questioning her with his eyes during the call, and she met his gaze with a shake of her head in the universal *It's bad* gesture.

Rapacine was shouting but her voice was cracked with pain. "But the trash men have come and gone, if that is where he put her. *Je te promets,* if he harms one hair on her head, I will cut him from his chin to his *couilles, je m'en fous!*"

"Listen, I'm in Brooklyn but I'm coming over right now. We're going to get her back." She hung up, wondering if she had just lied to Mme Rapacine for the first time.

She caught Gabe up, and without hesitation, he insisted on coming with her.

On the way to Rapacine's, Iris and Gabe learned that the closest sanitation garage to her brownstone was on Spring Street, off the West Side Highway near the Holland Tunnel, and that residential trash pickup had been that morning between eight and nine. It was now almost eleven, so if sanitation had picked her up, Jasmine had been in the trash bag for at most three hours. Not wanting to waste another minute, Iris updated Rapacine, and they went straight to the garage.

There they pleaded their case to the first sanitation worker they found, a husky guy named Dave. He was sympathetic but realistic. "Look, I'm an animal lover too, so I hate ta break it to ya, but a trash truck ain't just a rolling dumpster. It's a *compactor.* If they threw the bag with the cat into the hopper . . ." he grimaced.

Tears filled Iris's eyes. Gabe put a hand on her shoulder.

"I ain't saying there's no hope! But fair warning, it's a long shot." Dave tapped the screen of a handheld device. "The truck that serves 23 Bank Street is headed to drop off at the waste transfer center, it's a temporary holding location. If you want, you can go there and sift through whatever they got for a coupla hours before they load it up onto a barge, and then it's off to a landfill. It's a needle in a haystack, but I seen people pull lost engagement rings outta there."

While Iris took down the address of the waste transfer center, Gabe asked, "How big a haystack are we talking? How much trash do you guys pick up in a day?"

"Twelve thousand tons," Dave said. When Iris groaned in exasperation, he added, "But we're organized. We track our trucks with

GPS, so we know where and when each pickup is made. And when we drop it off, we organize the garbage by section of neighborhood it came from. So someone can help you narrow down the general area."

Iris and Gabe locked eyes. His dark brows tilted upward, as if to say *I'm down if you are.*

"Are you seriously up for this?" Iris asked, touched.

"A cat has gotta be easier to find than an engagement ring. We'll go down there and call her name."

"Jasmine is deaf."

Gabe's shoulders sank. "Do deaf cats still meow?"

Iris didn't know. But she knew they had to try.

They had already said their goodbyes when Dave called back to them, "One more thing—" His gaze fell disapprovingly on their feet, Gabe in Adidas pool slides and Iris in flip-flops. "I suggest ya change your shoes."

Thirty minutes later, they were at an enormous warehouse containing a massive pit of garbage. She and Gabe were both wearing plastic hooded jumpsuits, a poor man's hazmat suit, provided to them by DSNY, plus blue latex gloves and N95 masks. They had stopped at Iris's apartment so she could change into rubber rain galoshes, and Gabe wore a pair of old running sneakers (left behind by Ben). They both had scissors on a twine wristband to cut into the trash bags, which proved to be unduly optimistic that the bags would stay closed— the garbage was loose and everywhere. Even through their masks, the smell was fetid. A sanitation department supervisor explained that the trash was divided into eight sections and helped them figure out which quadrant to begin in based on Rapacine's address.

Gabe jumped in first and landed with a squish.

"How is it?"

Gabe gave a thumbs-up. "C'mon in, the water's fine!"

Iris had never loved him more. She waded in after him, her own leg sinking knee-deep into the white and black bags. "How is my ankle already wet?"

"I don't want to talk about it," Gabe said.

They called the cat's name even though she knew Jasmine couldn't hear. Doing *something* felt better than doing nothing as they stumbled through the ocean of refuse. At one point Gabe got them both excited when he saw a furry white leg, but it was only a soiled plush toy. As suggested by the supervisor, they cut open bags in search of mail with addresses to see if they were getting closer to Rapacine's at 23 Bank Street.

Iris sliced open a new bag that spilled wet spaghetti like entrails. "I don't want to think about the germs and bacteria."

"Do you think this is like getting a vaccine, or a thousand? Maybe we'll be invincible!"

Iris's heart leaped when she saw movement inside a nearby bag. "Jasmine!" She grabbed the twist-tie closure of the trash bag, yanked it upward like carrot greens, and cut off the top in one scissor snip. She frantically rifled through balled-up dirty diapers, a rotisserie chicken carcass, and mealy coffee grounds to get to the bottom where she heard rustling.

Her scream made Gabe bound toward her. "What? What is it?"

"A rat!" She pointed at the newly freed rodent streaking over Hefty hill and dale.

Gabe laughed. *"Euugh.* Welp, Godspeed, little dude. And hey, at least he was alive—that's promising!"

"Hey, I know that truck!" Iris pointed at a trash truck slowly rolling in to park in the queue. Unlike the row of identical boxy white DSNY trash trucks, this one was graffitied in a riot of Keith Haring–style text and graphics. From the busy labyrinth of black-on-white lines appeared words like COMPOST, DONT LITTER, STAY CLEAN, ESSENTIAL WORKERS along with pop art emblems of the city, like a hot dog, a boom box with legs, a basketball with a comet tail, a mouth with tongue wagging, and a pizza slice. It didn't always serve her neighborhood, but Iris had definitely seen it before.

Iris clambered through the heaping muck, harder than jogging through the ocean, and at last reached the ladder to hoist herself out of the pit, with Gabe not far behind. She jogged toward the Haring truck, leaving juicy bootprints in her wake, and flailed at the men who had just descended from it.

Iris caught her breath, pulled down her mask, and asked, "Excuse me, have you—"

The driver held up a hand. "Don't ask me about the cat."

They were too late. "Is she . . . ?" her voice caught.

He crossed his burly arms over his chest. "Whoever threw him out like that don't deserve him. And I'm already attached."

"She's alive?" Gabe had appeared beside her.

"You have her?" Iris's heart leaped with hope.

"Damn right I do. I was about to toss the bag in the hopper when it moved. So I sliced it open and there he was, a snowball of fur. He rode up front with us for the rest of our rounds, wasn't even bothered by the truck noise, my kinda guy."

"It's a girl, her name is Jasmine." Iris didn't burst his bubble by sharing that Jasmine was deaf, not simply suited to trash collection.

The driver narrowed his eyes. "You got pictures or something to prove this is your cat? How's I know you aren't the asswipes who threw him out?"

They explained the whole situation, and instantly the sanitation driver was on their side.

"Fuckin' scumbags. I thought someone in that building was messing with the trash before, but I draw the line at innocent animals. C'mon up."

Iris realized he meant up into the trash truck. The driver gave her a hand climbing into the cabin and Gabe hopped up behind her. The driver pointed to a cardboard box wedged between the seats. Curled up inside was Jasmine, stained and sticky, but safe and sound.

Iris removed her blue latex glove and stroked her soft head, and the kitty immediately began to purr. Then she felt Gabe take her other hand in his.

She looked at him with tears in her eyes, full of gratitude to have this man by her side, even, or especially, with them both smelling like a landfill—not her perfume.

When Iris and Gabe hand-delivered Jasmine back to her mom, Mme Rapacine embraced her beloved pet with tender kisses and murmured French, and when the cat had had enough of being cherished, Rapacine hugged Iris with enough force to nearly knock her off her feet. But after the happy reunion had taken place, Iris could sense a change in her friend's demeanor. Rapacine recounted in a dispirited tone taking the surveillance video to the police precinct, where she'd felt disrespected and ignored. She had wanted to press criminal charges, but the police hadn't taken the animal cruelty angle seriously and instead blamed her for letting her cat outside without a collar. Rapacine spoke to them hunched on her chaise, her distracted gaze glued to the cats reacquainting themselves with each other. She appeared enervated, more her age, as if this battle for her home had taken its toll. Iris had wanted Rapacine to soften her stance against the landlord, but not like this. It seemed the fight had left her, and with it her signature verve.

Iris assured her that she would find her a new tenants' rights lawyer, but for the first time, Rapacine appeared too tired to have an opinion about it. She gave Iris only a wave of permission or dismissal and left to draw a bath in the kitchen sink for Jasmine, letting Iris and Gabe see themselves out.

Forty-seven

I ris had been an official full-time employee of Wolff Development for only a few days, and she was still battling her "syndrome of the impostor" as she sat in her shiny new office in the
sky. It was an upgrade from her old job in every way. While Candela's
offices had been located on a low floor in a midtown Manhattan
building with perpetual scaffolding, Wolff Dev was at One World
Trade Center with panoramic views of the Hudson River and all of
downtown. At Candela she'd shared a long desk smack in the middle
of their open plan office, where she was interrupted so often that she
sometimes placed client calls from the women's restroom in order to
find quiet. At Wolff Dev, she had her own private office with a window overlooking the Battery Park Marina, a sleek desk with floating
drawers, and a brand-new desktop computer. Her office even had its
own thermostat, so she no longer needed the ratty cardigan that had
lived on her old chair. And the greatest perk of all, Wolff Dev offices
were dog-friendly, so Hugo didn't have to stay at home. Presently, he
was snoring at her feet.

After Iris completed placing an order for more than two thousand
hallway lights for Oasys, her next call was to Brianne Woolworth, the
attorney Jonathan had hired for James's sister, Veronica. She and Brianne first caught up on the progress of their eviction case, which
unfortunately sounded as though it could take months to settle. Iris
spun her chair to gaze out at the yachts and sailboats. "How long can
Veronica and her kids stay at the apartment they're in now?"

"Mr. Wolff has indicated they can stay until the case is resolved, however long that takes."

Iris was ever surprised at Jonathan's generosity. "But what if they lose, could they afford to live there permanently?"

"Oh no. It is in one of his mixed-income buildings, and the apartment is technically below market rate, but it's nowhere near public-housing-affordable."

"Ah." Iris sometimes forgot how astronomical "market rate" really was in Manhattan.

"But I'm optimistic for their case. Now that Mr. Wolff is poised to take on a leadership role in the Hendricks Houses redevelopment, there will be a place for the Pattersons."

Iris nodded, satisfied. "I'm also calling to get a referral from you for a friend of mine, Mireille Rapacine . . ." She filled her in on everything Rapacine had been put through.

Brianne cooed. "Aw, I have a cat, I'd be beside myself. I'm sorry your friend is going through this, it's absolutely grounds for harassment charges. My caseload is heavy, but I can refer her to a colleague."

Iris remembered Rapacine's words: *All rich people have cameras.* No one in Hendricks Houses was rich, but the housing project was surrounded by much more expensive residential real estate and businesses. "Just to go back to the Pattersons for a second. You know, we wouldn't have gotten the cat back if not for the neighbor's Ring camera footage. Do you think something like that could help with Veronica's case? The cause for eviction was that her daughter violated visitor policy and let in that group of guys, which she denies, but what if a home or business across the street had footage showing she was innocent? Have you looked into that nearby surveillance?"

Brianne scoffed. "We don't need a business across the street, Big Brother is alive and well in public housing. The problem isn't not enough surveillance footage, it's too much."

Iris swiveled her chair back to her desk. "What do you mean?"

"NYCHA buildings have on average one camera per every nineteen residents. More surveillance cameras than JFK airport."

"They can't even afford to repair an elevator. How can they afford security cameras?"

"Because it's not NYCHA that pays for them. It comes out of the police budget. And that's upwards of five billion dollars."

"I had no idea." Although she flashed on the expensive "toys" of the digi-dog search robots.

"You'd think with all those eyes, the projects would be the safest places on earth. But no one is manning the watch tower until *after* a crime happens. But NYCHA admin uses the footage to charge residents with petty infractions like the ones Veronica faces. I don't typically represent many public housing residents, but in my research, I found a case where an elderly resident in Brooklyn was evicted because she allowed her nephew to move in with her while she recovered from hip surgery, they accused her of lending her key to a nonresident. It's shameful. But as you know, NYCHA's finances are in dire straits, so they're cracking down on evictions."

"Rent revenue was never supposed to sufficiently fund public housing, that's the whole idea of subsidizing, no?"

"Exactly. But tenants are easier to squeeze than politicians."

Iris shook her head. "Would they ever let you access the footage?"

"Oh sure, they'll bury you in it! They were more than happy to give me six months of twenty-four-hour surveillance, thousands of hours of footage, which is unhelpful by design. And honestly, I only asked in case the threat of accountability inclined them to drop the case, but no luck. The complaint is imprecise about when exactly the infractions occurred, so it wouldn't be worth my hours to comb through it. It's only useful if you knew exactly the time and date you were looking for."

"Can you share it with us?"

"If Veronica really wants it, yes. But I hope she and Kiara won't make themselves crazy sifting through it. Tell them I have other grounds to fight this, okay?"

"Thanks. Veronica doesn't have a working computer right now, so why don't you send it to me instead, I'll give you my new work email."

They exchanged info and said their goodbyes.

She had just hung up the phone when someone rapped his knuckles against her open door, making her and Hugo jump.

Nate Childers was standing in her doorway with a messenger bag across his chest. "Working hard or hardly working?"

Iris rose to welcome him, warm but wary. "What are you doing here? Come in."

Nate bent to pat Hugo, who had shuffled over. "You thought you were free of me. But I'm just here to drop off some contracts for Oasys. Don't forget, that's still a Candela project."

"Aren't you a little high up to be playing courier? I thought they promoted you to partner."

Nate smiled. "Okay, I was curious. And now, jealous."

Iris followed his gaze to the cityscape behind her. It was spectacular—and yet she still felt a little melancholy. "You know I never thought I'd leave Candela."

"Yeah, you had to, though." His voice sounded wistful. "Frank should've promoted you earlier."

Iris was surprised.

He noticed. "Don't look at me like that. We all knew you've been ready for more. I certainly saw it. And Wolff saw it too."

"Thank you. What's different about you, you look . . . healthier?"

Nate brightened. "Allergy shots! It's the first summer in ages that I can *breathe*. Now I can actually wake up and smell my coffee."

The allergies—he couldn't smell her before, she realized.

Nate set the package on her desk. "I've been reading the gushing headlines about Wolff taking over at that public housing complex, HERO DEVELOPER SAVES PUBLIC HOUSING, and, what was the *Post*'s line? 'PROJECTS'-MANAGER. Great press, they make him sound like Bruce Wayne. But are you really excited to design the cheapest possible institutional lighting? You won't be getting into *Arch Digest* with that."

"You know? I'm genuinely looking forward to lighting those apartments. Those residents deserve as much warmth and good design as someone paying fifteen hundred per square foot. The budget will be a challenge, but I didn't get into this field to pick out Murano glass pendant lamps. I want to make buildings feel like homes."

Nate whistled. "Wolff's offer must have been rich!"

Iris chuckled. "Stock shares, baby."

"Oh!" Nate pantomimed a dagger to his heart.

"It pays to do the right thing. You should try it sometime."

He laughed. "Seriously, I'm gonna miss you. Will we still be friends?"

"Why not?" she said, feeling suddenly generous. "In fact, you should bring your family to this Italian Giglio festival in Williamsburg. My boyfriend, Gabe, is a lifter in it, they carry some big religious statue down the street—"

Nate's eyes lit up. "Like *Godfather Two*?"

"I don't know, but don't make that joke at the Giglio. I'm going on Wednesday night, but it's on the weekend too. Maddie might like it."

"Sounds cool. All right, so I gave you the Candela Oasys paperwork, and that's it. I'll finish my snooping on the way out, unless Scary Marilyn intercepts me." Nate gave her a last look. "Good to see you, Iris."

"You too. Give my love to Frank."

Iris smiled to herself after Nate had left. She'd thought his animosity toward her was deep-seated and unchanging because he couldn't smell the perfume, but his kind words today were hardly a snap judgment. Now she wondered if it had been only the competition keeping them from being friends, and maybe she'd had his respect all along.

She swiveled back to her computer, woke up the screen, and was delighted to see she already had a new email from Brianne with a zip file. She opened it and a deluge of files populated her screen. It was indeed an incomprehensible quantity of video. Even the trash depot was better organized. Without a time and date to search on, the footage was useless to exonerate the Pattersons in their eviction case.

Iris recalled what Nate said about good press calling Wolff the savior of Hendricks. She still believed that Kiara's heroism that day deserved to be a news story, one that would pressure the admin to back off with the eviction. Nothing helped a news story sell like pictures, or even better, *video*. Iris knew the gas explosion had occurred on June 29 at 3:58 P.M. thanks to Joshua Keaton's articles, the journalist she met at Hendricks on move-out day. She received *New York Times* alerts for his new pieces in her inbox, although disappointingly he still hadn't written about the Pattersons. Iris thought if she could find video of Kiara leading the evacuation, she could make Joshua reconsider.

Iris clicked folders with varying location names like "Tower A—N," and "Tower D—SW" to find the one trained on the entrance that had been destroyed. She oriented herself via cardinal directions and cross streets until she found the correct lobby camera. Then she opened the interior folder for June 29 and estimated where to toggle the playback on or before four in the afternoon. Iris landed just shy of two o'clock and watched with faster playback speed to see when the evacuation began, praying there would be a clear shot of Kiara.

The black-and-white video resolution wasn't the best, especially at 4x speed, and Iris wasn't sure she would recognize Kiara from the high angle, but she figured she was looking for somebody young, people moving extra fast, or any behavior out of the ordinary. She didn't expect to slow it down until she was very close to four o'clock, but something unusual caught her eye about a particular man entering the building.

Iris paused it; it was only 2:47 P.M. She rewound and replayed it at normal speed. Even when she slowed it down, the man was walking swiftly, with long strides, as if he was quite tall. She couldn't see his face; he was wearing a ball cap and surgical mask, but she could tell he was white. And still his race wasn't what tweaked her memory. Slowly Iris toggled the cursor, frame by frame, so that she could get a clear image of his feet—in some frames his shoe simply looked blurry gray, but when she stopped the video at the moment his leg was farthest forward, the shoe's design came into crisp focus.

A checkerboard.

The B/D, F/M stop at 47–50th St–Rockefeller Center was the only subway station that smelled better inside than outside, and not because it was cleaner. The platform was just as grimy, with the same objectionable puddles in the hallway corners, and the stairwell had particularly dated yellow tiles on the walls, or maybe they were once white. Nevertheless, a gourmand aroma of sugar, butter, and vanilla wafted down the soot-covered staircase, as if the MTA station were run by Keebler elves. The real source was revealed when Iris emerged on the corner of Forty-ninth and Sixth: Magnolia Bakery.

But no cupcake could comfort Iris after she received Veronica's text message that her lawyer, Brianne, had suddenly dropped their case. Iris knew she had to speak with Veronica in person, so she'd left the office immediately, dropped Hugo off at her apartment, and took the subway straight to the midtown Magnolia where Veronica worked.

Iris entered the bakery where a stacked line of customers was divided from the hustling employees by a row of fogged glass cases holding mini cheesecakes, key lime pie, red velvet cupcakes, chocolate mousse, and a battalion of banana pudding cartons. The Magnolia staff deftly took orders from between the large display cakes of every conceivable color and decoration that topped the counter. Iris scanned their faces, but no Veronica. She discreetly cut the line of tourists and got the attention of a staff member stacking trays of cupcakes on a metal rack.

"Hi, is Veronica working today?"

"She's on cake decoration. You picking up?"

"I need to talk to her."

"She's busy. But I got you, whatchu want?"

"I'm her lawyer," Iris lied.

The man reluctantly nodded his head in the direction of the back kitchen. "You'll see her. But don't touch anything."

With most of the staff distracted with customers, Iris slipped around the counter and squeezed between the rolling racks. In the cramped kitchen, Veronica was stationed behind a layer cake on a pedestal, with a blue hairnet over her braids, beads of sweat on her brow, and wired headphones in her ears. She held the long spatula perfectly upright and spun the cake against it, smoothing the pink buttercream with mesmerizing speed. Iris waved to get her attention, and Veronica pulled out her headphones and greeted her with surprise—but without slowing her icing.

Iris began, "I got your text, and I couldn't reply or call back because . . ." She didn't want to say the truth, that she was paranoid about her devices right now. "I was nearby. But tell me, what *exactly* did Brianne say?"

Veronica puckered her lips in disappointment. "Not much more than what I texted you. Just that she can't work with us no more, effective immediately."

"She didn't give you any reason?"

Veronica shrugged. "Mr. Wolff stopped paying her bills, I guess."

Iris felt a sudden dip in blood sugar. *He knows.* "Did she say why he stopped?"

"We didn't talk, she texted me saying I was no longer a client. I tried to call her, but looks like now she got me blocked." Veronica picked up a conical pastry bag and began to pipe green leaves onto the cake base. "To be honest, I was expecting this. It ain't the first time somebody trying to be a hero overpromised us. I don't want to be ungrateful, so I just never get too comfortable. Don't feel bad, it's not your fault, you did everything you could."

Actually, Iris thought, *this may be precisely my fault.* "Has Mr. Wolff contacted you at all?"

"No, but I figure our days at the apartment are numbered. It's the nicest place we've ever lived, I knew it was too good to last. I've been looking for another option since we moved in." Veronica's green vines crept up the sides of the cake. "Roman swears he can find us something, I know he's been busting his butt looking, and James said we could stay with them again—but there's no room for us. I don't know what we gonna do, I can't think about it."

Iris's heart broke for Veronica. Not to mention the wave of guilt that it was likely her asking Brianne for the camera footage that had caused Wolff to turn on the Pattersons. "I'm going to talk to Jonathan." Although as soon as she'd said it, Iris questioned when exactly Jonathan was going to turn on her, if he hadn't already.

Veronica switched to a bag of red frosting, and in seconds the cake was blooming with confectionery roses. "Don't. That's your boss, you gotta take care of that relationship, don't push it. We'll figure something out. I just hope we can find a place before school starts up again. My kids have already lost so much. I don't want them to start school feeling like their life's a mess."

"It's hot back here." Iris fanned herself. Or maybe it was just her blood pressure.

"It's the ovens. Nice in the wintertime, July not so much." Veronica wiped her brow with her sleeve. "But I like working here. The early morning shifts help me fit in my second job. And the cakes remind you of all the love in this city. I like being a part of people's best days."

The comment touched Iris. In contrast to the hand she was dealt, Veronica took pleasure in creating precise, controlled beauty and sweet treats for customers all day. Iris wanted the Pattersons to have their own cause for celebration, but at the very least, she couldn't live with herself knowing that she had been the cause of their latest setback.

"Don't worry. Everything's gonna work out." Iris prayed it was the truth.

. . .

Iris left Magnolia feeling worse than before. On the street, she wove through the herds of white-collar workers heading home at end of day. She'd been foolish to hope there was some benign alternative explanation for why Brianne had suddenly cut ties with Veronica. Only one thing had happened in the two hours between Brianne discussing active legal strategy with Iris and the lawyer and case being abruptly shut down: the Hendricks surveillance footage. Iris had seen something she wasn't supposed to. Now the only question was: Did Wolff know only that Brianne had pulled the Hendricks security footage for the Pattersons' case, or did Wolff know that it was Iris who had requested and viewed the tape? If it were the former, she still had time to plan her next move. The latter—

A gray Mercedes lunged to a halt on the curb beside her and both the driver and rear passenger doors swung open. The stone-faced driver sprang from the car and grabbed her. It was Esdras.

"Please get in," he requested, even as he forced her into the vehicle. Iris's feet scuffed the sidewalk as she struggled, and the car door's edge collided with the front of her hip as he muscled her around it. Iris yelped and buckled in pain while Esdras slammed the door shut. Her lower abdomen was so sensitive.

Jonathan was already seated in the back. "Forgive Esdras's clumsiness. We're in a terrible rush."

The car doors locked.

Forty-nine

I ris gripped the door handle as they zoomed up the FDR Drive,
but there were few lights or opportunities to ... do whatever
reckless escape her gut was screaming at her to attempt. Jonathan's mood was unsettlingly amiable. He apologized for startling
her and said only that they needed to have an "emergency meeting,"
with no mention that they had to have been following her. Jonathan
claimed he was treating her to dinner at "the best restaurant in New
York." Iris felt sick to her stomach as she watched the East River rush
by. They drove all the way to East Harlem.

Navigating through the unlikely neighborhood, Iris feared he was
taking her to a remote building site, but nothing they passed looked
sinister. It was not yet dark out, and people were everywhere, old
folks sat outside fanning themselves, one man hosing down the sidewalk sprayed a few game children. The car turned off First Avenue
onto leafy 114th Street, and Esdras pulled to a stop outside a modest
three-story brick building with a small, dark-windowed restaurant
that looked especially squat on a sunken patio, below street level.
The restaurant's simple facade was painted fire engine red with its
name in white capital letters: RAO's.

"Do you know this place?" Jonathan asked.

"I buy the tomato sauce."

Jonathan chuckled.

Esdras opened the door and offered his hand to help Iris out. Her only move was to play along, relieved at least to be in a public place. Jonathan told Esdras he would send out his usual and escorted Iris inside.

Although the restaurant looked closed from the outside, inside it buzzed like a secret clubhouse. The dining room was set away from the front windows like a hideaway, it had a low printed-tin ceiling, wooden booths with tall backs lining the perimeter, and large round tables in the center. The space was dimly lit by a few stained-glass fixtures and small table lamps. *Well,* she thought, *semi-public.*

The host in a fine gray suit greeted Jonathan like an old friend, kissing him on both cheeks and asking after Allegra, before allowing them to walk themselves to an empty booth against the back wall. The diners were older, whiter, and more male than average, the room felt full but not crowded. Music was provided by an old-fashioned jukebox playing Tony Bennett and the percussive cocktail shaker of a white-haired bartender standing behind a bar unseasonably festooned with Christmas garlands and string lights.

Jonathan directed Iris to slide into the booth with his hand at the small of her back, as if he was her date and not her kidnapper.

"Would you believe this is the most exclusive restaurant in New York, or in all of the United States? You can't buy your way in here. Elon Musk couldn't get a table here unless one of the regulars invited him as their guest." Jonathan explained that the coveted tables were meted out to "owners" like timeshares, and none were available for normal reservations or walk-ins. Jonathan had won his table—this booth was his the third Thursday of every month—in a game of high stakes poker with a fellow real estate scion who remained nameless. "That's what I love about this place. It's not about money or status, it's about connections, relationships, trust. That's where the real power lies, the kind that triumphs and endures. The joke about Rao's is, it's the only restaurant whose clientele is equal parts mob and law enforcement, sometimes at the same table."

"Must be some meatballs." Iris knew he was trying to intimidate her, and it was working, but she didn't want to let it show.

"They don't suspend their animosity for the sake of the veal. It's that here, behind the curtain, you see that the animosity is an act. We're all connected. All part of the same ecosystem. Doesn't mean we don't play our roles with conviction, but we need each other."

The host returned to personally take their order.

Jonathan raised his eyebrows at her. "Do you trust me to order for you? There are no menus. No bill, for that matter. They put it on your tab. The idea is, you're among friends here. And you trust your friends, don't you?"

"Sure." Iris remained wary. "Go ahead."

"We'll start with the seafood salad and the meatballs, and then let's do the orecchiette with salsicce and broccoli rabe, the spaghetti puttanesca, and ooh, the leg of lamb. And a bottle of Barolo. Ah, and please send an order of the lemon chicken out to my driver in the gray Mercedes."

The host nodded approvingly and left.

Jonathan smiled, taking in the scene, and gestured to the kitschy bar. "Christmas in July. It's fitting, as time stops here, and what better time than Christmas?" He turned back to her with a darker expression. "Although, forgive my insensitivity. You lost your parents at Christmas, didn't you?"

"Did I tell you that?" Iris asked, knowing that she hadn't.

"We look into all our potential hires' backgrounds. I remember the story because it was very affecting—a little girl loses both her parents on Christmas. I can't imagine how traumatic that must have been. Have you ever been able to enjoy the holiday again?"

She shrugged. "Christmas is always a little melancholy, isn't it? I still celebrate it. If I were bothered by Christmas decorations, I wouldn't be able to leave the house after October."

A waitress arrived with the Barolo and poured them each a glass, then left.

Jonathan swirled the wine in his glass. "No siblings, either, right? Just that cousin, the one who saved you, the one whose funeral Esdras took you to."

"Just me." Iris raised her glass, and they lightly clinked.

"My heart goes out to you. I think one of the worst things you can be in this world is alone. It's not natural. We're social creatures. We don't have big teeth, we don't have long claws, we don't have poisonous venom. We have only each other for protection."

"I do all right on my own. I had no choice."

"You do now." Jonathan sipped his wine. "You're a strong woman, Iris, that's one of the reasons I wanted you on our team. But another is that I could tell from your past, from your long time with Frank and Candela, that you understood the importance of family. That's how I run my business, truly. I know a lot of companies say that, but with me, it's not bullshit. It's real."

Iris nodded.

"And sometimes we get angry at family, but we work it out, and we stick together."

"Of course." Iris didn't want to show any more of her hand than she had to. She still didn't know what exactly Jonathan knew.

"And if I'm being completely honest, there's something about your aloneness that I find very attractive. It's politically incorrect to say these days, but I want to protect you. Even if that means protecting you from yourself."

A chill slipped down her spine.

The waitress returned with the appetizers. "Here ya go. *Buon appetito.*"

Jonathan scooped a steaming meatball onto his plate. "This looks great, doesn't it? Dig in."

Iris looked at the plate in front of her, the shiny, wet tentacles of an overturned squid reaching out like a desperate hand from the heap of shrimp, crab, and calamari.

Jonathan took a big bite of meatball and spoke through it, the gleam of tomato sauce shining on his lip. "So tell me, what were you up to today, before we ran into you?"

"I went to see Veronica. She was upset that her lawyer stopped returning her calls."

"Unfortunately I lost confidence in Brianne after she made an error in judgment, sharing privileged information imprudently. In fact, I had some of my people look into her career history, and they found some past ethics violations and indiscretions. It's likely she'll be disbarred."

Iris read the subtext. "I'm sorry to hear that. Will you be getting the Pattersons a new lawyer?"

"That depends." Jonathan fixed his turquoise eyes on her. "Are you going to keep sticking your nose where it doesn't belong?"

Her heart rate sped and everything in her body wanted to escape, but she was glued to the seat.

"I know you asked Brianne for the surveillance footage. I need you to tell me what you were looking for and what you think you saw."

Iris swallowed hard, the tannic wine chalky in her mouth. "I was looking for something to help with their eviction case. I thought if I could find video of Kiara helping evacuate people, someone might write a story about it, garner sympathy."

"And did you find any good footage for the press?"

"No, unfortunately. I couldn't see anyone's face clearly, the camera angle was bad." She hoped he'd take it to mean she didn't recognize anyone.

But Jonathan's mouth set in a stern line. "We're monitoring your computer down to the keystroke. I know exactly where you stopped the video, and you didn't even get to the evacuation. So tell me, what did you see?"

Iris felt like a child in the principal's office. "Patrick. I recognized his shoes."

Jonathan sat back with a smile. "There's that attention to detail I hired you for."

Her throat thickened. She felt overwhelmed with fear of Jonathan, sorrow for the victims, anger for being looped in with all of it, and self-recrimination for missing the signs before.

"Don't look so upset. You have everything you want right now. You have your dream job, a handsome boyfriend, a cute dog, and very soon, I'm going to make you rich. Unless you want to blow that all up. It's your choice to make." Jonathan reached for her hand across the table like a lover; she let him take it like a corpse. "Look, look at me. If you want to go to the police right now, I understand. See that man over at the center table? He's the new commissioner. I had a great conversation with him at the mayor's last fundraiser. I'd be happy to introduce you. In fact, if you want to know more about strategic arson, I can introduce you to that other man in the corner."

Iris had glanced to each man as Jonathan pointed them out. Off duty, they were indistinguishable.

"I know everybody. I take care of my friends and my friends take care of me. The police are satisfied with their investigation, they determined the gas leak and explosion were accidental. Bill and the NYCHA board are happy too. The tenants are thrilled about private development finally delivering the functioning buildings they have so long deserved, the chance to live with safety and dignity. Everybody wins."

"Except the people who died." The truth had a steadying effect on her.

"*Two.*"

"*People.*"

"You're right. That was an accident and a tragedy I never wanted to happen. But think of all the people who will get to live in safety and dignity when we rebuild. They would have gone on being slowly poisoned by lead paint, asbestos, and black mold. Who knows how many people those toxins have already killed?"

"It's murder."

"You think I'm a *murderer*? You've been to my home. You've met my daughter. I've cared about equitable, quality housing solutions my entire career, this is my cause, my passion." Jonathan looked like he genuinely believed what he was saying. "The tenants have long been on the side of private development taking over, they *want* us to step in and help them."

"Because they don't know you blew them up!" The force of her words jolted them both. Iris lowered her voice. "Those people died. They should be alive right now, it was wrong."

"There's a lot wrong. There's always gonna be a lot wrong. You have to pick your battles, try to do the most good that you can, and let the rest go." He moved his plate aside as if clearing an invisible chessboard. "Here's the reality. You tell the police about the existence of footage they already have, on an investigation that is already closed. The articles are written. The public and the politics have moved on. You have a positive ID on a pair of shoes, not a face. That's not enough for the DA to charge anyone, much less convict." He leaned forward urgently. "Nothing is gonna bring those two people back. And those injured will be taken care of by the Hendricks Victims Relief Fund, funded by me."

Iris recoiled, his hypocrisy like acid in her stomach.

"Just like I'm taking care of your friends the Pattersons for free. You go against me, you'll make them homeless. What do you think Kiara's odds are of graduating high school from a shelter? Do you think the streets are a nice place for Isaiah to come of age? These are innocent people, and you'll destroy whatever slim chance they had left."

But these words struck cold fear into her heart.

"Nothing will happen to me. No one will believe you, because it would be very costly for them to believe you. I'm too valuable to my friends to go down for this. There's no upside for anyone."

Iris had had enough. "You can't abuse people and then position yourself as their savior. You're only saving them from people like you. You rig and profit from the very system that keeps them trapped in shit housing like this. They need new homes because you destroyed theirs. You proved they were unsafe by murdering them. And now you position yourself as their hero? It's a gross manipulation, a betrayal of trust, it's *evil*. How can you bear to have them thank you, knowing what you did to them?"

Jonathan rolled his eyes. "Iris, grow up. We can't get to a perfect system. When someone's stock goes up, another goes down. But plenty of power players would crush the little guys and take all the chips without looking back. I'm actually offsetting the damage of this imperfect system. I'm one of the good guys."

"You are a homicidal profiteer."

Jonathan spread his hands. "And I'm the best they've got."

The plate with the leg of lamb landed on the table with a thud. "Whoops, careful, hot plate," said the waitress, as she quickly wiped up the bloodied juice that had splashed onto the table. The smell of rosemary and charred fat filled the space between them, and Iris felt ill. The excess of the food, the excess of his selfishness, all simmered in the searing truth that he was almost certainly right. He would win. The game was rigged. Men like him would always win.

Jonathan leaned close again. "So that leaves you. What will happen to you if you go against me? You won't work in New York again. Or LA. Or London, or Paris, or Dubai, because real estate is a small world, and nobody likes a rat. Or a slut."

The last word confused her.

"In every negotiation, there's a carrot and a stick. This is the stick." Jonathan pulled out his iPhone. "Surveillance cameras are easily overlooked. I guess we both learned that the hard way." He tapped the screen and handed her the phone. "Press Play."

Iris took the phone, the screen was black save for a Play triangle, but she recognized the date as the day they arrived in the Hamptons. The video had no sound, but she instantly recognized the outdoor shower at Jonathan's Hamptons house, and her blood ran cold. She watched as she and Gabe entered, giggling, looking over their shoulders. Even once they were inside the shower stall, the angle of the camera gave them no cover. Iris watched herself get undressed, her naked body exposed. The footage showed every intimate act she and Gabe engaged in. She even saw herself glance up, sickened to recall that she had fantasized about Jonathan at that very moment. By the time the video had ended, her entire body was shaking.

Iris gritted her teeth. "You invited me to your house to film me?"

"No, but I have cameras everywhere. It's not my fault you were blowing a guy outside my house in broad daylight. The cameras also caught you kissing me on my beachfront. And one of the hallway cameras caught you sneaking into the bathroom with Lindsay. So all in all, it was a very busy weekend for you."

Iris felt like she couldn't breathe.

"Again, as the father of a daughter, I hope no one else ever sees this footage. I wanted to earn your trust, Iris, but if you won't let me, then I have no choice but to ensure it. If this gets out, you will never work in this industry again. But if you see the bigger picture, and you can put the greater good ahead of whatever combination of ego and naïveté is driving you to self-destruction, then all is forgiven. I'll know I can trust you as a member of the team. And you'll never be alone again."

Iris sat trembling, adrenaline coursing through a body that couldn't move. She closed her eyes and tried to think straight. When she tried to think of herself, the shame was too searing to function. For now, she could only focus on someone else. "What about the Pattersons?"

"If you're on my side, they can stay where they are now."

"Their home has to be permanent, it has to be someplace that can't be taken away. Give them the apartment, sell it to them for cheap or something, but Veronica has to own it."

Jonathan stared at her, unblinking, but even his steady gaze couldn't hide his surprise. "You're not really in a bargaining position, but you've got a soft heart, like me. So I'll do it, *for you,* as a show of good faith." He clapped his hands, startling her. "Sold! For one dollar. I'll have my lawyer write up the contract, all right? Does that mean you'll stay in the Wolff pack?"

Her mind was spinning but she couldn't speak to answer.

"You know what? Don't answer me now. Think it over. Your next move is very important. I want you to make a measured decision of your own accord." Jonathan looked up past her head and beckoned for someone. "Esdras will take you home."

Iris stood, pressing herself up from the table on legs that felt like lead.

Jonathan stood too, leaning in as if to kiss her cheek, and added, "But do not play with me, because it can get worse. Much worse."

What happened after that was a blur. Iris was elsewhere, shut down, somewhere outside of herself. Esdras was leading her out of the restaurant, but she couldn't even feel his hand on her back. She was numb. She felt like she was sleepwalking. Her headspace was utterly at odds with the convivial spirit around her, she felt adrift, detached from herself and from the world. She followed him with her head down like a child.

Her first step outdoors was into a cloud of cigarette smoke. The smoker apologized, exhaling more through his nostrils like a dragon. He waved his hand but only sent the cloud billowing around her. Swirls of a familiar scent of a cigarette brand that Iris hadn't smelled in decades—the sweet, toasted tobacco mixed with the acrid notes of burnt rubber, camphor, and ash—summoning the memory of a freckled hand rapping the blue box with an image of a Native American against the heel of his palm, that same smell clinging to his fingers . . .

Iris turned her head, squinting as the smoke stung her eyes, and she saw the bleary Christmas lights through the window behind her. She stumbled, slamming her shin on the stair, the shock of pain bringing her into her body, and when Esdras's rough hands lifted her up under her shoulders, it all came back.

CHAPTER
Fifty

A waking dream, a missing piece of her recurring nightmare of the house fire, only instead of ending too early, she now realized the nightmare had always started too late.

She's in her childhood bed, and her body feels incredibly heavy, three times her weight. She wants to get up, she needs to escape, but she doesn't move a muscle.

She can't, because Jacob is on top of her. He's hurting her. She's confused and in pain and ashamed. But most of all, she's afraid it could get worse.

She wants to yell but she can't, because his hand covers her mouth. The other is where it should never be. She tries to breathe through her nose, but his fingers smell of those disgusting cigarettes. She wants to vomit, but it would choke her. He could choke her. He's so much bigger than she is.

Her gaze is fixed on the spot where the wall meets the ceiling, or the window with the neighbor's lights, anywhere but in front of her. Anywhere but on his face. Anywhere that her mind can escape when her body cannot.

The stenciled border with the barn and animals, the one she painted with her mother. She is desperate to slip out of the present and climb into that memory. To daytime, and to her mom, where none of this would be allowed to happen.

You didn't have to be careful with sponge painting. But her body is changing and the teacher said you have to be careful with boys. She didn't know you had to be careful with sleeping. Or that she had to be careful with Jacob.

Mommy loves you but she doesn't see. It only happens when she and Daddy are asleep. Jacob told you that you can't tell them. You don't even know how to say it, but you know that it's wrong. And you know you can't stop it from happening.

And you are so ashamed.

She'd tried staying awake. She'd tried pretending to sleep. She'd tried asking to sleep with her parents. She'd tried leaving the light on.

But she hadn't tried telling. And no one guessed right.

Poor, stupid kid.

When the smoke came, she thought she had summoned it. She thought it was the blackness in his eyes and in her stomach and in her mind infecting the whole world.

She wanted something to blind her eyes and make her sleep. She wanted it to stuff her nose to keep from smelling his filthy hand and make him and everything go away. She'd wanted to black out.

Because Jacob was the smoke creeping under her bedroom door. Silent, unseen, deadly.

It couldn't get worse.

But then it does.

Poor, stupid kid.

She never saw the fire until he carried her into it. Only the orange rim around her bedroom door.

Jacob didn't come in to save her. He was already there. In her bed.

He didn't see the fire that started right beside the couch downstairs, where he should've been sleeping, because he was upstairs with her.

Her door got closed when he closed it behind him.

When she saw the police lights and sirens outside, she thought they'd come for her. For the world's most wretched, nasty girl, bare feet and bare bottom exposed on a frigid night. Her pajama pants were left upstairs.

Then she thought they'd come for Jacob, and she felt glad.

Then she realized they'd come for nothing. It was too late. Her parents were never coming out.

You thought you'd rather die than tell your father, but then he died instead.

You thought it would kill your mother to know, but the fire killed her instead.

It's your fault. You didn't tell. You didn't ask for help. You didn't stop anything. And now they're gone.

Say thank you to the man who saved you. Say thank you to the man who hurt you. The bad thing is over. You survived. Be grateful.

No one would believe he did it, he's a hero.

He's your hero.

Isn't that nice?

Isn't that a miracle?

Isn't that a better story?

You're not a bad girl.

You're not a sicko.

You're not a victim.

He saved you.

And you can't be angry at him, you can't be angry at anyone.

You're lucky to be alive.

Be grateful.

You can be sad about your parents. You can be scared of the fire. But you cannot be scared of your cousin. And you cannot be mad at your parents.

You *are* sad about your parents. You were a bad girl and you kept a terrible secret from them and they were taken from you as punishment.

All your feelings, all your emotions, all your grief, all your anger— blame it on the fire. It was the fire's fault.

Yours is already the worst story people ever heard. You don't want to make it worse. What good would that do?

What's done is done. And you'll never be the same again.

It's better that nobody knows. As long as it's over. As long as you never have to see Jacob's face again.

Keep it a secret.

Bury it.

Burn it.

Burn with it if you have to. Light your shame on fire.

It's better than living with the pain of surviving.

But it's like you never got out.

"Miss?" Esdras's voice broke through the nightmare she was reliving, but this time it didn't make the memory disappear.

Iris blinked through tears, bringing herself back to her present surroundings by focusing on Esdras's deformed cauliflower ear, the cartilage rough and puffy, a physical manifestation of trauma, but no more real. And it was ugly.

"You're home."

Fifty-one

I ris pressed her key into her apartment's front door, and before she even turned it, the door creaked open. She froze, and the realization gripped her by the throat:

Someone had broken in.

Iris took a step back, scared to enter or even make a sound, in case the intruder was inside. The hallway was empty. She should call and wait for the police in the lobby. But then a thought occurred more fearsome than any danger to herself.

"Hugo!"

Her pulse thudded in her ears as she rushed through the apartment, which had been completely ransacked, but she couldn't process anything until she located Hugo. She called his name again with panic cracking her voice, but heard no sound in reply. Her world was already upside down, the last thread tethering her was tied to that dog.

Iris spotted his white-tipped tail on the floor behind her bed, and she leaped over her downed full-length mirror to reach him where he lay flat atop her strewn clothing. She dropped to her knees beside him and promptly scared the crap out of the poor dog. Iris cried out in relief and swept him onto her lap, burying her face in his stringy neck, and Hugo, recognizing Mommy's scent, wriggled with happiness.

Hugo was okay, so Iris could handle the rest of it.

Iris explored her home, that most familiar, comforting space rendered unrecognizable by chaos, and tried to deduce what had been stolen. Her bedroom mirror had been knocked over and cracked, her dresser drawers opened and tossed. Luckily, her jewelry box, tucked away on her bookshelves, was untouched, likely unnoticed. In her living room, her broken laptop lay open like a book, the joint between screen and keyboard snapped, as if it had been stomped. The kettlebell she kept beside her yoga mat had been thrown into the center of her television, shattering the screen. Framed pictures smacked off her shelves.

Her things had been destroyed, but not taken.

This wasn't a burglary.

It was a threat.

Jonathan had told her it could get worse. It terrified Iris that it had already begun.

But then her senses were soothed, her nose beckoned by the scent of Rapacine's perfume emanating from across the room. She walked toward the fragrance, which grew more potent with every step, and by the time she reached the bathroom, it was overpowering. She pushed open the bathroom door.

The beautiful perfume bottle—its century-old crystal lay in shards on the floor, its precious elixir spilled like blood. An unthinking stream of "No, no, no . . ." passed through her lips as she lowered herself to the ruin, careful not to disturb the spill's perimeter. Iris delicately picked up the partial base of the bottle, the cicada's graceful lace wing now jagged and sharp. Maybe two milliliters of the perfume remained in the bottle's tiny basin, as the rest pooled in the grout between her floor tiles. She racked her brain to come up with a way to preserve or salvage what remained. She ran to her kit of fertility supplies and retrieved an empty syringe, which she used in a desperate attempt to draw up the spilled perfume, but it was futile. None of the grout-rivulets were deep enough to be captured by the suction, and the rest of the perfume was spread too thin in an oily sheen over the pockmarked marble or had already evaporated, rendering the air thick and heady with the scent. Her last resort was to take a silk scarf and press it into the dark spot on the floor, hoping to capture a modicum of the fragrance.

Iris slumped against the bathroom doorjamb. She needed the perfume now more than ever. Iris couldn't report a man like Jonathan Wolff to the police without the perfume. No one would believe her without it. Her only weapon to match his money and power was the perfume. And now it was gone.

A cold, wet nose snuffled the back of her arm, and Iris threw out a hand to block Hugo from stepping on the broken crystal. She shooed him out and closed the door, then set about cleaning up the rest of the bathroom. Like everywhere else in the apartment, it was a disaster. The toiletries she kept on her vanity had been swept onto the floor or, as was the case with her electric toothbrush, in the toilet, and her medicine chest door hung open, its contents jettisoned into the sink. Iris cleared the sink and closed the medicine chest, but what she saw in the mirror made her gasp.

Scrawled in lipstick across her own horrified reflection:

SLUT

Iris lurched over her toilet and vomited.

Fifty-two

*T*he worst thing someone can be is alone. Wolff's words echoed in her ear. Iris leashed Hugo, packed an overnight bag, texted Gabe she was coming over, and set off for Brooklyn before he even replied. She couldn't go to the police. She couldn't risk further escalation until she figured out her next move. In the meantime, Iris needed to get herself and her dog somewhere safe.

But on her way to Gabe's, she thought of someone she could call.

Iris dug through the wad of receipts, CVS coupons, and loyalty cards in her wallet until she found the pink business card she was looking for. It was a long shot, a Hail Mary in case things went really bad. But it would be better than nothing. She dialed the number on her phone. An assistant picked up.

Iris cleared her throat. "Hi, I'm trying to reach—Yes, that's right. No, I need to speak with her directly. I can't, no, I have to remain anonymous. Please, just tell her I'm the friend of the perfumer, she'll understand. Dead serious. Yes, I'll hold."

Fifty-three

When Iris had texted Gabe to say she and Hugo needed to come over, she didn't say why. He'd replied saying he was at his mother's apartment in Williamsburg and that she should swing by and meet him there, and she agreed without much thought. She didn't expect the full house that met her when Gabe opened the door.

Everyone clamored to greet her—Gabe's mom, Angie, his aunt Donna, and her son, his teenage cousin, Matthew. They had obviously been celebrating something; the table had a Brooklyn Nets tablecloth over it and was strewn with empty glasses and picked-over paper plates. Balloons were tied to the chairs. Iris was struck by the strong family resemblance among Gabe's three relatives; all were short, tan, stocky brunettes with sparkly brown eyes and smile lines of varying depth. The main difference between the sisters was that Angie's hair was curly while Donna's was ironed straight. Matthew, who appeared to have Down Syndrome, was every bit his mother's son, with a slightly crooked smile just like hers. They welcomed Iris warmly but were clearly as surprised to see her as she was them.

"Girlfriend?" Matthew covered his mouth with his hand. "You didn't tell us you had a girlfriend."

"Yeah, you know why?" Gabe grinned. "Knock knock."

"Who's there?"

"Nunya."

"Nunya business!" Matthew exclaimed, jumping the punchline.

"That's right, bub!" Gabe made a tough guy face, making Matthew laugh.

His mom Angie said to Iris, "Don't take it personal, hon. Gabriel doesn't normally let us meet any girls, so you must be special."

"It's 'cause you all are so nosy. I don't want you gossiping about me more than you already do."

Matthew held up a finger. "Gabe, it's not *all* about you." They all laughed. Except Iris.

As much as Iris wished to be soothed by the cozy family atmosphere, the shocks of the evening had left her reeling. She had no bandwidth for social graces, clearly, as she'd not only crashed these nice people's party but brought her dog. "I'm so sorry to interrupt, do you want me to take the dog outside?"

Angie waved her off. "Not at all. We're happy to have you both."

"I love dogs." Matthew pushed his chair out, sat on the floor, and opened his arms. Hugo waddled over to him immediately, tail wagging, and climbed straight into his lap—and he was normally slow to warm up to men.

Angie crossed to the refrigerator. "It's Matthew's eighteenth birthday. I just put the cake in the fridge, but there's plenty left over. You want a piece?"

"It's red velvet!" Matthew called out, as if that settled it.

Gabe stepped in, "As soon as you cross the threshold of this home, you have to eat something, I don't make the rules. She does." He nodded to his mother.

Iris managed a smile. "I'd love a small piece, thank you."

Angie handed her a paper plate with a slice. "We had double to celebrate tonight, Matthew's birthday and his first Giglio as a lifter tomorrow!"

Right, the Giglio festival, tomorrow. Iris had completely forgotten.

Gabe put a hand on Matthew's shoulder. "We've been hitting the gym together prepping for it. You feel ready, right, bro?"

Matthew flexed his arm muscles like a body builder.

"Iris, are you coming with us?" Angie asked.

"I think so . . ." Iris took a bite of cake to stall.

Gabe came to her rescue. "So you'll have plenty of time to pepper her with questions tomorrow night. I should get her and the pup to my place. Okay? I'll take the trash out on my way."

His mom was already rifling through the fridge again. "Yes to the trash, but Gabriel, take the rest of the chicken parm home with you, it's takin' up too much room in the fridge." She emerged with a Tupperware container with a precarious tinfoil top. "Take it."

Hugo sniffed the air approvingly.

Gabe was yanking the trash bag out and motioned to Iris and the leftovers. "Can you grab that, babe?"

"'Babe,'" Donna repeated, nudging Matthew, who giggled.

"C'mon, we gotta get outta here before they start roasting me."

Iris barely spoke on the ride to Gabe's apartment, and by the time they arrived at his place, Gabe knew something was very wrong, but he didn't press her. He made her a cup of tea, cracked a beer for himself, and they sat on his fire escape to talk. Somehow, with his quiet, patient company, Iris found the energy to fill him in. Not on the revelation from her childhood, but on the surveillance video discovery, Wolff using Patrick to cause the explosion, Jonathan strong-arming her at Rao's, even the sex tape, but Gabe was most concerned for her and the violation of her home. He urged her to call the authorities.

"I can't call the police. I have no proof. I don't even have the surveillance footage anymore, I'm locked out of my Wolff Dev email."

"But the police already have the proof, it's *their* NYPD surveillance at Hendricks. Maybe you just tip them off, tell them to look at the video again. And what about your apartment? That's enough evidence of a crime, breaking and entering. And basically kidnapping off the street, the message in the mirror? That's stalking, harassment, blackmail, threats . . ."

"It's my word against Jonathan's, and believe me, his will count more. The apartment was a clear escalation, but how far is he willing to go?"

"I still don't get how they broke in. You said there was no damage to the door. Could you have left it open this morning?"

"It locks automatically behind me. I mean, Wolff is a huge player in real estate, he probably has a way to get to every building manager, or pay one off, for a key. Or his guys are pros at picking a lock."

"And the doorman didn't see anything?"

"No. I had Sammy go over the lobby camera and the back entrance by the bike storage, and there was no one suspicious. They must have found another point of entry. Jonathan already had one of his goons get caught on video once, he's not dumb enough to do it twice."

"I still think we should report the break-in, even if you don't want to share your suspicions of who did it. Just sleep on it. I'll go with you to the station tomorrow."

Iris knew she wasn't going to take him up on that, for Gabe's own sake. Jonathan had proved too good at tracking her movements, and she couldn't risk another "friend" of his at the police precinct.

They came in from the fire escape, and Gabe ran her a bath, making sure the water wasn't too hot, and left her alone to take it. He got her a toothbrush and Tylenol PM at the bodega on the corner. He picked out the softest of all his T-shirts for her to sleep in. And he took Hugo out for his last walk of the night.

Lying in bed, an exhausted Iris still occasionally experienced a passing full body tremor, her flight response short-circuiting on loop. Gabe intuited that she didn't want to be touched and lay facing her with a worried expression.

"You know you can stay here as long as you like. I'm gonna skip the Giglio tomorrow night, there's way too much going on and this is way more important."

"No, you go. Matthew's counting on you. And it's not like you can do anything anyway. I'll just lock myself in here. Hugo will protect me."

"He's cute, but I don't think he's much of a watchdog." Gabe nodded to where Hugo slept with his legs splayed out behind him like a frog's. "I don't think you should be alone. If you're up for it, maybe you should come with us. Honestly, there's no safer place than Havemeyer Street during the Giglio. The place will be mobbed with people, clergy, and cops. My whole family is going, plus Pax and Scotty from the shop. Believe me, that crew isn't gonna let anything happen to you."

Iris considered it. She knew Jonathan cared about image, maybe a public place was best. "Okay, but you can't tell them about any of this. We need to keep this locked down until I figure out what I'm going to do to get Jonathan before he gets me or hurts anyone else. I don't want to tip him off, provoke him to release the tape . . . or worse."

Gabe looked skeptical but acquiesced.

He didn't know what she knew:

It can get worse.

CHAPTER

Fifty-four

D usk fell on Williamsburg as Iris walked to the Giglio festival surrounded by a phalanx of Gabe's family and friends. Gabe was holding her hand, he and his cousin Matthew wearing their lifters' uniform of purple tanks and bandanas; with them were Angie and Aunt Donna, and two friends from the hot shop, Pax, a nonbinary glassblower Iris had met once before, and Scotty, their skinny roommate. North Eighth Street was crammed with old-school carnival rides, game booths, and food stands. The streetlights were decorated with giant tinsel daisies, their sparkly heads bent toward the street. They passed a Tilt-A-Whirl, Cuzzin Vinny's Sausage Stand, and a water gun game called Machine Gun Fun—something she didn't particularly want to think about at a packed public event.

Iris wanted to enjoy the sights and sounds, but she couldn't stop looking over her shoulder. Being out in a crowd made her feel exposed and vulnerable. She kept flashing back to her ransacked apartment and Wolff's threats over dinner. Who had he sent to break into her place? Were they following her still? She didn't know who she was looking out for—would it be Esdras with his cauliflower ear, or some hired thug she wouldn't recognize? All she knew was she needed to remain vigilant.

They turned onto the main drag of Havemeyer Street, and Iris saw the Giglio. Looming above the throngs packing the street spiked an enormous steel tower, even taller than the buildings beside it.

Iris looked at Gabe in disbelief. "*That's* what you're lifting?"

"Yup, that's the Giglio!"

Matthew jumped up and down. "Eighty feet tall and four tons, lifted by a hundred men!"

"Gabe, this is insane."

"They've done it every year since 1887, and nobody's died yet—I don't think." Gabe laughed. "The community coming together to do the impossible is the whole thing. It's a tradition that gets passed down, families participate in it for generations."

"Most everybody from the neighborhood has moved out, upstate, Jersey, lots in Florida, but they all come home every year for the Giglio. I see classmates from elementary school." Then Angie's expression turned wistful. "I guess I'll travel in for it next year, if I sell the apartment."

"We'll always do it, Ma, wherever we are," Gabe said, putting a hand on her shoulder. "All right, me and Matthew better get over there. We'll catch up with you guys after the fireworks." He leaned his head close to Iris. "You still feeling good?"

"Of course. Go. Be safe!" Iris didn't want to let on to the others that she was out of sorts.

Donna squeezed her son. "Have fun, and stay next to Gabe!"

Gabe bent and kissed Iris, and he and Matthew said their good-byes to the group before disappearing into the crowd.

Iris felt more anxious already.

Donna grabbed her arm. "You like sausage and peppers?"

It was hard to spot who seemed out of place in a sea of people this diverse. Many were Italian Americans: the old-timers in bowling shirts that draped over round bellies, their spotted heads topped with fedoras, Panama hats, and trecolore berrettos with pom-poms on the top; elderly ladies shuffling in sandals or pushed in wheelchairs by dutiful sons, wearing sleeveless housedresses that exposed their arms, soft as ricotta, and crepey, sun-freckled bosoms; and the younger generation with tan skin, French manicures, curb chains and crucifixes, and Giglio tanks and tees from past years. But they were mixed with Brooklyn hipsters, rich kids of Williamsburg, and probably the largest group: families, of every race and ethnicity—Iris heard Spanish, Italian, and Russian spoken to many a wailing or giggling child.

Iris made eye contact with a little boy about two years old sitting on his father's shoulders, playing the bongos on his dad's head. The boy had dark hair in a bowl cut, cherubic cheeks rosy as a summer peach, and enormous brown eyes that tilted down like a puppy's. She wondered if she and Gabe had a child, would he look like that?

Someone pushed her, and Iris snapped her head to see a man in a Mets cap, but she didn't catch his face. He was already moving away, but the contact gave her a bad feeling.

They made their way to the front of the crowd nearer to the Giglio. Iris could see the tower was a crude metal structure decorated with religious figures and scenes of the myth behind the festival, including, Donna pointed out, the *gigli,* Italian for lilies, that gave the tower its name. The lifters had gathered to form lines underneath the wide, flat base undergirded by foam-wrapped I beams; Iris got on her tiptoes to see if she could spot Gabe among them, but there were too many. The lifters were men of all ages, from eighteen to over seventy, all body types and ethnicities. The only uniform traits were their purple Giglio T-shirts and purple bandannas catching their sweat. Soon, men with brass instruments, drums, and a microphone mounted the Giglio's base and began to set up music stands.

Pax snorted. "No way! The whole band *stands* on the tower?"

"And the Monsignor," Angie added, waving to someone she knew.

The Monsignor mounted the Giglio stage with a microphone and, in a thick Brooklyn accent, welcomed the crowd. His reedy voice amplified through funnel-shaped loudspeakers on either side of the Giglio at an uncomfortable volume. He ended his address by gleefully shouting into the microphone, *"Maestro, musica!"*

The brass band broke out into the tarantella and suddenly the Giglio lurched off the ground with the grace of Frankenstein's monster and began to "dance" as the men beneath it bounced it up and down.

Eight stories over their heads, the robes of San Paolino shook with the music. Iris could see how the lifters carried the structure literally on their backs, with their right shoulder beneath the metal beam undergirding the tower and their left arm resting on the left shoulder of the man in front of them, so that all the lifters formed one cooperative human organism, exactly as Gabe said, banding together to do the impossible.

Then a *capo,* a designated old-timer on the street, shouted directions at the lifters to coordinate their moves, and the entire structure began to creep down the street and tilt toward the people watching. Iris was surprised as those around her cheered and gleefully walked backward out of the way, giving the looming four-ton structure a minimal berth to advance.

But tonight, what others found thrilling, Iris found frightening. The dense crowd of adults and children, distracted by food and friends, jostling her, crisscrossing the street, making her feel claustrophobic as she retreated. The *capo* yelling, the horn players blaring, the lifters grimacing with exertion as they struggled to keep their footing, and most of all the vertiginous tower tilting perilously over the onlookers.

And everywhere, Iris looked for the guy in the Mets cap.

By the time the Giglio had completed its journey up and down Havemeyer Street, night had fallen. The Giglio, now lit in Technicolor tones, pierced the Prussian blue sky. The lilies were cast in citron yellow and lime green, the Virgin Mother and Christ in warm tangerine, and the face of San Paolino at the very top glowed an eerie icy blue. The *capo* on the ground shouted his final instructions to the lifters in a voice so hoarse he was unintelligible, and they lowered the massive structure with arduous synchronicity. At last the Giglio had come to rest.

There was a great round of cheers and applause, and the Monsignor announced it was time for the fireworks and began a countdown as everyone in the crowd joined in.

"Will Gabe come find us?" Iris shouted to Angie.

"After the fireworks."

"Eight . . . seven . . ."

Every face and smartphone turned toward the sky above the church, a starless black velvet behind a Lite-Brite yellow cross strung from the phone lines.

"Four . . . three . . . two . . ."

Iris's heart lurched when the first fireworks exploded off the church roof, which at only three stories tall made them as loud and close as Iris had ever seen. The singer and band played "God Bless America" as the fireworks started out slow, sparklers loping into the sky and sailing back down, making arches of red, green, and white, then shooting with quickening tempo, until it sounded like a cascading firing squad, an aggressive *rat-a-tat-tat*, searing the smoke-streaked sky.

Only Iris wasn't looking at the fireworks display. She instead scanned the crowd, reading each shiny face lit like a camera flash. Her growing sense of unease had peaked, and Iris felt viscerally certain she was being watched. She scanned for a Mets cap, but there were all kinds of caps in the crowd, mostly New York teams, and all looked equally innocent and guilty. Ultimately, Iris looked for anyone who was looking at her, but it was hard from ground level. The church steps would give her better sight lines, but she would feel too visible and exposed herself. She needed cover, she needed protection, she needed a sanctuary.

Iris signaled to Angie that she would be back, mounted the church steps, and entered the vestibule. She passed the painted plaster statue of La Pietà, Mary's mournful gaze while cradling her grown son in His final moments of suffering—a tender moment cast in a lurid hue, lit from beneath by candy-apple-red electronic votives.

Iris quickly scaled the small winding staircase to the second-floor landing. The fireworks thundered even louder, as they were being shot off the roof just overhead, and she could feel the sound in her chest. Every explosion shook the walls, and a speaker blaring the bandleader's singing was mounted outside one of the windows, his voice distorted by the proximity: "My home sweet home . . ."

The landing was a mezzanine hallway between two locked doors, but the small stained-glass windows, cracked open for ventilation, provided just the vantage point she needed. She searched the crowd methodically, beginning in the upper left quadrant of the far side-walk in front of the Knights of Columbus and moving right to the zeppole stand, left and right, row by row. She paid special attention to every man in a ball cap, locating every Mets cap, but none of the wearers were Esdras or anyone doing anything other than eating, drinking a beer, or watching the fireworks with everyone else. She spotted Gabe and Matthew side by side in front of the Giglio. Their faces were angled to the fireworks, with Matthew's head resting on Gabe's shoulder.

Then Iris saw him—a man wearing sunglasses and a leather jacket. It was already dark and still well above eighty degrees, why was he dressed like that? He cut across the crowd with purpose, pay-ing no attention to the fireworks. She swiveled her head to locate Angie and Donna. It looked like the man in sunglasses was headed straight for them.

Iris's heart began to beat faster. Wolff wouldn't do anything to them, would he? Could he even know of their connection? But then, he had met Gabe, and Wolff had showed no hesitation using family against his enemies or even friends.

She retrieved her phone from her pocket and frantically scrolled through her texts with Gabe, trying to find Angie's number, cursing herself for not making her a contact. The man in sunglasses was get-ting closer, his right hand shoved in his jacket pocket.

Iris called the number and listened to it ring, but Angie had no reaction down on the street. "C'mon, pick up, *pick up*." The fireworks boomed overhead, the music, the chatter, the *oohs* and *ahhs*, Angie couldn't hear it ring. The call went to voicemail.

Someone clasped her shoulder, and Iris spun around, dropping her phone.

CHAPTER

Fifty-five

All evening Iris had been anticipating a male threat, and yet here she faced the most insidious enforcer in Wolff's predatory pack.

Marilyn bared her teeth in a smile. "Sorry, hon, I didn't mean to startle you."

Iris dropped quickly to grab her phone and sprang back up, retreating until her shoulder blades hit the wall. "Get the fuck away from me."

"Oh my God, Iris. I'm here as a friend."

"You are *not* my friend. Did you follow me here? Do you have people tailing me full time now?"

"Let's calm down, okay? You're upset, understandably, but it's making you paranoid—"

"Paranoid!" Iris scoffed.

"I said I understand your emotion right now, but you're not thinking straight. Hear me out. No one is tailing you. I heard you mention to your old Candela colleague that you'd be here tonight, and then I saw you during the fireworks. I just wanted to talk to you—outside the office."

"The office of your criminal enterprise? Jonathan snatched me off the street and blackmailed me over dinner, all while someone else broke into my apartment and trashed the place. So if you're suggesting the danger is confined to the *office,* you're wrong."

"Jonathan would never touch your home."

"So one of his guys did, what's the difference? As if the rest is fair game, but he'd draw the line at breaking and entering. He didn't draw it at *murder!*"

The last word silenced them both with its weight.

Iris stared her down. "Or maybe you just don't know as much as you think you do about what goes on at Wolff Development."

"I know about everything." Marilyn said it like it was something comforting instead of intimidating. "And I want to talk to you in a different way than Jonathan did. I want to talk to you woman to woman."

"Yeah, you're a real girl's girl, Marilyn. You happily oversaw Jonathan inviting me and my boyfriend to his house so that he could film us without my consent, make a sex tape to blackmail me—"

"Not blackmail—*insurance.*" Marilyn pointed a manicured finger. "Don't forget *you* were the aggressor here. Snooping behind our back, investigating, manipulating Jonathan's own lawyer to give you evidence that compromises the company. It looks more like you were positioning yourself to extort him than the other way around."

"Extortion and whistleblowing aren't the same thing. You killed those people to get a deal through."

"That was an accident, no one was supposed to be there. You might remember reading that someone on the first floor called maintenance to report a smell of gas well before the explosion, but the janitor on duty didn't bother to check it. Who do you think placed that maintenance call?"

Iris eyed her suspiciously.

"That's right. Me. We wanted everyone to be evacuated, that's how it was supposed to go. I called as soon as the Dante valve was removed, there was time to save everyone. But the very problems we are seeking to address were in full force that day, and that neglect resulted in tragedy. If not for that Patterson girl, the broken system would've claimed more victims."

"That community looks out for itself against the wolves."

"We all have to look out for ourselves, Iris. That's the most important lesson a woman can learn. No one is coming to save us. We have to save ourselves." Marilyn looked at her with an expression that was at once patronizing and full of sympathy. "I see you taking care of everyone around you. Using your leverage with Jonathan to bargain for the Pattersons' apartment—they signed the paperwork today, a family you're not even related to. I see you using your work contacts to get that very handsome but very unserious boyfriend of yours a real job. I see it because I see myself. I used to be like you. Doing for people to show that I'm good, I'm worthy. To *make* them love me—or at least, to make them stay."

The sincerity of her tone compelled Iris to listen.

"It's just a different kind of blackmail, Iris, an emotional one. Love without trust is only a transaction. A deal. And you're getting the short end of the stick. But when it comes to the deal Jonathan is offering you, my sincere advice to you is this: *Take it.* Jonathan isn't the monster you think he is. But even if he were, you're not going to get a better deal in your life than working with us, not against us in this moment. This is a turning point in your life." Marilyn surprised Iris by taking her hand; more surprisingly, Iris let her. "Choose yourself. It's not selfish, it's self-preservation. Choose your future child. You're pricking yourself every day, suffering for that baby. And you're smart, you're not waiting for a man. You think Gabe is gonna be the provider type? He's still struggling to parent himself, like most men. It will all fall to you. Trust me, I raised a child on my own. I know how hard it is, especially broke. I couldn't have done it without this job. A woman has only one lookout beyond herself, and that's when she's a mother. Let me be a mother to you now and protect you from making the biggest mistake of your life."

Iris broke from her grasp. "Protect me like you protected Patrick?"

"Yes." Marilyn cocked her head in confusion. "Yes, that's what I'm saying."

Iris took a slow step around her, and Marilyn mirrored it, like two magnets locked in attraction and repulsion. "You looked the other way while that man *used* your son to do his dirty work, because, why? Because he *pays* you?"

"What?"

"You didn't protect Patrick from him, you served him up on a silver platter. You *groomed* him for Jonathan. You let Jonathan ruin his life before it even began, ruin his innocence, ruin his fucking soul!"

"I don't know what you're talking about."

"It's Patrick on that tape at the Hendricks projects. He's the one who sabotaged the Dante valve on the gas pipe. It could've been any-body, but Jonathan used your son to hurt those people, used your kid to commit a heinous crime."

Marilyn shook her head. "No. You're wrong. Pat would've told me. It couldn't have been him."

"Yes, it was! Jonathan didn't show you the tape, did he? You didn't fucking know!" Iris scoffed in surprise at Jonathan's cunning. "He recruits your only child and he doesn't even let you in on it. Of course, because that way, he traps you both—Jonathan gets Patrick's silence and loyalty because Patrick doesn't want to let his mom down, and he guarantees yours because you'd never implicate your own son." Iris gathered strength like a forming tornado and advanced on Marilyn, backing her up with every step. "See it now? When you made a deal with Jonathan, you made a deal with the devil. And after twenty years, he fucked you. Because he did this to Patrick right under your roof. Under your nose. You sacrificed your only child for money, for security, for status—"

"No, I did everything for him!"

"—Before his life even got started, he did the worst thing he'll ever do. And he only did it because you told him to trust Jonathan like a father, you told him Jonathan would take care of him, just like you're telling me. But it's a lie. Jonathan is evil, and you let him into your house!"

Marilyn stopped abruptly as the mezzanine railing dug into her back. Her face was full of fear, not of falling, but of the truth.

"Wake up!" Iris raged at Marilyn, incensed with an anger that had smoldered inside her since her own parents had missed the signs. "It doesn't matter if you knew or not, either way, you failed Patrick. You didn't protect him. He's trying to protect *you.* He is keeping this se-cret for *you,* to spare *you.* And trust me, even if you all get away with it, the secret is going to eat him alive."

Fifty-six

I ris found Gabe gathered with his family at the base of the church steps. They fell into each other's arms, exhausted for completely different reasons. The fireworks had ended. It was time to go home.

After stopping at Gabe's place to pick up Hugo, the three of them drove back to Manhattan to Iris's apartment. She had left that day's fertility medication in her fridge and had to go back to take her shot. And they decided that, after a good night's sleep, they would tackle the cleanup in the morning. Gabe still urged her to report it to the police.

When Iris and Gabe arrived at her apartment building, her doorman, Sammy, was on the phone at the front desk, but he lowered it to give her a wave. He seemed about to say something but Iris gave him a friendly nod and walked swiftly by, with Hugo helpfully tugging toward their apartment. She was too exhausted for small talk. Iris just wanted to go home, even if it was a wreck.

Iris opened her front door to the sound of the vacuum running inside and stopped short.

Gabe put out a protective hand and shouted, "Yo! Who's there?"

The vacuum was cut. And Ben in a backwards baseball cap sauntered from her living room. "Iris! You're home."

"What are you doing here?"

"Cleaning. I wanted to get more done before you got here, but it was worse than I thought." His gaze fell on Gabe. "Oh, hey, man, I'm Ben."

Iris shook her head in utter confusion. "How did you get in here?"

Ben reached into his shorts pocket and pulled out his old key. She had let him keep it, premised on the idea that he might occasionally look after Hugo for her, but not to use it like this.

Gabe dropped Hugo's leash, and the old dog waddled over to Ben's knees for a clueless hello.

Ben ruffled Hugo's ears and put the other hand on his heart. "Believe me when I say, I am so, so sorry."

Iris squinted, uncomprehending. "What are you saying? Sorry for *what*?"

Ben gestured to the chaos around him. "For what Madison did to the place."

"Madison?" Iris repeated, shocked.

Ben yammered on, "I told her everything when I broke things off, and she went nuts. But I never thought she'd lash out at *you*! She stole my spare key! I got it back, obviously, but I might change the locks if I were you . . ."

Iris was frozen as this new information prickled her scalp and rippled down to the soles of her feet, when she realized the absolute worst person to be in audience for this conversation was—

Gabe held up his hands. "What the actual fuck is going on? Who is Madison? Who is this guy?"

Iris answered, "He's my ex-boyfriend."

"Oh, is this . . . ?" Ben laid down the vacuum cleaner and headed for the door. "I'll let you two talk."

After ushering Ben out, Iris briefly pressed her head against the locked door, gathering the strength to face her mess. When she turned, she saw Gabe slumped in the center of her sagging couch, crestfallen. She picked her way through her wreckage to go to him.

"So is this all a lie?" Gabe looked stricken. "Did you ever think Wolff broke in, or was that an elaborate cover story for having sex with your ex?"

Her shoulders sank. "No, absolutely not. I completely thought it was Wolff, it made sense at the time. It never crossed my mind it could be Ben's girlfriend, it's so random—"

"But you did have sex with him."

Iris lowered her gaze in shame. "Once."

"When?"

"After Shelter Island." After a beat of silence, she added, "But before you dropped off the Kintsugi vase." But that sounded even worse to her ears.

Gabe breathed heavily through his nose. "I saw him. I knew he looked familiar. God, I'm such an idiot. I fucking bumped into him leaving your place that morning."

"I'm so sorry. He surprised me by showing up here, I didn't know where you and I stood, and he said things that the most hurt part of me really needed to hear." She knelt on the floor by his knees. "But I know now that my feelings for Ben were always about stopping pain, stopping loneliness, or hiding from it. I didn't want to get back with him. Even when we were a couple, I'm not sure I really wanted him. Not like I want you."

"I feel so stupid."

"Don't, please don't—"

"I was doing arts and crafts while you're fucking some other guy. Worse, an *ex*."

Iris's heart wrenched. "It was a terrible mistake, I loved what you made for me—"

"Here I thought *I* had to prove to *you* that I could stick it out, I had to apologize to *you* for one bad night, and you let me grovel! You let me think I was the problem. When in reality, we had our first fight, and you went back to your ex. You know, you could've just told me I was your rebound and saved us both a lot of trouble."

"You're not a rebound. You changed everything."

"I'm supposed to believe that now? Just, what, take your word for it? How can I trust you?"

"I'm asking you to let me earn it back."

"Why should I?"

"Because you want to? Because I want you to. Because we want to take a chance on each other. It's always a chance, Gabe. Be brave and try to make something beautiful, knowing it might break—isn't that what you taught me?" Iris had been humbled by all she had learned about herself in the last few days, but with it came new clarity. "Getting to know yourself takes a lifetime, getting to know each other takes a hell of a lot longer than a few weeks. Trust means you don't know everything. All I know is how I feel when we're together, and when I'm with you, I feel alive, and safe, and beautiful, and . . . like myself."

Gabe clenched his jaw, holding back emotion. "So everybody lies, the truth is unknowable. What a bunch of bullshit. Convenient take for the day I find out you cheated on me."

"That's not why I'm saying it."

"You made me go against every instinct. You actually had me believing this could last, that *you* were different. But you're just the latest in a long line of people I cared about who bailed on me. You believe so much in feeling? I had a gut feeling we were wrong for each other on Shelter Island, and I wanted out. But then something made me change my mind."

"That something was what's good between us, what's worth fighting for."

"I'm supposed to let down my walls, get deep with you, worrying that one day, like last time, you'll see a side of me you don't like, and *BAM*—you're gone."

Iris picked up an overturned chair and sat down. "Now you know how I feel."

"Don't turn this around—"

"I've been living with that fear this whole time. Probably my whole fucking life!"

"Well, you didn't get it from me. I never wanted you to be anyone else. You were the one who put me in situations where I wasn't comfortable, where I couldn't be real."

"Not being comfortable isn't the same as not being real. Real is usually uncomfortable." Iris rubbed her temples. "But that wasn't why you were so unhappy with me on Shelter Island. That wasn't what was missing then. It's not what's missing now."

"Then what was it?"

Tears filled her eyes. "You don't love me. You don't even know me."

He softened, but only at the edges. "How can you say that?"

"You fell for a trick. A ploy." Iris felt emotion overcoming her. She tried to be tough, but she couldn't hide the heartbreak cracking her voice. "You're a *sucker.*"

Gabe eyed her warily.

"You wouldn't have looked twice at me if not for the *perfume.*"

"Huh?"

"You met me with it, you fell for me with it. We've barely had sex without it."

Gabe snorted. "I've had relationships that were just about sex, Iris, that was never what this was, this was different. And it certainly wasn't about perfume."

"That's why you couldn't get hard for me in the Hamptons, the perfume had washed off."

Gabe's cheeks colored. "I couldn't get it up because I felt like a broke punk compared to your boss—before I knew he was evil."

Iris shook her head. "After that, I was scared to test it, but I had to. I liked you too much not to know. So when we made up, I didn't wear the perfume, and I thought you wanted me for real, but then the next morning, you wore my scarf because it had the fragrance, you said you couldn't get enough of it. I thought I wasn't wearing it, but it was on the scarf all along!"

Gabe's eyes flared. "You don't believe I love you because I complimented your perfume? Are you insane?"

"Maybe I am! But it's not a normal perfume, it's magic! Rapacine made it for me. She's a perfumer, or a witch, probably both. It works on you without you realizing, it alters your brain chemistry. For the last few weeks, everyone has been responding to me differently because of it. And I loved it! Because it helped me do what I always do—hide! I've spent my whole life in disguise as a normal, chill, happy girl, I just never faked it so well as when I had the perfume!"

"What is this story you're telling? Just tell me the truth!"

Iris sprang up and went to the bathroom, tripping over the mess and Gabe followed. She dropped to her knees on the bathroom floor and began sweeping her hands over the spot where the puddle had been, but the perfume had evaporated and left only sparkling specks of glass behind. She bent so low to the floor that her nose touched the tile, but she couldn't smell it anymore. She grabbed larger pieces of the broken bottle and rose to meet Gabe in the bathroom doorway.

"Here, here, smell. Smell this! This is what you fell in love with!" Iris thrust the broken glass at him in cupped hands.

"What? I don't smell anything—oh my God, Iris, you're cut." Gabe caught her by the wrist, smearing a trail of crimson blood.

Iris opened her hands to see that the shards of cicada wing and the broken bottle base had sliced her palms, and though the perfume was gone, her blood had taken its place.

Gabe pulled her over to the sink and turned on the water, making sure it was warm, not hot, and held each of her hands under the running faucet, gently washing the glittering slivers and fragments out of her flesh. The water ran rosy pink.

After a little soap and a delicate pat dry, he closed the toilet seat top and sat her down on it. "Do you have a tweezer?"

"It's fine." Her energy spent, she slumped with her hands palms up on her lap. In seconds, the lacerations bloomed with fresh scarlet drops.

Gabe was standing, turning on every bathroom light. "Just tell me where I can find tweezers."

"Medicine chest."

Gabe turned to the mirror, pausing to read the slur still written there. With one forceful swipe, he smeared it to illegibility, before opening the cabinet to find what he was looking for. He sat across from her on the edge of the tub, her bathroom was so small their knees touched. "Believe me, little splinters hang behind, you have to get them all out. Give." He put out his hand. She reached hers out to him, and Gabe took it on his lap, opened her palm, and went to careful work.

Iris still had more to say. "You only like things that aren't broken. You liked me when you thought I was the together one, but now I'm coming apart. And you don't know how deep the cracks go, it would scare the shit out of you. It used to scare me, I was too afraid to look—but now I have. I'd been lying to myself for twenty-five years, and I'm done. No more. I'm done hiding my ugliness, and anyone else's for that matter."

Gabe dug out another splinter of glass, making her wince, and he whispered an apology.

But Iris expected this to be painful. "You want the truth? My truth has never been clearer. I love you. But I know how I got you, and I can't believe in us when we started like that. So that's it. You should just go." Iris pulled her hands back to her own lap. "I mean it. I have my own stuff to face, and you can't fix it for me. So maybe I'll heal myself or maybe I won't. But if we ever meet me again, at least we'll both know who we are."

Gabe exhaled, his broad shoulders sloping. "I never wanted you to be perfect, even if I did think you were pretty damn close. To be completely honest, your super-togetherness stressed me the fuck out. And I told you, nothing about you disgusts me or ever could." He ducked his head to make her meet his eye. "Because I did love you, Iris. I still do. And I don't smell any perfume."

Her breath caught.

"But I don't know if I can forgive you."

Fifty-seven

I f not for Hugo needing to be walked the next morning, Iris would not have gotten out of bed at all. She slowly began the job of putting her apartment back together, filling three trash bags with damaged items. She should have been angrier, but in some way, after everything, the purge felt good. Iris had begun to cleanse herself of the noxious lies she'd built her life around, and she wanted to keep it going. But the work, internally and externally, was exhausting. The hormones didn't help; Iris took her final "trigger shot," beginning the forty-eight-hour countdown to her egg retrieval procedure.

It wasn't her usual numbness slowing her down, but the opposite. Over the last several days, her system had been overwhelmed with feeling. She corrected herself: The feeling had started earlier—with the perfume. The perfume had kicked her out of her cerebral existence and back into her body. Wearing the perfume, Iris felt and gave in to her physical desires, heeded her gut instincts, and connected to a more sensual experience of the world around her, maybe for the first time. Rapacine had told her the fragrance would arouse her limbic system, the most primitive part of the brain that processes scent, memory, and emotion—Iris wondered if the witchy woman knew just how much would be unlocked.

When the initial frisson and fun had worn off, and the fragrance appeared to be wreaking havoc on her life, Iris began to think of the perfume as a Pandora's box. Now she understood the perfume was only the key—the Pandora's box was her body.

Iris remembered Rapacine's story about her mother, and the lesson that if you numb yourself to pain, you numb yourself to life's pleasures, passions, and beauty. And to make the trade even worse, it doesn't keep you safe like you think it will, it only blinds you to recognizing and reacting to the true danger. At some level, Iris now understood that she had learned to dissociate during the molestation, and the coping mechanism had never left her. She had learned to distrust her own body; her body hadn't been able to fight back or to flee, and the trauma had rewired her. Ever since, when Iris felt stressed, she retreated into her mind, strategizing how to behave perfectly and control outcomes, to only middling, unsatisfying success.

Not so with the perfume.

With Gabe, she had felt love. She wasn't sure if she could trust it, wasn't sure it was wise. But she'd felt it.

There was one part of her that felt lighter. Acknowledging what Jacob had done to her and what had really happened on the night of the fire released her from her lifelong shame about not being grateful enough. Her body had known what had happened all along, she just hadn't listened to it. Although now Iris substituted blaming herself for that instead. And what was she supposed to do with this knowledge now that she had it? How could she ever share it with an intimate partner? It was disturbing, it was repulsive, it was intimidating, it was *damaged.* How could she explain it to someone when she was just barely coming to terms with it herself? She knew she had a long road ahead of her in processing and healing, one long overdue. But she was thirty-five.

Would she ever be fixed enough to be loved?

Or, could she learn to love herself unfixed?

One step at a time.

Iris was gathering the clothes that had been pulled from her drawers when she saw Gabe's potted orchids overturned on the floor. The dirt had spilled out, the little bamboo stick propping the stems now bent them to the side, and a few of the purple flower heads had wilted or snapped off. But the Kintsugi vase—she bent to pick it up, turning the small blue globe in her hands—the vase was unbroken. Or at least, not rebroken. She ran a finger over the gold veins, checking for weaknesses, but the seams had held strong. Maybe even stronger.

It reminded her again of Rapacine's teaching: A flower's scent was most beautiful and powerful on the cusp of decay. Maybe what was dying off was the old ways that no longer served her. And the beauty of decay is the becoming something new.

Her phone rang. It was an incoming call from Hannah. Only when she answered, it was Mike, and he sounded scared. Hannah was about to have an emergency caesarean at Lenox Hill. Her water broke, and the baby was still breech. Hannah's blood pressure spiked and the baby's heart rate slowed. She was going into surgery—now. He was about to go in with her. Her family was on their way from Pennsylvania but might not make it in time.

Iris had ordered an Uber before she'd ended the call.

Iris raced down the hall of Lenox Hill Hospital's maternity floor, following the directions to room 416. She found it with the door ajar and peeked in; she could see only the foot of the hospital bed and Mike curled up in a nearby armchair, gazing sleepily into a bassinet. She knocked lightly, and Mike sprang up to meet her at the door.

"They're both asleep. Let's talk out here."

They went back into the hallway and took two chairs across the hall. Mike was wearing a long-sleeved T-shirt inside out, with sweatpants and loafers, like he'd gotten dressed in a hurry. Not that Iris looked any better.

"Is Hannah okay?" Iris asked.

"She did amazing. I mean, I was freaking out, but she was calm and so freaking brave—" Mike's voice cracked and his brow creased as his eyes washed with tears. "I didn't know a person could be that strong, but she is." He gathered himself with a sniff. "And they said it all went good. She was awake the whole time, and they said the surgery and delivery and sutures, everything went perfectly right. And we have a healthy, beautiful baby girl!"

"Aww, a girl!" Iris pretended she was learning this for the first time, but she didn't have to fake the emotion. "That's wonderful."

"Iris, I owe you an apology."

"Mike—"

"I haven't been myself these last few months. I've wanted to have a family with Hannah since our first date, but when the reality of this enormous change was coming, I panicked. I started drinking way too much, I acted out, I made a mess of my life at the exact moment I needed to be building a home." Mike's jaw clenched, his regret plain. "What I did to you the night at my party was totally out of line, and I'm so sorry. And worse was how I handled it afterwards. I was so embarrassed and ashamed and scared you were gonna tell Hannah that I gaslighted you, when I knew it was my fuckup and mine alone. And Hannah knows that too, I came clean, about everything. But I'm so sorry I did that to you, and to her."

Iris felt emotion welling in her chest.

"I did the same thing at work. I'd have two Scotches at lunch and act like an idiot. In my mind, I stayed on the right side of the line, but the line wasn't good enough. I pushed a flirtation on Toni and made her uncomfortable. When I realized I messed up, I told the partners I wanted her off my cases, I didn't mean to block her from getting an offer, but they mistook it to be because she wasn't up to snuff, and I didn't correct them. I behaved dishonorably, and I own it. So I resigned from the firm."

By this, Iris felt less moved. But she nodded.

"But with the baby here, everything is different now. I know that sounds like a line, but I feel it to my marrow. Today I felt what it would be like to lose Hannah, and it would end me. I love her more than anything, and I saw what she endured for our family, and I'm never gonna let myself fall short of her standard again, she deserves that ten times over. And when I held my daughter for the first time, the overwhelming love I felt and the instinct to protect her, it gave me instant clarity. I need to be the best father to her and the best husband to Hannah that I can possibly be. Nothing else matters. I will make it my life's work."

Iris took a deep breath. Mike seemed sincere, and she could tell becoming a father had moved him deeply. She just hoped he followed through on doing that work on himself. She looked him square in the eye. "You have to do better for Hannah or you will lose her, because she knows her worth, and I won't let her forget it. And you'll have to do better for your daughter, because she'll love you whether you deserve it or not. And if you don't deserve it, she'll never learn to love a man who does."

Mike nodded. "You're right. I will."

Then the sound of a baby crying from inside the hospital room caught their attention.

"They're awake! Let's go in." Mike led the way and Iris stepped gingerly into Hannah's hospital room. The nurse leaning over the bed straightened up and stepped back to reveal the most beautiful thing Iris had ever seen: her best friend holding the love of her life.

"Hiii," Hannah said softly. She was sitting up in bed with her back and legs propped on pillows, and in her arms was a tiny bundle in a pink-and-blue-striped hat. "Meet Olivia Grace Lefebvre."

"Oh my God!" Iris whisper-squealed and rushed to Hannah's bedside. "She's so beautiful, and I love her name! Welcome to the world, Olivia."

Olivia was perfect and pink. Her eyes were squeezed shut, and she had round, rosy cheeks with the faintest peach fuzz, her mother's button nose, and the beginnings of her dad's hair in strawberry-blond wisps at her temples. The baby turned toward her mother, nosing at her chest, and reached a tiny starfish hand out, then let it drape over her eye, as if to block the light. And suddenly Iris was mentally redesigning the maternity room lighting to better suit brand-new eyes.

"How are you feeling?"

"Shell-shocked, my legs are numb, I'm wearing bloody mesh undies, and I've never been happier. I didn't know I could love anyone so much. I feel like my heart doesn't fit in my chest. Actually I feel like my heart is on my chest right now." Hannah looked down lovingly at her infant daughter.

Mike came around the other side of the bed and kissed baby Olivia on the head, then kissed Hannah on the cheek, and Hannah watched him look at their daughter, both of their expressions soft. Taking in the tableau, Iris understood why Hannah was giving Mike a second chance. It wasn't denial, or because she had given up her job, or even because she didn't want to be a single mom. There was true love and trust between them. Cracked, but not beyond repair.

The nurse came over to change the bag on Hannah's IV and said, "Dr. Demchur is about to come in to check on Olivia, and I should check your sutures first."

Iris stepped out of the way. "I'll give you some privacy. Can I get you something from the cafeteria?"

Hannah widened her eyes. "Ooh, can you get me a *regular Coke*?"

"Abso-fucking-lutely. In a cup with ice, maybe ice chips?"

"Omigod, *yes*!"

"Does that make it that much better?" Mike asked.

"Yes," Hannah and Iris answered in unison.

Iris was just returning to the maternity floor with Hannah's icy Coke and a snack when she received a text message from an unfamiliar number. She opened it:

Hey, it's Sofia. Turn on channel
six right now!!!

Iris looked up at the TV mounted in the waiting area, which was on NY1 on mute. Luckily no one else waiting seemed to be watching it, all were absorbed in their families or their iPhones. Iris found the remote and changed the channel to Sofia's daytime show *Between Us*, where her news co-host, Kaitlin Cannon, was saying something above the chyron **EXCLUSIVE BREAKING NEWS**. Iris turned up the volume.

"—our own Sofia Morales brings you this exclusive report. Sofia?"

The camera cut to Sofia, looking beautiful as always but unusually serious. "Thanks, Kaitlin. Star real estate developer Jonathan Wolff has been taken into custody today on charges of felony murder, conspiracy to commit arson, and related charges in connection with last month's fatal gas explosion in a Chelsea public housing project, which killed two people and seriously injured six others. The gas leak was previously ruled an accident, but authorities now allege that Wolff masterminded the explosion in a scheme to push through a lucrative government contract to rebuild. My sources indicate that Wolff's own employees, longtime executive assistant Marilyn Hruska and her son, Patrick Davies, are cooperating with prosecutors. A grand jury will be convened next week to rule on Mr. Wolff's indictment. If found guilty, he could face life in prison. When asked for comment, the mayor, who has received campaign donations from Wolff Development and other real estate interests, had this to say."

The camera cut to the mayor with a microphone in his face. "I can't comment on an ongoing investigation, but housing throughout New York has been at the mercy of greed and corruption for too long, and now we see the terrible cost. That's why I'm calling all developers to sign an ethics pledge—"

Iris was distracted by a new incoming text from Sofia:

> Confirmed everything you said when Hruska flipped on Wolff this morning, and she's got the receipts! Son will plead guilty in hopes of a lesser sentence. Wolff's going down! My producer says it's my story, so I'm officially on news! Stay tuned. Thx again for the scoop!

Marilyn flipped on Wolff. Iris sat back in the plastic chair, stunned. If Jonathan was a cult leader, Marilyn was a true believer, and a well-compensated one. And yet she drew the line at her son. Nothing would make up for the loss of life caused by the explosion, and Marilyn and Patrick's involvement was unforgivable. But Iris was surprised that Marilyn had heard her that night at the Giglio, that she had taken in Iris's words and actually let them change her mind. Marilyn didn't let guilt, shame, self-preservation, or personal loss keep her from taking responsibility and doing the right thing— Patrick too—even if vengeance had more than a little to do with it.

A mother's first job is to protect her child, even if that means making them face the worst thing they have ever done. Because self-preservation bought with a lie is no life preserver at all; it's cement around the ankles. Jacob learned that. And the lie nearly drowned Iris with him.

And as ugly as the truth was, she was glad to be cut free.

Iris reentered Hannah's room with the soda and a bag of Herr's Sour Cream 'n' Onion potato chips. From Hannah's reaction you would've thought it was a Michelin-starred meal.

"Do you want to hold her?" Hannah asked.

"Can I?"

Hannah smiled. "She has to meet Aunt Iris."

Iris took a seat in the armchair beside the bed, and Mike gathered Olivia from his wife's arms. He brought the bundle over, eyes glued to his daughter, holding her like she was the most precious treasure in the world, because she was.

He directed Iris as he gentled the baby into her waiting arms. "Okay, hold your arms just like mine—nope, like this—yeah. Don't feel bad, I learned this an hour ago. Support the head, you got her— you got her? *There.*"

Iris melted under the baby's warm, soft heft. Olivia weighed not an ounce over seven pounds, and yet her body carried the weight of a woman's entire lifetime. Baby Olivia was tiny, fragile, vulnerable, and by far the most powerful person in the room. Every scrunch of her nose and attempt at an expression was cause for delight. Her yawn was phenomenal. Iris felt overcome with affection and optimism, imagining this little person's life at the very beginning, full of innocence and possibility. And just as Hannah was family to Iris, so too was Olivia.

"Smell her head," Hannah said.

Iris bent and sniffed Olivia's soft crown. She couldn't pick out a single note, but it was the most divine, delicious, heart-expanding, and soul-affirming perfume.

Fifty-eight

O n the day of Iris's egg retrieval, she skipped breakfast and arrived at Family Tree Fertility at eight-thirty in the morning, as instructed.

Nurse Dani greeted her with a hug. "Today is the day! How have the last few days been for you?"

Iris widened her eyes. It was an impossible question to answer, for reasons the nurse couldn't possibly imagine. "Intense."

"Yup, the hormones can really make you nuts at the end. They're an emotional roller coaster, I hear that from everyone. But after this, you'll even out."

Iris wondered how much the hormones had influenced all that had happened over the last two weeks. She changed into a gown, socks, and surgical cap and lay down on a bed. Dani wheeled her to the operating room, which was small and incongruously homey with floral wallpaper. Not that Iris felt at ease. She tried not to stare at the instruments on the side table, like the giant cervix-piercing needle.

Dr. Alsarraj entered and greeted her warmly. He introduced her to Dr. Parikh, the anesthesiologist, and Dr. Goldberg, the embryologist who would be evaluating and preserving the eggs after retrieval. Dr. Alsarraj explained, "This is called twilight anesthesia, you won't be fully under, but you're going to feel like you're falling asleep. You won't feel any pain or anything at all during the procedure. And in forty-five minutes we'll be all done, and another forty-five after that, you can go home. Do you have someone to pick you up?"

Iris nodded. "A friend."

"Great. As I said, you should feel fine but too groggy to get home by yourself." Dr. Alsarraj stepped aside so the anesthesiologist could take his place beside Iris.

Dr. Parikh put the plastic mask over Iris's nose and mouth. "I always tell my patients to think of something nice."

Iris closed her eyes and reflected on the better moments of the last few days. She thought about Olivia in her arms and prayed that what she was doing now would one day let her hold a baby of her own.

She thought about family. What makes a good one, a safe one, a happy one. She thought about her friends, and the family they had become for her.

She thought about the Pattersons, and how they got their sweetheart deal on the apartment in under the wire. Roman, acting as their real estate agent, had those papers signed and notarized in the nick of time.

Roman. No longer a sore spot for her thoughts to land. After visiting Hannah at the hospital, Iris had texted Roman asking him to coffee, and happily, he'd agreed. It was the first time they'd seen each other since the night they'd had their terrible fight, and the tension had taken such a toll on them both that nearly all was forgiven as soon as they shared their first hug. But they had important things to say to each other. Iris was able to apologize for being judgmental and dismissive of Roman and James's family plans. And Roman apologized for not duly considering the emotional weight of his request and treating her fertility struggles like "buy one, get one free." They both expressed how much the thought of losing their friendship pained them and promised to talk to each other and *listen* in the future.

Then Roman really surprised her. He slid a small velvet box to the middle of the table. "Not for *you*," Roman said with a smile. "But you have no idea how hard it was to choose this without your advice. Open it, I need your blessing before I give it to James."

The box contained a rhodium band with black diamond pavé. The ring glittered in the light. "Oh, Rome, he's gonna love it."

"You think?"

"I know." Iris wanted to have a do-over of the last time they discussed a major life change. "I won't doubt, and I won't assume, I'll just ask—what made you change your mind?"

"This summer, as difficult and stressful as it was, was a game changer for us. Because it burst the bubble that things were always gonna be pretty and easy, but we got through it together. It took James a while to trust I wasn't going to leave, which I wasn't helping by being so anti-marriage, but now he knows I'm not going anywhere, with or without a legal union. And once he backed off a bit, it gave me the space to rethink my stance."

"Growth—we love to see it!"

"I know, right? I saw how he jumped in to help his sister and his niece and nephew. He was so patient and devoted, he did everything to help them to make the best of a bad situation. And I realized making a family with him wouldn't trap me, it would make me the luckiest guy in New York."

"Aw, I'm so happy for you, that's so—"

"Wait, you're gonna like this part." Roman held up a hand. "I hate to admit it, but some of what you said that night resonated. I mean, why *was* I able to envision having a kid but couldn't let go of 'I'm never getting married'? I still don't believe it was the perfume, but it was my own childhood shit, that when I think of marriage, I flash to hearing my parents fighting and being desperate to fix it, but I never could."

"And it was never your fault. But if you're always running from your past, then it's still controlling you. You are not your most frightened version of yourself." Iris still needed to hear it as she said it.

"Exactly. I'm nothing like my parents, and James is from another planet."

Iris laughed.

"So I was mad at you for three days, and then I went and bought the ring." Roman sucked down the last of his iced coffee. "So I guess, thank you?"

"You don't have to thank me." Iris gave his hand a squeeze. "But you do have to let me pick my own bridesmaid dress."

"Oh God, we're not having anyone at the altar with us. Wear what you want and sit the fuck down."

"Cheers to that!"

. . .

When Iris woke up from the procedure, her head felt stuffed with cotton. The room she was in was dark, with soft light coming in around a curtain wall in front of her. She was covered with an extra blanket but still felt cold, and her mouth was dry.

Dani appeared from behind the curtain. "Glad to see you're awake. Would you like a cup of water?"

Iris nodded. Dani already had it in her hand. She helped Iris to sit up and take a sip. Slowly her brain fog began to lift. "Was it good?"

"Everything went great. Dr. Goldberg is going to evaluate the eggs retrieved today for their quality, so we try not to jump the gun until she calls you with her findings tomorrow morning. But I can tell you Dr. Alsarraj was pleased."

So, hopeful, but uncertain, Iris thought, *like everything.* At least she could say she'd done all she could. Lately that seemed like the best that Iris, or maybe anyone, could achieve.

"Why don't you rest in here a little longer, and I'll check back in twenty minutes or so. Is your ride here?" Dani handed Iris her phone to check.

Iris blinked at her messages. "Yeah. He's outside."

Iris said goodbye to the building's uniformed doorman and walked gingerly onto the sidewalk, squinting in the sunlight as she looked out to the street. The dented hot shop van was double-parked.

Gabe jumped out of the driver's seat in a white tank and jeans and jogged over to take her arm.

Iris flinched playfully. "Don't—with that van, they'll think you're kidnapping me."

Gabe laughed. "Just let me help you, will ya?" He gently took her elbow so she wouldn't trip on the curb, then opened the passenger door for her and helped her up into the van.

"Thanks. You know if Roman wasn't literally proposing to James on Fire Island today, I wouldn't have taken you up on this."

"If I hadn't had to deliver a piece uptown this morning, I wouldn't have offered."

Iris carefully buckled her seatbelt over her tender abdomen. The metal buckle was hot to the touch. "I forgot this van doesn't have air-conditioning."

Gabe hopped back into the driver's seat. "Yeah, but it *does* have an insulated container." He stretched between the seats and reached into the back, opening a boxy trunk and pulling out a plastic bodega bag. He handed it to Iris.

Whatever was inside was cold. Iris reached in and pulled out a frozen tub of Lucerne Rainbow Sherbet and a plastic spoon.

Gabe looked at her hopefully. "Is that the right kind? Like Aunt Sissy's?"

Iris could only manage a nod for the lump in her throat. She opened the top and saw the familiar swirls of raspberry pink, tangerine orange, and whatever green. She spooned a bite into her mouth. It tasted exactly like she remembered, and suddenly she was eight years old again, eating sherbet at the kitchen table at Aunt Sissy's house, her father sneaking a spoonful between innings in the Phillies game, her mother sitting beside her with her own bowl, having been the original recipient of Aunt Sissy's frozen treats. One sense memory encompassing love, safety, loss, and love again. "It's perfect. Thank you."

Gabe smiled and started the engine. He turned down Fifth Avenue with Central Park to their right. It was a glorious morning, and the park was vibrantly alive. Iris looked out the open window and inhaled the accord of linden blossoms, freshly cut grass, carriage horse manure, and car exhaust. Her belly was tender and she was still headachy, but she was done with the injections and the hormones. She didn't have a job, but she'd get another one. She wasn't married, but she had time to find someone, or not, the choice was hers. She definitely needed therapy, but she'd gotten a referral from Dr. Alsarraj.

Iris didn't have the perfume, but she had something more powerful: self-knowledge. She knew she had the strength and the courage to face the ugliest parts of her lived experience. That trauma was a part of her, but not the defining note. She would not disconnect from the body or the world that had once hurt her. She couldn't heal without connection, first to herself and her body—that was her first home. She would trust herself first, and then others. Her gut instinct, her heart's desires, her mind's memories and fantasies, fully integrated and embodied. Getting there would be an ongoing process, forever, for everyone.

"So, am I allowed to ask, how'd it go?" Gabe glanced at her at the red light. "What happens now?"

"I don't know yet." Iris kept her eyes on the road ahead. "We'll have to wait and see."

The light turned green.

EPILOGUE

The morning sun rose high enough to warm the roofs of the buildings, the glossy glass towers that bounced awake with reflective shine and the tarry black roofs that absorbed it as if to beg for five more minutes. The sun yawned its golden arms up and out to reach farther down each block, its fingers combing through treetops, rousing the birds to sing in a new day. This early in the morning was the only time when the city was quiet enough to hear birdsong, before the rumble of traffic and the din of people. Light filtered through the leaves, dappling the lush dark foliage in luminescent lime. Most of Bank Street still slept under its shady canopy, or slept elsewhere, having decamped to fashionable beach towns from the Hamptons to Mallorca. Only the early dog walkers and the most committed runners were out, and they were barely awake themselves.

No one noticed anything amiss at 23 Bank. The first-floor windows were dark, the interior shutters latched. The stately double doors stood as proud as they had for the last century. But underneath them, just below the shiny brass kickboard, water began to silently creep. First it spread and seeped into the landing, darkening the brownstone like a terra-cotta pot. Once that porous sandstone was saturated, a thin and shimmering sheet of water began to move, spilling down over the rounded lip of the top stair, forming a curtain of rainfall to the next stair, where it again soaked, pooled, and spilled down the next, and the next, until it had created a small and tranquil urban waterfall.

It would be hours before any passersby noticed the water soaking the stoop and pooling on the sidewalk. The vast majority walked by oblivious, their ears plugged with headphones that muted the splash of their feet through the mysterious puddle, their eyes straight ahead or glued to their phone screens, their busy minds ever elsewhere. Of the observant few who did register the wetness, most assumed the plants had just been watered or the sidewalk scrubbed of dog excrement; fewer still realized it was leaking from inside the house. And as all New Yorkers unfailingly mind their own business, save for the most ignored classes of the very young, very old, or very crazy, it wasn't until the next-door neighbor's living room baseboards began to buckle that anyone called anyone at all, and even then, the neighbor called their lawyer first. By the time someone reached a human being over at the unlisted shell corporation that owned the brownstone, and a part-time super was sent over to check on 23 Bank Street, the water inside Rapacine's apartment was up to the windows.

The super said that in his thirty-two years working in the city, he had never seen anything like it. When at first he couldn't get the front door open, he got a ladder to peer inside the windows, and he saw the water inside was four feet high. All of Rapacine's beautiful, curated belongings were either drowned or bobbing on the surface. The cognac leather Eames chair, only visible at the very top, was submerged, the once shiny patina on its leather cushions now matte black, waterlogged, and ruined. The television on the bar stand peeked out of the water, short-circuited, the Baccarat tumblers clinking against its dark screen. There were sunken books whose pages fanned out like anemones, same for the Moleskine journals whose secret recipes were blurred forever. A large wicker basket drifted like a life raft among a flurry of skinny white test strips of card stock soaked to a pulp. And then there were the bottles. Bottles, bottles everywhere. An abundance of brown glass apothecary bottles whose fragrant oils and essences had spilled and scented the water and whose handwritten labels had bled beyond legibility. A vast collection of vintage crystal perfume bottles bobbed on the surface like floating gemstones. Her entire home—shipwrecked.

They would find out how it happened only after the door had

been pried open and the apartment emptied itself in a rush of water that sloshed into the hallway. Every faucet in the first-floor apartment had been turned on at full force, with every sink drain plugged, and an exterior hose had been snaked inside a back window and left on for days. Every crack and seam to the exterior had been stuffed, blocked, or otherwise sealed shut, from the back door to the window-sills, which had allowed the water to rise and rise. The kitchen floor had begun to sink into the basement, and the water had seeped deep into the walls, where mold would soon take its place. The building's very foundation was likely compromised. It was said the property was unsalvageable.

Neighbors with even a passing acquaintance of Mireille Rapacine refused to believe that the glamorous older lady who had lived there for longer than any of them could remember was the source of the vandalism; they couldn't believe she would destroy the home she had so dearly loved. The building's new owners had been harassing her, neighbors told reporters, they had driven out a beloved and elderly rent-controlled tenant, a city tale as old as time. The landlords had only themselves to blame for no one being home at the time of their final prank gone wrong; their avarice and heartlessness had destroyed their own asset. The drowned brownstone became a symbol of capitalistic greed and inhumanity in New York real estate.

What they didn't know was that it was Rapacine's garden hose. The drain of every sink and the tub in her apartment had been intentionally caulked shut, including the drain of the darling antique toilet, its valve turned open to run and run. The wallpaper in the powder room that Iris had once admired had come to life, the sirens now dragging the sailors under real water, and the scenes themselves peeling at the corners, breaking free.

When, months later, it was reported by less scrupulous tabloids that Mireille Rapacine likely was behind the flooding, the *New York Post* headline read HURRICANE GRANNY, and she became a folk hero. But she and her cats had left and were never found.

When Iris stood with Hugo on the sidewalk regarding 23 Bank, that most precious jewel of New York real estate—the brownstone—with its neoclassical details, leaded glass windows, and elegant molding as intricately carved as Lalique crystal, she saw things differently. She saw it through Rapacine's eyes. If Madame Rapacine had taught her anything, it was that if you wanted to capture a time, a place, a feeling, you needed to make it into a perfume. Iris understood, Rapacine hadn't destroyed the home she loved—she had bottled it.

But for those few passersby who resist the dissociation the city begs of its residents, those who are more in touch with their bodies, or sensitive to whimsy, or at the very least not in a terrible rush, they had a surreal experience. A Pilates instructor and former principal dancer with the Alvin Ailey company walked by and smelled the water and was reminded of the glamorous patrons at her first professional dance gig, opening a new club called Studio 54. A Japanese chef on holiday passed by and thought it smelled like the yuzu and rosewater cake he once baked for his sister's wedding. And a small child simply thought it smelled like her mother when she was going out for the evening. The perfume that poured from the brownstone could evoke a different memory for every person in New York. But all of them were beautiful.

ACKNOWLEDGMENTS

Writing is a solitary task, but book publishing is a team effort, and storytelling calls on the whole village, so I have many people to thank for bringing *Full Bloom* to, well, you know.

Kara Cesare is the editor who feels like a best friend. Her energy is so warm and positive, her edits so smart and incisive, that every meeting makes me a better, braver writer. I can come to her with a spark, and Kara breathes oxygen into it until it's a hearth fire that could warm the whole house. I am the luckiest author; to make art with Kara is a joy. Likewise, Jesse Shuman took time from his own stacked list of authors to lend his clear-eyed perspective to this book, and his margin compliments are so funny and satisfying that I repeat them to my friends. And thanks to Gabby Colangelo who keeps all our spinning plates in the air.

This is my first novel published by Ballantine, and I am privileged to work with this dream team. Thank you to Kara Welsh, Jennifer Hershey, and Kim Hovey. Thank you to my publicists, Emily Isayeff and Katie Horn, who gave *Full Bloom* the book launch and tour I missed out on when my first novel, *Ghosts of Harvard,* debuted during Covid lockdown. Thanks to marketing geniuses Taylor Noel and Emma Thomasch for shepherding this book through the labyrinthine and ever-changing online landscape to find the readers who would best connect with it. And the most important first impression of any book is the cover, so I'm indebted to gifted artist Sarah Horgan for dressing my book in the most perfect cover short of being scratch-and-sniff. Interior design is always one of the most surprising and delightful parts of production for me because I pore over the words, and Ralph Fowler did an amazing job making every page and every line look more beautiful, more readable, and, to the little girl who dreamed of seeing her words in print, *more real.*

Thank you to my brilliant agent Rebecca Scherer, along with the amazing Andrea Cirillo and Amy Tannenbaum, at Jane Rotrosen Agency. Rebecca gets the most unfiltered, insecure, anxious, and ambitious version of me and still answers my calls on the first ring. Thank you for the reassurance, guidance, and for never telling me I dream too big. I know that together we can lasso the moon—and tell the best story about it. And special thanks to Berni Vann at CAA for all of her efforts.

My love affair with perfume began as a little girl marveling at the faceted perfume bottles on my mother's dresser. She gave me a mini bottle of Lancôme's *Trésor,* likely a free sample gift-with-purchase type thing, which I treasured as a magical elixir that held all the secrets to womanhood. Today, I own an enormous collection of fragrances that I keep in a hundred-year-old French vitrine. Perfume is the only thing I put on that makes me feel more beautiful but has nothing to do with how I look. It conjures memories and fantasies in equal measure. Its magic is almost impossible to put into words, which is why I knew I had to write about it.

But passion and knowledge aren't the same thing, and this book required a great deal of research. I started my journey in the capital of perfumery: Grasse, France. I traveled to Grasse and studied the origins of perfume at the Musée International de la Parfumerie, I visited the fields where flowers and other raw materials are grown, I explored the factories of perfume manufacturing at Galimard, France's oldest *maison de parfum,* founded in 1747, and even consulted with their in-house perfumer, Caroline de Boutiny, to compose my very own fragrance, which I named *Près de Moi.* The trip was all I had dreamed of and more, and what I learned permeates this novel. I took many videos and photos that can be found on my website FrancescaSerritella.com and social media @FSerritella across most platforms.

If you're interested in learning more about perfume, fragrance composition, or the science of scent, the books that informed my research were: memoirs by noses, *The Diary of a Nose* and *Perfume: The Alchemy of Scent* both by Jean-Claude Ellena, and *Aphorisms of a Perfumer* by Dominique Ropion. Luca Turin is the premier perfume critic and scientist, his book *Perfumes: The A-Z Guide* is a nostalgic review of the scents you know and love (or hate), and *The Secret of Scent* is a fun and informative read. On the science of scent, I greatly enjoyed *Nose Dive: A Field Guide to the World's Smells* by Harold McGee and *Revelations in Air* by Jude Stewart. And for the history of fragrance in a social and political context, *Smells: A Cultural History of Odours in Early Modern Times* by Robert Muchembled is a fascinating and engaging resource.

I review fragrances and generally geek out on Fragrantica.com, my handle is @FrancescaInFiore.

Thank you to the artists on staff at Brooklyn Glass who taught me rudimentary glassblowing, Thomas St. Amand and Ali Feeney. They shared more fun facts than I could plausibly cram into this dialogue, and for that I am sorry. Everything cool about the fictional studio "Brooklyn Gather" is from Brooklyn Glass, and anything inaccurate is because I couldn't hear them over the furnaces.

I am blessed by many brilliant friends who are experts in their fields and who aided me in my research. Thank you to Drs. Deborah Doroshow and Nora Demchur for answering my medical questions related to fertility and egg-freezing. Thank you to one of my best friends and one-man support system, Ryder Kessler, who is also a dedicated advocate for fair and abundant housing in New York City. He has taught me so much about the housing crisis and parsing these complicated problems with clarity and compassion. Thanks to my lifelong friend, Courtney Yip, who is pointedly *not* Iris, but who has always impressed and inspired me navigating her career in architecture as a lighting designer with ambition, tenacity, and grace. Rebecca Harrington, my best friend from college and a brilliant author in her own right, remains the only friend I can bear to let read my drafts, because she is the gentlest reader and the most enthusiastic brainstormer.

Thank you to my entire family for their enduring love and support, including the friends whom I consider family: Laura Leonard, always my first reader and best sounding board, who has taught me so much about this business; my godmother Franca, who radiates love for me and cheers my every endeavor; and my lifelong best friend and chosen-sister, Katy Keating. My friendship with Katy has sustained my soul for nearly thirty years, and we're just getting started.

Love and thanks to my father, a lover of language who read the classics from Charles Dickens to Michael Crichton aloud to me as a child. Today he foists signed copies of my books on everyone he knows, and his pride still makes me glow from the inside out.

And of course, all my love and gratitude to my mother. There is no book long enough to contain all I want to say and hear from you.

I dedicated this book to Pip. Pip was my dog, my best friend, and my baby for fifteen too-short years. I wrote this novel when Pip was alive, although I knew he wouldn't be with me for much longer, and every day with him was a gift. But Pip saw me through, like he always did. He saw me through my twenties and most of my thirties—that glorious, terrifying, precious time when it was just us—and his radiant sweetness softened every edge this city had. He saw me through heartaches and trauma, and he healed me with his love. He saw me through building my career and building myself. I loved him, and I loved life with him, and, though I miss him to my marrow, he left me with a life I loved.

Every description of Hugo's behavior, his sweetness, his soothing effect on Iris, and the constancy of their love was inspired by Pip. And every draft, my editors had to gently suggest I trim those sections for word count, because my loving descriptions would go on and on—and they were still an understatement. Any praise for a dog's love is an understatement. And my love for Pip could fill a library. Writing him into this book was just one more way that Pip could live forever, in my heart and in my pages. Love never dies.

Finally, to my readers, whether you've followed me from the "Chick Wit" columns and memoir series, or if you took a chance on an unknown author with this book, thank you. Reading is a generous act; it takes your time and asks you to open your mind and heart to the writer's mind and heart, and I never take that gift for granted. I cherish the connection a book can create between strangers. If you've read this far, you aren't a stranger anymore.

And for all the single women reading this, who feel proud and grateful for all they have accomplished and survived and built on their own, but who still want more—

I see you.

I applaud you.

I am you.

Let's get it.

ABOUT THE AUTHOR

FRANCESCA SERRITELLA is the *New York Times* bestselling author of *Ghosts of Harvard,* nominated for Best First Novel by International Thriller Writers, and a nine-book series of essay collections co-written with her mother, author Lisa Scottoline, based on their Sunday column in *The Philadelphia Inquirer.* Serritella graduated cum laude from Harvard University, where she won multiple awards for her fiction, including the Thomas T. Hoopes Prize. She lives in New York City with her eighteen-year-old cat and her new puppy.

francescaserritella.com
Facebook.com/FrancescaSerritellaAuthor
Instagram and X: @fserritella

ABOUT THE TYPE

This book was set in Celeste, a typeface that its designer, Chris Burke (b. 1967), classifies as a modern humanistic typeface. Celeste was influenced by Bodoni and Waldman, but the strokeweight contrast is less pronounced. The serifs tend toward the triangular, and the italics harmonize well with the roman in tone and width. It is a robust and readable text face that is less stark and modular than many of the modern fonts, and has many of the friendlier old-face features.